Avilion

Avilion

—

ROBERT HOLDSTOCK

GOLLANCZ

LONDON

The right of Robert Holdstock to be identified as the author
of this work has been asserted by him in accordance with the
Copyright, Designs and Patents Act 1988.

First published in Great Britain in 2009 by Gollancz
An imprint of the Orion Publishing Group
Orion House, 5 Upper St Martin's Lane,
London WC2H 9EA
An Hachette UK Company

A CIP catalogue record for this book
is available from the British Library

ISBN 978 0575 08299 1 (Cased)
ISBN 978 0575 08301 1 (Trade Paperback)

1 3 5 7 9 10 8 6 4 2

Typeset at The Spartan Press Ltd,
Lymington, Hants

Printed and bound in the UK by CPI Mackays,
Chatham, Kent

The Orion Publishing Group's policy is to use papers
that are natural, renewable and recyclable products and
made from wood grown in sustainable forests. The logging
and manufacturing processes are expected to conform
to the environmental regulations of the country of origin.

www.robertholdstock.com
www.orionbooks.co.uk

To Sarah.
Twenty-five years on from *Mythago Wood*, you are still
cariath ganuch trymllyd bwstfil

But now farewell, I am going a long way
With these thou seest – if indeed I go
(For all my mind is clouded with a doubt) –
To the island-valley of Avilion;
. . . Where I will heal me of my grievous wound

From 'The Passing of Arthur':
from Idylls of the King by Alfred Lord Tennyson

The ghost is as the man

ibid

Echo: Mythago Wood

Ryhope Wood is as ancient as the Ice Age, primal, undisturbed for twelve thousand years; and it is semi-sentient. As small as Ryhope Wood seems, it contains a vast world. Within its apparently impenetrable boundaries, legendary figures and landscape come alive, born from the collective memory of those who live in its proximity.

In 1948, Steven Huxley returned to England from France, to his home, Oak Lodge, at the edge of this remote patch of woodland.

His older brother Christian was waiting for him there. Their father, George, had disappeared into the wild two years before.

George Huxley had discovered the secret of Ryhope Wood. He had called the ancient ghosts that lived there *mythagos*: the images of the myth.

One of these figures of legend was the Celtic Princess, Guiwenneth of the Green. George and Christian Huxley had become entranced by this beautiful and feisty echo of the Iron Age, this 'image of a myth', after she had emerged from the edge. They had fought over her, but had lost her.

Soon after Steven's return, his brother also disappeared into the wildwood, trailing his father and searching for the woman he desired.

But Guiwenneth of the Green re-emerged for Steven – and their love was sudden, genuine, and profound. Sadly, it was a short-lived love at the edge of the wood.

Christian, aged by many years and remorseless in his search (Time is strange in Mythago Wood), returned with armed men and took his prize, leaving his brother for dead.

I

Yet Steven survived, and he and Christian met again at the very heart of Mythago Wood, and in a bitter winter. Steven exacted revenge. Christian was dead. But so was Guiwenneth, cut down by one of Christian's mercenaries. She was taken to Avilion, also known as Lavondyss.

Steven held faith in her return, however, waiting at the top of the valley known as *imarn uklyss*: 'where the girl came back through the fire'.

He was rewarded – old love was reignited, and two children were the consequence, named Jack and Yssobel, both of them half human and half mythago.

What follows now is a story of Blood and the Green.

And of Resurrection.

PROLOGUE:

Yssobel

The stone stood stark against the moon, towering over Yssobel as she stared at the monument from the edge of the wide glade with tears in her eyes. The journey here had been long, far longer than she had expected. There had been times when she had despaired of ever finding the true trail to this place. But she was here now. She had found it at last.

Pale light illuminated the stone's flanks, showing by shadow the old script carved there, a different tale on each side, four in all, four echoes of the life of a great man, and a great king.

The monolith whispered to her, greeted her. As she walked towards it in the night, it seemed to lean slightly, as if to embrace her, the illusion of welcome.

I've found you, she thought in triumph, and then gave voice to the words. 'I've *found* you!'

Yes, she was sure of it. This was Peredur's Stone, the marker of the man's grave. This was where her mother had died and been taken to Lavondyss; this was close to where her mother had returned, renewed and vibrant with life. This was the place of ending and beginning.

Yssobel reached the stone. The smells of night and earth enveloped her. She touched the first of the cold sides, feeling the smooth carvings in the rough-hewn rock. She traced the patterns, her mind a dance of recognition as the images blossomed in her imagination.

Peredur and the Nine Eagles. She smiled as she recognised a part of the legend that was her mother's. It was a story with which she was very familiar.

Walking round, setting loose her tumble of hair as she did so, she embraced the second flank.

Peredur and the Song of the Islands of the Lost. This was strange. She didn't recognise it, though she recognised the song. Her mother, Guiwenneth, had often sung it. But for all that she had learned and dreamed about Peredur, she had never heard of his link with this tale, these islands. She moved away from it.

At the third face, her heart started to race a little: *Peredur and the Shield of Diadora.* This, she knew about: the shield that reflected the past, and if viewed carefully could show a glimpse, at the edge of its inner, polished centre, a hint of what might come. It had been one of Peredur's prized possessions.

Yssobel stood for a long time in front of the fourth flank, that side of the tall stone that lay in moon shadow. Here she sang quietly, words composed whilst on her journey. When that small celebration was done, she whispered a chant of promise to her mother and promise to her father. She blew a kiss to her brother Jack, who would, no doubt, be following his own path, somewhere else in the land. She missed him. Then, with a smile, she reached to feel the carvings, tracing them as she had done with the others, reading the marks and spirals, her fingers so expert that they could have read them in complete darkness. But she frowned again as she traced:

Peredur and Yssobel.

'That can't be right,' she said to the stone. 'I don't belong to your time. This isn't the rune that I dreamed. I dreamed of you at The Crossing Place of Ghosts.'

But perhaps this was one of the changes that could occur in this world, she thought to herself. Perhaps this signified that Peredur would look after her on her journey inwards. It was a comforting thought.

A dark bird, perched on top of the monument, suddenly stretched its wings and drifted silently away, across the clearing and into the forest edge. Yssobel saw it, but was not made apprehensive by it.

She had been so engrossed in her inspection of the stone that she failed to hear the stealthy approach from behind. The first she knew of it was when her tumble of hair was yanked gently but firmly. Stifling her cry of surprise, mind and limbs suddenly sharpened, she drew her long-bladed Greek knife in a blur of speed and swung round ready to strike. She immediately relaxed and laughed.

The face that watched her was benign; it blinked, sighed, and the horse turned away. *I'm here too. And it's late.*

The moon lowered, the glade darkened. Now Peredur's Stone was a shadow against stars. Yssobel lay in her small shelter, wrapped in a long sheepskin, and stared and thought and remembered. She had fed her horse; the packhorse she had brought with her towards the heart of the wood had perished on the way, not from the exhaustion of carrying her supplies but from predation by the creatures that stalked the valley down which she had ridden. She was glad that Rona, her favourite – a small mare, with a long black and white mane, her flanks grey – had made it this far.

Peredur and Yssobel. She hadn't expected that.

But she had dreamed long, long ago that the rune-marks would be there, the patterns, the codes that signified the tales; and when she had told her mother, her mother had cocked her head, stared at the child of five summers, smiled, and said nothing. A look that signified she was thinking very differently.

The sun rose and Yssobel rose too, prepared herself and the horse for the day, then walked to where the sun was casting the Stone's shadow. She looked along that shadow towards the leaning trunk of a broken oak – blown down by a storm wind, no doubt.

That is where I go. That is where I go to find him.

She led Rona to the narrow space below the tree, led the way through to find a narrow track that widened to a grassy trail. It might almost have been a road. The road was in a hollow. Tree-lined earthen banks rose on each side. She was puzzled; this wasn't right. She swung herself onto Rona's back and cantered forward, watching and listening, and she had travelled a long way, lost in her own thoughts, before she thought to slow down and rest the mare.

There should have been fire here, marking the way through. She had seen fire in her dreams, and her father's account of this place was that a wall of fire guarded the deepest of the lands in Ryhope Wood. But there was just the forest trail, and the sense that human hands had built the way. The world had changed. The wood had changed its mind.

Yssobel rode for most of the day and was about to rest when she caught the scent of a lake. The wind had freshened. The smell of the fresh water was clear and sharp and clean. Intrigued, she pressed forward.

The wind shifted and she stopped suddenly. Faintly, then more loudly, she could hear the din and clatter of battle. She kicked the mare on and the trail began to curve. The horse was straining slightly. She could smell the lake as well, and was thirsty. Yssobel hauled her back. The battle was very close now, and its sounds made her stomach clench and her senses sharpen. The beat of shields, the ringstrike of iron, the wailing departure of men, the screaming triumph of killers, the noisy protesting of horses ridden through the fury, these signs of vicious struggle waxed and waned on the air.

Yssobel's copper hair billowed out like a cloak behind her as the wind strengthened, bringing with it the sharp tang of blood, and she took a moment to gather it and knot it to the side, using a silver ring. She was about to kick forward again when a horse burst through the undergrowth above the bank and stumbled its way down and across the track. A man lay slumped on its back, arms dangling, features obscured by a small helmet that covered half his face, which now was red from a strike. As the horse leapt up the opposite bank, so he fell heavily to the ground, rolling back to the road. For a moment gleaming eyes watched Yssobel, a hand moved towards her. Then brightness became blur.

She rode on. The battle was loud now, and she dismounted, crawled stealthily up the bank and through the sparse woodland until she could see the hill, and the swarm of men on that hill, the sky filled with streaming pennants and clouds of fine yellow hair, blowing across the site of battle, glittering elementals engaged in the fray.

She saw the man at the centre of the action. His face-helm was black, his banner green. He was bloodied and raging. He rode with others as a troop, but even as Yssobel watched, so he was struck by a javelin, pushed back on his horse, then struck off it. Ravens rushed towards him and the struggle over his body

8

became fierce. The tone of the conflict had changed. It became static, pressing, urgent.

Yssobel pulled back. She had seen enough. But as she sat, huddled, at the top of the bank, she began to realise just what it was that she had seen. She looked towards the lake, remembering the stories she had been told by her father, remembering the dreams she had inherited from her mother. Quickly, she returned to the fallen rider and stripped the corpse of its armour and face-helm.

Yes – she would stay here tonight, in hiding, and watch events unfurl.

PART ONE

Jack at the Edge

Wood Haunter

The man materialised from the edge of the wood so suddenly that the two boys, fishing from the opposite bank of the brook, almost slipped into the water with shock. He stood midstream in the shadows for a while, the water bubbling around his crude soft leather boots. He was wearing buckskin trousers, had a jacket or cloak slung casually over his right shoulder, and a pack over his left. His filthy shirt was open to the waist, revealing a heavily tattooed torso.

The boys scrambled back onto the bank and stared at the stranger, who met their look with a cool, pale, searching gaze of his own. His face was lean and lightly bearded, scars on the skin visible in places through the black hair. On his left arm a strip of white fabric, bulging with moss that dangled from its edges, was stained with red, suggesting a recent wound. He seemed unbothered by it.

After watching the boys for a while he looked towards the spire of the church in Shadoxhurst, squinting against the sun.

'Shadokhurze?' he asked, still staring at the distant village. Though his pronunciation was strange, they recognised his meaning.

'That's right, mister,' said the older of the boys, a gangling, ginger-haired youth who spoke nervously.

'How far in paces?'

The boys exchanged a confused, wide-eyed look. The younger, much smaller boy, said, 'A thousand, maybe.'

'Maybe a million,' the other added.

The man looked quizzically at each of them before his face

broke into a broad grin. 'Depends on the size of the paces, I suppose.'

The boys smiled as well, one less willingly than the other.

Now the stranger came towards them, tossing his pack onto the bank, bundling up his odd-looking jacket and crouching down between them. He ran his free hand through the water as it flowed beneath him, towards the edge. He inspected the moss patch on his arm briefly, then glanced up quickly. 'What do you call this stream?'

'We don't call it anything.'

'It's the *sticklebrook*. Do you know where it flows to?'

The boys shook their heads. 'Nobody does,' said the older one. 'Can't follow it in. You try and follow it in and you end up coming back. It twists you about in there. I've tried it. It's scary. When did you go in?'

The man glanced up. 'I didn't go *in*,' he said softly. 'I came *out*.'

'Came out of where?'

'Came out of what's in there. There's a lot to see in Ryhope Wood. That *is* its name, isn't it?'

They nodded agreement. Then the older boy made a sound of surprise, his mouth gaping. 'You're one of the wood haunters! You're speaking English, so I didn't realise it. But that's what you are. A wood haunter.' He hesitated, nervous. 'Aren't you?'

The stranger considered the question, then splashed water onto his face and slowly stood up.

'Perhaps. Perhaps not. I don't know what you mean by that. But you'd be amazed,' he went on, 'at what this little stream becomes a few thousand paces in. It's very big, very deep, very rough. There are tributaries that run into it and I used a boat to get here along most of it. From inwards. Hauled it onto a sandbank in a beech forest, maybe four thousand paces from here. Hid it among rocks. The *Muurngoth* hunt in those places, not far from the edge. The rivers run in all directions; and they know how to trim a sail too. I don't want to lose my boat.'

He smiled then, and stepped onto the bank. 'This is where

14

the stream goes in. My father's directions were right. I'm on the right side of the wood.'

He looked around, inspecting the landscape. 'Do you know the house here? Oak Lodge?'

The boys watched him blankly, then shook their heads. Again, it was the older one who spoke. 'There's no house near this wood. Just fields and pastures and sheep. And old fencing. And some earthworks. The Manor House is over the hill.'

'Oak Lodge? You've never heard of it?'

'There's no house anywhere near here, mister. That's the truth.'

'Oh, but there is.'

'What makes you think so?' the other boy asked, with a frown.

'What makes me think so? Because my father lived there for a lot of his life. And so did my grandfather, who was a scientist and an explorer. His name was George Huxley. My father's name was Steven. And I'm John Huxley. Jack, if you like. And I've come a long way to find my home. What are you two called?'

'Eddie,' said the fair-haired older boy.

'Won't tell,' said the younger, with a glare.

'I understand. More than you might know.' He smiled. ' "Won't Tell." '

He gave the boys a friendly look and turned away to pick up his heavy pack, then thought of something and came back. He reached into the pack and pulled out two odd circular objects, bits of twig and small thorny briars, interwoven intricately, with two longer twigs curling out and down like inverted tusks. He tossed one of the objects to each of the boys, who caught them and studied them curiously. They looked up and the older one, Eddie, asked, 'What is it?'

'It's what we call a *daurbrak*.'

'What's it for?'

'It's a shield. It keeps a Green Man away if he comes at you. You put it in your mouth with the twigs pointing down. It confuses him. They're called *daurog*. He doesn't have very good eyesight, you see?'

With a wave and a twinkle in his eye, Jack Huxley turned

away and began walking briskly round the edge of Ryhope Wood. Looking back after a few seconds he called out, 'There *is* a house here, you know. It's just that you boys can't see it.'

Oak Lodge

The two boys had been right. No house stood *outside* the dense edge of trees. But Jack was an insider. He had lived all his life in the heart of Ryhope Wood, very far indeed from the sight and understanding of the people who lived outside. Now he searched the shadows of this forgotten forest, peering with expert eyes into the gloom, seeking form that was alien to the tangle of trunk and branch. Soon he saw it: a perpendicular wall of brick, forty paces or so in.

Jack noticed something else. Where he stood, the earth was recently healed. He stabbed at the grass with his toe, drew his foot along the ground. There had been roots here – he could feel their echo. Until recently this had been on the line of the edge, twenty paces from where it brooded now.

The wood was shrinking, drawing in her skirts.

It was a strange thought, an unexpected one. Oak Lodge had once been even more thoroughly consumed, it seemed, but was now being given back to the land.

He would have to ponder this later. Now he merged with the undergrowth, the part of him that was human giving way again to that part of him that had been generated in the womb of the forest. The part of him that was *mythago*: born of the wood. Wood haunter, as the boys had referred to it. The reference had startled him. *Haunter* was how he himself thought of the mythago side of his life – the green side, as his sister Yssobel called it, not the *red-blood* side.

From the overgrown garden, in the embrace of oak and ash, through the tangle of briar and creeper, Jack peered at the tall house, with her three ivy-shrouded chimneys, her shattered windows, her grey brick walls. For a moment he thought he could hear the echoes of children running and laughing, the shouts of a mother to slow down and do something constructive, the grumble of a father's voice complaining about the noise when he was trying to work.

The house, in silence, was vibrant with imagined life. The echo passed away.

Jack picked his way to the back door, which now leaned heavily off its hinges and was rotten. Pushing into the building through the kitchen, he was surprised to find that far from the musty, tree-invaded rooms that he had expected, the interior of the house was almost as if it had only just been locked up and left empty. The air was fresh and warm. There was nothing faded here, though the light was gloomy.

How long had it been like this, he wondered? How long since the last occupant had crossed the garden towards the wood and disappeared inwards for all of time?

This place would be his base. All his life he had longed to see the outer world, the world of his family's origins, spreading away from Oak Lodge in a wide arc, over hills and along roads. The excitement he felt was intense, but he suppressed it for the moment.

He would be especially intrigued to see the study. He had tried to imagine, whilst in the heartwood, what this grove of learning and understanding had been like. He had seen many sacred enclosures as he and Yssobel and his father explored the wood around their home: the remnants of 'enchanter caves', sanctuaries devoted to certain mysteries, and, in some of the more civilised ruins they had come across, a room where scrolls littered the floors or the walls were a confusion of hieroglyphs and signs. Those were places where long-gone minds had sought answers, with chalk or graphite, to the secrets of whatever aspect of life, the stars or nature had obsessed them.

These were his father's words, more or less, but they had fired Jack's young mind. Answers, yes. But what questions to ask?

Finally only two remained: what is the outer world like? How do I get there?

He was here now. He stepped tentatively into the enchanter's cave and looked around. Cracked and shattered glass-fronted cases of weapons, tools, exquisitely patterned bowls and fired-clay beakers lined one wall. Clusters of spears, rusting swords and wooden weapons were stacked in the corners. Several shields, oval and bright with design, were hanging from hooks on another wall. Skin clothing, cloaks, long colourful tunics and bone armour were piled in a tangled and musty mass in a recess by the chimney breast. Huxley's office was a cramped museum, filled with the chill of survival, the rage of territory, the warrior, the hunter, the clay-shaper, the little songs of life: a wardrobe of the past.

Jack smiled. He was more than familiar with many of these exhibits, if not these exact ones. For all of his short life he had encountered weapons, domestic items and clothing very similar to these fragments collected by his grandfather. And he had seen them used.

A broad, heavy desk and chair were at the centre of the room and Jack imagined the man working there, bent over his journal, obsessed with the terrors and wonders to be found within the edge of Ryhope Wood.

Jack's father had suggested that before he do anything else, should he arrive safely at the 'old family home' (said with a laugh), he should go to the main bedroom, where he might find, in a drawer or cupboard if the place had not been ransacked, a photograph of the 'man' himself.

The stairs were creaky and Jack went up slowly, following a sketched map of the house. The ceiling in the bedroom was dull with time, the bed enormous, covered with bedding that was not rotten, but rank and damp. Wardrobes and chests of drawers lined the walls. They were mostly full of clothes, objects wrapped in paper, boxes of implements, and albums. He had opened several of these out of curiosity, recognising his father from the black and white pictures in one album he found, when he glanced up and saw the brooding face of a lightly bearded man, framed on the wall.

The picture was covered with filthy glass, but the moment he rubbed the dust away he saw an image very like the sketch he carried: broad-chinned, high-browed, eyes narrowed and the skin around them lined, thin lips neither scowling nor smiling.

And the gaze, though straight, was clearly focused elsewhere. This was a portrait of a man who seemed indifferent to everything around him.

'Hello, George,' Jack said.

He stared at the face, stared into its eyes, talked to it, engaged with it, memorised it. There was a moment, as he stood there, when something downstairs shuddered. He realised he was standing above the man's old study.

'Goodbye, George. Time to try to raise you.'

Jack went downstairs again, out of the house and across the garden. When he was in the gloom, feeling that familiar and welcome tug of the earth at the soles of his feet, reaching a hand between trees for the comfort of the murmuring he could feel there, he shouted, 'Grandfather! George!'

Comfortable though he was with tracks and rivers and open spaces, Jack was equally at home in the tighter, tangled womb-like copses and spinneys that formed so frequently and so suddenly, even though they were often the forming-places of mythagos.

He repeated his call, perhaps his summons. He waited; and called a third time.

He decided that that would do for a start.

Jack went upstairs again, prowling, searching, memorising for his father, and completed his second task before the dusk began to darken the house.

'A book,' his father had said. 'There's a book somewhere in my room, probably in a pile with other books. If it's still there. The whole house has probably been looted, stripped. But if not, I'd like to have it.'

He struggled to remember the title for a moment, and then found it. *The Time Machine*, by H. G. Wells.

'And something of my brother Chris's. Some small thing. I'll leave it to you. Nothing too heavy. You'll need to take care. You will take care . . .'

'I'll take care.'

Jack went to the room marked on Steven's sketch map as 'Chris's room' and after a look around found a small box of light, shiny chess pieces. Intrigued by the material from which they had been fashioned, he tucked the box into his belt. His father had carved chess pieces from wood, back in the villa, and had made a board, and it was a game that Christian had loved and at which he had excelled.

Tired now, and hungry, Jack decided that the study was the best place to make his camp for the night, and after eating a small amount of his meagre supplies he curled up gratefully in the corner where the room seemed warmest.

Beyond the Edge

With first light came the sound of his name being called. Jack had been more tired than he'd realised. Those last days on the river had been a test of strength as well as of nerve as he had approached the edge but found himself fighting against the elements; as if the wood were reluctant to allow him home.

His name again. He sat up, rose and went to the shuddering tap, with its hesitant flow of water, and washed his face.

Leaving the house, he made his way to the field, and as he emerged from the wood again so he saw the older boy, Eddie, standing at a distance. He smiled when he saw Jack and held up a bag, then approached, less apprehensive than the day before, but still cautious.

'What brings you here?'

'I told my mum about you. She asked a lot of questions. She thought you might want some food and milk.'

Jack was pleased. He accepted the bag. 'Thank you. Thank your mother.'

'Just milk and some bread and eggs.'

'That's very kind.'

The boy hesitated. He was more smartly dressed than the day before, and when Jack commented on this, Eddie said, 'You know what today is?'

Jack said that he didn't.

'It's Easter. We always go to church on Easter Sunday. I go early so I can get away and do other things. There'll be a big party on the green this afternoon. Do you like beer?'

Jack laughed. 'I've heard of it.'

'There'll be beer and a hog roast later. But you'll need money.'

'Money, alas,' said Jack, with a smile. 'Money and I are strangers.'

'Well.' The boy was thoughtful. 'Maybe you could tell some stories. About what it's like in there?'

'Maybe.'

'My mum wrote a small book about the wood. Maybe she'll interview you. I know she's interested in you.'

Eddie must have been talkative indeed. 'I'd like to meet her.'

'I'll tell her.'

Distantly, a bell sounded, a single strike followed by several others, and then a cascade of notes that had Jack entranced.

'Eight o'clock,' the boy said, glancing at something on his wrist. 'Fifteen minutes to go. In at eight, out by eight-thirty. No sermon. It's the only way to do it.'

He grinned, turned, and half ran, half walked towards the distant town, but suddenly glanced back. 'You look strange. Jack.' He had hesitated before calling the stranger by his name, as if he felt it impolite. 'You don't look right. You need different clothes.'

And then he was gone.

How should I look? This is my look. These are my clothes. This is my skin, decorated in the way we decorate our skins in the villa, in the inner home, by the fires, facing the hunt, facing the hunter. This is the way I look. How else should I look?

Jack brooded for a while, seated at the desk in the study, drinking milk and cracking the raw eggs. They were bland compared to what he was used to, but he was glad of them.

There was an apple in the bag as well, a russet, rough-skinned fruit that had a flavour like none he'd ever tasted before.

How should I look?

He decided then to shave his beard. He found a knife in the kitchen and sharpened it, but discovered that it was useless. He had made things worse – the curl of his light beard was now a hacked mess. He severed what he could, trimmed it as best he could, then combed his hair straight back, plastering it to his scalp in the style that Eddie had worn.

Then he thought: why am I doing this? I haven't come here to look like a prince. I am here to make contact with the world of my father's childhood, and my grandfather's life.

The sun was high, though the day was cool, and Jack set off again towards the town, following the iron rails of the old railway track, following his young advisor.

Almost at once he was thrilled by the new perspective.

As he strode away from the edge of Ryhope, he truly felt that he was entering another land. The air smelled different. The sounds were muted and eerie; and yet delicious. A single huge oak stood on a rise to his left, what he would have called a 'signal' tree. He sensed history in that solitary growth, in the wide spread of her spring branches. As he topped the rise, so he could see distant hills. There was the glitter of a river, pastures, enclosures, scattered farm buildings. A tamed land, unlike anything he had experienced.

The old tracks curled away between high banks, and he found a small gravel road which seemed to lead towards the sound of distant noise from the town, and the tall grey tower that he could see, and the rise of smoke.

Behind him Ryhope seemed small and distant, and Oak Lodge was invisible.

If he felt disorientated at all, it was a passing dizziness, a moment's hesitation. The blur of sound was enticing. A stringed instrument was playing. Only when he turned to look back did he hear the melancholy hum of the forest, a deep murmuring that seemed to shift and fade.

The road became firmer. A group of children, with two adults, came past on bicycles. He knew about such vehicles. He hadn't realised they could move so fast. He saw the frowns on the adults' faces as they stared at him. The looks were not welcoming.

Soon he was at the town's entrance. The music was very assertive and rhythmic. The air was heavy with conversation and laughter. The smells of roasting meat were sublime. The grey church tower was stark against the clear blue of the sky. Its bells were silent now.

Jack was hot and he stopped to splash water on his face from a trough at the edge of the town, where water spurted from a carved face. He felt dizzy for a moment, almost as if his head were being twisted on his neck; a sensation of being *pulled*, pulled back the way he had come.

I'm not having this!

He took a few steps forward. Now he could see the open space where people were gathered. There was a large fire, and a pig hung on a spit above it. Bales of straw were scattered everywhere, and a group of musicians sat in a semicircle, playing jauntily. Again he started to walk, but his legs suddenly felt dead. He stood quite still, astonished at the sudden sense of being locked inside his body. His vision blurred, his head began to make nonsense of the sounds.

Nothing would move. A deep, mournful moan blew through Jack's consciousness – a summons! He was able to turn, to look back along the road. Ryhope Wood could not be seen, and yet he sensed that it had reached a great hand towards him and was grasping at his heart and liver, squeezing him, tugging at him.

No! I must go further!

One more step and his world exploded. He fell heavily, shaking like a man in a fever, screaming with pain, though the pain was not in his body, just in his mind.

Jack was aware of the disturbance around him. The voices that sounded now were crow voices, taunting, the shrill shriek of the scavenger. Something hard struck his cheek, and he tasted blood. Another blow to his stomach. Laughter. He was being mocked, though the words, the abuse, meant nothing to him in sound, only in intent.

Something stinking landed on his face. Then something wet. Another blow, and then a stone, cracking against his cheek.

The disturbance ended as suddenly as it had started. Gentle hands eased him into a sitting position. A voice was saying, 'That's him. The wood haunter. He's called Jack.'

'Everything's all right now.'

A woman's voice. The clouds were scudding behind the high grey tower. Roast meat and the smell of wine were strong. The music, which had faltered, had started again, and the murmur of voices inhabited his mind, like the droning of bees.

'Everything's all right. I'm just going to wash your face.'

Again, cold water, a gentle touch. The cooling sensation calmed Jack's heart. Slowly he focused on the pale face before him, kindly, a delicately featured woman with ice-blue eyes and fair hair.

'I told him he looked strange,' a boy's voice said.

'He didn't know any better. Go and get a shirt and some soap. And here . . .' She was fumbling in a polished leather bag, 'Get a good thick pork roll, and a pint. Tell them Julie sent you.'

'Yes, mum.'

Now a different pair of hands lifted him, strong hands, helping him stand, leading him away from the music, beyond the water trough and to a wall, where he sat. And gradually the world came back into focus. And with it the pain of his bruises.

'Why was I hit?' Jack asked quietly.

'Because of what you are,' the woman said. 'I'm so sorry. Not everyone behaves that way.'

A man's voice: 'You've come a long way, I think.'

Jack nodded. 'A long journey.'

'From Europe?'

The words signified something, but not enough for Jack to respond. The woman said, 'Not from Europe, I think. From somewhere older. More distant.'

Jack sighed, trying to take in the face that regarded him so earnestly. She was trying to smile, but there was a frown on her, indicating a curiosity and an anxiety that made him uncomfortable.

'It has, yes . . . it has been a long journey. I've dreamed of being here. I was warned that I wouldn't be allowed to leave. But I'll try again. I'll keep trying.'

The man's hand was heavy and reassuring on his shoulder. 'Don't judge us by the teenagers. They have nothing better to do. What they called you: forget it. Just words. Just names.'

What they called me? I don't remember.

Eddie came back. He was a blur of speed, a whirlpool of activity, arriving and skidding to his knees, holding out a fragrant piece of meat in a soft dough. Jack took the food and placed it in his bag. The proffered drink smelled sour and unpleasant. The offered shirt was accepted.

'It will cover those tattoos,' Julie said, with a smile. 'And here. You rather need this.'

It was a piece of wax that smelled like pine. Jack knew what it was, and how to use it.

'I'm going back.'

'Be careful.'

He stood shakily, his legs only finding their strength again as he reached the tracks. He didn't look back, aware that the bells in the grey tower had started to ring again. Aware of anger; and kindness. And that he had found the limit of his adventure.

He had hoped to go so far. He was devastated now to realise that his father had been right. There was too much of the *mythago* in him to allow him into the world of his human origin.

He reached the Lodge and sat down in the corner of the study, touching the bruise and the cut on his face, staring at the cooked meat, cold now, and feeling like a corpse.

Jack cried for a while, tears of anger and confusion. Then he left the house and went to the same enclosed place where he had called for his grandfather the night before. And staring into the darkness, thinking of Huxley, he called again. It was a moment when he at last broke from his own turmoil, from his own self-doubt.

He went back to the house, ate the meat and drank the milk that Eddie had brought for him that morning and later that afternoon. And he began to rethink his situation.

Huxley's Shadow

Jack spent a disturbed and restless night. The shock of the day played on his mind, in particular the terrible feeling of being dragged back to the house, a wrenching sensation that seemed to have bruised him more deeply than the physical attack upon him.

When he tried to think about it, huddled in the darkness, he could only explain it by the sense that something was coming alive in him, something that he had always known was there: his mother's side of him, which afforded him insights and sensations in the deep forest but which had always been suppressed beneath the human part of his existence.

The wind was strong, and the house was noisy. The hanging clothes shifted spectrally; floorboards creaked and doors swung on their rusting hinges. The house seemed unhappy. The moon vanished, and the small light that Jack had enjoyed for the early part of the night faded into a thin starlight.

He tried to sleep, and perhaps had drifted off just briefly when he woke to the sound of voices. They were a distant murmur, a man's voice and the chatter of a child who was being told to 'huuish'.

Rising quickly, Jack went to the window that looked out across the garden to where he knew a gate had once marked the exit from the property. A tall hooded shape stood there, featureless but staring at the Lodge. He held two staffs, one in each hand, each as tall as the man himself. Beside him, the pale face of a boy – perhaps a girl – also stared at the building, and suddenly this smaller figure pointed excitedly and directly at Jack and began to babble in a language that Jack didn't recognise.

The man took both staffs in his right hand and used the left to pull the child to his side, silencing him. Then they turned and walked away, neither into the wood nor away from it.

For the rest of the night, Jack sat by the window, watching the gloom and the waving of branches against the dark and glittering sky, waiting for another visitation; but none came.

He did sleep at last, but woke to the sound of his name again. The call was not the boy's; it was the woman's, Julie's, or so he thought, and when he picked his way to the field he was proved right. It was a brisk day, and the field was damp with dew.

She smiled at him. He recognised the same kind face from yesterday. She was wearing a loose white jumper and tight blue trousers, and had clothes over one arm and a bag in her hand.

'Good morning,' she called. 'How are your bruises?'

'Sore.'

'I've brought some antiseptic . . .'

Jack didn't recognise the word.

'For the cut,' Julie went on. 'And breakfast. And two old shirts and some trousers that might fit.'

She was frowning as she approached, then she smiled brightly and held out the gifts. 'I'm sure we can find something for you to trade. If only your story. Your history. If that would be all right with you . . .'

Again the uncertainty, and when Jack didn't respond she looked crestfallen for a moment, slightly embarrassed.

'Well, something, anyway,' she said. 'I hope the clothes fit.'

'Thank you.'

She brushed a hand through her hair and looked over her shoulder into the distance. 'Well . . . I'd better get to work. First day of the week.'

On impulse, slightly dazed from the night's restlessness, and perhaps from the kick he'd received the day before, Jack said, 'Would you like to come and see the ruins?'

Julie bit her lip, glancing beyond him, thinking hard.

'I've heard there is a house there, but no one goes there. Most people think it burned down. This is a very strange woodland; it feels dangerous. I don't like my son playing near here, but he fishes in the stream.'

Jack nodded. 'It's where I met him. And his friend who wouldn't tell me his name.'

Julie pulled a face. 'A nasty piece of work, if it's who I think it is. Eddie shouldn't mix with him. He's the boy who kicked you. Did you understand what he was calling you? The word? The name?'

Jack shook his head, hardly able to remember anything. 'Just as well,' Julie went on. 'Not to be repeated.'

'Someone said that to me yesterday, but I was too dazed. Come and see the house. It's not far to walk . . .'

She hesitated for a moment. 'All right. I *am* interested,' she added more brightly. 'I've written a small pamphlet on Ryhope. About some of the figures that have been seen here. Haunted Wood.' She folded her arms, again looking beyond Jack and frowning. 'All right. But I mustn't be long.'

He led the way through the scrub and over the low bank that seemed to mark the edge. Following the narrow track through the trees, it was a matter of moments before the wall of the house could be seen. But already Julie was shaking, her arms held tightly across her chest, her breathing oddly laboured.

Jack hesitated, watching her. Perspiration was beading her face. 'Can you see the house?'

She looked at it and nodded. As Jack walked on, she followed nervously, then suddenly cried out. 'Where am I going?'

'To the house.'

She shook her head violently. 'No, this isn't right. It doesn't want me. I'm going to be sick.' She started to turn and twist, looking frantically about her. 'This isn't right.'

She stumbled away from him, bumping into trunks, tripping over roots, and Jack chased after her and led her out to the field. She was shaking.

'I'm sorry,' she whispered in a small voice. 'That was very unpleasant. I'm sorry. I hope the clothes fit . . .'

And with that Julie started to run back towards the old railway line, and the road that wound through the farms to the town, only slowing to a walk when she was about to disappear from view. She didn't look back. Jack watched her go with some sadness.

It doesn't want me.

What had she meant by that? What had she been feeling? The house was just a ruin; a very intact ruin, certainly. It gave no signs of having been burned or ransacked, used by wayfarers. The wood had grown around it, embracing the bricks and mortar. Jack had the uncanny feeling that the house was being protected. But from what? Against what?

Ransacking, perhaps. Or curiosity?

He returned, that morning, to the 'sticklebrook', and though the shallow water was cold, he stripped and washed, feeling invigorated by the action. The clothes felt strange on him. He was not used to buttons, but understood them instinctively. He tucked the blue-fabric trousers into his boots. The garment felt loose around the waist but he managed to tighten it through the belt loops with some twisted ivy. He had rope in his small boat, but that was a good stretch inwards and along the dangerous riverland where the Muurngoth had their enclosures. He wanted only one visit back there, and that was to find the inwards river and return to the old villa that was his home.

Jack walked along the edge of the woodland for most of the afternoon, watching machines at work on the land, fighting the urge to run down one of the absurdly woolly sheep he saw in a flock (for its meat), standing for a long time by a field, admiring the fine, lean horses grazing the pasture, beasts that would have towered above the ponies that his family had accumulated as pack animals. They were creatures from a vision-dream, drawn out, extended, long-necked and long-legged, and when they ran they were so graceful they might have been birds in flight.

With the coming of late afternoon he returned to Oak Lodge. He had not hunted but he would open one of the metal containers in the cupboard, an experiment, anything to keep the hunger pangs controlled. He had long since learned not to acknowledge hunger, only to satisfy the craving when the opportunity arose.

He was in the kitchen, staring at the shiny cans, knife in hand ready to jab one of them open, when he heard a sigh from deep in the house, and the sound of a chair scraping on a wooden floor. His heart raced for a moment, then calmed.

Jack put the knife down. Intrigued, but not alarmed, he walked quietly along the corridor towards the study where Huxley had worked so intensely in the past. He heard another sigh, almost a grumble. Then the sound of a hand being slapped several times on the desk – a sound of frustration, he was sure.

At the entrance to the study, Jack stopped. The old man sat with his back to him. The late-afternoon light cast a beam across the wide desk and the scatter of papers and books that were piled there. They had not been there yesterday. The man was writing and sighing, writing and sighing, shaking his head, looking up and drumming his fingers on the mahogany surface as he paused to consider his words. Jack knew at once who it was.

Seen from behind, this shade of George Huxley looked hunched and old. He wore a faded green jacket. His hair was mostly grey, long, curled over the jacket's collar. There were bits of leaf in his hair; his skin was browned and desiccated, and small strands of briar were caught in the jacket and in his trousers.

There was a pause and Jack heard the whispered words: 'Familiar. All very familiar, but not right. Not right. The vortices have shifted; the places of power are not there now. The tracks are not the same. Everything has shifted . . .'

The scribbling began again, the head bowed to the task.

Jack whispered, 'I know who you are. Let me see your face.'

Had Huxley heard that murmur? He stopped writing, sat up a little, cocked his head; puzzled. After a moment's listening he turned in his chair, arm resting on the back, and peered down the corridor past his watching grandson. Jack was leaning against the frame of the door, hands in pockets, motionless.

'Steven?' Huxley called. He listened again, then repeated, 'Steven? Christian? That you? Steven?'

'It's Jack. Steven's son. His brother, Christian, is a long time lost in the heartwood.'

'Steven?' the old man murmured again, his voice fading as he leaned to peer further along the corridor, seeing nothing. Then, with a twitch of his eyebrows and a shake of his head, he turned back to his work.

Jack walked carefully into the room and stood on the other side of the desk. Huxley was heavily and scruffily bearded. A streak of white marked his chin. His eyes were red-rimmed and watery. The hands that rested on the desk, one holding a pencil, the other holding down the page of a battered journal, were skeletal, almost woody. There was tremor in the fingers, and the handwritten words were shaky.

'You can't see me,' Jack said softly. 'I wonder why?'

Huxley responded to the sound, but again looked over his shoulder, frowning deeply before continuing his scrawl.

Jack stood there for a few minutes, then came round to stand behind his grandfather and read what was being written.

It is strange to feel belonging. Yet not belonging. It is curious to feel summoned, but to not know the summoning entity; neither its nature, nor its purpose. I believe I have been ill and in a state of dreaming. Certainly, I am abundant with experiences from my explorations of the wildwood and its strange landscapes, though many of them are hazy. Perhaps an effect of my sudden awakening.

The house is not right. It is familiar, but overgrown, and there is a ghost here. I sense its presence. Perhaps the ghost is that of my own existence, returned in frail form. And summoned.

All is familiar and yet not right. The study is not as I re-member it, though it contains memories that I can relate to. It is as if clever hands have put the pieces of a jigsaw back to-gether; the jigsaw is wrong, but the pieces, for some reason, fit together.

There are books here. But all randomly placed. I do not know if my earliest journals are still intact. I cannot remember where I hid them. I write in the notebook of a schoolboy, found among Steven's effects in his room. The room has been disturbed recently. Again: I cannot fathom why or how I know this.

What shall I make of the ghost in the lodge? Is it a mythago? The oak vortex, once accessible only after an hour's walk inwards, has perhaps shifted out to encompass this rotting build-ing. I had always believed that the points of power, the fluxes of time and space that are scattered around the edge of Ryhope, were flexible in their position, their movements as unpredictable as a storm.

I remember a different season, cold and harsh, heavy snow and mindless savagery, a huddle and a hiding for survival as I journeyed. That was not long ago, but I remember nothing in between. Yes, I believe I am surfacing from a state of dreams, and must accordingly make a record of my experiences with all accuracy and concentration, especially if whatever, or whoever, has summoned me has a purpose in mind.

Jack gently touched the old man's shoulder, noticing the flinch. But it was a flinch ignored. The pencil was hovering over the page, caught between thought and the haunting presence.

Jack said, 'I'm Jack. Steven's son. I summoned you.'

No response from the strange figure at the desk.

'The why and the wherefore of that summoning is not import-ant at this moment. But the name Yssobel is a name I want to whisper to you, and ask you to imagine. Yssobel. She is your granddaughter, and she is lost; she is searching for a life that will take her into danger. That is what your son Steven believes. And of all her family, you have gone furthest and deepest into the sorts of places that Yssobel might have travelled. There is so much to explain to you, George. Though not yet. But hold Yssobel in that ghostly mind.'

Huxley was staring straight ahead. His flesh had gone cold and pale and his hands were shaking more than before. He didn't even look at the page of the notebook as he wrote – as if in the dream state to which he had previously referred – the letter Y.

Thinking that his visitor was here for a while yet, Jack went to the kitchen and quickly opened a tin of what turned out to be soup of indeterminate nature. When he returned to the study, he found it empty. The window was open and a breeze was making the primitive clothing on their hangers twist and turn. The simple notebook was still open, the pages fluttering, held down

34

by a stone. It was as if they were inviting inspection, and Jack peered at the entry for the last time that day.

All Huxley had added was a question mark after the letter Y.

Between Worlds

During the night, Huxley returned to Oak Lodge. Jack lay quietly in the darkness, watching the figure as it stumbled about the study, touching here, staring there, breathing hard, whispering from time to time; and occasionally making a forlorn sound, a sound of loss.

This very solid 'shade' of his grandfather roamed the house. Jack listened to it as it climbed unsteadily up the stairs and visited each room in turn. Furniture was shifted, objects were dropped.

Finally, Huxley came downstairs and looked out of the study window that faced towards the open land, and the world in which he had been born.

Again, he seemed to be silently crying; and then, without showing any awareness of his grandson, now crouched close by, he turned and crossed to the French windows to the garden, opened them and was gone.

Determined to try again to reach the town, Jack dressed in the new clothes but tucked his cloak into his pack. He always felt comfortable with the cloak. A glance in the mirror suggested that he was still wild-looking, his hair long and still showing the signs of the tight braids he usually wore. The boys' hair had been cut very short, as had Julie's husband's.

On impulse Jack sharpened his knife on a stone step and this time cut with more vigour, lopping off the locks and saving them carefully.

A second glance in the mirror suggested that he had made

things worse, not better. He looked as if he had been in a skirmish, his head intact but his hair having taken the brunt of the assault.

It was too late to reverse the damage but, as if she had intuited his next move, Julie had clearly come to the path either earlier that morning or during the evening. A second bag was hanging from the branch of a tree at the edge: another shirt, another pair of trousers, shoes that seemed to be made of soft leather, a box containing cold chicken and slices of a rich meat, and a strange hat.

The hat was flat on his head, with a stiff peak. It was patterned in green and black. Inside was a handwritten note: *Your hair needs trimming; meanwhile, advise you tuck it under this (if it fits). J.*

Jack laughed and called out, 'Why, thank you again. I'm glad someone's looking after me!'

The cap was strange. He pulled it down as far as he could. The sky was becoming dark and, glancing up, he saw rain clouds. The smell of rain was strong, sweeping over the hills that lay towards the setting sun.

And now he noticed something else: the edge of the wood was not where it had been two days before. It was further towards the ruined lodge. The ground was rough, scarred, though coarse grass and stubby thistles covered the marks. But now, when he turned to stare back into Ryhope, the human part of him could see the traces of the old house, even though just faintly: a touch of dark red and grey within the shadows.

Why, he wondered, was Oak Lodge being returned to the open world? Who or what was guiding this passage back to the light?

The rain started to fall, at first just a shifting shower, a freshening of the air and the pasture, then a heavier downfall below gloomy, sweeping clouds that seemed to coil above him, watching for a while, before fleeing on, away into the distance; and behind them the sky brightened and the rain eased.

By then Jack was soaked. This was nothing new, but the fabric of the clothing he now wore was so thin that it turned cold against his skin, and the cloak came out, and he buckled it at the shoulder, and felt happier at once.

Shadoxhurst was quieter today than on the day of the festival. He reached the water trough and looked along the road to the green, with its central stand of oaks, where the musicians had played, the hog had been roasted, and the brutal little boys had come for him. There were a few people walking dogs, a group of children standing outside the church, listening restlessly to someone talking to them. The shops were quiet. A few cars, mostly coloured silver or dull green, murmured their way along the streets. Jack watched them with fascination. He had always longed to see such a vehicle, but these were like nothing his father had painted for him. His father's drawings had shown black, squat machines. The vehicles he watched now were more like iridescent beetles.

He was also disturbed by how quiet it was. This was a strange thought, when he addressed it, because he had lived all his life in a quiet place, a villa with a farm, close to a deserted fortress; the sudden eruption of noise and life, of visitations or people passing by were always exciting (sometimes frightening). He had sometimes experienced the sort of vibrancy that he had witnessed during the festival, but it was a rare thing. The festival, however, had seemed to him to have a true life, to be how things should always be. Until his collapse and the attack upon him, he had felt the first suggestions of having 'come home'. Of having made the transition between worlds.

A few minutes of pleasure that had been disrupted by aggression.

Nevertheless, this quiescent and subdued town brought out feelings of sadness in Jack. He longed for noise! He longed for a swirl of life.

How long he stood by the water trough staring into the distance he didn't know. He was aware that he was hoping to see Julie. She would recognise him and come and greet him. Perhaps she would turn out to be the guide between the worlds, just as he – for her – could be the guide inwards. Both she and her son had suggested that she was intrigued by Ryhope, and that she had an insight into its inner realm. Jack had had little experience of women during his later formative years in the villa and the wild lands around it, but he had enough instinct to recognise interest in him.

The encounters with Julie had been shy, yet revealingly intimate. When he allowed these thoughts to wander aimlessly as he scanned the town, so what he saw was the look in her eyes, the way she had looked at him rather than the way she herself looked.

Jack took a deep breath, unbuckled the cloak and packed it away, glanced down at his saturated shirt, shivered with the cold, then took the next step. Literally, the next step. He walked past the trough towards the church. He waited for the clutch at his bowels and head, the wood-scream that would turn him round and draw him back. He kept walking.

The scream didn't come. He reached the centre of the green, and leaned against one of the oaks there.

It had started to rain heavily again; the group of children dispersed quickly, and the streets emptied suddenly. Jack was startled by the sound of a car starting up and driving off, its tyres screeching. Voices shouted, followed by laughter. Doors slammed and three people, hidden below wide rain-shades, ran quickly to a building where a sign showing the crude image of a Green Jack was hung. A moment later Julie appeared from the same building, running in the same direction. He started to call to her, but found he couldn't speak the name. Even so, she glanced back, quickly, querulously, before entering the same building, which Jack knew was where food was served and where the sour drink that had been offered to him two days before was sold.

I can walk there. I can make it there. I can join her, talk to her. I can extend the edge of my world . . .

He repeated this thought many times, but all the time he stayed where he was, in the half-shelter of the oaks, almost as rooted as the old trees themselves. He was brought back to consciousness by a quiet voice, a man's voice, saying, 'You look very wet and very lost. Can I help you at all?'

For a moment as he looked around, Jack saw nothing but the green, the oaks, the distant hills, the hints of forest. He had looked through the man several times before the figure came into focus. He was standing very close, wearing a long coat and a black leather hat, from which rain was dripping. His face was grey with a stubbly beard, his eyes dark-rimmed, narrowed, possibly curious, certainly tired; but not old.

'Can you see me?' the apparition asked.

'Yes. Yes, I can.'

'It took you a while, though. Quite a while.'

'I didn't see you at first. That's true.'

'I know what you are,' the grey man said. 'I know your nature. They rarely come here. I usually find them in the fields, or out by the railway tracks. Sometimes in the river. You are the first that has tried to come into the town. There must be something special about you.'

'The first? The first what?'

'You know exactly what I mean. Eddie hasn't exactly been discreet about you. You remember Eddie?'

'The fair-haired boy. Yes, I met him. He was good to me, brought me some food. His mother brought me clothes.'

The other man glanced up and down at Jack and smiled. 'The rain makes them fit, at least. They don't really suit you. It wasn't so much the clothes you wore, you know – the other day, when the vermin in this place treated you so badly; it wasn't the clothes. It was the smell. But the rain has helped with that.'

'And soap,' Jack added. 'You said: "the first". I asked, "The first what?"'

'Wood haunter. You're a wood haunter.'

'That's what Eddie called me.'

'It's what you're all known as. Generally.'

All of us?

'My father has a different name for it,' Jack said. 'But how much of that name I am, I don't know. I just know that I have a "haunter" side, and that he sees the wildwood differently.'

'I understand. And your father's name for it,' the man asked carefully, 'myth imago? Would that be right?'

'Mythago,' Jack whispered.

The black-coated man thought about that, then nodded his head and took off his hat to reveal a long length of grey hair, tied back in a plait. 'I'm something of the wild myself,' he said quietly, 'though not as wild as you. A wild life ended in humility, tucked up inside grey stone. Vows taken, counsel accepted, especially among the middle-aged. Services unattended, and an

40

odd witness from one temple of new practices, to older practices on the green, an even older temple. Do you understand what I'm saying?'

'Not a word,' Jack said.

'I'm what is called "the vicar" here. I came to it late. It's a long story. A very long story. But that's my church now, built of good local stone by long-dead craftsmen from all over the land. And a bit of local labour. Nearly a thousand years ago. I'd like you to come into my church, dry off, and have something to drink and something to eat. What do you say?'

'I'll try.'

'You'll try to eat?'

'I'll try to get to your church.'

Greybeard frowned for a moment, then seemed to understand. 'Haunted. Haunting. The ghost is never far away from the grave. Ryhope is your home and your grave. I think I understand. There are chains on you. Chains made of vines and briar.'

Jack stared at this strange man and all cold in his body had gone. This was his second encounter during which he had suddenly felt a sense of being known, understood and welcomed. Perhaps the bridge between worlds was not in the steps taken, but in the encounters made. Julie had touched his heart. This man had inspired courage.

'I think I can make it.'

'Good. It's Jack, isn't it? Jack of Ryhope? Jack of Leather? Jack the Haunter?'

'Huxley. Jack Huxley. And you?'

'Caylen Reeve. Some call me "The Reverend" Caylen Reeve but, as I said, there's a story behind that. For another time. If you can make it into my grey-stone mausoleum, please regard the tomb as your home. All wooden pews available for sleeping. Sacrifice what you like upon the altar. I deal only in church wine and Indian takeaways. Only one rule: don't ring the bells. It's a job I love and guard jealously. And if the stone walls start to sweat and swell, leave fast and go back to Ryhope. I mean that very seriously. But for the moment – if you make it – a mere three hundred paces! – shall we have some Indian cuisine?'

'I have no idea what that is.'

'No. I don't suppose you do.'

Jack remembered his father talking to him about the Indian Nations. 'Buffalo?'

Caylen laughed. 'Buffalo? Ah, I see what you mean. Well, I can ask. But it will come in a spicy sauce.'

Courage!

Caylen walked ahead of him, a confident stride, the wide-brimmed hat now settled upon his head again, catching the light rain. Jack followed, focusing on the door to the grey building, aware that he could hear a whisper of urgency, the moaning song of return.

I've come this far. I'll go that small step further!

He fought the sudden urge to turn and run. He reached the steps, five of them, that led to the open doors of the church. Hard-eyed now, and solemn, Caylen watched him as he hauled his feet up those five simple slabs of stone. His stomach was hurting, his head contained a sound like the raging of a river, the rushing of water over rocks, the crash of waves against the steep cliffs where the river turned. He was shaking.

'You're doing well. You're doing very well indeed. It's important to stretch the chain.'

Calm words from the expressionless man, his grey eyes seeming unblinking as Jack reached the door. 'Stretch the chain and you can find the dream. You will never break the chain. But stretch it, stretch it: that is in your own power. Ten more paces, Jack. Stretch for ten more paces. Come on.'

Ten more paces!

He felt as if stones were dragging at his feet. His head was hammering against a wall. Branches whipped him, water sucked him down. The screech of elementals was unbearable – almost There would be peace in running back. There would be silence and relief in returning to the lodge.

'Five more paces, Jack.'

He flung himself forward, then screamed in pain, embracing a cold marbled floor, feeling strong hands on his shoulders.

'Far enough. This is far enough.'

The hands pinned him down, but this was not aggression: the hands were holding, supporting, fingers pushed into his muscles to relax them. He had twisted round and faced the spill of light from the open doors of the church, and a woman was standing there. She hesitated only for a moment before running to him, crouching down and whispering words he couldn't take in. Two gentle fingers on his face; soft breath on his lips. The flow of words between the woman and the priest were murmurings of urgency, then calm.

'You've done well, Jack. You've extended the edge of your world.'

'Julie . . .'

'Yes.' She leaned down towards him, bright and smiling. 'The little brats are in school. And the clothes suit you. The hat doesn't. And what in the name of all that isn't holy have you done to your hair?'

'Cut it. Your suggestion.'

Laughter. Julie said, 'I'll find a way to rescue it. Just stay calm, Jack. Altar wine for the boy!'

This last was addressed to the vicar.

'I'll see if I've got any left.'

More laughter.

Courage!

He was cold now, and the space he was sitting in was high and wide, and cold and grey, and the light that struck his face came through shaped windows, and some of it was coloured and confusing. A gentle hand was entwined with his, and still there was the soft breath, sweet breath. The grey-haired man was bustling about, but mostly writing in a book while almost simultaneously spooning a stew into his mouth. The food was fragrant and unusual, the texture of the meat so soft it might have been a flavoured bark fungus. Jack had eaten a little, but the pungent spices and the burning sensation of one of the meats had made him retch. A cooling drink, not unlike a weak goat's milk, had helped his stomach calm down.

Earlier, Julie had fussed at his hair, using scissors and a very fine comb to cut away the tangle that he had left, leaving nothing on his neck and scalp that he could touch with any confidence. But she had kept every length of hair in a paper bag – he

43

remembered crying out that she should do so – and he clutched the bag as if it were a container of life itself.

'I need to go home.'

'Yes,' Julie said. 'You've come further than before. That took some doing, I imagine.'

'It was . . . easier at first. Then hard. My head is a rage of noise.'

'Go home. You've come very far.'

Jack suddenly became aware of her, turning sharply, his face so close to hers that she pulled back slightly, then smiled, leaning forward again. He said, 'I pushed further. But I can't push much further than this. Perhaps it's enough. I feel cold here.'

She listened to him in silence; stayed silent; then said, 'I can't be sure of what you're feeling. But when I tried to come to the old Lodge yesterday, I was terrified. You forced your way here against your fears. I'd like to try again: for the house. Tomorrow. If you'll help me.'

'Of course.'

'Help me overcome the terror.'

'I understood what you meant.'

'And we can talk?'

'Yes. Of course. You might even meet my grandfather.'

He noticed the way Julie's breathing changed, how her whole body tensed, her heart racing for a moment, her sweat changing odour suddenly, exuding excitement.

Whatever it was he had eaten, Jack was suddenly wretched again, and crawled to the huge stone bowl where he had earlier emptied his stomach. He retched for a second time, clinging to the carved edge of the basin, then pressed the metal button with its little cross for a flow of water to swirl away the mess. And after that, without looking back, he picked up his pack and ran, cumbersomely but with increasing strength, out of the town and towards the wood.

Back in the tranquillity of the study, he wondered if Huxley had been there during the day.

It was clear that his grandfather had returned to Oak Lodge, however briefly, since the notebook had gone, and Jack doubted that anyone else would have removed it.

Iaelven

Shortly before dawn Jack had visitors. He had been expecting them.

The flickering light of torches appeared at each window of the study, the flame burning a strange green. At the same time the soft trilling of pipes began again, their rising and falling tunes entrancing and distracting. It was the sound of pipes that had alerted Jack earlier to the arrival of a band of Muurngoth.

He had seen the signs of them along the river, close to where he'd been forced to hide his boat. It didn't surprise him that they had now come to the edge. It was what they did: seeking to steal from the outside world, to abduct and remove, to pillage life to take back to their own enclosed realms, where time was ruled by a set of whims different to those of Ryhope Wood itself.

Jack was prepared for the visit and had armed himself with iron and arrows. He had found a bow among Huxley's museum artefacts that could still pull efficiently, although he wouldn't risk using the willow to its full capacity. There was something about everything that Huxley had collected that suggested life, but brittle life; newness, but a certain fragility due to age.

He knew how to handle Muurngoth in small numbers, though they were dangerous. If the pipes began to shrill and the Muurngoth began to sing in their distant, echoing voices, the human part of him would be as susceptible as any other human to their summoning charms. They had been called by many names, he knew from his education at the villa.

He tried to assess the size of the group, first by listening to the bone pipes – he heard four – and then by counting torches: two at the windows, but a further four on the woodland side of the lodge. When the torch at the outer window vanished, he darted there and scanned the darkness, noticing three altogether. Eight, then, which probably meant ten or twelve, since some would be hugging the darkness, unlit, waiting.

Jack strung the bow, found an iron-tipped arrow – silver would have been better – and strode to the flame at the double doors to the garden. As he came to the glass panels, reflection confusing him for a moment, he saw the eyes of the creature that was searching the interior. They were looking down at him!

He took an involuntary step back, startled to realise the height of this investigating *Iaelven*. Not Muurngoth, not the small, teasing creatures he had often come across during his youthful years in the wood: these were Amurngoth! They were a far more dangerous species of Iaelven. He had seen them only once before.

He thought back to the signs, the traces he had seen on the river. Yes, now he remembered that the fire-pits had been large, the temporary wooden enclosures too wide for the less robust form of this life.

But they would still respond to his defences. Jack stepped forward again and unlatched the French windows, pulling them in with his bow hand as he thrust the iron-tipped arrow forward with the other.

The Amurngoth looked at him through the narrowed vertical slits of its eyes. The stink that came from it was overwhelming. Its pursed mouth stretched into a parody of a human smile and it shook its head slowly, the long frill of its hair flowing like weed in water.

It made a whispering noise, then sang briefly, a sound that set Jack's skin crawling and which made him falter, almost dropping the pointed and drawn arrow.

But his shadow stepped forward, screeching loudly, drew back the bowstring and pressed the iron point of the arrow against the Amurngoth's bare-boned chest.

It retreated, dropping the torch. Shrilling sounds, and a chatter like magpies, signalled the sudden and rapid departure of the raiding band, though Jack noticed, with human eyes and

Haunter instinct, that they moved along the edge, rather than retreating inwards.

They were out for prey, and they clearly had Shadoxhurst in their sights.

The Amurngoth were the true 'stealers'. Change-hunters. They stole the new and left their own behind. They carried a supply of shards, unshaped pieces of wood, usually rowan or willow, and when they found the opportunity to steal, they were adept at shaping the shard to reflect the stolen life, usually that of an infant child, sometimes an older child, though that involved a great deal of effort. In Jack's father's time, the Amurngoth had all but disappeared, though, in the generations before, the Amurngoth had become a considerable and tangible presence in the outer world. It was akin to a slow invasion. It had worked well for many generations; but the Amurngoth had been frustrated by the one thing they could not control: change.

They never changed, and they lived by different rules of time. The world they coveted changed and was steady in the passing of days.

The days, eventually, had passed the Amurngoth by. On the outside world, at least.

But they were here again now, and Jack couldn't help but think that they had been following him. This was more of his Haunter's instinct. Having seen the traces of them by the river, mistaking them for the smaller kind, he'd assumed they existed at that location. But perhaps they had merely overtaken him.

His journey from the Villa to the edge had been an opening of a channel, perhaps. He felt alarmed at the thought, since it meant he might have put the small town over the rise in danger, all because of his curiosity.

Could they move that far from the edge of Ryhope Wood? It was a consoling thought that if a half-human could only just make it, a non-human would be drawn back far more quickly. Nevertheless, he would have to find a way of warning the priest without alarming him, and suggest he find a way to quietly spread the word: there is danger at the edge.

*

The torch that the Amurngoth scout had dropped had ceased to flare, but it would still be useful. It burned again as Jack picked it up, but the flame died as he placed it in the kitchen sink. The chaotic chorus of birds was signalling first light and he made a rapid inspection of the dew-frosted land, walking rapidly as far as the silent outskirts of Shadoxhurst itself, inspecting the pasture and the rough tracks for signs of the Iaelven, but he saw nothing but animal traces.

Returning to the sticklebrook, he stood at the place where twin alders crossed and let the Haunter look for signs of the band.

They had been here. This was where they had found the open land. But they had not progressed further than this, returning instead to the deeper wood, and moving towards the Lodge on one side, and . . . yes . . . they had divided into two groups, the other exploring away from the house.

Everything was silent now. There would be no piping, no singing, no enchanting summons. Not now, not in the day. But the Haunter was uncertain. It sensed that the Amurngoth were still close, folded up in their nests, awake and canny, listening and learning.

Tired and hungry, Jack returned to Oak Lodge and savaged open another of the cans from the larder. The contents were soft and smooth, tasting of very little that he recognised, and he ate it with the chewy but sweet bread that Julie had brought him the day before. Once again, he tried to remember the joy of his mother Guiwenneth's sharp-flavoured cooking, the solid, fatty meats, the belly-satisfying grain cakes, the scalding and soothing broths.

He finished the can and the bread and made a quiet decision to go hunting later – but beyond the edge, not within it. There might well be new game to find in the hinterland around Shadoxhurst.

As the empty can clattered into the sink, so a sound came from above, as if an animal had been suddenly startled.

It surprised Jack as well, and he reached at once for his bow and arrows, wiping the blade of his iron knife clean and sheathing it.

The sound had come from the room where – he tried to remember the way this house was constructed – yes, where his uncle Christian had stored his belongings, slept, and prepared for the day.

Jack went upstairs; there was little point in being quiet since the wooden boards creaked loudly, several of them threatening to give way beneath his hesitant step, so much so that he almost ran to the landing and then walked purposefully to the open door of Christian's room.

He saw a bed that was now dishevelled, a scatter of books, an open wardrobe, the clothes scattered.

A voice whispered, 'Chris?'

Turning, he saw his grandfather standing at the top of the stairs. Huxley was staring at him, yet through him. The old man held shirts and trousers in his arms; in his right hand he held the school notebook in which he had begun to keep his latest record. He had a vacant look and was wildly unkempt, his trousers creased, his feet bare. He had shaved his beard roughly, and there was dried blood on his neck and cheek. His hair was sticking out in spikes, perhaps the result of a restless sleep.

He had been here all night. While the Amurngoth had probed the edges of the Lodge, Huxley had been upstairs all the time!

'Hello, George. Hello, Grandfather. Can you see me?'

'Chris?'

'Jack. It's Jack.'

'Steven?'

'No. Not Steven. Jack.'

Jack approached the man cautiously. The rank odour from the man's body was suddenly overwhelming, no doubt the same smell of sweat and travel, of distraction and the wild that would have greeted the two boys on Jack's first appearance at the edge of Ryhope.

'You need a bath, old man. A good wash.'

'Chris?'

Huxley was staring into a different time; whether into a truly remembered time, or a time created out of the mythago's dreams, Jack had no way of knowing. Was this the real man, returned after many years' absence? Or a mythago drawn from

Jack's human side? Haunter, the wildwood aspect of Jack, whispered: not real.

And yet this Huxley, this risen presence, knew what he had had, knew what had been in his life, knew his sons, and knew that he had given his life to documenting the apparitions and the phenomena, even the nature, of Ryhope Wood.

In his right hand he clutched the simple journal in which he – a mythago – was accounting for his new existence in the home from which he had vanished in 1946, a disappearance that had not resulted in a *reappearance* until now.

Jack stared hungrily at the tattered notebook. Had his grandfather been writing during the night? He had obviously been curled up on Christian's narrow bed; he had raided the wardrobe for clothes; he had surrounded himself with the tangible memories of one of his two sons.

But had he written in the journal? And had he proceeded beyond that question mark after the letter Y?

Was there anything, yet, about Yssobel?

George Huxley seemed to wake from a daydream. He became aware of the clothing he was clutching and let it drop. His gaze still vacant, still not aware of his grandson, he stumbled awkwardly down the stairs and into his study, sitting down heavily at the desk, smoothing out the pages, staring for a moment at the garden windows. Then he plucked a pencil from the holder and started to write.

Jack found a cushion, tossed it to the floor in front of the cabinet of flint and bronze artefacts, and sat down, folded his arms and watched Huxley. They were face to face across the room, and occasionally Huxley looked up, looked directly at Jack, but in a distracted way, as if thinking rather than seeing, returning quickly to the rapid scrawl of words.

There was something of a fever in the older man. His breathing was loud, with long pauses, gasps of understanding, little sighs of satisfaction, and the occasional groan of frustration. And he talked constantly, though the words were uttered so sibilantly, and in so low a voice, that Jack could make out very little.

I made you, Jack thought, and with that thought there came a moment's affection.

Old man: lank hair, grey, rough-hewn cheeks and scarred chin, sagging eyes, clothes dreamed out of nightmare; and the pulse of blood in his temples, and the odour of moss and undergrowth on the breath.

I made you. I summoned you. And you came, equipped with memory. My father was right. You would come equipped with memory. And you have it, though you think of it as jigsaw.

Each time gaze met gaze, Jack felt his heart race. It was impossible to tell whether Huxley was seeing him or not; and yet, there was the distinct sense that the older man was aware of the presence of his half-human, half-Haunter descendant.

'Yssobel,' Jack finally said aloud. 'Your granddaughter, my sister. Yssobel. She is the very image of a woman you once loved: my mother. *Guiwenneth.*'

At the sound of the name, Huxley frowned, though he did not look up. He paused for a moment before continuing to write.

'Yes, Guiwenneth,' Jack persisted from his sitting position, almost taunting the man now. 'So beautiful. You loved her. You summoned her. You summoned love, because you wanted it, as I have summoned memory – memory of you, grandfather – because I need it. Guiwenneth!'

Huxley made a keening sound, his eyes closed, his body hunched, the hand that held the pencil now shaking. If he spoke words, Jack again could not hear them. And after a moment, the spasm of grief, or whatever was causing the distress, passed away.

'Yssobel,' Jack repeated now. 'I know you can help me find out where she went. I saw you talking to her, at the edge of the villa, when I was younger. Was it you? Or a shade of you? How do I know? But Grandfather, you know of your granddaughter. You know of Yssobel.'

Yssobel, the shade of Huxley murmured, and Jack leaned forward.

'Yes. You remember her.'

Huxley looked around as if seeing his surroundings for the first time. 'Yssobel.'

'What happened to her?'

'Yssobel,' breathed the ghost.

Jack spoke softly: 'When I was a boy, I saw you. I saw you many times at the villa, where your Steven lives now. And a few seasons before she rode off, before she disappeared, I saw you talking to her. You came and went, just as you always do. You came out of the wood and you whispered to her. She remembered nothing of your visits, but I do: I saw you so many times. Whispering, whispering. You know, you alone know, where she went, and why she went, and what drove her away. Talk to me, George. Talk to me. About Yssobel!'

'Yssobel,' the man repeated quietly, sitting up straight, as if he had just seen something startling. 'Oh no, oh no . . .'

The forlorn voice, the forlorn whisper, were the last words the mythago spoke.

Huxley pushed back from the desk and stumbled to the French windows, pushing them open and staring into the gloom of Ryhope. As Jack struggled to his feet, the old man lurched away. He could not possibly have walked so fast as to have vanished into the wood by the time Jack reached the garden. But Huxley had gone, absorbed yet again.

Jack called for him twice. Silence was his only reply.

He went back to the study and sat down at the desk, leaning close to the scrawl of words, deciphering them as best he could.

I have been dragged from the grave. The ghost-lit boy has dragged me here. He stinks of the wood, a stink I know so well.

Dragged from the grave, but also dragged out of time. I was lost. This haunting 'boy' has resurrected me, and I begin to remember the LIFE before.

So much reconstructs itself. The jigsaw shuffles, the pieces turn and twist and shape and fit. Bit by bit, shape by shape, echo by echo, memory by memory, all begins to congeal. I am . . . Huxley. I can shape my life.

I am reborn with the flesh and mind and recollection of my first incarnation. That is to say – as far as I can tell. I can shape it, both the flesh and the dream. In order to remember. And the ghost-lit boy will recognise me. But will I recognise the ghost-lit boy for what it is?

Is it attached to me? This boy? A version of myself? I have no way of knowing yet.

The genesis of 'myth imago' forms is more intricate than the Ur-Huxley, the original form of me, could possibly have understood.

I am more aware than him, though it is his struggle to understand that drives my own curiosity.

Ur-Huxley? Jack stared at the word, bemused by it. 'The original form of me.' Did he mean the real man, the true man, the man who had been a child, had grown, had learned, had lived in the Lodge, had explored, sired two children; had pursued a strange dream; and died in the heartwoods?

So the memories and dreams of Ur-Huxley also rose in the mythago, just as the ragged clothes were re-formed, just as the flesh and bone, the blood and beat and pulse of the heart were shaped again.

But from whose memory? From the human side of Jack? From Steven? Or from Jack's 'haunter' side, the aspect of him that was silently in tune with the timelessness of the wildwood.

Haunter was quiescent inside Jack, understanding nothing of this. Haunter was instinct.

Jack turned back the pages of the notebook to see what had been written during the night when the Amurngoth had visited and distracted him, while all the time his grandfather was upstairs in hiding, sketching his visions in words.

This scrawl was even harder to decipher, but underlined several times was his sister's name. And under that bold statement, which signified either confusion or realisation, were the words: *Yss. Her birth. Eagles.*

The name Yssobel, or Issaubel, is whispered to me, and I have remembered a small story relating to the later life of Guiwenneth, though I cannot remember who told it to me, nor where it was that the story was spoken.

She was born in the early evening. Eagles flew around the fortress during her mother's labour, and with her first cry of life they scattered, though one came back later and stayed. The child was in distress. At dawn, when she was taken to the spring to be drowned and reborn, the child reached and wailed, watching the solitary eagle through eyes that showed awareness, but no comfort, only anxiety. And yet – piercing through the misty, infant blue – curiosity!

Yssobel was the daughter of Guiwenneth, who was known as 'the Green' and was of noble birth, being the daughter of the Warlord Peredur and his wife Dierdrath.

In her childhood years, Yssobel and her mother were close and affectionate, and Yssobel learned much about her mother's hardships, and the loss of her father under cruel circumstances. But in later years, the friendship between mother and daughter was broken.

Guiwenneth wounded the girl with her words, and the house became angry.

Although Yssobel continued to live in her parent's house, hardly any words were spoken between them, and when they were, they were brief and usually harsh.

There came a day when Guiwenneth went out from the fort and never returned. All that is known of her is that she was heard singing the Song of the Islands of the Lost, which are reached by one of the five valleys that lead away from her father's memorial stone at the edge of Lavondyss.

Distraught at the loss, her daughter went to search for her, and in doing so found a new world of her own. She, too, disappeared.

There is another story about her, almost as small, but more intriguing. It is unresolved. I must try to reimagine it.

At this point, the entry had been underlined and it ended; the journal was closed over the pencil. By the harsh light spilling into the room, Jack could see a handprint, made perhaps from sweat. He pressed his own hand against it, not truly knowing why he did so.

The account was a shadowy reflection of the true events – they had not occurred in a fort but in the Roman villa where the family had lived until its abandonment. And Jack was intrigued by certain things, particularly the reference to the memorial stone. And *The Sons of the Islands of the Lost* was a favourite song of his mother's. But he needed more if he was to find his sister and, in that finding, understand what had happened to Guiwenneth.

He sat down and read the entry again and again, until his eyes closed and he drifted into dreaming sleep.

Elf-shot

During the night, the wood around the house was restless. The floor beneath Jack's feet trembled and grumbled on occasion, then went quiet. The moon was a strange colour, ruddy; he had never seen such a moon. The wind was strong, coming from the west, but it didn't hold the scent of a storm.

Despite his intentions to rise at first light and try and make his way to Shadoxhurst, exhaustion must have caught up with him. He fell into a deep sleep and woke from a vivid dream well into the morning. He washed, gathered his pack, and briskly left the house into what he expected to be a tangle of undergrowth.

Instead, he found himself staring out into open space, across the remains of a collapsed stone wall towards the fields that led to the ridge and the road to the town. The whole area contained within the wall was scattered with shards of terracotta pottery and coloured ceramics, almost certainly the remains of decorative pots.

And Julie was standing there, just beyond the wall, silent and absorbed in looking at the newly revealed façade of Oak Lodge.

In the night hours, the wood had pulled back from the old house as far as its front wall. The ivy-covered grey brick peered from the undergrowth, face-like and haunting. The windows were dark; the tall chimney stacks could be seen through the branches. For a while Jack took in the sight, comparing it with the model he had made when he'd been a child, noticing the details he had got correct, the details both correct and missed, all based on his father's description.

What had it been like, he wondered, when the house stood

tall, square, alone in its grounds, reached by the single track from the main road that ran beyond the hill, between the villages and the bigger cities, and people had come here in their cars or on horseback, and sat in the grounds, in the sun, talking and discussing mysteries? It struck him that the building must have been remote and isolated, silent in the landscape, almost a lonely place.

And he remembered what his father had told him: the house *had* been a silent place except, towards the end, for the shouting and the anger. Its visitors were mostly stiff and surly men of science, who shut themselves away behind the study door and conversed in low voices with his father. 'It was not a house where laughter was a commonplace, unlike our own home, Jack.'

Though, sadly, neither had there been much laughter in the villa, in the wildwood, in the years before Jack had left.

'This is so weird,' said Julie from behind him. 'If I wasn't seeing it, I wouldn't believe it.'

He walked up to her, then glanced back again. 'When my father lived here, many years ago, when he was alone here, one night the house was swallowed. You can still see the traces of it inside. There's a room where a tree grew right through the house. But that's gone now.'

'What a strange place. Much stranger than I'd realised. It's really quite frightening. And I let my son come fishing here.'

'I wouldn't do that for a while,' Jack cautioned, but didn't feel this was the moment to go into detail about the Iaelven.

'So weird,' Julie repeated. Then, looking at Jack, 'I think you can expect some sightseers. People will be curious.'

'Don't tell them for a while. If you don't mind.'

'No. Of course not.'

She was carrying a bag, and suddenly remembered why she'd come. 'I brought you some books. I thought you might be interested to see what the world out here looks like. They're . . . picture books.' She seemed uncomfortable. 'I expect there are a lot of books in the house.'

'Very many. Very leathery, and full of words. Not many pictures. I'd like to see yours.'

She had brought a book showing famous sites in Britain and

Europe, and another with views of the Americas. There was also a book of planets and stars, which astonished Jack as he leafed through it. Saturn? Jupiter? And that's Mars? This is what they look like close up?

Julie explained how the pictures had been taken and his mind reeled.

'And more milk and bread, and some meat in tins that are easier to open. You don't have to stab them with a knife,' she added with a smile.

'Thank you. Again.' Jack caught her eye, that slightly intense and interested stare that made him slightly nervous. 'Is everyone in this world as generous?'

'No. They're not. By no means.'

'Neither in mine.'

'But this is not generosity, this is just a little help for an interesting – if weird – woodland man.'

'Some of the help tastes good,' he said. 'Some is – weird.' He smiled as he repeated her word.

He realised that Julie was shaking. He'd noticed it when she passed him the books. She was also very pale. Perhaps she saw his question before he could ask it, and she said, 'I'm quite frightened of what's happening. There is such a strange feeling about this place. Everyone talks about Ryhope Wood as being dangerous; lots of old mine shafts and boggy patches where you can sink down into the mud. And the kids talk of "wood haunters", but are they real or not? Probably just itinerants.'

He frowned at the word.

'Travellers. People who roam the country, no fixed home.'

'That's certainly me,' Jack said. 'Though I have a fixed home a year's struggle away.' He was guessing at the time he'd taken to get here – it had certainly been long.

'I should be going mad with what I'm seeing,' Julie added. 'But I'm not. There is something very otherworldly about you, but something very calm. It's as if . . .' She struggled to find the way to put her confused thought. 'As if you're a gate, a safe gate, into the . . .'

'Weird?'

'Yes. Into the weird.'

'Perhaps I am. Thank you again, Julie, Now to try and find the churchman.'

'Caylen? I can bring him here, if you like.'

Jack thought about the proposition, then decided against it. He was half thinking: one more try to break the hold of Ryhope. Just one more try.

They walked along the edge of the wood, to the stream which flowed from the heart. It was wider now, and by listening carefully Jack could hear how it dropped steeply and became faster. All the rules of nature were subjected to the whim of the unnatural.

He made it as far as the edge of the village before his heart began to race and his chest tightened. Another step, with Julie watching him anxiously, and he was dragging himself forward against ropes. Then the sound of roaring in his head, the scream of a storm, the raucous cries of carrion birds, urging him back, back to the green.

He'd managed further than this the second time he'd tried.

Julie's hands were on his face, her eyes wide with anxiety. 'It wants you back, doesn't it? It doesn't want you here. You don't belong here.'

Jack managed to nod in agreement.

'I'm sorry,' she said.

'I've seen a little of it,' he muttered.

'You'll have to make that little go a long way.'

He sat on the bench by the water trough, and calmed down a little, closing his eyes. A while later, he realised that Caylen Reeve was sitting next to him, holding out a mug of hot drink. Jack accepted it. It was sweet and strange, and Caylen told him it was 'tea'.

'Something's happened,' the churchman said. He was wearing ordinary clothes, not his vestments; thick leather trousers and a hunting jacket. His wide-brimmed hat was hooked on his knee.

'Something very dangerous is in the area,' Jack told him.

'What sort of dangerous?' The man was very calm, steely-eyed as he watched Jack with an intensity that was quite disturbing.

How to explain? 'Have children ever gone missing from the town?'

'Runaways?'

'Just missing.'

The churchman didn't break his hard gaze. He watched Jack as if he was curious about the younger man's words. 'Not for many years. But yes, there are reports of children disappearing, families broken apart by it. It goes back a long way, too. The church has a small stone plaque in it. Come and see.'

Jack shook his head. 'This is as far as I can get.'

'Not with me, it isn't. Come on.'

Caylen hauled Jack to his feet, put his hat on his head. There was a shotgun leaning against the bench, and he grabbed this too. Jack recognised it for the sort of weapon it was and was puzzled.

The draw to the wood was strong, the sense of disorientation the same as before, but weaker. Caylen Reeve took his arm and the two men walked slowly to the church and entered its cool, silent confines. 'There. See? With me, the evil gets shouted away.' Caylen was smiling. Jack was confused. How did this man manage to weaken the bond with the wood?

'This is the plaque.'

It was a small rectangular piece of grey stone, with shallow inscriptions and the date 1643, though that meant nothing to Jack himself. Caylen read it out: 'On This Day of Our Lord, our children Betheny, Crispin, Oliver, Samuel and Joseph were lost to us, taken by an unnameable evil. May God protect them from harm.' He looked at Jack, half smiling. 'It's an unusual sort of thing to find in a church, I'm told. Lists of war dead, yes; memorials to knights and bishops, yes. But this has been carved by amateur hands; each name has a different signature to it. This was carved by the parents of the lost children.'

'An unnameable evil,' Jack repeated. 'And what do you think that was?'

Caylen hesitated for a moment, before saying, 'I suppose in 1643 they'd have called them "faery folk". But I call them Amurngoth.'

Older and younger man stared at each other in silence. Jack's mind was a whirl of thoughts, not just the effect of being so far from his home. The churchman was smiling slightly, his grey eyes twinkling.

'What are you?' Jack asked.

'More green than you,' replied the other.

Mythago! Now Jack understood what the man had meant by 'I'm something of the wild myself. Though not as wild as you.'

Caylen was nodding gently. 'Let's get out into the air.'

'I don't remember coming here. I just remember opening my eyes and I was in this church, and there were people fussing over me. I was just a boy. But I stayed here, grew, learned the church ways, and the real priest, who lives in a grand house behind the church itself, made me his ward. And then warden. I'm no reverend, though people call me that sometimes and maintain the illusion. I've been a part of the community for so long that nobody takes any notice any more.

'I knew the Iaelven were close. I have a gift for smelling them. Or perhaps sensing them would be better. I think that's why I was born. To protect the people against dealers in changelings. Have you seen them?'

'Yes. Last night. I used iron elf-shot. That's what my father calls it. It drives them back, or at least away to somewhere else. Scares them, anyway.'

'Let's hope so. Meanwhile, I've quietly told all parents to make sure they know where their kids are at all times. That *is* what you came to see me about, isn't it?'

Jack agreed.

The priest looked all at once uncomfortable. 'Strange feeling: to know suddenly what you're facing, without having encountered it before, and without having seen it this time. But knowing it's there.'

'When you come to the Lodge, I'll give you elf-shot. Or show you how to make it.'

'I think I already do. But thanks, any way.'

They were strolling along the road out of Shadoxhurst, Caylen with his hat tipped back and the shotgun, broken, across his shoulder. Jack, with his ill-fitting clothes and leather sack, was no less incongruous a figure. It was a gloomy, cold day.

'Your grandfather is quite a legend here, around this place as well as other villages or small towns. But only among the elderly. People who lived here when he lived here. They always talk about the house in the wood, but no one younger takes them seriously.'

Jack thought about that. 'The wood is vast. I know it doesn't seem it, but it is. It has an awareness all of its own. And it feeds on people. On their unconscious minds, as I understand it.'

'You're well educated for a wood-haunter,' Caylen said, a curious note in his voice.

'My father is an educated man. He taught me a great deal. My sister too. Poor Yssobel.'

'Poor Yssobel?'

'Like those children in the church, she disappeared one night. But of her own will, we think. We're not sure. Broke my father's heart.'

'I'm sorry.'

'It was probably broken again when I decided to come to find the outside world.'

'Twice sorry. Jack: how can it be that when we come alive we are not just the legend, but we *know* what we are as well? Is that unusual?'

'No. Not unusual at all. I live in a Roman villa, surrounded by caves, fortresses, other places, and the mythagos that inhabit them believe they're in the real world. But I don't have an answer for you on the "how" of it, reverend.'

'I'm not a reverend, remember? I'm *mythago*. Settled at the edge.'

There was a moment's silence. Caylen added with a shake of his head and a grin, 'Brings a whole new meaning to a village-bound life.'

Jack turned and gripped the older man's arm. 'Watch out for faeries.'

'Born to the task! I know they can't return to their hill without something to show.'

Jack strode off ahead, breaking into a run as he returned to Ryhope. He had only gone a few paces when Caylen called out to him and he turned round.

The man was standing there, gun over shoulder, hat now held

next to his leg. 'What do you think brought the Iaelven to the edge this time?'

It was an uncomfortable question, but one that Jack had considered before, 'I don't know,' he called back. 'But it occurs to me: they were following me.'

Armour of a King

Jack approached the house, fascinated by the brick face it presented against the shroud of green and shadow. He mimed opening the gate (now gone) and admiring the wild rose and fruit bushes that probably had once adorned this approach to the front door. He plucked an imaginary plum from an imaginary plum tree – he could see the pit and root marks where a small tree had once stood – then shook hands with an imaginary grandfather, who greeted him at the door.

The door was open. Had he left it that way? Probably. He went inside into the hall, then walked through to the back of the house. There was a strange light there. No, not strange: just brighter than when he'd arrived. And there were animal sounds which he instantly recognised as the noise of chickens. Chickens? There were two ways to the back: a main door to the lawns and garden; and through the kitchen to where the chicken runs had been, and the vegetable garden had been planted. He went through the kitchen. The coops, fallen and rotting, were exposed, but five chickens were pecking around them. There was a fence at the bottom of this garden, and a rusted iron gate. The wood abutted that gate, and spread around the property, but the gardens were exposed again.

I must be doing this, Jack thought. Like I drove back the Iaelven, I'm driving back the forest. Or is it welcoming me home?

Back in the house, he noticed that the kitchen had been disturbed. It had been untidy when he'd found it, and had become worse while he'd been here. Jack was not a tidy man. An animal, perhaps, had been in. On the floor were cans which he had left on the work surface. For a long moment he stood in silence, listening, but there was only the sound of the hens clucking as they pecked at the ground, and of the rustling breeze.

He went to the study. His bedroll and blanket were as he'd left them, in the corner, but the exercise-book journal was gone. And there was a rank smell in the room. And the sound of soft breathing.

He turned and nearly fell backwards across the desk as his face almost touched the face of George Huxley. The man was standing an inch away from him, and staring so deeply into his eyes that Jack felt overwhelmed, almost paralysed by that gaze.

'Who are you?' Huxley whispered. 'Are you the ghost-lit boy?'

Gently, Jack pushed the old man back a little. 'I believe I am.'

Huxley looked scared. He was clutching the exercise book to his chest with both hands. The fabric of his tweed jacket was crumbling. His beard had grown coarse, his hair longer and wilder, hanging around his shoulders.

'Who are you?' he whispered again, then looked around the study as if seeing it for the first time. His gaze back on Jack's, he said, very softly and uncertainly, 'You've been here before. I could tell you were here. I couldn't see you. But now I see you. I have a son. Steven. You look very much like him.'

'I'm Steven's son. Your grandson.'

Huxley mouthed the word silently. Aloud he said, 'Yssobel . . .'

'Your granddaughter. She takes after her mother. Guiwenneth.'

Again, the silently mouthed name, repeated several times, eyes distant as if summoning memory. 'So beautiful. So beautiful. I remember when she watched me from the garden, curious and lost. So beautiful. She went away again, back into the wood. I followed her and found her, but she ran from me. So beautiful. Out of a dream.'

His speech had been dreamy too. Now he frowned. 'Yssobel. Who has been whispering to me about Yssobel?'

'I have. My sister is lost. Something has taken her; or she has gone to destroy something that was *trying* to take her.'

65

Huxley was thoughtful, cocking his head as if listening to a distant voice, brow furrowed, eyes questioning. Then, in his ghostly, distant voice, he repeated what he had perhaps remembered, the bare bones of a tale. 'Yssobel stole the armour of a king. She fought in the armour of that king. And she died in the armour of that king.' He paused, searching. 'She followed the shadow of the king's stone – and came to the night-black lake. She crossed to the underworld in the king's boat. There she exacted vengeance. There she healed a wound that had cut deeply. Yssobel . . .'

He stepped back to the desk and put down the book, stroking the cover almost regretfully, his hair obscuring his face and his expression. 'Yssobel,' he repeated, as if relishing the name. 'The image of her mother.'

She followed the shadow of the king's stone . . .

An odd change was happening in Huxley. He sat down in the desk chair and stared at his hands. The skin was dry and cracked, the knuckles showing hard and swollen like the knots on the branches of trees. The aura around him was of mould. Tears glistened in the corners of his eyes, though he showed no signs of being sad.

Looking up at Jack, he searched the young man's face, then smiled affectionately. 'You are! Yes. The image of my son. But then – how do I remember?'

He went into a huddle of thought, staring at nothing. Then in an authoritative and firm tone of voice he suddenly said, 'There are parts of the wood where the generative powers are very strong. I call them vortices. They are associated with springs, or trees, usually oak and elm. Sometimes with clearings, especially those with shrines at their centre. Sometimes with very ancient tracks. They are the birthing places of the images, though I was never privileged to witness such a moment of generation.

'But I have come from deeper. Far deeper. Someone drew me here.' Huxley looked sharply up at Jack again. 'You? Would that explain Yssobel? Your need; me; your needed mythago. My regenerated mind, my experience of wandering, the tales I've heard . . . somewhere in me there is a memory of the girl I never knew, a memory from stories I had heard about her. Your father was right. Huxley, when he was pure flesh and blood, would

66

have been delighted to know that he could be brought back with a fragment of his intellect and memory, as well as his tweed clothing and ragged boots.'

Suddenly the old man shrank into himself again. The moment of resurrection was gone. Whatever sustained him, whatever sentience, whether inside him or acting from around him, was maintaining this mythago form of the scientist; it was not powerful enough to hold him in full life.

He was speaking words that Jack could hardly hear.

'Mythagos . . . weaken at the edge. Whatever draws them there . . . once they are there, they are trapped. Insects in a web. The world sucks them dry. They become brittle. Fragile. They dissolve back into earth. True power for this form of creature lies at the heart of the wood. Lies where it begins. The place I have heard called *Lavon d'yss*.'

Jack sat down on the floor, as close to his grandfather as he felt he could. Huxley peered down at him through watery eyes. 'I think I'll sleep for a while. Where do you sleep?'

'Over there,' Jack indicated his bedroll and furs. 'Sleep there if you want. It's not as comfortable as the bed upstairs, but far less damp and rank.'

Huxley shuffled out of his chair and walked to the corner, kneeling down, then lying down, curling up on his left side, knees drawn up. A bony hand reached for a fur and tugged it over his legs.

He became very quiet.

Jack watched him for a while, and then must have dozed off. He was awoken abruptly by the pressure of a spear-point in his chest, and in the darkness was aware that Huxley was standing over him, weapon in hand, growling, 'Where is he? Where is he?'

Acting by instinct, Jack slapped the shaft aside, struggled to his feet, only to be pushed down by his grandfather whose strength seemed to have returned tenfold.

'Where is he?' the frail, rank spectre insisted, holding Jack's neck, face so close to Jack's again that he could smell the forest.

'Who?'

'Christian! Christian! Where is he? Tell me now!'

'My father's brother?'

67

'The killer. The killer. He took her from me. He took the beauty from the wildwood. He took my dream. He killed her. He killed her. Where is he? Where is he?'

'George . . . let go. Go softly. I'm Jack. Steven's son. I don't know where Christian is. My father thinks he's dead.'

A lie! But it seemed appropriate.

'Go gently, grandfather. Grandad. George. Gently. I'm half mythago. As fragile as you.'

Though his grandfather didn't feel so fragile at that moment.

Gradually Huxley quietened down, kneeling back, staring at the spear from the cabinet, then casting it aside.

'I was dreaming. A rage dream.'

'We all have them.' Jack sat up and embraced the old man. 'It's the middle of the night.'

'It's the middle of nothing,' was the bleak reply.

'A friend of mine called Julie has given me a herb called tea, which tastes sharp and bitter when boiled in water, but is what another friend of mine, from where I was born, would call "the welcome taste of strangeness". Would you like to try some?'

'No!'

Huxley began to ramble, suddenly wild-eyed again, emphasising certain words and phrases as if rehearsing them. 'When the *pre-mythago* begins to form it is first glimpsed at the edge of vision: a flitting shadow, a shape, a flash of colour. As for the other senses, a fleeting odour, of sweat or sex, or a swift breath, a whispered nothing, an *elemental touch* to the cheek, or hand, a brush stroke of contact. This indicates that the sentience that abides within this primordial stand of *wildwood* is beginning to engage with the manifested forms of the *archetypes* accumulated in the human mind over *many hundreds of thousands of years*! Whatever governs this primary mythagogenesis—'

'Huxley!'

Jack stopped the old man in his incoherent flow, and George Huxley glanced up sharply, almost angry in the dim light. 'Go gently,' his grandson urged. 'You'll break a twig.'

'Too many broken already,' was Huxley's rather gloomy reply, and Jack laughed quietly, though at something he

68

remembered from home, from his growing up, not at the old man's grim demeanour.

'Yes. Yes indeed.'

It was dawn. A thin light began to illuminate the study and Huxley's hunched, sad shape. Jack lay on his side, head in hand, watching the man who had haunted his childhood, and who had been one of the reasons for his longing to find Oak Lodge, and the world of science.

Distantly, there was the sound of two sharp 'cracks', short pulses in the air that made the Haunter side of Jack start with shock. Huxley sat bolt upright, then glanced to the window.

'What was that?' Jack asked.

'Gunshots.'

For a moment Jack was too confused to think. Then he scrambled to his feet, pulled on his boots and raced to the outside world.

'Stay there!' he called back. 'Don't go away. Please!'

The dawn air was fresh. The dew lay heavy on the fields, glistening as the light began to strengthen.

Which way? Which way?

Instinctively he ran towards the brook, brushing the tiredness from his eyes as he skidded on the wet grass. When he came in sight of the stream he saw the solitary figure of a man standing there, legs braced apart, shotgun hanging limply in one hand, wide-brimmed hat drawn down over his face.

When Caylen Reeve looked up, his eyes were bright with tears, his mouth set thin. 'I failed,' he said as Jack walked up to him. 'I failed in my task.'

Jack looked down at what was sprawled on the bank of the stream.

Blasted twice through the chest was a creature of hideous shape and appearance, its mouth stretched open in agony, its eyes sunken, its tongue protruding, its long bony fingers clawing at the wounds in its shallow frame. There was no blood in evidence, just gaping holes where the shot had ripped it open.

'A changeling?'

'Mature form,' Caylen said, agreeing. 'I hadn't expected that. Infants are their normal prey.' He looked grim. 'They leave wood dolls behind and if they're allowed to the dolls grow and take on a human feel. I was warning against infants. I chased this one all the way from the village. But I'm afraid the Iaelven have got what they came for. I can't sense them now. They've run deep, looking for the way back to their hill.'

The dying changeling began to ooze glistening sap from its mouth. It shuddered and keened.

Caylen Reeve drew a machete from behind his back and with a single brutal stroke he cut off the eerie sound.

The not-reverend regarded the corpse with sadness, then glanced at Jack. 'I don't know what you expected to find when you found the open world, but I don't imagine it was this.'

Jack sighed and shook his head. 'I expected something magical. Something peaceful. Castles, cathedrals, seashores. A child's dream, I suppose. But I don't regret the journey.'

'Good luck,' said the churchman. 'I hope your dream gets you home. As for me, I'd better go and see if anything is lost . . .'

He dropped his gun, reached down and picked up the creature by hair and heel, dragging its remains into the trees.

As Jack walked back to Oak Lodge, Caylen made his way back to Shadoxhurst. At the top of the ridge the man turned and waved. Jack had been watching him, and he raised his hand. The change-hunter disappeared over the horizon.

'George? Grandfather?'

Jack walked into the study, only to find it deserted. He searched the house quickly. The man had gone. The exercise book was on the desk, however, and Jack flipped it open. Huxley had left a last entry, its writing testifying to his sudden decay.

Many paths lead into Lavon d'yss, but they twist and turn with time. Yssobel followed shadow of the stone where her mother died. She found the Crossing Over place by a bold act. Treacherous act.

J is image of my son. More of the man than wild. Sentience of the man and sentience of the old wood.

* what power in combination to bring me alive, ghost from ghost.*

* and with half remembered life. Knowledge of work on first*

70

discovery of mystery of old wood, and same passion to under-
stand secrets of this strange place.

are there other Huxleys? Do they think same thoughts?
Regeneration beyond understanding. But incomplete. Life force
not strong
fading
rotting faster than usual degrading of myth form
if only could see Isabel
image of mother—

It was here that the scrawl finished. Jack had great difficulty
reading it, though Haunter helped intuitively. The last few
words were almost childlike, exaggerated in shape, as if Huxley
had been summoning every last ounce of strength to force
through the thoughts.

He knew, perhaps, that he was being drawn by a much
greater force than he could control, back into the shadow of
Ryhope Wood, to be absorbed and finished.

Jack went to the rear garden. He called a couple of times,
but was not surprised when he received no answer. He felt
oddly forlorn. The encounter, for him, had been intense: he
had touched the past; and perhaps he had learned a little about
what had happened to his sister.

Returning to the study, he read again everything that his
grandfather had written, then carefully folded the notebook
into his leather sack, packing it along with the copy of *The
Time Machine* and the little chess set.

Suddenly his name was called. It was Julie's voice. He went to
the front of the house. She and Caylen were running towards
him. He waited for them to come to the wall. Julie was looking
frightened and desperate. 'You have to go,' she said, as she
caught her breath.

'I'd advise it,' Caylen added, looking at the house. 'They'll
strip this place. And if they take you too, you'll die for reasons
you know too well.'

Jack was confused, shaking his head. Caylen went on, 'There's
a boy missing from the town.'

His expression, a direct look at Jack, indicated that the reason
should not be revealed to the townswoman.

Julie said, 'It's the Hawkings' boy. Eddie's friend. The police are in the town, asking questions, and they'll come here as soon as they hear about you. And *everybody* is talking about you. I'm sorry. I'm so sorry.'

With a last sad glance, Julie turned and half ran, half walked back towards the road.

Jack watched her go, then caught the look in the churchman's forlorn gaze. 'I haven't taken the boy. Why should they suspect me?'

'Welcome to the edge of the world,' Caylen said grimly. 'You *must* go, Jack.'

'That was my intention. I have half of what I came for. There is nothing left for me here now. But I had nothing to do with the boy's taking.'

'I know that. They don't. Come on!'

They walked swiftly along the edge of Ryhope Wood to the stream. Caylen followed Jack beyond the edge, and responded as did Jack to the sudden pull and tug of the interior. At once Jack's human side felt disorientated, but the Haunter side emerged and focused through the distortion of space. The first thing they encountered was the gruesomely slaughtered carcass of a horse, no doubt stolen from a nearby field.

The Amurngoth had slaughtered the beast and stripped away most of the flesh. They had taken the head, no doubt as a trophy or to hang in the Iaelven caves. The kill was too recent to be rotting. Jack drew his knife and cut strips of flesh for himself, finding a thin branch, sharpening it and threading the strips so they would dry.

There was a murmur of human noise some way away, but he was safe here.

Then Caylen said, 'If you hurry you can travel behind them. They know the short cuts through the earth, the openings, the under-realm, and they close some distance behind the band.'

'It depends on where they're going.'

'With their new Change? They'll be going close to the heart, to one of their hills. And if they *had* followed you here, as you think they did – then the hill must be close to your home.'

Jack stared at the other man, the full Haunter, and shook

his head. 'You amaze me. What it must be like to live your life I can't imagine.'

Caylen Reeve smiled thinly. 'Strange. And strangely wonderful. I live in a kind of hinterland. There are times that I want to go back into the wood and just quietly die. But where do I die? Where do I belong? And sometimes I dream of pushing further from the edge. But if I become unstable, then I'll die in a different way. That I know! So I stay here, comfortable and happy. Except for today. Today I failed.'

'For the first time.'

Caylen shook his head. 'For the first time? No. But for the first time in a *long* time.'

They made their farewells again. Whatever the fate of Oak Lodge, Jack would never know about it. He walked along the bank of the stream, slipping down into the water, crossing the natural stone bridge where the stream suddenly became a river and the greenwood began to swallow the light for a while.

Haunter whispered: I sense them. Sit back. Don't try so hard. I'll take us on their trail. Concentrate on Yssobel and what Huxley said about her.

And the entity that was Jack relaxed into its wildwood side, thinking:

She followed the shadow of the king's stone . . .

Under-Realm

The Amurngoth were slow travellers. But Caylen Reeve had been right to urge Jack to follow as soon as possible. As they moved, the forest widened slowly ahead of them. When they approached a sheer cliff it became the ghost of a cliff. Along a river, the very air itself seemed to open like a cat's eye.

Their traces were obvious, those of their 'stolen' more so, since Iaelven left a different spoor to humans'. Jack followed them fast. They left a stink behind them that was unmistakable, so he was confident of being on the right trail. They had taken the stream to where it became the river, walked along one side, crossed over, then settled for a while. This was the place where he had hidden his boat. They had found it, inspected it, and clearly rejected it as useless.

They didn't need the river. They had the Iaelven trails.

But that pause in their passage inwards allowed Haunter to catch up, running Jack like cloud shadow, weaving through the wood, through the rocks, through the tangled masses of briar that seemed to flourish towards the edge, almost as a defence.

They had entered a stone gorge, leading inwards though not downwards. He could see the sides beginning to contract, shaping back to normal form. As he ran, stumbling on the rocks and clutching at his two leather packs, he was almost sucked in as the space closed behind him.

This was a very different channel, darker, colder, and it echoed: he could hear the whistling, clicking language of the Iaelven ahead of him, and the muffled but angry objection of a boy.

In this dank defile Jack's breathing became laboured. Twice he stumbled and the sound of displaced stones seemed to echo for ever. Ahead of him, the movement of the Iaelven was un-interrupted.

Stop trying so hard, Haunter urged him. Look straight ahead. What do you see?

Jack stared into the gloom. Then, at the edge of vision, shapes began to form, some human, some animal, some seeming to peer at him, others running past. He had experienced this before.

That world is always there. Remember what your father told you? That at the edge of vision we can glimpse the early forms of mythagos.

I've seen them before, but never so clearly.

That's because I am seeing them for you. This is one of those places where the generation of the mythago is strong. Your mind is in a turmoil of generation. Let it do its business in the wood, and let your body relax. Let me take us on the trail, silently.

I need to be aware.

You ARE aware. I am you. I just know the trails better.

I reached the edge. I managed to see the Lodge.

With a lot of help from me. If you had tried the journey without me, it would have taken you years. I knew the way.

I know you did.

Persuading you to give way to the *haunter* is very hard.

I'll give way now.

Good. And now we have the chance of a very swift return. This Iaelven band smells familiar. They will lead us home. Let go, let Haunter have the limbs. Sleep, dream, create. I'll feed you as we travel.

He passed through trees, through hills, the world twisted around him, and he turned giddily as the whole landscape stretched and warped.

He ran from grassy slope to underground passage, with a raging torrent of water carrying him in the dark, until suddenly ahead:

The dark shapes of the Iaelven, doggedly walking their trail, the small boy walking in the middle of them, a pack on his back, a staff in his hand, his head turning this way and that as he took in the strangeness that surrounded him.

Haunter roused Jack. They were in a vast cavern. Sound echoed and echoed again. The walls were patched with phosphorescence. A river ran through the centre, but there were stone banks on each side, and the Amurngoth had built a fire in the distance and were crouching at the edge of the icy water itself. The sound of their talk was shrill and unpleasant. The boy was sitting under the guard of a small Iaelven. He was wrapped in a leaf cloak. One of the Amurngoth was washing his clothes.

Where is this?

A crossing place, Haunter said. They are waiting for another clan. They are close.

Jack watched from hiding as a strange act of care occurred. Spears were joined at the point to make a rack, and the boy's wet clothing was hung there to dry. Two of the Iaelven went to the bulging water-scoured walls and scratched marks, using dark stone knives. The whistling and clicking was constant, a persistent chatter which suddenly stopped.

A second band of Amurngoth emerged from what Jack had thought to be a shadow on the rock wall, but was most likely the exit from a separate cave system.

These were more colourful and taller. The two bands spread out cautiously across the sloping bank of the underground river, and sat down, facing each other on either side of the boy.

An argument occurred. Much slapping of the cold rock. Much shaking back of the long hair. Several times small stones were scattered angrily between the two groups, one or other of the two sides reaching to a pouch to grab a handful of the pebbles and throw them.

After a while there was silence. The new band stood and stalked, without referring to the others, across the icy water and disappeared into a cleft in the rock again.

The boy crowed with laughter. Whatever he understood of the situation, he had at least comprehended that something had failed for his captors, an exchange perhaps, a trade. The wet clothes were taken down and flung at the lad.

He pulled them on without demur. The band rose and

gathered their weapons and sacks, and were soon lost at the far end of the cavern.

They are stuck with him, Haunter laughed. I think we should stick with them.

I agree.

Later, they were walking through sun-dappled woodland. The Iaelven seemed almost to fly as they passed through this place, moving so fast that Haunter was breathless. The guardians of the boy lifted him and lowered him, like two parents with their child. Their progress was so fleet that at times Jack/Haunter found himself in silence, aware of nothing but shadow and sun through the canopy, streaks of light and silence.

Then a whistling cry would alert him to the direction they had taken. Soon he could smell them again, and soon they were descending, but not before Jack had seen the state of his body, his limbs obvious to his inspection, his face reflected back when he stooped to drink from a shallow pool of water.

His hands were brown, the bones gnarled, his skin so translucent that he could see the network of thin veins deep in his flesh. When he touched his face he felt no flesh at all, just carved wood, dry-lipped and stark.

I'm a corpse! I'm drying out!

A corpse in good hands, Haunter reassured him. Give me control. You are in good hands. Now get back to dreaming. Create! Bring life to the wood. You, the human. We are going deep again, and this will be difficult. But I think the journey is almost over . . .

He slept and he dreamt, and in his dream he saw the king's stone, though it cast no shadow. He had an idea, now, of where his sister had gone. But he had been gone a long time from the villa. In his dream he began to question whether he had done the right thing, forging his way to the edge of the wood; on a whim; with the idea that he could summon the spirit of his grandfather, and in doing so 'read' the memories of the man, in the hope that the old man would have found stories to do with Yssobel.

You were right, Haunter whispered through his dream. Your intuition was right. How we go from here, I don't know. Stay sleeping. We're almost at the cavern. These Iaelven are even more familiar to me now.

When Jack woke next it was with a start, an unvoiced cry of fear.

The Amurngoth's face was close to his, long fingers gripping his shoulder, foul breath dizzying and vile as he became more aware and focused.

The cat's eyes were wide. Jack became aware that he was in a rock-walled hall, from which hung bones, skulls and shapes fashioned out of wood. And as he looked harder, he saw the petrified forms of both Amurngoth and human. There was a dull glow in the place, and the echoing of movement and voices, the familiar song of the Iaelven.

This was the trophy hall.

Almost out. The stone figures are dead heroes from the Iaelven wars. I can hear their whispered memories.

The *haunter* side of Jack had withdrawn when this Amurngoth had approached, though not completely. Its whisper came to him: *Female.*

Another Amurngoth passed behind the female, glancing down. There was the smell of fresh winter air. The creature that held him offered him a carved bowl of pungent fluid, and he realised it was water. Jack sipped it reluctantly, though the taint was of nothing more than moss. When he had drunk a little, she cast the bowl aside and as if by magic produced the polished iron elf-shot that Jack had been carrying. She looked at it carefully before casting it aside too. Transfixed by the fierce eyes of the Iaelven female, Jack was only vaguely aware that his leather packs were still beside him, opened but not ransacked.

Knew we were following.

No danger. Stay calm.

The Amurngoth rose to her feet and pointed back into the hall. Jack felt weak as he struggled to stand, and was still shocked at the skeletal nature of his body. He was aware also that his beard and hair were long and matted, coarse with sweat and mud, and stinking powerfully.

In the distance he heard a boy's wailing cry. It broke down not into sobs but into growls of rage. A fighting spirit.

The female Amurngoth never let her gaze shift from Jack's, but she was watching him restlessly.

'Let the boy go . . .' he started to say, and at once her hand clutched at his throat, the long fingers finding pressure points and causing him pain. The hold did not relax, but again he managed to gasp:

'Just let him go back. He doesn't belong here. What good can he bring you? He's unhappy . . .'

A series of clicks in his face, accompanied by a fetid stench, seemed to signify that he should be quiet.

Haunter, distantly, unnecessarily, whispered: *She says no.*

The Amurngoth picked up the water bowl and squeezed liquid from a sack that she carried. The sludge was dull red, and smelled of fruit. She offered this to Jack but he turned his face away. Placing the bowl down beside him, the female rose and departed, but as she did so she revealed to Jack's view a slim and silver woman, a pale gleam in the trophy hall. She was as thin as a willow, and it was only the grey of her hair and the pallor of her face that made her seem silver. Her dress was grey as well, although it picked up the phosphorescence of the cavern. Her eyes were green and seemed not to see. They were blind eyes, blinded by time and sorrow. They saw Jack, but from a soul that had long since become weary. And yet she was lovely.

She stood above him for a moment before slowly kneeling and taking his hand in hers.

'You saw me once,' she said. 'There was a fire in the field behind your home. You were young. The change-hunters let me out into the air and I saw you. Did you see me?'

Jack struggled to find memory in this hall of chaos. He scoured his childhood dreams. He couldn't remember.

'Who are you?' he asked.

She didn't answer him. Cocking her head, she touched his cheek with a slender finger; ephemeral and sad.

'Jack, you are at the edge of your world again.'

'You know my name?'

'I know your name. I watched you play, I watched you grow. You are home now, a field away, a wall away; your villa is there, beyond this hill. You must not try to save the boy. The Iaelven have a task for him.'

He stared at her, confused. 'Who are you? Do you have a name?'

'Nothing, no one of importance,' she said dreamily. 'I was taken as a small child, and sometimes I think my name in the old world was Deirdra, though perhaps that is just a wish. Here, they refer to me as Silver.'

'You're a Change. That much is clear.'

'Yes. Like the boy you followed, but older. Much, much older.'

She didn't look old at all. Jack was again struck by her elfin beauty. 'Why did they steal you?'

She smiled, leaning back on her haunches. 'For a task that I refused. They brought me here, yes, a Change in swaddling: to be a bride.' She laughed quietly; leaning forward, she whispered, 'To go willingly is one thing. The Iaelven do not understand resistance.'

Again she sat back, moonglow in frail body, ancient beauty sustained by the under-realm.

She sighed. 'I know what is going through your mind.'

'That you should escape?'

'That I should escape,' she echoed. 'But my time is gone. I am now in limbo. I age very slowly. And your son, if he fights, will be in limbo too. You should go back into the fresh air, Jack. The Iaelven have been tolerant of you. That tolerance is a rare gift.'

His son? She meant the Hawkings' boy.

'What do they want with him?'

Silver shook her head. 'Nothing until he's grown. The Iaelven travel the under-realms and sometimes they need the strength of men like you, like the boy. Human strength. If they've taken your son . . .'

'He's not my son.'

She seemed surprised. 'If they've taken the nameless boy it's because they have lost one of his kind. There is nothing you can do for him, Jack.'

'And for you?'

'Nothing,' she repeated, with a shake of her head. 'I am the ghost bride. I denied the Iaelven warrior who fetched me. I wax and wane with the moon now, but they will never let me die. Go on, Jack. Go home.'

She rose, serene and gentle, translucent. Turning from him she walked away, but her left arm stretched back, the pale hand reaching for him, and he stood and took that cold hand. She walked him through the trophy hall.

Echoing distantly, he heard the sound of a boy's voice, still angry, defiant.

Fight, he thought. Fight for your life.

The trophy hall narrowed and became no more than a ferny and dank crevice in the hill. Silver stepped aside and pushed Jack forward. He caught the last glance in her eyes, the last sallow smile, the subtle movement of her lips as she whispered goodbye.

Then he stepped out of the hill and onto the open land. It was icily cold, and in the dead of night. The field that stretched away from him, down towards the villa, was frosted. The villa was a dark sprawl of buildings with bright torches along its outer walls. There was a sense of desertion about the place. The moon was crescent. The surrounding hills were dark in the gloom, though against the pale night cloud the valleys that led away from here could be seen as cuts in the ridge.

A man was standing in the middle of the field, holding a guttering torch. He was leaning forward, peering hard at the hill, at the cleft in the hill where it opened below the tree line.

Silver gave Jack the lightest of pushes with her finger. He glanced back to acknowledge her as she withdrew into her own darkness. Then he stepped out into the frosting night and called for his father.

Steven Huxley dropped the torch and bowed his head, and Jack went down to greet him.

'I'm home,' he called. 'I'm home! And I know where Yssobel has gone.'

PART · TWO

The Villa

The Valley

At dawn on the day of her fifth birthday, Steven took Yssobel to see the valley through which her mother had returned, several years ago, after her time in *Lavondyss*, the land beyond time, the place of healing. Yssobel was a strong and robust child. Steven had hoisted her onto his shoulders for the walk, and she gripped his hair with small fists of iron. Her legs, clamped around his neck, threatened to strangle him.

'Easy, girl. Easy. My neck's not as young as it used to be.'

Yssobel was excited by the dawn treat, although as yet she had no idea of why she was being taken to see the valley known as *imarn uklyss*. All she knew was that *imarn uklyss* meant 'where the girl came back through the fire'.

The air was fresh, the light stark and clear.

'The valley! The valley!' she chorused as her father walked her through the enclosures, towards the tall gate that separated their homestead from the wild. And though she shouted the words in English, she also called them out in other languages.

Aged five, Yssobel could already speak in tongues, and her favourite was the language of her mother Guiwenneth, which had a ring to it and which could be used effectively in arguments with her older brother Jack because of its rich content of abusive expression.

The valley opened before them, forested on both sides, wide, with the silver gleam of three rivers that seemed to flow from nowhere, disappearing into the distance to where the valley narrowed. There it curved away to the right, taking its secrets with it, to begin its dangerous course towards *Lavondyss* itself.

But here, beside a stream, in the overhang of willows, sitting on the smoothed grey edges of rocks, Steven let his daughter down to survey the passageway through which her mother had returned. There were no creatures to be seen this morning, other than birds: a flock of starlings, the usual crows, and a solitary eagle circling in morose fashion, as if half asleep.

Yssobel stared into the valley. The sharp breeze caught her auburn hair and she brushed at it; but her green eyes searched only for the unknown. Her feet kicked at the rock, her hands clutched the cold stone; curiosity made her pale face glow.

Steven watched her for a while.

How like Guiwenneth. That half of you that is Guiwenneth. The wildwood half.

It was not the same with seven-year-old Jack. The boy, tall and edgy for his age, was human in all respects; or if not, then the wildwood had not yet exerted its force upon him.

This was not Jack's day. This was Yssobel's.

The sky brightened, the valley shed its gloom. Slowly.

'That eagle's seen its prey,' the girl announced suddenly, just as Steven was about to speak.

'How do you know?'

'The gleam in its eye. It flashes with the sun. It's cocked its head three times now, in the same circle. Breakfast is on the ground. The eagle is pretending not to know.'

'You can see that from here?'

Yssobel laughed and looked up at her father. 'Can't you?'

When he looked back, the eagle had disappeared, only to reappear a moment later, rising with speed, legs dangling, wings beating, its prey hanging limply in its talons.

'Sometimes,' Steven said, 'I believe you know this world better than I do. And I've lived here for twenty years.'

'I dream that I've lived here for ages,' the girl said quietly, then kicked the stone seat again with her heels and said in a sing-song voice: 'The valley. The valley. Tell me. Tell me.'

'Have you heard of the giant known as Mogoch?' Steven asked. The girl frowned, then said brightly, 'Yes. From Jack. He used his tooth to mark a great man's grave.'

'It is a big tooth,' her father agreed. 'And it marks the grave of Peredur. And do you know who Peredur is?'

86

'An eagle!'

'He transformed into an eagle, certainly. But he was a great king. And . . . *and* . . .' The two of them exchanged a stare.

'And?' Yssobel prompted.

'He was your grandfather.'

'My grandfather was an eagle?' The girl looked delighted.

'More than that. Much more than that. But about the valley: this is the short and simple story:

'At that time, in the life of this people, Mogoch the giant was set a task by the Fates and walked north for a hundred days without resting. This brought him to the furthest limit of the known world, facing the gate of fire that guarded *Lavondyss*.

'At the top of the valley was a stone, ten times the height of a man. Mogoch rested his left foot on the stone and wondered for what reason the fates had brought him this far from his tribal territory, to the edge of the Unknown Region.'

'What's the Unknown Region?'

'It's what I call Lavondyss. Now be quiet and listen . . .

'A voice hailed him. "Take your foot from the stone."

'Mogoch looked about him, looked down, and saw a hunter, standing on a cairn of rocks, staring up.

' "I shall not," said Mogoch.

' "Take your foot from the stone," shouted the hunter. "A brave man is buried there." '

'Peredur! Peredur!'

'Yes, Yssi. Peredur. Now be quiet.'

' "A brave man is buried there."

' "I know," said Mogoch, not moving his foot. "I buried him myself. I placed the stone on his body with my own hands. I found the stone in my mouth. Look!" And Mogoch grinned, showing the hunter the great gap in his teeth where he had found the brave man's marker.

' "Well, then," said the hunter. "I suppose that's all right."

' "Thank you," said Mogoch, glad that he would not have to fight the man—'

'He would have won – the hunter would have won!'

'Yssi! Quiet! I'm trying to tell you the story.'

She jumped up and down on the rock, her face beaming, hair swirling.

' "And what great deed brings *you* to the borders of *Lavondyss*?"

' "I'm waiting for someone," the hunter said. "Someone of importance to me."

' "Well," said Mogoch after a moment, staring down at the hunter. "I hope they'll be by shortly."

' "I'm sure she will," the hunter said, and turned from the giant.

'Mogoch used an oak tree to scratch his back—'

'*An oak tree ? He should have used a pine!*'

'*Quiet!*'

'—then killed and ate a deer for his supper, wondering why he had been summoned to this place.

'Eventually he left, but named the valley *ritha muireog*, which in his own language meant: "where the hunter waits".

'Later, however, the valley was called *imarn uklyss*, which means: "where the girl came back through the fire".'

For a short while after he had finished recounting this tale, Steven was silent, his gaze on the steep-sided valley, his mind detached from the purpose of this visit to the place where he had finally settled.

It was not a dream that had drawn him in, nor even a memory; it was an uncertainty. He could remember the long journey through the valley, from the place of fire, from the stone, to this quiet place where he had waited. He could remember the horrors and the struggle against the unseen and unknown presences that inhabited this land, sufficiently so to feel an echo of that terrible time.

But he could also remember the joy and delight, the hope and calm that rose in him when, sitting on this very rock, he had seen a shadow become a shade; and a shade become a form; and the form shape itself into the a woman he had known.

The woman had stepped out of the valley and come to him. And her wounds had healed, though she was bedraggled and scratched by a journey that had taken her through her own hell and hardship.

But the blood and bruising on her body had not mattered, only the smile and glow of relief when she had seen him.

'I've found you,' she said.

'Yes. I knew you'd come.'

Steven remembered how she flowed into his embrace, all strength gone, letting his own strength hold her. She seemed so small. So light. Her fingers sought his hands, clutched them hard. Her breathing became calm. Her hair was matted with time and travel, with forest and river. It was a mat of copper, long, unkempt, smelling strongly of toil.

'The return was very difficult,' she whispered. 'The return was very difficult. I hope I'm safe now.'

He remembered how he had held her, pressing his face against hers, opening her mouth with his, welcoming her with all of his body and clutching her to him, not letting her go, tasting and remembering everything about her.

And when she started to cry he picked her up and carried her home.

And when she slept, he sat by her and listened to the words she spoke in her dreams, the same words, over and over.

'The return was very hard. I hope I'm safe now.'

A small foot gently kicked Steven on the shoulder. The valley cleared in his mind's eye and became the steep-sided shadowy pass that he had brought his daughter to see.

Yssobel was standing on the rock, looking down. The breeze was catching the tassels on her fur leggings. Her hair, red like fire in this strange light, was flapping over her face. The look in her eyes was questioning, not alarmed. 'Where were you?'

'Dreaming,' Steven replied.

The girl looked down the valley.

'I liked the story. I'd heard some of it from Jack.'

'You told me.' Steven had taken his son through the same ritual two years before.

Yssobel stretched out her arms in front of her, fingers pointing before she turned her palms so that they seemed to embrace what she was seeing. A moment later she let her arms drop.

'The girl who came back through the flames was my mother.'

'Guiwenneth. Yes.'

'But who was the hunter? Who was waiting?'

'Who do you think?'

'Jack didn't tell me. But it's obvious. It was you.'

'Me. Of course.'

Yssobel shivered. She was still standing and Steven could see that she seemed uncomfortable. So small a girl, so much expression in her face. He asked, 'What is it?'

'I was just thinking. I was thinking about how long you waited.' She looked down, meeting his gaze. 'How long did you wait, daddy?'

The innocent question was like a blow to his head and heart.

'If I knew the answer to that, my darling, I'd have been able to move away from this place. I waited a long time. But I don't know how long. All I know is that I waited too long. By the time Guiwenneth came back, I was too much a part of the valley. I can never go home.'

Yssobel frowned. 'But you *are* home. This is your home.'

Realising that he had made a mistake, Steven stood and gathered the girl into his arms. 'Yes, of course. This is very much my home. But we've talked about my childhood and you know I had a home a long way from here. At the edge of the wood. That's all I meant. I can't go back to the old place. I'm happy here.'

'Do you want to go back?'

'I'm happy here, sweetheart. With you and Jack and Gwin. This is my life. This is my world.'

The girl stared at him long and hard, still frowning. Then she shook her head and took her father's face in her hands. What she said next shocked him.

'But you're not. You're not happy.'

'Why do you say that?'

She looked sad now. 'I don't know. I think it might be because . . . because . . .'

'Tell me.'

'Because . . . you wonder what will happen when we're grown up. Where do we go? When will we go? We can't stay here for ever.'

No, darling. We can't. My God, you understand my fear more than I understand it myself.

Steven said, 'Let me put it another way. I'm happy with you. I can't think of a greater happiness than to have my family with me as I get old and creaky—'

'And can't hunt like you did!'

'And can't hunt like I used to hunt—'

'Can't throw your spear and hit anything other than a rock!'

'I most certainly can.'

'Can't shoot straight; always putting funny smelly infusions on your shoulder to ease the pain.'

'The pain is called arthritis, and if you keep reminding me of my infirmities I'll wish a touch of it on your tongue!'

'Can't even wrestle the calf down to the ground.'

'But Jack can. And do I not make excellent vegetable juice and bread? And do I not tell you great stories? About the people who live all around us, and who sometimes we can see? And a few of whom you've even met?'

The girl nodded enthusiastically. 'I like your stories. I like Odysseus best of all. He makes me laugh. I wish he wasn't so lost.'

'Be careful of Odysseus.'

'He's lonely, though he has a lot of visitors and they talk for hours. He's learning all the time.'

'Be careful of him. I don't like you riding off to visit his cave.'

'I know, I know. He's a trickster. But he makes me laugh.'

'Your mother and I think he's dangerous. And he's older than you.'

'Two years? He's Jack's age, daddy.'

'Even so . . .'

This was not the time to readdress his concerns about his daughter's meanderings, her acquaintance with the people who had gathered at this end of the valley, this stopping place for the spirits who had crossed back from Lavondyss. It was time to go back to the villa.

'Come on.'

Steven reached up his hand to help Yssobel down from the rock where she was standing, but again she stared into the valley. And was looking puzzled.

'What is it?' he asked.

'You *weren't* the hunter,' she whispered. 'You *weren't* the one who was waiting.'

Something about her demeanour, perhaps the way she was trembling, arms limp by her sides, alarmed Steven and he found himself unable to move. 'What do you mean? I waited for Guiwenneth and after a long time she came back, and here we are.'

'You can't have been the hunter,' the girl said softly.

'Why not?'

'Because he's still there. The hunter is still there. Still waiting. I can see him. He's only a shadow, but I can see him. The hunter is there. He's sad, he's confused, and he's calling to me.'

The girl's hands were icy cold. Steven reached for her and after a moment she allowed him to take her down from the rock.

'There's no one there now. No one who should concern you. This is just . . .'

Just what? Dream? Fantasy? Imagination?

Before he could find a way to express his thoughts, Yssobel said, 'I'm not imagining things.'

'Sweetheart: in the world in which we live, imagination is everything. Of course you're not imagining things. What you see is what you've made. With this . . .' Steven tapped her head. 'The hunter in the valley is not me. I'm here. It's you. Do you understand me? Do you understand what I'm saying?'

Yssobel hugged her father. 'Yes. Yes, I do. There is no such thing as a dream. A dream becomes life. You've told me this.'

'Good girl. Five years old, going on twenty. Good girl. Now tell me: the hunter you can see, if indeed he is a hunter. The hunter in the valley. Does he have a name?'

Yssobel was silent, shivering. Suddenly she became strong again, pulling herself away from her father's embrace. She was small and stout, strong and sturdy, and she walked away from Steven, towards the twin pillars that seemed to mark the entrance to the valley.

'His name is resurrection. He is held together by his scars. And he needs to be healed of his wounds.'

Was this Yssobel speaking?

'There's no such name as "resurrection".'

The girl was silent. She looked suddenly sad. 'It's not his real name. Anyway, he's gone now.'

92

She came back to her father and took his hand, leading him away from the valley. They walked along the track that led to the villa, and Jack was waiting for them at the gates. The tall, thin boy looked anxious.

'Gwin's gone,' he said. He always called his mother by her name. 'She got upset by something.'

'What do you mean, "gone"?'

'She took the grey and a packhorse and rode through the east gate. I think she's gone up to the old stone *Dun*, her father's fort. But I'm not sure. She took Hurthig with her.'

Hurthig was a mute young man, a Saxon, strong from working the villa's forge, with a good protective arm.

Steven was stunned for a moment. The boy had watery eyes. Whatever had happened, it had been upsetting for him.

Behind Jack, Rianna appeared, walking across the courtyard from the villa itself. She was one of several older women who came to the villa occasionally, and who were trusted to look after the children. She had come, with others, from Dun Peredur, the fort of Guiwenneth's birth, and now a haunted place a half-day's ride away. They lived most of the time in shelters along the edge of the river that flowed into the valley, but overwintered in the greater company of this old Roman ruin.

'I was at the river, listening to the water,' she said. 'Guiwenneth came to find me before she left. Jack is right: she is very disturbed.'

'Did she say anything?'

'Nothing.'

Yssobel whispered: 'Is mummy upset?' She held her father's hand tightly.

'I think so.'

She hesitated, frowning slightly, but only for a moment. 'Is it . . . is it because of that man in the valley?'

Steven looked down at his daughter. She was strangely bright-eyed and brightly curious. 'I don't know, Yssi. I'll have to find out.'

The Villa

Steven had discovered the ruined villa in the fifth year of his wait for Guiwenneth; five years, that was, as far as he could estimate. The valley itself was a dangerous place. He had had no horse. It took him many days to make the journey from one end to the other, and he was constantly aware that other beings were walking the same tracks: some shadowy, real and curious of him; others ephemeral, often giving themselves away only by their movements through the woods, or the disturbance of the river.

As he wound his way through the wide pass, he often saw boats or small colourful barges, floating down towards the stone. They were eerily silent as they passed, and as still as death, though sometimes a face would appear from beneath a cowl and stare at him forlornly.

He had always found some form of shelter, and manageable hunting, fruit orchards and wild crops, and the makings of fire.

He was not unaware that what he encountered was surfacing from his own memory. He tried to suppress the darker thoughts he carried. To think of romantic stone castles and armoured knights was to think of war. The brightest notion he carried was of a Roman villa, terracotta tiles, whitewashed walls, colourful mosaic floors in every room, a place packed with animals and laughing children; and with stores of grain and wine.

Some forgotten part of legend embraced such a farmstead, and one day he had discovered that it had formed there, at the top of the valley – though not exactly as he had expected it.

The outer gates were broken and rotten, the courtyard

cracked and weed-infested. The villa itself was in disrepair. Most of the roof tiles had slipped and were broken, the mosaic floors of the ten rooms grown through with roots or scrubby trees. The two gardens, at the side and the back, were growing wild, though the trees were mostly fruit trees, untended, knotty with calluses on their bark, and thick with fungus. But still producing.

The gates faced the deep valley. At the rear, a field led to a steep hill, rising to thick wood. There was a small gate to what Steven called 'the east', and outbuildings to the 'west'. All around, there were smaller valleys, leading away into smaller unknowns.

Several of the rooms were habitable and Steven spent time cleaning them, and sealing them against whatever weather this end of the valley might choose to throw against the place. After he'd cleared the gardens and the central courtyard of the square-shaped villa, the land began to grow flowers among the fruit trees, and it attracted bees, and wild fowl, and small wild pigs that rooted and ran when he approached but seemed almost to embrace the villa, as if once they had been a part of it, and their very tangible spirits were returning.

And people came too. At first just drifters, seeking shelter before continuing on whatever journey was taking them to their final destination. Once, ruins of this sort had been the living spaces of all manner of migrating peoples, after the Roman oc-cupation of Britain had ended. Eventually the villas had fallen, returned to earth, been covered by new land.

Not this one.

Steven tried hard to locate some clue as to the nature of the family that had lived here in the centuries when the old stone and river gods, and the gods of hearth and home, had still been invoked. A family of four, he discovered: parents; the children a boy and a girl. And each had had their own sanctuary, a fact he surmised from the statuettes and wax remains he found; and each had had their own servants or slaves.

The villa had also been a place of horses. He found the collapsed stables in the woodland behind the villa itself.

There was one group of arrivals he recognised at once, having seen them when he had first entered Ryhope Wood. They arrived at night, waving torches to signal that they were there, calling out in a language of Germanic dialect with which Steven had become vaguely familiar. A man, a woman and a boy who didn't speak, and they were called Ealdwulf, Egwearda and Hurthig. They had with them six scraggy and tired horses, on one of which was a leather bag containing the mummified arm of a tattooed man, a beautiful, ornate gold ring on its middle finger. The relic of their warrior king, Steven discovered later.

They were seeking a place they had heard of; a place of healing. They refused to say its name.

Steven smiled, thinking to himself: *That's a lot of healing.*

But Ealdwulf and Egwearda stayed, and Hurthig grew, became strong and great fun with his antics, and told wild tales in mime from his own dreams. Hurthig seemed less concerned with the family's journey than with his curiosity about the strange land in which he found himself.

And they were still living in the villa when Steven took his five-year-old son Jack to the head of the valley. They were still there, protecting and involved in the everyday routine of living in Villa Huxley, when Steven returned with Yssobel to find his son upset and confused, and Guiwenneth fled to her father's fort.

'Can I come with you?' Jack was anxious.

'No. You stay here with Egwearda. Have you finished the repairs to the drainage channels?'

The boy shook his head. It was work he hated and Steven knew that, but it had to be done. 'I've seen him again. The old man. I've seen him.'

Steven had slung a saddle and supply sack over the back of one of the horses, and Ealdwulf had supplied a second. He was ready to go after Guiwenneth, but realised now that his haste was due more to concern for the woman than care for his son.

Ealdwulf took the horses to the gate and tethered them, and Steven took Jack to the shade of an olive tree, where they sat down for a while together.

'Where was he this time?'

'Across the river, standing in the shadow.'

'Did he see you?'

'He was watching me. He didn't say anything.'

'What were you doing by the river?'

Jack hunched down a little. 'Just fishing.'

'Catch anything?'

'A rainbow. It slipped the hook.'

Steven waited for a moment, knowing that Jack's disturbed state of mind was because of his growing obsession. 'Was it my father? Are you sure?'

The boy agreed silently. 'He's very grizzled and very scruffy, but I can always tell it's him. His eyes, the way he looks at you . . . it's just like you. He stands and stares, then turns and disappears. It's like he wants to come in, but can't cross over. I feel sad for him.'

Suddenly alert to his father's frown, Jack sat up. 'I'm not afraid of him! I don't think he's dangerous.'

'I know you're not.'

'But it's as if . . . he's lost.'

'We're all lost, lad. We've been lost since birth. We're in a place of the lost. But you and I, and Yssi and Gwin, we're alive, right? We're alive. We live well. We can't get out, but who needs to? When you're older you can leave home and make of this place what you will.' Steven reached an arm around his son. It was so hard sometimes to make joy out of their situation, to encourage in the lad a sense of belonging in a world in which they did not, truthfully, belong. And soon, no doubt, he would face the same difficulty with Yssobel. She had just forewarned him of that.

Suddenly Jack asked: 'Is Huxley alive? Or just *mythago?*'

'My father? My father is dead. The Huxley you see at the edge? Mythago. Yes. You've seen him in too many shapes and forms for it to be anything else. Some are formed by me, some by you, some by Yssi.'

'Why does he haunt us?'

'I don't know, Jack. I truly don't know. You have to remember: it's only you who sees him.'

Jack took his father's hand for a moment, holding it tightly, staring across the garden. 'I think my sister sees him sometimes. She pretends not to. Do *you* want to see him?'

'I don't know. I don't know. I think that if he'd wanted me to see him he would have allowed it. As it is, I'm glad that my young man, my drainage-hating son, is in touch with a memory of a man who once meant a lot to me.'

'Can I come with you to find Gwin?'

'No!'

It was a good day's slow ride to Dun Peredur, through difficult country. Ealdwulf rode ahead, heavily armed. Steven followed with the packhorse.

They passed through a change of season, and for a while were in a place of never-changing dusk. Sometimes they could see fires in the forest. But mostly they rode in summer and the day.

Steven still thought of time as minutes and hours, having been born and raised outside the wood. His body innately sensed the steady passage of time.

The fort was overgrown now; most of the buildings had collapsed or were ivy-covered. The gates were hanging on their hinges, and it was certain that Steven's approach could be heard. Dun Peredur was a small fort: it had once been a crowded place, and there were signs of casual occupation everywhere, including the use of the place by wild dogs, which Hurthig had driven off.

The young Saxon had tethered the horses by one of the forges and was sitting close by, leaning back and drinking from a small jug. When he saw Steven he nodded to his right. Ealdwulf tended to the horses, then went to his son and crouched down to talk. Steven sought Guiwenneth in the chaos of vegetation and building.

She was sitting among the overgrown stone walls that had once formed the king's hall, but she was sad, her knees drawn up to her chin, her fading red hair a tangle, partly of the feathers she wore in them, partly of leaves and sweat. She was anguished. Steven noticed she was sitting on the circular stone slab that had once formed the feasting table. She glanced up as he approached, smiled wanly, then straightened, stretching back, lying supine and gazing at the sky.

'You're not a happy woman, Jack tells me.'

'I am not a happy woman.'

'May the man who loves her ask what has happened to turn happiness into fear?'

'Fear?'

'You're afraid. I've only seen it in you once before, but you're afraid.'

'I'm not afraid.'

'What, then?'

'Lost. Angry. Thinking of the kill.'

He was shocked by that. 'What kill?'

'The man who stole me! The man who raped me! The man who sent his guard to kill me! That Fenlander. Hunting me through the forest, in the snow.'

For a moment Steven couldn't respond. Was she talking about his brother Christian? As if she had seen his confusion, as if she had guessed his own train of thought, she looked up and gave him the briefest of smiles. 'He's in the valley, Steve. The moment Yssi called to me from the valley, I sensed him too. It was like a knife turning in my belly. A storm of thunder. Silent, but terrifying thunder. I had to go! I couldn't stay there, in the villa.'

Yssobel had called to her mother? Steven had noticed the moment, but it must have been when she had declared that her father could not have been the waiting hunter. The connection between daughter and mother was strong. The 'green' side of the girl was very strong indeed. They communicated through the very earth itself.

'You're safe in the villa,' Steven said. 'You're safe with me. With Ealdwulf and Hurthig.'

'Yes! Yes! But not in the valley. And not from *what*'s in the valley. He's coming for me again. And I'm older, now. And you're right . . .' She reached for Steven's hand and held it to her breast, clutching tightly and starting to shake with tears which she then forced back with will and strength. 'I am afraid of him. And therefore I must kill him. I will not allow myself to be taken again.'

'You won't be.'

Guiwenneth was quiet for a while; then she kissed the hand she was holding, not looking up. Then she whispered: 'Steve . . . something else. I find this difficult. Please don't be angry.' Tears touched his skin as she squeezed the fingers. 'I'm not sure who I am,' she said in a small voice. I'm not sure I'm yours. I think – I dread to think – that I'm his. That's why I'm lost. That's why I ran. That's why I've come here, to my father's house. I can't dream my own life. Only you can. What happens to me has already *happened* to me in your own mind. Only you can know.'

Steven was shocked by what she had said. It had never occurred to him that the woman who had walked out of *imarn uklyss* might not be the same woman who had emerged from his own memory. It had certainly never occurred to him that she might be his cruel brother's.

'What makes you think this, Gwin?'

'I don't know. I feel haunted. It's happened before and I said nothing. But earlier, when you took Yssobel to the valley – it was very strong.'

'Have you seen him?'

'I don't think so. But he's close again. I just know it.'

Resurrection.

'Come back to the villa.'

Guiwenneth shook her head. 'Not yet. I'll stay here for a while. Hurthig will stay with me. My father's ghost sometimes walks here. I'd like to see him.'

There was nothing Steven could really say. He kissed her, called for Ealdwulf, explained what had been said and the two of them rode back to their home.

Yssobel

Guiwenneth changed after that day. Her moods turned darker, she became distant in a way that saddened Steven. She often left the villa for weeks at a time, though when she returned she was usually radiant, almost her old self.

'I've been shedding ghosts,' she would always say, with a smile.

'It's certainly time to shed clothes and take a wash' was the joke that soon became established.

Steven never asked Guiwenneth where she had been, and apart from a pronouncement that she had been 'inwards' and 'shedding ghosts', she volunteered nothing. He guessed she went up to the old fort, hoping to see her father's ghost. When she was asleep in the villa she would often cry out for help, or murmur: '*I hope I'm safe now.*'

It took only a gentle kiss to quieten her, though.

Yssobel was also greatly affected by her father's walk with her into *imarn uklyss*, but in a very different way. She became obsessed by the place. Steven was educating the children to the best of his abilities and memory, but Yssobel turned every lesson into *Lavondyss*. She painted from imagination, wrote childish stories, made links between the historical characters that her father spoke about and the place beyond the fire. Ealdwulf had made her a small harp. It was crude, though intricately carved; the sound it produced was raw rather than sweet. And yet, in Yssobel's hands, it produced tunes that were mellow and sad, echoes of lost music, all flowing from the mind and the fingers of the half-girl.

Her room was in the heart of the villa and was the warmest. She had hung several painted skins on the walls, and tapestries that had been found in a storeroom, but she had left room for art.

Indeed, Yssobel's large space, with its purple and red mosaic floor lovingly reconstructed from the scattered tesserae, had become a gallery of her art and creations. Faces and figures peered from the walls, from among the tapestries, or ran around them in ancient chases. Clay figures were grouped on small shrine tables, their bodies elongated and weird. She had made a model of how she imagined the valley to be, and tiny men and women were placed within it, marking places where she dreamed the openings from *Lavondyss* could be found

As she grew older the art became more sophisticated. Steven watched with fascination. He and Ealdwulf repaired other rooms in the sprawling villa and Yssobel eventually had three: one to sleep in, and two in which symbolic beauty and savagery crowded the walls and the rough-hewn tables around her workbenches.

It came as a shock one day, when Steven went to see his now-teenage daughter, to be confronted by a death mask, life-sized and painted in the true colours of recent mortality, and to recognise his own brother, Christian.

'That one scares me,' Steven said gently. The girl shrugged, holding it up and staring at the closed eyes.

'There's nothing to be scared of. This is just how he was. But he's back now.'

Steven shivered. 'Back where? In the valley?'

'No. Not at the moment. Further away than that. He's very strong now. But there's something sad about him. I can't tell what it is, but he's searching for something. Or perhaps for someone.'

Yssobel turned the death mask left and right, then put it down, glancing up at her father. 'Come to criticise or to help?'

'I don't criticise.'

'Yes, you do. You do it very carefully, but I always know when you don't like one of my paintings, or masks.'

'Some of them *are* a bit grim. But as I've said before: your talent is remarkable.'

She shrugged. 'It's a forest talent, not human. It's the green in me, not the red. I wish you could see my dreams, daddy. Sometimes they're so wonderful I wish I would never wake from them.'

'I'm glad you do, though.'

Yssobel was now tall for her age. Riding, swimming and the necessity of participating in the villa's more robust tasks had made her lean and very strong. Though she had inherited her mother's features, there was something harder about her look.

Guiwenneth had noticed it develop. 'She has the look of her grandfather Peredur, I'm sure,' she had once said. 'I've only glimpsed him, but I think there is softness in his manner, but not in his features.'

'Tell me a dream,' Steven asked his daughter. 'One of the wonderful ones.'

'Well, I have a dream that keeps coming back . . .'

I'm very young and I'm playing in the garden with a wolf puppy. Three women are sitting, guarding me, talking and laughing. It's a bright day and there are seven birds circling overhead.

Then the birds dart down and one of them picks me up and carries me very high. They play a game with me, swooping and soaring and one drops me – the feeling of falling is not frightening at all, just startling. And another catches me. Down below, the women are running around through the gardens and groves, staring up, but I'm being well protected by these huge birds.

Then suddenly we fly to the edge of the forest. I'm dropped and this time nothing catches me. That's the only frightening bit. But I land on the back of a young hind and she runs into that wood, with me clinging on. And she brings me to a river, or sometimes it's a lake, where there are armoured men sleeping. Only they're not sleeping. They've been killed in battle. They're very young. They look like they are dreaming, but they're very still and very cold. Their armour is wonderful, bright, some of it bone-white, some spring-leaf green, some dusk-red, and one set the sheen of patterned copper, the colour of my hair, the colour of my mother's hair. (Where it isn't greying.)

This man is a prince. And I don't know why I do this in the

dream, but I kiss him on the cheek, and remove his helmet and his armour and put it on, and lie down beside him.

After a while we both sit up and he seems angry. Why have you stolen my armour? he asks.

Because you were pale and cold and I thought you were dead. I wanted to wear it so that you would be remembered.

He laughs. Do you know me, then? he asks

No, I say.

Then why would you wish to remember me?

For a moment I have no answer. Then I say in the dream: I need to remember something of someone, or I will have nothing to remember. I need to wear their skin.

And he asks with a smile, My armour is my skin?

Your armour is the mask, I reply, and he's silent for a moment, dark eyes watching, brow furrowed, thoughtful.

Would you have worn it in battle? he asks, and I reply that the armour is not even as strong as a boar's-tusk cuirass and helmet, or three layers of bull's leather stitched through with thin shards of the hard, black thorn. But the armour is beautiful, and it fits me to perfection, and I tell him so.

Then you may take it, he says. And I will find armour of leather and bone and thorn. And wherever you go, I shall follow you until I find you again. But for the moment I must sleep. It has been a hard day, and a gruelling challenge. The tip of a sword is inside me and it is as cold as a winter's waking.

And he lies back and closes his eyes. But as he closes them, and becomes pale again, he sings softly. It's the song I've often played on the harp that Ealdwulf made for me. Though the words change, and sometimes I can't remember them, but only because I wake at a later time in the dream.

> *I came to the strong place which I knew I must hold,*
> *I came to a time in my life, and I knew I must hold,*
> *I came to the hill where the harnessed host was waiting*
> *And the wind was waiting*
> *And a storm of rage still silent, waiting.*
> *And I knew that I had to hold on to what I had been given;*
> *And that the world was changing, and that I had to hold;*
> *And everything that I had once been given was gone,*

Yet everything I had been newly given was with me.
  Under gloom-grey sky, and over red-green earth,
  We held and held until we broke.
But in the breaking, we held, and in the holding we will find
Avilion.

Suddenly Steven could see Guiwenneth more clearly in the girl. Part of the dream, the first part, echoed Guiwenneth's own story, her own mythic past, in slender detail. Guiwenneth's own childhood had been a tale of growing up in sadness and then strength. For Yssobel, for the girl's dream, the events were encompassed with pleasure and childish joy.

But in Yssobel, he now realised, there was a strong echo of a more violent beginning. He looked around at her room, and what had been beautiful in her art as he had seen it before became suddenly darker, though he suspected that his daughter herself had intended only the lighter shade of her creative efforts.

'Finding dead warriors by a lake doesn't sound very wonderful to me.'

Yssobel shook her head. 'It's just a beginning. I wake up feeling very good. It's always a feeling of something that's going to happen next, and I like that. Jack dreams of running in the forest from huge wolves and suddenly coming to the outside world. I've never had that dream. I do have bad dreams, but they're from the red side, not the green.'

'Why don't you tell me about them? Or your mother?'

'I tell Rianna a few of them, now that she lives here. But I've sworn her to secrecy, so don't even ask her. When I'm ready I'll tell you. When I understand them.'

Steven smiled and left her, adding, 'Thanks for the Dead Prince story, at least. Just confirms what I've always known.'

'That I'm weird?'

'Exactly.'

'If I had a chicken for every time you've told me that—'

'You'd have a palace-full of eggs and feathers. I know. I know. Don't be long. The table's already set, and something smells good in the kitchen. And it isn't chicken.'

She doesn't confide in me. And she doesn't confide in her woodland mother. She talks to the High Woman. Maybe all of them. I don't mind her talking to them. They carry wisdom. But I wonder why she doesn't talk to us? Perhaps because Guiwenneth has changed so much. She has become so haunted, so distant. And perhaps because I've been too reticent. If so: why the reticence? Perhaps because I'm afraid of my children. Afraid of what? Perhaps of what exists on what Yssi calls the 'green side'. And she can tell it in me. She can sniff it as she can sniff the pungency of the earth where it hides little treasures for the table; or the remains of the long-dead. She knows I'm afraid of what might emerge from her one day. Or what might be lost from her. Or what might take her away.

Jack

Families have their rituals. They celebrate in their own ways. In the villa the seasons were celebrated, as were the passing through of strangers, the slaughter of old hogs, the birth of foals. Birthdays were greeted with wild gifts and teasing, and Yssobel always composed a song for the occasion.

The song she always sang for Jack was a deliberately created piece of nonsense, though it echoed the sense of loss that was to come. Everyone clapped their hands to the rhythm. As she rose to sing it, Jack groaned, head in his hands, imploring, 'No. Please, no.'

Yssobel grinned. Her hair was tied high and she wore a colourful bell skirt, which swirled about her as she twirled as a prelude to the performance.

> *Jack, yes Jack, my brother Jack,*
> *Hunts in the wild, chases at the run,*
> *Brings back a kill, but dreams in his heart*
> *Of reaching the edge,*
> *Where our family was begun.*
> *Where a father met a mother,*
> *Though from forest mind she came,*
> *And a brother loved a brother,*
> *Though this wouldn't stay the same . . .*

It went on like this for some time, dogged, doggerel, sometimes amusing – to everyone but Jack, though he played up his irritation. But it had become a tradition. Each year, on Jack's birthday when she played and sang it, she added a verse, ignoring the eye-rolling from Jack, who seemed to be saying: yes, yes, I know, I *know* that I go on about it, but the joke's wearing thin.

The verses were teasing, but pleasing – especially for Steven as he could detect shadows of the poems that he had related to Yssobel as a child. And some of the songs he knew.

She eventually took a bow, to cheers and applause.

Yssobel had written the first verse when Jack was eight and she had been six. By then he was only mildly curious about the outside world. By eleven he was obsessed by it. By thirteen he was demented at the thought of it, at the thought of never seeing it.

Once in a while he saw his Huxley grandfather, and it was these encounters, brief but clearly profoundly affecting, that shaped his life. Unlike Yssobel, it was the human side of Jack that was challenged in the villa, in the wood, at the head of the valley *imarn uklyss*. What he called his 'haunter' surfaced only occasionally, usually when he had become lost, or needed to survive in extremely hard deep-wood situations, where elemental forces could play all kinds of havoc.

'Do you speak to him? Does he speak to you?' Steven had asked him some years before.

'No. He just watches for a while from the shadows. He seems to be thinking. It's not as if he knows me, just as if he's curious. I think he's trying to find out where he is. Or perhaps why he's here.'

'Has your sister seen him?'

'I don't know. I don't think so. But once I saw him sitting by her when she was painting. She didn't notice him. He wasn't there for long. He went back into the wood.'

'I've never seen him, Jack. And I'm his son. Can you describe him?'

'Ragged. Gaunt. His eyes are strong. He's wearing strange clothes. He hasn't much hair, though it's long at the back. There's a scar on his chin, but not much of one. Not like yours.'

Steven was quiet. His own scars were not on his face but on his body, from his time during a war he had almost forgotten, when he had been shot in the chest, surviving because of the luck of the wound, not the power of the shot. The older Huxley, his father, had been struck by a sword in a skirmish in a war that Steven could not remember. A shallow cut, usually masked by the man's beard. But the beard had turned grey along the line of the strike, and it had been exactly where Jack was able to describe it.

So if his father was here, was it the real man? The man Steven believed had died many years ago. Or just an image of him? If so, who was summoning him?

It had to be his son.

Whenever Jack claimed to have seen George Huxley, Steven went to the location and scoured the underbrush or the river's edge, often searching for a whole day before giving up. There was a feeling of agony in the act: he was half afraid to encounter the mythago, and yet he longed to touch at least something from his childhood. Although his father had been a difficult and remote man, there had been times of great happiness, at Christmas and in the school holidays especially.

But Steven was never rewarded with a glimpse.

Jack began to ask questions about his grandfather. He pressed his father to repeat, time and again, what he remembered from his journals. Steven had read only parts, but they came to him clearly. And he still carried a fragment of a journal that he had torn out when he'd been called up to army service in one of the wars, a memento of his father, taken in anger from a man who had become, by then, distant and unfriendly.

Steven eventually gave this sheet to his son, who framed it and placed it above his bed, not understanding it but fascinated by its reference to 'the woodland aura reaching as far as the house', and his grandfather's assertion: 'Am distinctly losing my sense of time'.

Time and the seasons were all askew in Ryhope Wood. But the family was able to live day by day, except when they left the confines of the villa. While Yssobel's rooms became shrines to her imagined Lavondyss, Jack's sprawling chamber became a museum to the outside world, aided by his father and by his own imagination.

Ealdwulf helped him to build a model in wood of Oak Lodge, complete with gardens, hen runs and workshops. Jack made fields out of painted cloth, criss-crossed with the tracks and roads that led between the villages. He modelled the church at the town of Shadoxhurst and the railway station at the oddly named Grimley. His floor became a map of where his father had been born, and in his mind's eye he walked those fields, danced on the village green, sipped beer in the public house and rode the train to Oxford.

The place called to him strongly. He felt he belonged there, and soon he began to feel claustrophobic and confined in the villa and its surrounding landscape. His heart ached for adventure, for the journey outwards.

From his father's own stories Jack was certain that the river in which he fished, and from which they obtained their water, would lead him out if he followed it against the flow.

He determined that one day he would make that journey. But not yet.

Jack's fifteenth birthday occurred, that year, in crisp winter. There was no snow as yet, and the air smelled November-fresh, the sky was clear, the stars brilliant. A bonfire had been built in Hazel Field, the name given to the field behind the villa, a patch of land scattered with stunted hazel and rowan. The pigs were penned up for the evening, the bonfire struck, skewers of meat roasted as the flames died down, but not until after the Saxons, the Highwoman, the family themselves, and two others had danced around the fire, holding hands and teasingly singing a reprise of Yssobel's 'Song of Jack'.

The two outsiders were a Hood-form, who called herself Morwen, and who brought gifts of game and straight arrows on her irregular visits, and Odysseus, who had been enticed to the party by Yssobel herself. He was taller than Jack, the same age, and as moody as the Huxley boy.

He lived in a deep cave, high on the slopes of Serpent Pass, making icons and wood carvings of gods, goddesses and strange creatures, all from his imagination. Steven had discovered him some years ago, and he was a regular visitor, and Yssobel had always been fascinated by him.

Whatever had kept him in the cave for eight years, how he had come to be in such a remote place, this particular time in his legendary life was ending. He was dreaming of Ithaca, his island home in Achaea, by a great ocean, which he remembered as a young boy.

Steven had never let Odysseus know that, as a man, he would have a scant few years with his wife on the island before his name would become associated with the greatest siege of all time, held before the walls of Troy.

There was certainly romance in the air between daughter and Greek, but Guiwenneth, maternal and tough, made sure that her daughter did no more than dance with the young man, though their dancing – which made him smile at last – was certainly a swirl of passion and an embracing of arms.

Ealdwulf drank heavily. Egwearda was a very fine brewer of a liquor that tasted very like beer. Its strength was not reliable. This barrel was clearly potent. The old Saxon chanted a long poem in his own language. From his movements – striking, holding, demonstrating fear, then ferocity, acting out a great amount of laughing and cheering – this was a mead-hall tale. And no familiar name was detectable, save for Ealdwulf's own.

He was singing a tale celebrating himself!

Guiwenneth had learned to play Yssobel's harp, and now sang a soft song about her father, not one she had composed herself but a song that she remembered from her own childhood in the fortress.

As the fire died down and the mound of wood fell to a sprawling glow, with everyone sitting around it, Jack stood and told the tale of Jack his Father, a story that had come to him one day while he was working in the fruit orchard. He had hardly begun the tale when he stopped, staring into the darkness.

Standing in a line, not far away, were twenty of the tall, lank-haired, cat-eyed creatures that were occasionally seen near the villa, but always – until now – in solitary form. They were carrying short bows and bone knives. All were clad in what looked like clothing of leaves, though there were furs around their shoulders. Their eyes seemed to glow with anger, but it was probably the fire.

One of them spoke, if the term speaking could describe the whistling and clicking that came from its thin-lipped mouth. It kept repeating the sounds; with increasing irritation, it seemed.

'What are they?' Odysseus asked. The hooded woman, Morwen, rose from where she was crouching and motioned everyone to be quiet. She picked up her own bow and reached into her pouch for what looked to be a silver arrowhead. 'Silver best. Iron will work.'

Again she motioned stillness. 'Iaelven. Amurngoth,' she said. 'Danger.'

Amurngoth? The name sounded close to that of the Muurngoth who inhabited parts of the surrounding valleys, and had nests in the forest from which they raided. But the Muurngoth were more nuisance than danger, and were easily handled. This band looked sinister.

Morwen walked away from the fire, towards the group, flinging her cape back to expose her shoulders. The creatures watched her as she approached, then one signalled to her to stop.

They spoke, she spoke back. The whistling conversation lasted a long time.

Abruptly, the Iaelven turned, strode up the hill and into the dark wood. Morwen returned to the fire and crouched again. In her awkward English, she said, 'Amurngoth, like elves. Many different ones. They are asking what are we doing so close to their hill. This is their land and their hill. They have been away hunting for a long time. Now returned. They don't like fire so close.'

'What did you say to them?' Jack asked. He was still staring at the place where they had disappeared. He was sure they had been swallowed by the earth and not by the woods.

'That this fire is for a celebration and will be extinguished. Next fire, further away. They also want to know what the building is doing here. It was not here when they left for the last hunt.'

'And what did you say to that?' Steven asked.

Morwen shrugged. 'It came from the valley. Many things come from the valley. They agree to you staying. Do not climb the hill, do not enter the wood. Do not harm any Iaelven you see in or near the building. They will do you no harm. But there are entrances close to you.

'They also said: they will keep watch on you. Be careful.'

After the unexpected interlude, and after a pause for reflection, Jack clapped his hands together to draw attention and concluded his party piece. He was determined that the night should be long and enjoyable, though Ealdwulf was now sleeping gently.

But it was not the only encounter of the night, though the festivities were almost at an end. Yssobel and lithe-limbed Odysseus were dancing gently to the music of the harp, though they were scrutinised intensely by Guiwenneth as she played. Steven was fast asleep and the others had all gone back to the villa.

Jack was lying on his side, staring at the hill and the ragged edge of the tree line. He sat up suddenly.

A pale face, faintly illuminated by moonlight, was watching them from the darkness of the wood. At first he thought it was one of the creatures, but the figure that emerged was not Iaelven. It was human. And it shambled halfway down the hill before stopping.

Jack recognised him at once. 'There he is!' he said in a low voice. The others hadn't noticed. They seemed lost in their own world.

Jack stood and ran across the field. As he arrived, so the man withdrew, lowering his head. He was clutching a book. He looked more dishevelled than ever.

But he whispered, 'I'm going home. Have found a way. It will take me time.'

'Wait!' Jack pleaded. 'Please stay and talk. Your son is here. Look at the fire. The woman playing the harp. Don't you recognise her?'

George Huxley lifted his head, but he only had eyes for Jack.

'Have found a way,' he repeated, then turned and walked more briskly back along the route he had come. Jack tried to follow but a voice hailed him and he turned to see Steven running towards him. Looking back at Huxley, he called, 'What way?' but received no answer.

The moon had long since set, and the sky was dark with cloud. For the second time that night, the earth rather than the wood seemed to swallow a life. Huxley had gone.

113

Steven arrived behind him, breathless from his sprint on a full stomach and heady drink. 'Was it him? My father?'

'Yes,' the youth said morosely. 'I don't think I'll see him again. He said he was going home. Something has changed.'

'You're not to follow him.'

Jack glanced round angrily, eyes like fire. 'Not now. Of course not now. But I can't stay here for ever. I feel trapped. Sometimes I feel dizzy with the sameness of everything.'

Steven was hurt. 'I'm sorry you feel that. But I can understand it. It's not easy for me either. I've settled here, I risk encounters from the valley, I try to find new places to explore. Best of all, you and Yssobel, bringing you up and teaching you what I know has been a pleasure. It's kept me going.'

Jack shook his head, puzzled. 'Then why don't you leave yourself? There's the river,' he pointed into the distance. 'Isn't that how you came in?'

'There are too many rivers to know the answer to that. I'm rooted here now. I don't think I could leave even if I wanted to. When your mother was returned to us, I became a part of the valley just as much as she is. This is our place now. If you and Yssi aren't bound to it, then you must go. Of course you must go. If that's what you want. But not yet.'

'I said that, didn't I? Not yet. But one day certainly.'

Jack softened his tone and smiled at his father. With a rueful glance back into the forest, he returned to the fire, kissed Guiwenneth and his sister, and with a courteous bow to Odysseus, who was watching him curiously, walked away from them, back to the house and his own quarters.

Painting the Past

The winter that followed was extremely harsh, one of the worst they had encountered. The wind blew from the valley, hard and cold as frozen steel. Guiwenneth had sensed it coming and they had filled a whole room in the villa with firewood.

With the snowfall, the women who lived in their huts along the river came into the villa and found winter quarters, joining Rianna. Steven and Ealdwulf, and their sons, had made the rooms as winter-tight as possible, but most of the villa was still in a state of disrepair, and though much of it now had the hypocaust in place, this was inefficient and dangerous. Hearths were constructed, and every animal skin and fur available was hung across the walls and doors.

The arrival of Odysseus was anxiously awaited. He always came down from the pass when the weather turned cold, usually with two or three companions, young men unknown to Steven from his understanding of the past, but no doubt once of importance in their countries' legends.

Yssobel found her father in his own room. 'I'm going to find him,' she said.

'Who?'

'Odysseus. I'm worried about him.'

She was already wearing her heavy furs, thick boots and tight cloak. Steven watched her, then sighed. It did no good to argue with the young woman these days, despite her youthful years. And she knew the pass as well as she knew the villa. She was an expert at arms, thanks to the training of the young man she was going to visit.

'Take Hurthig with you. And spare furs. And dry food.'

'Of course.'

He watched her ride out through the gate, his heart heavy with anxiety. Hurthig led a packhorse and leaned down to kiss his mother goodbye. She stood there, arms crossed over her chest, probably as anxious about her son as was Steven about his daughter.

The gates were closed after them, against the storm.

Serpent Pass was becoming difficult, more difficult than Yssobel had expected. The track was treacherous with ice, and there was a heavy, patchy fog that made progress slow. Rocks tumbled from the slopes, and already trees were down and had to be moved or circumvented. Then, after two days, Hurthig pointed ahead of them and Yssobel saw, through the gloom, the white marble columns and high stone wall of the Greek temple that guarded the winding track to the cave.

They spurred forward, found the path and called for the young Ithacan, but there was no answer.

The mouth of the cave was still covered with skins. Yssobel dismounted, lit a torch and, still calling, went inside. The cave was deep. It was a clutter of pots and weapons, rough-hewn furniture, clay statues, coarse-woven rugs and discarded clothing. A mess. She went to the back of the cave, to the small shrine to Athene. Two Roman-style candle lamps were alight there, and in a bowl before the goddess were the remains of a burnt offering.

Heavy-hearted, Yssobel accepted what was clear: that her friend had departed. He was on his way to begin his adventure, though what he had been doing in the hills, in a rough cave, was a mystery to her, as indeed it was to Steven.

Sadly, she went back to where the Saxon was waiting for her.

'Gone?' he asked by gesture.

'Gone.'

'How long ago?'

'Not long, I think. I hope he makes it.'

Yssobel took a last look around. And then saw it; the small round clay plate, painted with the face of a smiling auburn-haired girl. She had never noticed it before when she had come to play games, or ride and talk as best she could with the young man who made her laugh. She took the plate and tucked it carefully into her saddlebag.

The wind suddenly picked up and the horses whinnied nervously. Hurthig looked down the pass. 'Storm coming. I think we should overnight here.'

Yssobel agreed and they made themselves comfortable in the cave, though it took some effort to persuade the horses inside.

Sitting by torchlight, listening to the howling wind, silent and reflective, Yssobel suddenly felt a rising of her spirit. For a moment she couldn't identify it, and then she began to remember the face she had once dreamed of, and for some time had forgotten.

The face of the man who called to her. The lost man.

The man she had called *resurrection*.

And her sadness lifted, and she began to feel warm.

Yssobel's safe return was greeted with relief and an understanding of her sadness at the disappearance of her good friend Odysseus. The courtyard was thick with snow, though for the moment the blizzard that had until then raged all day had ceased. It was after dark and they had approached with torches, following their line of sight to where fires struggled against the wind on the walls of the villa.

Shivering and half-starved, Yssobel and Hurthig were glad to leave the feeding, rubbing down and stabling of the horses to others. The beasts had done well in the conditions. Now it was water from the well, to be heated at least to warm, that Yssobel craved.

After bathing, and allowing Rianna to comb through the tangle of her hair, she went to the dining room to join the others. Most of the winter visitors had already had their small meal and departed. Only the Saxons remained and the Huxleys. The dining room was at the back of the villa, away from the head of the valley, and therefore warmer and cosier, with its open-hearth fire and goat-skin carpet. Everything in the room had been crafted by Ealdwulf, from the long table to the hard chairs, from the drinking cups to the carved wood platters on which the frugal fare was served.

Yssobel told her parents what she had found in the Odyssey cave, as they called it. She showed them the portrait that Odysseus had painted of her, which she believed to have been his way of saying goodbye. But there was no grief in her, she explained, when Guiwenneth asked her the question, and no, no sense of loss other than that of a lost friend.

Realising what her mother was intimating, she said very pointedly, leaning across the table: 'We were friends. We were not lovers.'

Steven murmured, 'Good. We won't have to be bringing gifts to a little Greek, then.'

He went on, 'If it's any consolation, though nothing is certain this deep in Ryhope Wood, I'm sure he'll be safe. I don't think anything has survived of his story between, what, five and fifteen? We shall never know why he has chosen to be in the wilderness, in a cave, making images of the various gods and goddesses. A strange isolation. But we know he went to his home at Ithaca. And we know he helped win a great siege.'

'I know, daddy. You've told me the story. The hollow horse. You've also told me that whatever is created from our minds in this place is created with that person's strengths and weaknesses. Not every mythago will follow its true track.'

'I hope this one does,' Steven said gently.

Yssobel forked up the last piece of meat from her platter, agreeing silently as she chewed, pushing the plate to the centre of the table. The Saxon family gave their thanks for the meal and left, and Yssobel thanked Hurthig again for his companionship on the ride. Then she said, continuing the previous conversation, 'But suddenly I'm aware of the man in the valley again. The man who calls to me.' She glanced at Steven. 'Your brother.'

At that, Guiwenneth's fists clenched and her voice rasped, 'You've not mentioned him for years. What makes you mention him now?'

Her face had become ashen and drawn. It startled Yssobel. She had been talking out of the red side of her life, the human side. But it was the green side that regarded her mother now, and it was shocking for her to see.

Guiwenneth's features had become like a wood skull, coated

in translucent skin. Yssobel could hear the crack of wood, the creak. It was as if her mother's whole body was being broken, resisting only because of its residual strength. Glancing at her father, Yssobel could tell that he was seeing nothing of this.

Jack had seen it, though. What he called the 'haunter' in him, the forest part, had perceived the terrible change in his mother. He watched her in consternation, then glanced at his sister and shook his head.

Yssobel didn't know what she had said. She remembered that years ago Guiwenneth had fled the villa for her father's fortress, upset by the man in the valley, but Steven had never told his daughter why. And eventually she had forgotten about it.

After a few moments Guiwenneth returned to normal, though her look was still that of an angry woman. 'You should leave him alone,' she whispered. 'He is a rotten man.'

'He doesn't feel that way to me . . .'

'Leave him alone!' Guiwenneth shouted. 'Get him out of your mind, if you can that is. If he hasn't already snared you through the branch and root that winds through your insides.'

Steven reached out and took Guiwenneth's hands in his. 'Gwin. Take it easy. You'll snap a twig!' He smiled at the family joke, but Guiwenneth snatched her hands away. 'More twigs snapped than you know,' she said coldly, pushing back from the table, almost stumbling as she stood and walked from the dining room and out into the snow.

Steven came and sat next to Yssobel. He tried to put his arm around her, but she felt angry and confused, hunching into herself, dismissing the gesture. 'What did I say? What made her angry?'

'The man you talk about, the man you paint, the man you dream about – you do dream about him, don't you?'

'Not for a long time. But I still feel he's there . . .'

'He's a hurtful man. He began as a child as a lovely child, though we scrapped a lot, and he usually won. He began as a man as a kind and colourful and competitive and funny man. And then he went into this wood from the outside . . .'

'From Oak Lodge?' Jack asked quickly.

'From Oak Lodge, yes. He followed his father into the

interior. He was curious to know what George Huxley had discovered; and he became transformed.'

'Transformed? Into what?'

'Something evil. A man who had become possessed by a dark element in the wood, if I can put it that way. His heart was cold, but his need was a furnace.'

'That's a strange way to talk,' the girl muttered. 'What was his need?'

'Can't you guess?'

Yssobel leaned forward, head in her hands. With a glance at Jack she nodded vaguely. 'I suppose it was my mother.'

'It was. And she still hurts. And you are wrong about him, Yssi. He is not lost, nor sad. If that resurrected man *is* Christian, then you should never go near him. He is harmful.'

'I didn't know,' she said. 'You should have told me before.'

'Well, I'm telling you now. Never go near him.'

'I'll never go near him,' Yssobel agreed in a dull tone of voice. She stood up. 'I'm tired, now. Tell mummy I'm sorry.' And with a kiss on his cheek, she left for her rooms.

Jack was flushed in the face, partly from the heat in the room, partly from Egwearda's concoction, which he'd diluted but perhaps not sufficiently. He rolled the empty cup between his palms, staring down into the bowl as if scrying the future, or perhaps the past.

Steven watched him. The log cracked and spat on the hearth, and he knew that soon he would have to open the room to the others so that they could sleep. He might even join them, though there was a good fire in his own room.

Jack looked up, breaking his thought. 'What was your brother – what was Christian searching for when he entered Ryhope?'

'Love, I imagine. A love that he'd already lost.'

'I don't understand.'

'I told you about the war in Europe. I told you how I stayed in Europe after the war. Chris came home. He found our father deluded – or mad, in fact: overwhelmed by his discovery of the nature of this immense realm, immense, even though we occupy only a tiny corner. One day a woman came out of the wood. She was very beautiful. She had flowing auburn hair and was dressed in hunter's clothing, and was a princess, running from pursuers.'

'Gwin,' Jack said, with a smile, glancing round at the door.

'Gwin but not Gwin.'

'How do you know?'

'Because the Guiwenneth who came to Oak Lodge on that particular day was either a mythago created by Christian or by the man of your own obsession: my father, George.'

'Ah, I see now. They fought over her.'

'Fought over her, and one of them killed her.'

Jack sat back in surprise. 'Killed her?'

'Buried her in the earth by the chicken sheds. I found her bones. Only they weren't bones by then, just scraps of cloth covering decayed wood.'

Thinking hard for a moment, Jack asked the obvious question. 'Which one killed her?'

How Steven would have loved to have known the answer to that. Long ago, when he had returned home from France, to find his father lost in the wood, his brother edgy and different, finally becoming lost himself, Steven had been shocked to dig into the grave and find what was left of the woman from the greenwood. It was certain that both other men had been passionate for this beauty from early Celtic times.

So now, for Jack, he filled in the missing piece: that when he, Steven, had been alone in Oak Lodge, Guiwenneth of the Green had returned, in new guise, with different traits of behaviour and humour to the other, no doubt, but essentially the same legendary woman. And they had fallen in love, and that love had been intense. And yet they had had only a few happy days before Christian, much aged and with a band of hawk-masked slaughterers, tracked her down to the Lodge and abducted her, leaving Steven for dead.

It was now too hot in the room. Father and son rose and went out into the freezing air of the garden, stepping into the darkness through the star-illuminated snow, breath frosting, welcoming the ice of the night on their overheated faces. The moon was low and only a crescent was visible. The edge of the wood across the rise of the Amurngoth hill was a dark wall, though it was possible to make out several sets of criss-crossing tracks, some animal, others human. There was always much movement from the valley and into the surrounding hills and passes when winter came, as if the bite of winter resurrected the life that had been gathering in *imarn uklyss*, sending it on its various paths; summoned by human mind and sentient wood, it was dispersed at random, probably to fade and die just as the echoes they were.

'You found Guiwenneth dead,' Jack said. 'But she was taken into *Lavondyss*. Taken by whom?'

'I shall never tell you. That secret dies with me.'

Jack stared at his father, almost too curious for words. When he tried to question him further, Steven cut him short.

'But you waited for her. And she came back.'

'I waited for her. And she came back.'

And with an inward shudder, Steven thought of what Guiwenneth had said to him, in her father's stronghold, the deserted fort that rose on the hill above Eagle Valley.

I'm not sure who I am. I'm not sure I'm yours. I think – I dread to think – that I'm his.

Winter in the land had ended. It ended as suddenly as it had arrived, and the villa was in spring sunshine between one day and the next. The animals were let out of winter quarters, but there was no confusion in them. From shivering in misery they were suddenly frisky, and breeding was in the air.

If winter had left the valley, it had not left the family, and the relationship between Guiwenneth and Yssobel became bleaker by the moon. As Yssobell's fascination and obsession with 'the resurrected man' increased, so did her mother's anger and fear; there were times when Guiwenneth walked the grounds of the villa by night, and when Steven saw her he felt he was looking at a ghost, that her body had become translucent; as if she was losing all substance, all connection with the world.

This would change, though for a while only, and it changed when Yssobel began to dream of her grandfather, Peredur. One evening when Steven passed her room, the door was open and he saw her painting in a fury. She had made her own brushes, and had traded skins and meat from her hunting for pigments with the bone-shapers, tent dwellers who regularly passed through from the valley. She was always complaining that she could never get enough yellow. Red, green, black and white, but never enough yellow.

'One day I will try and create the National Gallery,' Steven said from the door.

She waved the brush at him dismissively. 'Not now. I've got him. I can't hold him.'

'Who?'

'Go away.'

He stood in the doorway, watching her. 'The National Gallery in London is a famous place for famous painters. I would like to take you there.'

'Create it, then,' she snapped, not looking up. 'I know several painters in the region. A boat painter, a cave painter and a woman who paints bodies with iron pins and skin dyes. We can make a feast of it and discuss our work. But not now!'

My my, Steven thought; sharp-tongued, sarcastic, irritable, dismissive . . . fevered.

Yssobel was painting on parchment. He could see the black marks on the written side. 'Where did you get the scrolls?'

'There are thousands of them,' she said. 'Most of them just fall to pieces when you touch them. A lot are painted, really beautiful paintings. I just took a sackful of ones with writing on.' She turned the strip of parchment over. 'It's what you call hieroglyphs. I get a small sense of their meaning, but that's from the green side. It's not very interesting.'

Steven could hardly speak for a moment. 'And what does your green side tell you they say?'

'Just lists of battles, names of warriors, lists of weapons and chariots. There's one that has a list of boats and the number of men who went to war in them. Really boring.' She flipped another small pile of flattened parchment fragments, as yet unpainted in her workshop. 'This one, in fact.'

Suddenly she leaned back, chewing the end of her paint brush, gazing intently at the man in the doorway. 'There really *are* thousands. A few won't matter, will they?'

What had she found, and where had she found it? He asked the question, and Yssobel pointed vaguely in the direction of the

Serpent Pass. 'It's like a huge palace, built right back into the hill. Green marble on the outside, polished corridors and rooms, packed with all sorts of things. Including hunting equipment.' She indicated with a glance the sturdy bow she used, and the tall quiver of arrows, which Steven knew she could fire with great accuracy. He realised he had assumed that Ealdwulf had made them for her.

She was quite a lesson in surprise, this girl.

She was painting again. 'I found the place with Odysseus. It's further up the valley from his horrible cave. I suggested he moved in. Warmer, for a start, but no: he had to stay in that hole in the rock. Such an odd friend. But a good friend.' She finished the painting with a flourish, turned it round. 'There. Got him. But you never saw him, did you? Nor Gwin.'

'Who?'

'My grandfather from the green,' she said, intoning dramatically.

'Peredur?'

'War chief and hero. He has a strong face. And I can see where mother and I get our hair.'

The portrait was astonishing. It might almost have been a photograph. Thoughtful, a careful gaze, the hint of a smile in a lean, young, lightly bearded face, copper hair curling from below a simple crested helmet, the only decoration being two panels showing chariots in full attack. The man's face was slightly scarred. Around his neck, an eagle's head in profile, on a leather cord. In the background, sketched in light detail, rose the hill with its high towers where Guiwenneth had been born. He was a striking-looking man.

'You saw him? Or dreamed him.'

'Dreamed, of course. Greenside dream. But he was very clear. He was laughing and drinking, with friends, somewhere out in the open, close to a small fire. I don't think he was aware that I'd come so close. I think they'd been fighting. Not each other. I could smell blood. But they were triumphant. For the moment, anyway.'

'He's very handsome.'

Yssobel turned the portrait back and considered it. 'Yes. He is. I'm sorry he had to die so horribly. Shall I show it to my mother? Or will she rage at me again?'

Steven considered the question without knowing what to say. Guiwenneth was in a black mood again, for reasons he could no longer fathom, though he knew that fear and anger were at the root of it. She was so often like this, dark and despairing, though she certainly had her brighter moments; cheerful and active, full of life and energy, and eager to leave the villa for a look at the land around.

Since there was no 'red side' to Guiwenneth, only the green, Steven, in the dark hours, was inclined to think that she was slowly being called back into the wood, back into Lavondyss, death in the place of creation. He couldn't bear the thought of it, so he chose – being full of everything that was the red in man, and able to avoid more difficult issues – to put it from his mind. Although he spent as much time with Guiwenneth as he could, and as he was allowed.

'I think she'd like to see it,' he said. 'She never knew Peredur, nor her mother—'

'Deirdrath!'

'Yes. Deirdrath. Killed shortly after the birth, but she talked of him from the world of the Unhappy Dead. She had loved him very much. What a life she had had with the princeling. Yes, I think Gwin would like to see it.'

Yssobel gave a little sigh. 'I hope so.' And she added: 'Shall I try to find Deirdrath?'

'I don't know, Yssi. Ask her. Sometimes we like to live with the memory we have and which we hold precious, even if what we remember is just a ghost. We don't want them changed. But Gwin has always been curious about her father. So your portrait might be a lovely gift or it might hurt. Your choice.'

The girl nodded, picked up a piece of charcoal and quickly adjusted a contour. 'I believe he would have made a good impression,' she said, with an admiring smile. 'I think I'll take the chance.'

Ealdwulf suddenly appeared in the doorway, annoyed and flushed of face. 'Dried meat. And fruit,' he stated slowly. 'On the table! I called you.'

'Sorry, Ealdwulf. Didn't hear you.'

Father and daughter exchanged a quick smile as the Saxon moved irritably away. 'Dried meat and fruit,' said Yssobel softly, holding her head in her hands theatrically. 'Oh no.'

It was Ealdwulf's way of signalling that the meal was frugal, and badly prepared. Something had gone wrong in the kitchen. Probably an argument.

Later, Steven went to Guiwenneth's room, the small alcove where she liked to stitch hides together to make hunting out-fits, or create small images in clay or bark of the entities and memories of her childhood. Yssobel had inherited her artistic talents. Guiwenneth's shapes and forms were stranger, far more sinister in appearance, even though she claimed they were benign.

Yssobel was sitting on the floor, leaning back against her mother's knees. The room was illuminated with candles, and Guiwenneth was holding the portrait of her father and talking softly.

Everything was peaceful.

'I think, yes, he must have been very like this. I saw his image on a coin, and scratched on a piece of slate. I don't know who scratched the lines.'

Yssobel leaned back, eyes closed. 'Probably your mother Deirdrath. When she and Peredur were in love.'

'I imagine so.'

'Tell me what happened. What you were told had happened. It's time I knew.'

A mother's hand raked gently through a daughter's hair.

The portrait was placed aside.

Sadness and memory hung heavily for a moment, then Gui-wenneth, her voice almost as weak as the frail, ghostly body that contained it, whispered what she knew of her birth. Every-thing she remembered. Some of it, Yssobel and Jack had already been told.

'Deirdrath met Peredur after a battle. She tended to his wounds. I think he was just a boy then, not yet the king. He hadn't yet fought for the war chief's seat at what would become Dun Peredur.

'Deirdrath's sister, Rhiathan, was barren, but her consort, a

Roman of rank, wanted very much to have his own child. He planned to stay in Britain after his time of service to Rome was finished. So when I was born, Rhiathan killed my mother and took me for her own.

'I'm not sure where my father was at the time. Peredur was always away. War was commonplace; or perhaps he was taking hostages from another island. Ship raids along the coast were common, from another island, further west.

'When Peredur came home he knew at once what had happened. But Rhiathan's husband had gathered a force of men to guard the fort. Peredur and his shield-men, nine in all, went to a place and summoned the Jagad, a dangerous thing to do. She rules the pathways to the underworld. She rules ice and fire. She hunts what lies between the land and the wasteland. She can misdirect the dead on their way to the otherworld, so that a brave man can find himself stranded in nowhere rather than rejoining his fellow horsemen and heroes and starting life again.

'The Jagad exacted a great price for her help, but she allowed Peredur and his companions to transform into any three animals they wished. That was when they became *Jaguth*, which means: bound to the huntress.

'They first chose eagles. The Romans used an eagle as their standard, so I can see the pleasure he must have taken as he swooped and took me, just an infant, from the unsuckling false-mother.

'Sadly, a bowman of great skill, as great a skill as yours, Yssi, shot him down from the air. That was that. I was passed between the others.'

'My dream,' the girl whispered. 'That's my dream.'

'I know. The Jaguth,' Guiwenneth went on, 'transformed and protected me until I was old enough to ride. But then the Jagad called them back – she took back what she had believed to be hers.

'Without their protection, I was lost. But I survived. And the Jagad, terrible woman, showed one small morsel of compassion. Every year on the day of my birth she allowed the Jaguth to find me, for a night only. And the last time I saw them was at Oak Lodge, at the edge of the wood, after I had met your father and was still happy. Before I was taken again.'

'What is the day of your birthday?' Yssobel asked, suddenly shivering.

Guiwenneth smiled knowingly. 'Soon. I sense it.'

'Because?'

'Because I can hear them again. After all this time. Their voices are on the wind. They are coming again. But they bring a cold fire with them. Urgency and danger.'

The room had gone cold as well. The mood had changed abruptly.

Yssobel said stiffly, 'What danger?'

'You know what I mean,' said her mother softly, meeting Yssobel's gaze with cold eyes.

The girl almost screamed with irritation, twisting round to kneel facing Guiwenneth, a flame-haired, furious-faced image of the older woman. She snatched the portrait back. 'You hear danger in everything! You smell danger in everything! What has happened to you?'

And with a loud groan of frustration, she stood and started to walk from the chamber, hesitating only when she saw Steven standing in the doorway.

Suddenly humbled, she turned back and placed the painting on her mother's lap. Guiwenneth stared straight ahead, pale and unmoving. Yssobel walked grimly past her father, though Steven saw there were tears in the girl's eyes.

But enough had been done by the donation of the portrait of Peredur to ease the tension between the two women. Yssobel became fascinated with her grandfather, forcing her dreams to bring him to her sleeping mind, and she painted him vigorously; and in those paintings were reflections of his history, of his life, even – once – of his childhood.

She used sheets cut from a scroll that recorded part of *The Iliad*. Since the paint did not penetrate through to the text, Steven ignored the disrespect for the poet who had recorded the story of a fateful few days in the siege of Troy. He couldn't read the language anyway, and occasionally Yssobel – when 'green' – would rattle through some of the lines, sighing heavily with boredom. To Steven this was magic from his daughter's mouth, even if what she read was simply the list of ships and men who had gathered from all over the Greek world to savage the city of Troy itself.

The Cretans came in eighty black ships. All these were under the command of Idomai, who carried ten spears and two shields. He led the ships from Gnossos of the two-bladed axe, from Great Walled Gortyn, from all the hundred towns of Crete.

'Where's Crete?'

'An island. A long, thin island, with mountains and valleys, rivers and wilderness.'

'I like wilderness.'

'It was famous for a labyrinth that had a very strange attribute. For sacrifice. For a creature that was made of one part man, one part woman, one part bull and one part wood. Once a year, this monster ate a meal of Greeks, fourteen in all.'

'Quite a feat.'

'Quite a *feast*. Four times a year, at the turning of the seasons, the creature was allowed to mate. It gave rise to strange offspring.'

'You're making this up.'

Steven laughed. 'A little embellishment, perhaps.'

'But the island existed?'

'It did. Oh yes.'

'And the strange attribute of the labyrinth?'

'I made that up as well.'

Yssobel smiled. 'I don't think you did. There is something forceful about what you said, something of truth in it.'

Another few lines from the ancient text caught her by surprise.

Twelve ships, painted with crimson bows, came under Odysseus, master of all the masters of Ithaca. This was a great host, a great force, in awe of Odysseus, whose life-force and cunning rivalled that of life-engendering Zeus.

She stared at the words, and without looking up asked, 'Twelve ships?'

'He took part in that great war. Against Troy. You know this.'

'So this is part of what happened to him later. It's strange to find it written. Master of all the masters of Ithaca. He'll be very regal, then. Is Ithaca like Crete?'

'Yes. A territory, a part of a greater land. Not an island. Our young friend Odysseus is destined for long memory and fame; probably most of it wrongly reported.'

'Meaning?'

'Time creates confusion. Time changes memory.'

'Well, of course. Don't treat me like a child.'

'Sorry.'

She sighed. 'I miss him.'

'You might find him again.'

But Yssobel looked up and shook her head, sad and also knowing; accepting. 'He's moved on. Dad, you know that. If he remembers me, I'm pleased. But he's moved on. I know that.'

Steven was quiet for a moment, trying to find the right words. He couldn't find them.

You don't know anything of the sort, he thought to himself. *Not in this place. Not in this world. But then: I only know half of you, even though you're my daughter.*

Red side, green side. What must it feel like to have that mix? What colours your dreams?

Yssobel looked up suddenly, sharply. 'What's the matter?'

'What do you mean?'

She stood and came round to him; she was curious. Shorter than her father, she put her arms around him and rested her head against his shoulder. 'What were you thinking?'

'I was thinking,' Steven said, 'that I'd like you to paint a picture of Guiwenneth; and of Jack; and of me. On fragments of *The Odyssey*, though *The Iliad* will do if needs be.'

'Why do you want pictures of yourself?'

'To be remembered by.'

Yssobel laughed. She stayed where she was, holding Steven tightly. 'But I know you. I can remember you. Peredur, Deirdrath – I need them because I can't know them. Why would anyone want pictures of you? Especially of Jack! I'd have to paint him conceited and cocky.'

'He's not conceited and cocky.'

'You don't know him like I know him.'

'Then you misunderstand him.'

'I'm teasing.' She looked up, pulled away a little. 'Why? Why pictures?'

'What if the green side of you should die? How will you remember us? If we've all gone.'

'The red side of me will have everything that I need to remember. It's blood that comes out of me when I fall and cut myself. Blood at the moon time. The wood is not in my veins, just in my head.'

'And if the red side of you dies? What about the green?'

'You will be legend. What else? But then, what is legend to a tree in the middle of the wild? If only the green in me survives, there is no need to mourn the passing of a father. Or a brother. Or a mother. You think too much, dad. You worry too much.'

'I'd still like you to paint us. If all of you go, and I'm left: a small icon helps. You've worked so hard to bring an image of your grandfather to life. I love it. I think Gwin does too, despite your row. Use your skill to leave a little of the rest of us behind. And put something from your dreams in each painting. OK?'

'Ok,' Yssobel said without a pause, and with a smile.

'And in exchange I'll find you a horse to rival Caliburn. A better horse.'

'For when I go?'

Steven hugged his daughter. 'Yes. For when you go.'

'Caliburn is a wonderful horse. But he's getting old. He changes when we enter Serpent Pass. It's as if he's going home. He knows exactly where to tread as he winds up through the rocks. When he dies I'd like to place him in Odysseus's cave.'

Steven was pleased by the thought. 'So you'll stay and terrorise the villa at least until the old war horse kicks his last?'

'Yes. Of course. And Rianna has already promised me a new horse – a special horse, she says. So you don't need to go trading.'

Game and Promise

Yssobel found Jack in the forge, helping Hurthig to beat out a new sickle blade from one of the pieces of iron that they gathered, as well as forage for the fire, from the surrounding valleys.

Her brother, dripping with sweat, was distracted. Hurthig concentrated on his job, talking to Jack with his fingers and gestures. The coals flared and water hissed in the tempering barrel, and Jack was clearly proud of his efforts.

He was learning a lot from the silent Saxon youth.

'If you've come to be shod, you'll have to wait your turn. Horses come first. And besides, I don't know how big your feet are.'

'Very funny.'

Jack hammered the edge of the blade, then tested it with his finger, passing it to Hurthig, who twisted it this way and that, and then nodded approval.

Wiping the sweat from his face, Jack grinned at his sister. 'I'm getting to be quite good at this.'

'I'm glad to hear it.'

'Aren't you supposed to be rubbing down the horses?'

'All done. The horses are happy.'

'That's good to know. I do like to hear that our horses are happy. And so: you've come to see your brother master his skills at . . . sickle making.'

He lifted the blade, made gestures as if using it as a weapon. Hurthig looked bemused.

'Do you like doing this?' Yssobel asked.

132

'I love doing this. Oh yes. Take something old, shape it new. Bring the gleam back to the dead. Bring the cut back to the edge that was blunted by neglect.'

'Eloquent. I suppose.'

'Thank you. Anyway. What makes you stand here watching me? Something of iron for you? Or of bronze? I have bronze. Ask me to make it, I'll make it. With a little help from Hurthig,' Jack added quietly and with a confidential smirk, as if speaking quietly mattered. The Saxon was far too busy with his own thoughts and skills. 'I'm good, but not yet good enough.'

'Do you have silver?'

Stripping off his leather apron, untying his long hair from the strap that held it back as he worked at the fire, Jack frowned. 'Silver. Silver? Why silver?'

'Do you?'

'Do I? Have silver?' He walked to a box and opened it, peering down at the loose metal contents, moving his fingers through them. He was thinking hard. He picked out a small figurine, a woman diving as if into the sea, then a coin, turning it in his fingers. He dropped them back into the small hoard. 'Yes, I have silver. Not much. I could probably find more. Why do you ask? I don't waste it on horseshoes, not even for my sister.'

'I don't want to be shod; nor bridled.'

'I didn't think you did. Why silver?'

'I want a silver ring to hold back my hair. When I ride through the deeper wood my hair catches in the branches. In the briar, if I'm hunting, I need to tie it down. Hard. A ring of silver.'

'I tie my hair with leather. Or strips of fleece. Or strips of thin metal. Or thin rope. You could tie yours with any of those things. You could tie it back with a sharp word! Tie a parchment picture of our grandfather around it. Anyway, I know you tie your hair with bands of leather.'

'But now I want silver.'

Jack leaned back against the brick wall that contained the fire, quickly standing up as the heat began to burn him. He swore, brushing at his backside, and Yssobel was amused. Her brother laughed too, then said, 'All right. Silver. You have something in mind?'

'Something thin, something designed. Something that if I end up on a field of battle, and my scalp is taken as trophy, the ring will be admired. Something that when I've completed my days can be passed on to my daughter. Something that will mark me as Yssobel. Something to be loved by.'

Jack stared at her, eyes wide, face expressionless.

Then he said, 'Well, that sounds easy enough.'

After a moment, they laughed again, and he said, 'Yssi, I'll do my best. A ring to hold your hair. And in exchange . . .'

'Anything.'

'Then show me how to find the edge of the world.'

'That, alas, I can't do.'

'I know.'

'And so in exchange: what? Not another verse of that song!'

Jack turned from her. Hurthig had slumped down, sipping water from a clay flask and brushing some of it across his sweat-saturated face. Over the coals, Jack stirred the fire with the same blade he had just shaped, the reaping knife. He was not a man given to easy thought.

'I don't want to lose you,' he said. 'I don't want to lose this home, this villa. But we must move to the place that calls us. We have to.'

'I know.'

'How will we keep in touch? How will I know you're safe?'

'And how will I know that *you* are safe? And how will our parents?'

'Gwin will always know. But Gwin is fading. I feel it.'

'I feel it too.'

Jack looked up from the fire. Yssobel met his gaze.

And the young man said, 'I don't know why, or for what reason, or purpose, or because of what dream, or vision, or hawk's cry of warning, or hound's growl in your waking dreams, you want a ring of silver for your hair, but I will make it for you and pattern it as you require. With a little Saxon help,' he stated. 'In exchange, never let me go. And in exchange I will never let you go.'

Yssobel had slumped down by the wall of the forge, knees drawn up. She was staring into the dusk, towards the darkening sky that came from the valley, from *imarn uklyss*.

'Winter's coming.'

'Winter?' Jack said with a frown. 'We've only just had winter. Not so soon.'

He walked away from the heat, out into the cold, stepping beyond the glow of the forge. He raised his head and took a deep breath. 'You're right. Winter. Again. So soon.'

He came back and sat down next to his sister. Hurthig walked past them, shivering suddenly, then used his hands to signal goodnight, and could Jack please make sure the fire was controlled until it was reduced to embers, ready for the blow of the bellows tomorrow.

Yssobel said, 'I want to play the game. We haven't played it for a long time, Jack. But I would like to play it now.'

'Yssi . . .'

'Jack! I want to play the game. This might be our last time. And this time, it might be important.'

'I have to look after the fire.'

'The fire will die on its own. It can look after itself. It's going nowhere.'

'I'll play the game. But not where we used to play it. I'll play it here. The fire is still too fierce for silver.'

'Then we'll play it here.'

The fire had dropped to a glow. The winter was coming in fast, as it usually did, and in the darkness Jack could see flakes of snow. He had put out the torch, and rearranged the coals with tongs. Yssobel was curled in the corner, waiting for him, a blanket of stitched sheepskin covering her against the wind from the valley. Jack found a small crucible and embedded it in the heat.

'I'll melt the silver now. How big a ring do you need?'

Yssobel had already released her hair and tossed him the strap. He fitted his fingers through the loop of skin, stretched them out. 'You do know that silver won't be as strong as this. I'll have to make it thicker; heavier.'

'Do you have enough silver?'

'I'm sure I do. But it will weigh on you. You'll notice it.'

'That's what I want. As long as it keeps my hair out of the branches.'

He scrabbled through the hoard. The diving woman. A figurine of a lost god; two coins, quite large; an actual silver ring, with poor decoration, designed for a large finger. And two arrow points, though clearly weapons that had been symbolic and not practical. One of these he kept back. He placed the rest in the earthenware crucible, used the bellows on the coals beneath it, let heat and metal meld and melt. Silver would start to run at a lower temperature than iron. He blew air over the surface for a while to help bring impurities out of the true metal.

Wrapping his own sheepskin around him, he dropped down by his sister, shivered and reached for the water jug. 'I'm ready. For the question. Who goes first?'

'Same rules?'

'Same rules. One question, two answers. One answer truthful, one answer not.'

'I'll go first,' Yssobel said, leaning forward to bring her face close to Jack's. 'Are you ready for this?'

'I'm ready.'

'Why do you want to go the edge of the world? First answer.'

'I long to go to the edge of the world because I will find a life there that belongs to me. Now you: why do you want to go to the centre of the earth?'

'I want to go to the centre of the earth because I think I will find there who I am. Why do you want to go to the edge of the world?'

'Because I will find my way home there. I will find someone I care for.'

Yssobel sat back, frowning. 'That's a strange answer.'

'Why?'

'I don't know. It's just . . . strange.'

'The game requires that we don't question the answers,' Jack said with mock severity. 'Now you: why do you want to go the centre of the earth?'

'Because . . . because there I will find an answer to the question; the question of why what should be dead is alive again. I will find everything I care for, everything that ever mattered to me, and will always matter to me. I will find Avilion. And you, Jack, brother Jack? Will you find everything that matters to you at your world's edge?'

'That's outside the rules of the game. And talking of strange answers . . .'

'Forget the game. Will you find what you're looking for? At your own world's edge?'

'I don't know. I don't have your confidence, Yssi. I wish I did. When I get there, I'll know better.'

Yssobel made a sound of disapproval. 'You didn't play the game. Both of your answers were true.'

The silver had melted. Jack could tell by the sound it made that it was ready to be cooled, ready for the reshaping. He dragged his sheepskin around him. It was cold in the forge, despite the fire. Yssobel huddled, watching her brother. He lifted the crucible carefully and inspected the contents. The silver hadn't been pure. Though it gleamed like moonlight, he could see the tarnish of copper, and black specks of sand.

'It will have to be skimmed. And I've melted too much. I'll make you a second, smaller ring.'

'Just as long as it doesn't drag me backwards off my horse.'

'What pattern do you want?'

'I have said already. Any pattern you think fit.'

Jack tipped the crucible this way and that. The hot metal shone at him, despite the impurity that stained its surface. He had a ring mould to hand, but it would be too large for his sister's needs. Placing the crucible back on the coals, he broke the mould, snapped off part of it and pushed it back. The mould was clay. The silver would leak from it, but silver could be shaped, beaten into shape, marked.

He skimmed the silver, let it heat again, skimmed it again. All the time he thought of the hand that had made the small figurine; the hand that had shaped the arrowhead, though a point that was unusable; the hand that had struck the shape into the coin. They were echoes of other lives, condensed into what would soon become an echo of his own.

Jack poured the silver into the mould. Snow blew into the forge, a thickening blanket of cold, helping to cool the coals, though the fire still gave heat enough for the task.

It was a rough-looking ring of silver when, later, he eased it from the mould. Yssobel had left by then, tired and thoughtful.

Jack took a small hammer and began to work the metal. As the sky brightened with dawn, he took an awl and began to engrave it.

Hurthig came into the shelter. He inspected Jack's work and by the raising of eyebrows signified that Jack was doing well.

—A bracelet?

—A hair ring. For my sister.

—Then don't close it completely.

The young Saxon turned away and began to use the bellows to fire up the crude furnace.

They were making blades and horseshoes. Everything in the villa had its time, and this was forge time, and Hurthig was an expert at iron-making.

What to say? What idea to put on the small, thin ring? He would do it in runes. He and his sister understood rune-writing. But what to say?

After a while he gave up the struggle and just carved the silver with the only thoughts he could summon.

Yssobel looked at the ring, peered closely. On one side she read: *Avilion is what we make of it.*

She was thoughtful for a moment, then nodded. 'I like that. I wonder if it's true.'

Jack shrugged. 'Avilion belongs to you, not to me.'

'Does it?'

'It's your dream, Yssi. It's you that sees it from the edge of vision.'

'From the corner of my eye.'

'The gleam in the corner of your eye. Whole worlds are there.'

'I know.'

She turned the ring round, peering hard at what Jack had rune-scrawled on the other side. *What we remember is all the home we need.*

With a shake of her head she said, 'That's a bit . . . what does dad say? Corny.'

'Best I could come up with. Anyway, not as "corny" as your birthday song about me.'

Yssobel laughed. 'How long do you expect to live?'

'Twenty years more at least.'

'Twenty more verses. I don't think I can bear the thought.'

'*You* can't bear the thought? Who's the one who has to sit there listening as he's dissected by his sister's tongue? Anyway, you'll find a way. Just make the last verse count.'

'Thank you for the hair ring.'

Jack tossed her the smaller ring. He had not formed it completely, not joined it. It was ragged and uneven. Broken. He had inscribed: *Here to there. There to here.* Yssobel clutched it and held it and smiled.

'I like this very much. I'll find a use for it.'

'It's nothing. It's just raw silver, twisted. Nothing to it.'

Yssobel stood and glanced out into the growing storm of snow. Walking away from her brother, she said, 'That's what I find good about it. Goodnight, Jack.'

Winter came in. And with winter came a brief greeting from the past, welcome in its way, yet unwelcome for the news it brought.

The Jaguth came. Only Guiwenneth was there to receive them at the time, and Ealdwulf and Egwearda. So that when Steven came home, and his son came home, and Yssobel came home, they found a villa that had changed.

Ghost Rising

The stink of hounds was on the wind, the stink of fear. Bright in the moon, the villa was outlined in snow. Ealdwulf had closed the gates, but Guiwenneth pulled on her boots, wrapped herself in a sheepskin, and walked to where the ageing Saxon was trying to secure the grounds.

'Leave them open.'

'Something's coming.'

'I know. Leave them open.'

'I don't trust the night. Something is coming. I heard hounds calling. Can you smell that stink?'

'They're friends, old friend. Just friends. Leave the gates open.'

'It's blood, my friend.' He took her by the arm. 'They are not coming with good news.'

'I know.'

'When my father died, there was a storm of wolf's breath on the wind. There was blood shadow. There was crow calling. And the moon was bright, like this moon.'

'This moon doesn't frighten me. I've been expecting them. Ealdwulf, I am not afraid. But, please, old friend: stay beside me.'

'Will you protect me?'

Why was the Saxon so anxious? He was a strong man, a carpenter of skill, well fed and in robust health. And yet suddenly he looked drawn and was breathing hard, his face creased by the harsh silver light.

'Ealdwulf. There will be nothing to protect. Not from what is coming. Later? Yes. Then there may be some difficulty.'

As Ealdwulf faded, Guiwenneth strengthened. The snow-storm began to blow hard again, and the moon disappeared. They shivered in the villa; the heating was beginning to fail.

The women from the river had come scurrying in, hooded, cloaked, carrying their belongings in their arms. Three of the horsemen who had recently been using Dun Peredur as a temporary haven on their journey also turned up at the gates, laying their weapons down and leading their animals through the snow to the stables when Guiwenneth indicated they could come in. She had met them before, and was easy with them, though they were of a later age to her. She was glad to see the ancient old hunter she called Flint, wrapped in his furs, making his way to the kitchens. He glanced up as he passed, a miserable remnant of many a savage winter in a land far from his own. He was carrying wood on his back, and Guiwenneth directed Ealdwulf to go and help him. The two couldn't exchange words, but soon there was a better fire, the sound of laughter, and the welcome smell of simple food.

Rianna approached Guiwenneth. 'Where is Steven?'

'I don't know.'

'Your children?'

'With their father. Serpent Pass, I imagine. But I don't know.'

'Let me go and find them,' the older woman said, resting her hand lightly on Guiwenneth's folded arms.

Guiwenneth shook her head. 'Too dangerous.'

'I can shift my form. I can run. I can fly. I've not tried it for a long while, but the memory is there.'

'And be taken by a moon eagle before you make the valley? No.'

'Moon eagles? Have you seen them.'

'I've seen one. He's above the snow. With this storm, you can't see him, but he's there. And you wouldn't have a chance. Thank you, anyway.'

'Then the drums.'

'I was thinking of that. But Ealdwulf says there is movement in the earth. I'm not sure the signal would get through.'

Rianna crouched down, placed her hands, then her face against the bare ground, where the snow had been cleared.

'Yes,' she said. 'Movement in the earth.'

And quite suddenly Guiwenneth felt it too. A tremor that she had experienced before, nothing alarming, nothing threatening; a vibration that seemed to have a rhythm. She was always reminded of an army on the move.

'Try the drums anyway.'

Rianna disappeared. The snow began to ease. Darkness had taken the land, sliced through by the bright curve of the moon. Ealdwulf's guttural voice, and Rianna's insistent commands, sounded from the drum enclosure and almost at once the drums began to beat their own rhythm. The Saxon himself had made them, as he had made almost everything that was new and useful in the villa, and the sound managed to echo in the dark. Would it carry far enough to alert Steven and the others?

It certainly alerted the hounds that had been approaching stealthily. They began to run.

Two of them leapt onto the wall, one each side of the gate. They were huge, grey-backed, white-bellied, howling, hanging onto the stonework with their front paws, peering hard at Guiwenneth. Two more came through the gate, bounding through the snow, slowed by the snow, but determined to reach the woman who waited with open arms. When they reached her they almost struggled to get the first embrace, and Guiwenneth was left wet, licked, pushed over and laughing with the fierce and fond attention of the beasts.

'Enough! Enough! Good to see you, but you're rough!'

They sat down beside her, panting. The hounds on the wall scrambled over and approached; younger, leaner, they simply watched, eyes curious and wide, waiting for their masters.

Torches were flaring beyond the gate. A horn sounded, strident and deep, blasted in rhythm with the drumbeat from the signal shed, where Ealdwulf was still frantically signalling to the valleys.

Men approached. Guiwenneth stood and counted the dark shapes against the snow, counted the torches. Only five!

And the villa shook, almost throwing her off balance again. The drumming stopped. The dogs leapt up and looked to their masters, unnerved and alerted. Tiles were shaken from the roof

of the villa. One of the women from the river came running
through the cloister. 'What's happening?'

'I don't know.'

And then another. 'There's something happening in the field
behind the villa. Ghosts. Rising.'

What should she do? Old friends coming from the south. A
mystery rising from the north.

'Stop that damned drumming!' Guiwenneth screamed, and
her voice made the distance. Ealdwulf appeared, ashen in the
moonlight, shambling, terrified by the hounds, which merely
stared at him.

The torch bearers had stopped beyond the villa's gates. *What
to do?*

'Something in the field. Come with me!'

The old man ran with Guiwenneth, through the villa, out into
the gardens, to the low wall which separated the enclosure from
the field and the wild wood beyond. White, and gently rising,
the field was host to figures struggling into the early evening.
They came, all silver, some bright, some dark, some on horses,
some dragging carts, some burdened with packs of supplies; an
army, surfacing from the underworld.

Tall riders struggled up through the snow. Horse breath
misted. Riders looked around. The whole field was filled with
men-at-arms, all shivering, shouting, laughing. Flames flared as
some went towards the wood, others towards the villa, most
just huddling.

The army seemed to be moving east, towards Serpent Pass,
but there was confusion, clear confusion.

A rider came through the churned snow, a heavy-set man
wearing furs and leathers, his hair piled on his head and bound
with two copper rings. He was young, though hard of feature.
But his smile was easy. Two others followed him.

'I didn't expect winter,' he said

'Winter happens,' Guiwenneth replied. 'And too often in this
place to get comfort from it.'

The young man looked to the east, standing in the stirrups of
his horse. Then, looking back across the wall, he said, 'If I asked
you for food for this rabble?'

'We have enough food for only twice the rabble you see standing before you. That's ten at most. We have enough for a few days; fire for a few days more. I'd offer hospitality to a band of twenty, but so many?'

'I understand. Believe me. I understand very well. I've lost count of how many we are. Several hundred for sure. We move through strange realms. We move through worlds defined by time. We have, I have to tell you, seen very strange sights.'

'Good sights? Bad sights?'

'A lot of both, my shadow lady.'

'Delights?'

'Oh yes. But to surface in winter? That's no pleasure.'

'Some love winter, some don't.'

'Summer is a feast. Winter?'

'A beast. I know. Our beasts are dead, all but a few. I will gladly give you food and drink for a few of you. I can't do more than that. Unless you take it by force.'

The young man smiled, dipped his head. 'Lady, the man who commands this Legion would scour land for the last blade of grass. But he's old now. We're still confined to our movement through the world, sinking, surfacing, fighting in wars that we don't understand. There is something about us that is beyond our comprehension. But that is what we are. Legion.'

'Lost.'

'I suspect so. But when I referred to "rabble",' he added brightly, 'I meant just my own small group of companions.'

'A friend of mine,' said Guiwenneth, 'makes good beer. A barrel is at your disposal.'

'Accepted gladly. I don't suppose . . .'

'A little food?'

'Enough for a few. If you can spare it.'

Guiwenneth looked at Rianna. 'A ham. Fetch a ham.'

The woman gave a look of surprise and scurried away. 'How do you feed your Legion?' Guiwenneth asked.

'It's hard. We didn't expect to surface in winter. But something, something beyond my understanding, sustains most of them.'

As he waited for the gift, the young man beyond the wall

looked down at Guiwenneth, leaning on his horse's neck, half aware of the rise and fall of the Legion behind him as they surfaced and descended.

'I'm not going to ask your name,' he said.

'I wouldn't give it.'

He grinned. 'And I'm not going to give you mine.'

'I wouldn't ask it, though perhaps I already know it.'

He laughed. 'Once your hair was as bright as copper, gleaming. I can tell that.'

'Soon your hair will be grey, bright in the moon.'

'That's true. But not yet. Not until the bull turns and charges.'

'I think I understand. I'm not sure.'

The ham came, and Flint and two women from the river carried a barrel of Egwearda's ale. The young man stepped down from his horse and leaned over the wall, taking the ham first and then, with the help of his two companions, the barrel.

They rode away. He looked back, raising a hand in respect. 'It's the old song,' he called. 'When you're young, the bull pounds the dirt, but at a distance. Later, the bull and you are equals. Then, later still, the young bull is charging at you. What once was easy is now a challenge. As I said, it's the old song. And when you find the music, you'll find the words! I can't remember the poet who wrote it, but he was right. And what keeps us alive, beyond our time, is keeping that old bull at bay.'

'I'll find the music,' Guiwenneth called back against the noise of the rising Legion. 'And I'll keep the old bull at bay.'

'I'm sure you will.'

'Are we threatened?' she shouted.

The young man's voice was faint. 'Not now. Not this time. We're in the wrong place.'

The earth shuddered again, throwing Guiwenneth off balance. The wall against which she stood cracked, bricks fell. The villa itself twisted. The whole land seemed to distort. And in that moment, this strange army of disparate and moonlit men surged down into the snow, drowned by the earth – carts, horses, fires, all of it, all of them, moving away.

*

Rianna was tugging at Guiwenneth's arm, the look on her face one of panic. 'Strange men at the gates. I can't understand what they're saying, except that they keep saying your name.'

Guiwenneth consoled the older woman, though she herself was shaking.

She returned to where the Jaguth were waiting and beckoned them in. They waded through the snow and their hounds stood up, stretched and yawned, moving back as the men came forward in their heavy clothing. Five. Only five. Where were the other four? They were so heavily bearded, so lank-haired, so grimed with travel that they all looked the same, but one said, 'You've aged well.'

'Thank you. Magidion?'

'I'm Magidion.'

Guiwenneth cried out, 'I didn't recognise you! But I'd recognise that voice!' And she ran to him and tried to embrace him; the hounds growled. Her arms wouldn't reach around the broad body and bulky clothing of the man, so she tugged his beard. The others laughed at the action.

'Come into the villa. There's a fire there, and food.'

Magidion shook his head. The five crouched down in the snow, working the torches into the hard earth so that they were a semicircle of figures, eerily illuminated by the tar flames. They seemed exhausted, sad. Guiwenneth went to them and sat within the half circle, but not before she had signalled to Rianna for broth and bread. The old woman was certainly terrified of these tall, ragged apparitions, but she did as she was told and scurried back to the villa. After a while of silence, Rianna returned with a wide bowl of stew. She placed it on the ground. For a woman normally so resolute in the charge of adversity, she was strangely worried. She had brought two large heavy loaves as well, and Guiwenneth broke them with her hands, passing the chunks to her friends, who scooped the fragments of meat and vegetable from the bowl, ate quietly, and at last relaxed.

'Have you come from *imarn uklyss*?'

'From the valley? Yes. An army was ahead of us, but it seems to have passed you by.'

'I saw it. Legion. They seemed lost.'

'They're not lost,' Magidion said, licking his fingers. 'They just don't know where they're going. We came to warn you of the danger, but you are indeed Peredur's daughter. They moved around you and left you standing. Sometimes,' he added, with what Guiwenneth just discerned as a smile below the huge moustache, in the middle of the beard, 'Sometimes I wonder why we bother.'

'Bother with what?'

'Watching over you. As Peredur instructed us.'

'If you've been watching over me for the last few years, I haven't noticed much watching.'

'Then you were looking in the wrong direction.'

She smiled. Then she said, 'I've been happy, you know. Not always. Not recently. I have two children. I have a man in my life that loves me and has stayed in this place, this wood heart, because he knows I can't leave it. He gave up his world for me.'

'A good man. I remember him. But he's not enough, not strong enough, to hold you now. Not enough to protect you.'

'I don't understand.'

'Legion passed you by. We saw it. We were too slow in the following. We should have been here first. But it passed you by. You were lucky this time.'

His words echoed the parting words of the young rider.

Guiwenneth scooped up snow, made a ball and tossed it at the man. It shattered on his head. 'I'm glad to see you.'

He shook the ice from his ragged hair. 'This has been a long walk. We're glad to find you in good spirit.'

'Better now that you've come. But tell me what has happened. Peredur, my grandfather, died on the wing. I know that much.'

'Shot down, carrying you,' said Magidion.

'But the others? I can't make you out through the whiskers and hoods. Who remains here?'

One of the Jaguth rose to his feet. 'I am Amri'och. This is Cunus. This Orien. And here is Oswry.'

'And the others . . .'

She stood and looked at them, her heart racing as she

147

remembered how young they had been when she had been in their charge, and how they had been transformed into creatures as wild as the wildwood itself. 'You've been halved in numbers since I saw you last.'

'The Jagad is taking us back,' said Magidion. 'It was the agreement we made with her for holding you safe as a child.'

'I know. But why have you come?'

'To take you with us, if you wish. To protect you from what lies at the heart of Legion.'

'Your time here is done,' said Amri'och.

'My time is done?' Guiwenneth shook her head emphatically. 'I don't think so. What time I have left, I need to spend it here.'

Even as she spoke the words she felt their falsity.

Bread was thrown into the empty bowl. The Jaguth rose to their feet, shaking snow from their clothing. Magidion looked forlorn.

'The choice is yours. Whichever of us is left will watch for you.'

There was no anger in his voice, though Guiwenneth heard disappointment. She stood up and reached out for him. When he entered her shallow embrace, he smelled strongly of earth.

'I must go my own way,' she said.

'You are that man's daughter.'

'And his granddaughter lives here now.'

She added: 'When Peredur was shot down, when he dropped me, you were the one who caught me. Would that be right?'

'Lady, we all caught you as you fell. It's not the order that matters, it's the saving. The Jagad is taking us back, one by one. But as long as one of us is left . . .'

'If I fall, there will be one to catch me.'

He bowed his head in agreement. 'Perhaps this wasn't such a wasted journey after all.'

'Just to see you has given me courage. Please stay longer.'

But Magidion raised his hand, declining the invitation. He drew his torch from the snow.

'Then goodnight.'

None of the Jaguth responded except with a nod of their heads.

They turned. The hounds rose, yawned, shivered, shook the snow from their hides, looked mournfully at the empty bowl of broth but quickly turned to the gate, leaping through the drifts, leading their masters back into the winter wilderness.

The Crossing Place

We held and held until we broke, and in the breaking we found Avilion.

For a while Guiwenneth sat and stared at the torches as they dimmed with distance. She cried a little, then Ealdwulf stopped the drumming. The sudden loss of sounds startled her. She stood. The old man came towards her, his face flushed with effort and fatigue. 'I need to rest. I hope they heard the drums.'

'I'm sure they did. Thank you. Use my room, it's warm.'

He entered the villa.

What had she been thinking of? Why had she sent her protectors away? Her time here was done: she'd known it for several winters without really thinking about it.

Guiwenneth sighed. She walked into the back garden, went to the low wall where she could see the churned field, where the army had surfaced and descended. And for reasons that she didn't understand but which seemed completely natural, she called for the young rider. She felt very calm.

The snow parted, the earth parted, he came up, his horse struggling, finding its balance. He was attentive to the animal, no eyes for Guiwenneth until horse and rider had made the hard ground. He shifted his shield onto his back, reached down and stroked the broad cheeks of his mount. Behind him his shield companions surfaced, one of them leading a bridled, harnessed, saddled mare, bringing her forward to the wall, leaving her there before retiring.

The young warrior said, 'I wasn't sure if you'd call, but I waited.'

'I'm glad you waited. I wasn't sure if I would call.'

'I shan't give you my name,' he said.

'I shan't give you mine.'

'Not yet, at least.'

Guiwenneth clambered over the wall and hoisted herself onto the ice-cold saddle, holding the horse's mane, reassuring her. A fur-lined cloak was thrown to her by one of the companions and she hauled it around her shoulders, securing it at the neck with the heavy bronze clasp.

The young rider asked, 'Are you sure? Are you sure you want to come?'

'No. Not at all. But for some reason it feels right.'

'You have a husband, children.' It was a statement, not a question. He knew who she was, then.

She stared at the villa for a moment, then slumped across the horse's withers, crying softly. 'I know. I know. I belonged with them for a long while. Now I don't know where I belong.'

'There is an answer to be found. I'll help you find it. Be strong. Hold your ground.'

Hold your ground?

'Who are you?' Guiwenneth whispered, and he answered, 'I've already told you: that I'll not tell you. But I'll tell you this. It's a song I know, though I'll not sing it. My singing voice is terrible. And it's a terrible tune.'

His companions made a low sound, almost like a muttered cheer.

'But I like the words, and I like them partly because I don't understand them, not all of them. Shall I speak the song to you before you freeze to death?'

'Yes. Yes, do.'

One of his shield men leaned so far back in his saddle, groaning, that he fell from his horse. The young rider watched him for a moment, then turned back to Guiwenneth.

'Since I'm not permitted to indulge in story or song by those who claim to protect me, let me say just this . . .'

He reached out his hand; she took it. His gaze was inquisitive

151

•

and uncertain and pleasant. He said, 'It's as if I've met a ghost; and know at once I know her.'

Guiwenneth shivered but laughed. 'Well, strangely, I feel the same.'

'So what are you doing here?' he asked.

'I could ask the same of you.'

He let go of her hand and stared across the winter hills. 'This is my world. Isn't it? I feel that it is, and yet . . . I'm not sure.'

'It's mine too,' Guiwenneth responded. 'And yet – I'm not sure either.'

'Then we've met where, at what? A hinterland?'

She looked at the villa, at the moonlit ridges of the hills, at the dark road to the valley, to *imarn uklyss*. 'Yes,' she said quietly. 'A crossing place. A place of meeting. And of parting.'

He stared at her, curious, before smiling; he glanced round at his companions, then back at the woman. 'Ghost – will you come with me?'

'Will you keep me safe?'

'In Legion? I wouldn't volunteer that promise! My best is all I can promise; and the strong shields of my men here. And your own courage.'

Guiwenneth sighed. 'I wonder if I'm dead.'

'I can't answer that. You look "quick" enough to me. So now decide,' he said in a formal tone. 'Shall I step aside? Or hold you?'

Guiwenneth now reached out her own hand, which was quickly taken. The horses were feeling the cold, the stillness. Riding was needed. Warmth.

'That's from your song,' she said, and he agreed. 'Hold me,' she went on. 'You say you've met a ghost. I feel the same. I'm not sure if you're from my own world of dreams, or you from mine.'

'Who is the ghost – who the host?' he responded with amused understanding.

His companions rode up, restless. Each acknowledged Guiwenneth politely again, but frowned at the young rider.

One of them said wearily, 'We have to go. We know you like words. You're better than the two of us put together in just about everything; when it comes to words. But for the moment, for all our sakes, stop the mead-hall romancing!'

'And we'll never catch up unless we go now,' said the other.

'Yes. Yes, of course. One of you ride at the front, one stay at the rear.' He looked at Guiwenneth. 'Until we're settled, perhaps you should ride ahead of me.'

Snow began to fall again, though lightly. A torch flared and circled in the grounds of the villa, though Guiwenneth couldn't see who was waving it. She started to sing, a song she had always loved. The Song of the Islands of the Lost.

The four made their formation and found their way back into the earth.

Parting

During that same night, Ealdwulf and Egwearda died. Yssobel, Steven and Hurthig rode back the next day to find Egwearda on her knees in the snow, face pressed hard into the ground, as if grieving, as if to freeze her tears.

'What's happened here?' Yssobel whispered.

'I don't know. But it's not good.'

Jack was elsewhere, but Yssobel was certain that her brother had also heard the summoning of the drums and was finding his way home.

She dismounted, took the horses and led them to the stables. Steven went to the Saxon woman. He put his arms around her, to raise her up. He imagined she was in pain.

'Egwearda . . .'

The woman didn't move. She was cold and hard, like rock. He sighed, then lifted her from the snow and carried her to the villa. Yssobel came running, shedding her cloak, a quick glance telling her father that she had understood the situation.

'Find your mother,' Steven said.

Yssobel went to Guiwenneth's room and it was there that she found Ealdwulf. He was lying on the bed, quiet, cold. Now she understood the reason for Egwearda's grieving death. She knelt beside him for a moment, then realised with a moment's profound shock that something was wrong beyond the death of the Saxons. Nothing was missing from the room itself; but the room had begun to turn grey: surfaces and walls were shedding a light ash.

It was Rianna who brought the news, arms crossed, face

distraught as she stood in the doorway. Yssobel rose slowly to her feet, face darkening as she saw the look in the old woman's eyes.

'My mother?'

'She went with them,' Rianna said softly, on the verge of tears. 'I watched the whole thing. A young rider and his companions; out on the hill. We gave them food and drink as they passed, just enough for a few. But they came back later, during the night. They took her with them.'

'They took her with them? Where were they going? Do you know?'

'I don't know. How can I know?' The woman was crying. 'Downwards. Into the earth. They seemed to melt into the earth. Riding east, towards Serpent Pass. I saw the whole thing. She was unhappy, I could tell that; but she was not taken against her will. She didn't struggle. It was almost as if she wanted to go.'

Yssobel was silent. She touched the cold, calm face of the dead man. Inside, she too was feeling cold and dead. *What have I done?* There was a long silence as she thought about what to do. Then to Rianna:

'I dropped my cloak in the snow. Fetch it, please.'

'Yes.'

'I'm going to my quarters.'

Yssobel covered the body of the old man, looked around at her mother's private room, once a warm place where she had told stories, combed hair, made clothes, cried whilst awake, cried whilst asleep. All, now, becoming dust. Yssobel walked about the chamber, searching. She found something of importance and folded it, tucking it inside her heavy clothing. Then she went out into the frost, walked round to the wall at the back of the villa and stared at the hill. It was churned up and rough, as if a battle had been fought there. Among the trees on the ridge, a few torches glowed, the ever-watching Iaelven.

She shouted at them. Then she shouted at the night sky, at the stars she could glimpse. Then she screamed and struck the wall with her fists until she felt them bruised.

'What have I done? What have I done? Gwin! Mother! Come back, come back.'

Tears of anger flooded her face. The red side of her was in

a fury, but at herself. The red side felt guilt. Argument was remembered. Her mother's anxious anger that her daughter might be summoning Christian from the deep. Her own unwillingness to accept anything other than a sad and needful nature in the resurrected man.

Her mother had 'gone willingly'. Or had she? She had taken nothing, no winter clothing, no personal items, no supplies. She had just gone.

Yssobel slumped against the wall, head between her outstretched arms.

'We must not lose you. We must not lose you.'

After a while, she returned to her own rooms, her anger gone, a strange pain inside her still insistent.

When Steven found her, she was slumped on her arms on her table, painted and unpainted parchments scattered on the floor, swept there with indifference, only the image of Peredur in place; and her hand was on the painting. Her hair was a veil across a woman who was clearly weeping softly.

'Yssi?'

The hand clawed at the image of her grandfather. Auburn hair shook as she rocked from side to side. 'I'd like to be alone for a while.'

'Don't do anything rash. Promise me?'

Yssobel sat up, tearful eyes glaring, mouth hard, as if she were about to shout some fierce rebuke to her father. But she softened her look, frowned, then nodded agreement.

'I won't do anything rash. I just have to think. This is my doing. This is my own doing.'

'Why do you say that?'

'The falling-out. The anger. Her unhappiness.'

'Guiwenneth had been unhappy for several years. She's a mythago. She's *all* from the green side. That's the side that calls the strongest; and when it calls, you have no resistance to it. What has happened is simply a part of the cycle of her story. We have to understand that.'

'Simply? Simply? How easy to accept that. Aren't you sad she's gone?'

Steven could hardly speak for a moment. The words choked in his chest as he tried to suppress his own emotion. 'Of course I am,' he managed to say. 'But I understand it. I don't like it. I wouldn't have wanted it. I would do anything to have her back. I love her. But I understand why it must happen.'

'You waited so long for her to come back to you. How can you let her go now?'

He had no answer except to say, feebly, 'I waited once, and I was rewarded with a great deal of hardship and joy. I couldn't wait again, Yssi. I'd rather follow her.'

Yssobel stood and came round to her father, looked him in the eye, then put her arms around him. 'What if I could get her back?' she whispered.

'Don't! Don't even think about it!'

'But what if I could?' she asked, stepping back.

'Then I'd lose you too. Yssi, winter's coming to an end. Can you smell it?'

'Oh, yes.'

'Tomorrow, the day after, the snow will be gone. Cold makes us think only of the cold. Soon we can think of the future.'

'I understand.'

She kissed him gently, looked at him gently. Steven read that look – he knew it from years of experience with her. She would agree at first, before disobeying.

He sighed. 'I'd better go and comfort Hurthig.'

Yssobel wiped her eyes with her hands, agreeing. 'I'll come with you.'

The young Saxon had arranged the bodies of his parents so that Egwearda lay curled up, facing Ealdwulf. The old man's arms held the strange relic that they carried with them, but the ring had been removed from the hand, and Steven saw that Hurthig now wore it.

Hurthig rose from kneeling and turned towards Yssobel. 'I hope you find your Odysseus, no matter where you travel.'

These were the first words he had ever spoken. In English, with an odd accent, but comprehensible. He repeated them in his own language. His voice was mellow and deep, soft, unlike his father's.

'You've been silent since we knew you,' Yssobel said. 'What brings the voice now?'

'These deaths.'

He didn't elaborate. Steven asked, 'Then you'll be leaving us?'

But Hurthig shook his head. 'This is the place we came searching for. We found many like it, but this is where they belong. And where I belong as well. I would like to build a funeral pyre, in the field.'

'The field is yours, Hurthig. It doesn't belong to the villa. It belongs to the Iaelven.'

Hurthig nodded his understanding, then turned away. Steven left him to his contemplation, though Yssobel remained, watching the man at his ritual. Steven heard her ask, 'Who are you? Who are you really?'

He answered in his own language, guttural and resonant. Then he said, 'They were the last of the old kingdom. I am the first of the new. I don't know any more than that. Like you, like Jack, I dream of myself in future times. But there is never a name.'

All night the pyre had burned and it was still glowing when dawn came. The snowfield was alive with the colours of fire and Hurthig was still in the saddle, slumped forward in sleep.

This was two days after the deaths, two days after Guiwenneth had disappeared.

Several tall armed Amurngoth had appeared during the night funeral and watched curiously, but they had not interfered. The silvery ghost of a woman had also been seen, standing at the edge of the wood, staring down at the pyre, but for moments only.

Jack came back early the following day. He had been trying to ride up Serpent Pass to the museum, to bring back more easy metal for the forge. The Haunter side of him had detected the heavy beat of the summoning drum. He had been about to turn back anyway. For ages, Serpent Pass had been in winter.

He found Steven in his mother's room, in distress, confused, almost unable to speak. The room was coated in a strange ash, which did not feel or smell as if it had come from burning. 'She's gone,' was all his father would say.

Jack stalked the grounds, searching for any sight or sign of

Guiwenneth, or of what might have happened. His face was flushed with the effort of the ride, and with anxiety. Another fire had been lit on the field behind the villa; and the field was in ruins. What was going on?

The human side was not coping. Haunter whispered to him, and the sound of summer streams and stillness calmed Jack down.

He went to find his father again. Now he was in the room where they took their meals, sitting at the table.

'What happened here? What happened to Gwin?'

Steven looked up, shaking his head. 'Egwearda and Ealdwulf are both dead. Hurthig is alive. Rianna says Gwin was swallowed by the earth. Riders came past. Night riders. She went with them. But, according to Rianna, willingly.'

'Willingly? I don't believe it. That's nonsense. She's been taken.' *Calm!* Jack took a few deep breaths, his heart still racing. 'Where's Yssobel?'

'Still in her quarters, I expect.' Steven looked suddenly alarmed. 'How long is it after dawn?'

There was no need to answer the question. They ran through the villa's corridors, to the rooms where Yssobel's gallery was still intact, exactly as she would have left it. But of Yssobel herself there was no sign.

On her table, spread so that they could be seen from the door, were the portrait of Peredur; next to it a sketch of Guiwenneth herself; and the shallow porcelain dish that Odysseus had painted, the image of the girl, which she had taken from his cave.

As his father started to bend forward, his breathing becoming desperate, Jack took his arm. 'You go to the stables – see if her horse is still there and I'll look for tracks.'

'Yes,' Steven said, and walked quickly from the room.

Jack went out into the wide courtyard and asked Haunter for help. The green side of him scanned the snow, as far as the gates, and then beyond, where the track wound towards the beginning of the valley.

Hounds had been here, and men, five of them, judging by the impressions in the frozen ground. The men had sat in a semicircle. Something hot had been placed on front of them; a

159

cauldron, no doubt. Another figure had crouched on the other side. His mother, he imagined. Why had they sat in the snow? Why not in the villa? He didn't understand; but he was careful to remember that pattern, and the numbers of men, and the numbers of hounds.

There were tracks, too, of the riders who had come home: Yssobel herself; Steven; Jack and Hurthig. But all tracks led inwards from the gate. There were none – and he searched the snow carefully – that suggested any departure.

His father called to him. 'Jack? Rona is gone. Yssobel's horse is gone. All the other packhorses are here.'

They met at the rear wall and looked at the field, and across the field at the hill. Haunter whispered: *Nothing to see. But in this mess of tracks and chaos, I can't be sure. If she went this way, she went towards the hill, or Serpent Pass. But I can't be sure.*

Had she gone to the valley?

Jack walked through the main gates, out into the cruel day, and stared at the far hills, the winter woods, the place from where his mother had struggled to return. He saw there the same hound tracks and the man tracks; they led in, then out. The outward traces suggested they had turned into the pass. There was no sign of any horse or horses going anywhere but into the villa.

Jack stood there for a long time, feeling the ice wind, listening to the silence, searching the distance for movement, seeing only the movement of cloud and the swirl of gusting snow, picked up by an elemental wind. This winter had lasted too long. Too many winters, too much wasteland. Distantly, he could hear a woman softly crying, and recognised the mourning keen of Rianna, who perhaps was sensing the end of the home.

And then his father's voice: 'I'm going to lose you too! I know it. Everything about you tells me that's what's going to happen.'

'What about me?'

'Your anger.'

Jack turned from the gate, walked to his father and took him in his arms. Steven Huxley was a shade of himself – dark-rimmed eyes, deep frown, shivering with cold and something more: fear, perhaps.

He was taller than his son, but now Jack felt taller. 'We should go into the warm.'

In the villa, in Jack's room, surrounded by his son's models of the edge of the world, Steven started to smile. He looked at the model of Oak Lodge; at the landscape of the fields and woodland; at the small wooden buildings that represented Shadoxhurst – the church far too prominent, the spire too high. It was such a small town in the land, even though it called to all the villages around. Shadox Wood. And what had Shadox meant? Not even his father had been able to understand the meaning behind the name.

It sounded like shadow.

Steven said, 'The edge of the world is shadow, Jack. To me it's memory. To you, a place to find. I've always known that.'

He exchanged a long and silent look with the young man whom he loved. 'But do you really need to go there now?'

'Yes. And for a second reason.'

Rianna appeared at the door. At Steven's signal she came in and sat at the table. 'I didn't see her go. I didn't hear her go. But the horse was mine, my gift to her. And the horse was charmed. I can believe that in riding out, before dawn, she would have left no signs.'

'Do you have any idea where she might have gone?'

But the High Woman shook her head. 'If I'd known what was in her heart I could have followed, but it's too late now.'

'My thinking exactly,' Jack said. He looked at the gaunt woman. 'Will you look after this man in my absence?'

She seemed surprised and insulted. 'Where else can I go? Of course. This is my home.'

'This is my home too,' Jack replied. 'And Yssobel's. To find where she's gone I need to find my grandfather.'

Steven shook his head. 'That makes no sense.'

We can find him. We can summon him. We can explore what he has seen. He has been close to us for years, and might have the clue to where she has gone. This may be instinct, but instinct that should be obeyed. Go to the edge, Jack. Your Haunter will get you there.

'I think . . .' Jack began, but paused. He corrected the word: 'I'm certain that I can find Grandfather George.'

'You'll find no more than a mythago. He'll be an impression, an echo of your own needs, your own passion. What is the point? Raising a man who is not the true man?'

'But dad: Guiwenneth came to you with memories of her past. They weren't yours, they were hers. You've always told me this. You brought her to life. You brought my mother to life. She came with life! A memory of life. So can George. If I can call him.'

'Why do you think my father would ever venture near the edge of the wood?'

'Because that's where the Lodge is. Because that's where he began. Because for him, that's the place where he can cross between worlds. All he needs is the call. I'm guessing, of course. But I'll try. If I can bring him back, I can ask him about my mother and Yssi.'

'And see the world you've dreamed of so obsessively at the same time.'

'But I'll come back. I promise.'

'What would bring you back? What reason would you have to come back if you find the world you've dreamed of?'

'You. This place. This life. It's so intriguing. But, that said, I will leave again, eventually. But not before I've said a proper goodbye to you.'

Rianna interrupted. 'Would you like me to prepare food for your journey? Hurthig can saddle the horse. You'll need a pack animal too. Are you leaving now?'

'The day after tomorrow. I smell spring. I want the snow to go away. I'd like to be alone with my father now.'

Rianna rose and smiled, vanished like a ghost.

Jack said: 'Well: now we can talk for a while longer. And I'll call to you when I return.'

This was the end of the villa. Rebuilt from ruins, now it was ruined again, by the loss of so much of the warmth of the life that it had contained.

Return

Steven stood in the middle of the field. It was night, and a brisk early-autumn wind was blowing. The field had healed itself; no sign now of the passing of Legion those many seasons ago, that confused passage of time. Silver gleamed on the hill, between the trees. The silver was woman-shaped.

He watched, aware that he should go no closer.

A darker form appeared, masking the silver; man-shaped, weary. The glow of the woman made a halo around his body. Steven heard her words:

'A friend has returned.'

And then the call of his son: 'I'm home. And I know where Yssobel has gone.'

Silver faded, that enigmatic glow he had witnessed before, not understanding it, but gone now. His son came down the hill, a gaunt man, stinking of travel and the wild. None of that mattered. Afraid though he was of walking too far into the ground belonging to the Iaelven, Steven approached his son and held him.

'Where has she gone?' he asked.

'Beyond the fire.'

'And my father? Did you find him?'

'I did. Not a good encounter, but good enough.'

'Did he remember me?'

'He remembered you. And your brother. And for a while he confused me with you, but he soon understood who I was. And he knew of Yssobel.'

Steven smiled. 'You were right. There was a good reason for going to the edge.'

'And I've brought you your book. *The Time Machine*. I've read some of it. It's so strange! I like it, though I don't understand the world in which it's set. Such a strange future. And I've also brought a chess game. From Christian's room. It's all I could think to bring.'

'Chris liked chess. Thank you.'

'And I don't propose to leave again for several weeks.'

His father smiled now. 'I'm glad to hear that. But food is scarce.'

'Food can be obtained.'

'Not much warmth in the villa.'

'We'll see about that.'

'This was a hard trip, I think. For you.'

Shrugging off his leather packs, pushing them into his father's arms, Jack said, 'Not hard at all. There's a part of me that can pursue trails through anything that's hard. I'm pleased to see you.'

Fading eyes brightened at the words, then the frown in the gaunt face again. 'Who was the silver woman?'

They looked back towards the hill. Jack said, 'Someone from the past. When I've found our Yssobel – should she need finding – I'll come back for the silver woman. And someone else.' He shivered with the cold. 'Why are you asking me so much? Out here. In the field! I need to sleep and see you in the light.'

The hill was dark now, but Rianna had lit a torch and was waving it, a fire of welcome by the outer wall. Exhausted, but with his arm around his father, Jack went back to the comfort of his first home.

The Crossing Place: Moonsilver

Jack stayed with his father for several days, enjoying both the comfort of the villa and the awareness that Steven Huxley was transformed by his son's return. It was quite clear that Steven had not been looking after himself. He was dishevelled and ragged, his eyes rimmed with dark through lack of proper sleep, and he had developed a substantial belly.

But now he was a fury of activity and chatter. And laughter.

Hurthig had maintained the villa as well as he could, though there were distinct signs of change, and Rianna had kept it clean, though she had failed to persuade Steven to wash more often and trim his hair. It was as if he had wanted an excuse to clean himself up. And that excuse had come back into his life. Apart from the paunch, he was a new man.

On the second day of Jack's reappearance, Jack told of everything he had found at Oak Lodge.

'You found my father? You found old Huxley?'

'He was just the ghost of the man, I'm sure of that,' Jack said. 'I don't know from whose mind he was resurrected. And it was the ghost of a journal. But he wrote about Yssobel when I whispered in his ear.'

'And you know where she's gone?'

'Where she's gone, and how she got there. But if I'm right,' Jack had been thinking hard about what Huxley had written, about his sister's transit to Avilion, 'that way is not open to me.'

To the extent that he could, he recounted the scrawled contents of the notebook. Steven was fascinated and perplexed in equal measure.

Jack described the Amurngoth, and his failed attempts to walk beyond Shadoxhurst.

His father was not surprised. 'It's true; we would find mythagos dead on the land. They would come to the edge of the wood and peer at us, but those that tried to move outwards always perished. I didn't know this until I read my own father's journals, long after he had disappeared.'

Jack shook his head. 'At least *one* mythago made it to the outside and survived.'

Steven was surprised. 'Oh? What was it?'

'*Who* was it! His name is Caylen Reeve; he's been with the Shadoxhurst church for generations.'

For a moment, Steven was speechless. 'Good Lord. The Reverend Reeve. He used to conduct the harvest festival every year. That's the only time I ever really met him. How in the name of . . . how do you know he was from the wood?'

'He told me. He recognised me for what I am.'

'Tell me more.'

When Jack had finished filling his father in on the details of his journey and his edge-world experiences, he presented Steven with the two items he'd requested.

Steven looked at the copy of *The Time Machine* and shook his head fondly. 'This was my favourite story when I was a child. I must have read it fifty times. Maybe more. It makes me shiver just to think about it now.' He opened the book, read a paragraph or two to himself, then closed it and kissed it. 'You must read it before you go again, Jack. And I know you're going to go again.'

Jack passed his father the chess set. 'Ah,' said Steven. 'He was a good player, your brother. Better than me, though not as good as George. When our father deigned to leave his study and come and spend time with us, that is. The pieces are made of something called *bakelite*. It was quite new.'

'They feel strange to the touch. I would have expected ivory.'

'Ivory or wood. Yes. This was a birthday gift from a friend of my father's, his great companion and fellow scientist. A man called Wynne-Jones. Heaven alone knows where he is now. In our different ways, we all became lost.' He placed book and game to one side. 'Thank you, Jack. These are precious souvenirs.'

It was warm in this room, in the villa. It was as Jack remembered it. When his mother and Yssobel had shouted at each other, the room could seem cold. But when the family were quiet, eating and laughing together, this place of simple furniture, decoration and open hearth had been comforting and enclosing. Or was this nostalgia at work, the constant draw to home? Life in the villa had been hard, and his and Yssobel's growing frustration at their confinement had been harshly expressed.

Perhaps it was just that he was pleased to be away from the journey, feet up, sipping Hurthig's strange brew, appetite satisfied with Rianna's meat stew; and seeing his father with a glow upon his face.

He stayed for seven days, helping Hurthig at the forge, Rianna with the running of the smallholding, and with her cooking. Several visitors came and went, all entertained, none particularly entertaining.

But Jack was getting restless. Something Haunter had heard whispered as they had followed the Iaelven through the under-passages of the wood kept coming back to him: that the Iaelven could traverse all boundaries.

Each evening he went up onto the slope between the villa and the wooded hill and wondered if they would appear. He called out at times. Only once did he hear anything from that mysterious, invisible entrance below the ridge, and it was not the whistle-speak of the Amurngoth but the angry and frustrated shouting of the boy, the human boy.

And only once did he see anything. The silvery glow of the young-old woman who was the eternal prisoner of the Amurngoth.

At the end of seven days Jack realised that he was now ready to go; it was not a feeling he perceived in himself, but only by looking at the signs of anxiety and sadness in his father's gaze. Steven Huxley could tell what was in the wind, and his heart was breaking again.

'Why don't you stay? Yssobel will come home when she's

achieved what she needs. She has no reason to stay in that part of Lavondyss once she has found Gwin.'

Jack thought about that. 'If she finds Gwin, she will probably find Christian. From what you've told me, that might not be for the best.'

Steven sighed, looked away. He couldn't disagree. In the garden of Oak Lodge, where he had met Guiwenneth for the first time, his brother had emerged from the wildwood with fierce and mindless men, brutalising him before taking Guiwenneth; there was a part of Christian that was deeply twisted. His obsession for Guiwenneth, when the brothers had been young men, had been overpowering. Charming, unpredictable, besieged by thoughts of her, and capable of murder: yes, the encounter would be dangerous.

But Yssobel had been convinced that her uncle was a gentle man, and that he was calling to her more out of need than anything to do with desire. Yes, this might have been the way she rationalised her own obsession with Avilion, her passion to see the very heart of the wood. But whatever had happened to her, just like Jack she had been unable to suppress vision and a dream with common sense.

For several nights more Jack walked across the field and called for the Iaelven. Only the occasional screaming of the boy from Shadoxhurst could be heard. It was not the sound of punishment but of defiance.

He was half asleep, watching the stars through his window. It was a warm night; the cooking fires were now just embers, though the drifting smell of woodsmoke was soft and pleasant.

Jack became half aware of the glow of silver, as if the Moon had just surfaced into the night sky. And then his name was whispered. He lay quite still.

A hand touched his shoulder and he reacted with a startled cry, rolling off the padded bench and staring at the apparition that watched him. 'You! You frightened me.'

Silver stood there, looking down at him. She put a finger to her lips, then smiled. The room was in strange light, but he had met this many times on his way back from Oak Lodge: sometimes golden, sometimes silver, it was light that emanated rather than shone.

'They wish to speak to you,' the woman said.

'The Amurngoth?'

'They wish you to come to them. Will you follow?'

'I've been calling to them for days,' Jack said, with a frown. 'Is it because of my calling?'

'It is because of the boy. And your calling. Will you follow? You will be safe, I promise you.'

Ethereal but very tangible, she walked from the room. As Jack dressed quickly he saw her pass through the gate in the rear wall and walk up the hill. He followed at a run, but she moved fast, and she had long disappeared from sight by the time he arrived, breathless, at the ridge.

Then Haunter whispered, *We have company. Stay very still.*

The Iaelven, two of them, had walked out of the darkness behind him. They towered over him, their breathing wheezy, their eyes a glitter of unwelcome in those ragged-hair faces. But they were not armed. Without any sound, none of the whistle-speak, they turned and walked towards the tree line. Jack followed, aware that this pair stank in a way he had never experienced before. Haunter said, *That's anger and fear. But why?*

Silver suddenly greeted him. He had moved back into the Amurngoth hill without even noticing the transition.

He was in a wide fern-lined chamber. Four Amurngoth crouched there, watching him. The boy was sitting between them and he frowned when he saw Jack. Silver was seated on a low wooden stool to the side. Jack was invited to crouch. He did so, but kept his gaze on the boy's.

There was whistling and whispering, a mouth flutter. Silver said, 'The boy will not tell them his name. He is very obstinate.'

Jack tried to remain expressionless, but he narrowed his eyes and gave an almost imperceptible nod to the lad: *Keep it that way.*

And the Hawkings' boy, as Jack knew him, with the merest twitch of his mouth, the merest hint of a smile of recognition, signalled that he understood.

The Iaelven were agitated. The conversation was heated. 'What are they saying?' Jack finally asked.

The silver woman thought for a moment. Then, with a deep breath, she said, 'They do not wish to keep this boy. He is too difficult. They took him to trade him, but they cannot trade him. He is violent and aggressive; he does not cooperate. His anger screams through the minds of the Iaelven, causing pain. He is a mistake.'

Jack glanced back at the Hawkings' boy, remembering his assertion: 'Won't tell you my name!' He smiled as he remembered the defiance when they had first met.

'Do you understand what's being said?' he asked. The boy shook his head.

'She speaks really strange. You've got a funny accent, but I can get most of it.'

Jack glanced at Silver as if speaking to her as he warned the boy, 'Keep your name to yourself.'

The lad laughed. 'Won't tell! Never will.'

Jack looked around at the dark, straggling creatures, listening to their subdued whistling. 'What is it they want?' he asked softly.

Silver replied, 'They want you to take him. They want you to accept him. Return him home. They cannot tolerate him.'

Torn between concern for the child and his own selfishness, Jack was silent and confused. There was opportunity here, but at what price? Then Haunter spoke: *Refuse the request*.

To the woman. Jack said, 'No. I can't do it. Where would I take him? How? I have a journey to make. The boy is to live in the villa? With my frail father? That's not possible.'

Silver was speaking Iaelven, translating as Jack spoke, and his words were not well received. Jack persisted: 'If they are unhappy with the boy, then kill him. Dispose of him. Or let them take him back themselves.'

Silver said, 'They can't kill him. That is not in their nature. Human adults, yes. But not a child. They wish to dispose of him to you, to place him with you. Then they will take back the Change they left behind.'

Jack stared at the floor of the cave, wondering what to say to that, if anything at all. He had no idea how the Iaelven would react if they knew their hideous Change was in a shallow grave.

'Leave him with me? No. At least . . . not yet.'

The Iaelven asked through Silver what he meant by that, and Jack said, with Haunter's prompting, 'I will take him home if the Amurngoth will take me to Avilion. I need to go there, but I don't know how to get there. I need to pass by Peredur's Stone, at the bottom of the valley. Ask them if they can help me.'

There was a long exchange. The boy stared at Jack, calm now, but suddenly slightly frightened. The anger and resistance in him was subdued as he struggled, from the look on his face, to understand what was happening. The first answer, conveyed by the woman, was that they knew about the stone, but that the stone was a crossing place. A myriad of paths led away from the monolith.

'But can they get me to Avilion?'

Yes. But they would have to know the direction.

'If I can find the direction, will they get me there in exchange for me keeping the boy and taking him home?'

Silver listened to the chatter and birdsong for a long while. When it fell silent, she looked at Jack; she seemed sad, but was smiling. 'They say yes.'

From the gloom of the cavern behind the Amurngoth, an Iaelven appeared, carrying a wide wooden bowl. This was placed in the middle of the circle. The bowl contained a thick grey mass, studded with the reds and purples of small fruit. The odour was unmistakably that of fungus.

Silver said, 'This is a rare privilege. They are inviting you to share their food. They must be very desperate for your help.'

Jack looked at her. 'What is it?'

'Their staple meal. They have very little variety.'

'It looks disgusting. Don't tell them I said so.'

'It is very nourishing.'

And probably poisonous, Jack thought. Then Haunter nudged him. *Would they want to poison us when we've offered to help them? That doesn't make sense.*

They may not intentionally want to poison us, Jack said to his green side. But what is tolerable to the Iaelven might cause madness in a human.

Let go, and let me eat. If I detect poison I shall spit it out discreetly.

Silver had already reached into the bowl and moulded a small ball of the mash, eating it slowly. Jack did the same, and then

171

the group who had greeted him all spooned handfuls of the slimy cake.

To his astonishment, the food was very palatable. Pungent, unusual, with the sweetness and bitterness of the different fruits contrasting with the earthy taste of the mould. Haunter was reassuring. *They have picked carefully. You can expect a wild dream, but no damage. You've eaten enough. Indicate pleasure and thanks.*

Jack did as his alter ego suggested.

To Silver, he addressed a quiet question. 'Is there anything I can do for you?'

She touched a delicate finger to her lip, brushing a small morsel of food away. 'I told you, I have nowhere to go. I am now a part of the underworld. I serve a simple purpose: to communicate between the Amurngoth and other forms, including human. There is nothing you can do for me, Jack. But the boy? He can be taken home.'

In fact, Jack had been having very difficult second thoughts about the Hawkings' boy. To play with the lad's life was wrong; to use him as a bargaining counter was deeply wrong. The boy would be perfectly safe in the villa. Steven and Rianna could take care of him; he would be well fed – indeed, he would be nurtured. And he might even find a trade, under the expert eye and hand of Hurthig, at least until the young Saxon decided it was time to move on, to find his true destiny, the founding of a new kingdom.

The lad belonged with a family, living within human company.

The meal was finished. The Iaelven rose to their willowy heights and disappeared into the cavern. The boy whispered, 'Don't leave me.'

Leaning forward, thinking hard, Jack said, 'I want you to stay with my father. You'll be well cared for. I have a journey to make, and I have no idea how hard it will be, no more than I know where I'm going! Will you stay with my father? You'll be warm and well fed.'

There was a long silence. The boy's face twisted between confusion and anger, sadness and determination.

Finally he said, in a voice that was almost a growl of despair, 'No! I'm staying with you. I want to stay with you.'

Surprised at the ferocious certainty shown by Won't Tell, Jack urged him to reconsider. 'A warm villa, good food; and I *will* be back. You'd be better off here.'

Again, an angry 'No!' There was panic in the boy's eyes.

'The reason?'

'I trust you,' Won't Tell said. 'You came out of the wood once, you can come out again. If I stay here, and you die, where do I go? No, I'll take my chance with you. And make life very, very difficult for these monsters.'

'Are you frightened of them?'

'I was. But not now.' He frowned, looked down. 'This is just a dream. A horrible dream. But I'm not afraid, not really. Just a little. I want to stay with you!'

'Then stay you will. But for the moment, you stay here.'

Jack left the hill. Despite Haunter's reassurance, he was feeling distinctly strange. The villa glowed with torchlight. His feet embraced the hard earth, but he was moving with speed. He was running, and breathless. He flung himself against the perimeter wall, turned and sunk down into a sitting position.

He began to extend. He felt engaged with something deeper, something below him, a network. Haunter whispered, 'I may have misjudged.'

'I think you did. I feel very strange.'

'It isn't poison. I can detect poison. It's no more than an influence. Jack is a little more Haunter than he's used to being. Follow where it takes you. I'll follow too.'

Where it took Jack at that moment was over onto his side, retching violently. When the spasm of sickness passed, he breathed deeply.

His limbs were drawn towards *imarn uklyss*. He felt himself to be a spread of roots, surging in their growth towards the bottom of the valley. There they embraced the tall stone he had never seen, only heard about, witnessed only in the furiously sketched drawings of his sister. Peredur's monument.

This is madness. This is poison. Does it mean anything?

He was still sitting by the wall as dawn began to strike the sky with gentle light.

'No more than you already knew,' Haunter said. 'Yssobel passed beyond the stone. How she did it isn't clear, but we agree: that way is not open to you. The Amurngoth will take us. And a little of the grey cake they've fed you might occasionally show us the way.'

'Show us the way? To Yssobel?'

'We are connected. We should do everything we can to maintain that link between us.'

Slowly Jack's senses revived; his focus became clear again. He felt hollow and hungry, vaguely alert yet weary in his body.

A while later, in the villa, his father found him. 'Good God, you look dead. You're yellow, Jack. Good God, good God. You've done something to your liver.'

Steven was suddenly anxious, but Jack waved him quiet. 'Mushrooms. The wrong kind. I promise you, I'm a survivor.'

'But you're yellow!'

'I'm also strong. It will pass.'

'Nonsense.'

Rianna was suddenly beside him, tipping his head back and making him sip a thin foul-tasting liquid, warm to the tongue. Quite soon his body had recovered. He felt cold, but clear-headed. The sharpness of his senses had come back, not all at once but in stages. Only the Haunter side of him had escaped the chemical effect. Haunter was laughing, but there was certainly a lesson to be learned if Jack was to travel with the Iaelven. 'I'll be more careful,' Haunter promised.

During the brief time of disorientation, Jack had revisited Oak Lodge in full sensory detail. Walking with Steven round and round the villa, he described again the strangeness of the place.

'It was covered by woodland. There is no question of that. But in the time I was there, the woodland pulled back, exposing the front walls, then the whole house. I didn't see it happen, though I felt it. A very unreal experience.'

Steven listened, intrigued and agreeing. 'When I returned there, after the war, something similar happened. It was after

Chris had disappeared, though he would shortly come back with his brutal troop of mercenaries and take Guiwenneth.

'But in the time I was there alone, a whole orchard grew overnight, taking over the garden. It was amazing to watch. Some trees even grew into the house. Did you see signs of tree damage inside?'

Jack thought back to what exactly he had seen as he'd explored the Lodge, but answered that he hadn't. He was very quiet, very dreamy.

'What is it?' Steven asked after a moment. 'What are you thinking? About the Lodge.'

'I was wondering if it was *not* everything it seemed. It was ramshackle, yes, and damp, but could have been abandoned only a season or two ago, not thirty years in outside time.' Jack turned to look at his father. 'I think your old home lies in a sort of "tidal" zone. Not that I've ever seen the waves on a beach. But there was that feeling of the house being first swamped, then exposed – a slow, steady movement.'

'Not that slow when it's exposed, from what you say. But what *are* you saying? Oak Lodge . . . a mythago?' It was clear to Jack that Steven had never considered this possibility.

But then, Jack was not sure of his own reasoning; all this was coming from his encounter with an Iaelven food gift.

'It just did not seem to belong there. Right there, at the edge of the strangest forest. Why would it have been built? Why does Ryhope hide it, then release it?'

After a moment, Steven sighed, turning back to the villa. 'I wonder if that's right? If that *is* right, then it must have changed its shape over many thousands of years.' He took a breath, then looked hard at Jack. 'When my father moved in, when he took the Lodge, it was to write a book analysing the ideas of Charles Darwin on evolution. I taught you about him, if you remember: as much as I could, since I didn't really grasp the principles myself.' He smiled, recollecting his own dreadful ignorance as he had tried to give a reasoned and careful heartwood's education to his offspring. 'He very quickly dropped that task and started to explore Ryhope. That was when it all went wrong, for him and for us. He was a changed man. His language was all "zones" and "vortex" and "ley pathways and matrices", all short cuts through the forest, defences against intruders, and manipulators of the weeks and months and years. He aged very rapidly when he should have aged very slowly. I wonder if you're right? Perhaps Oak Lodge was Ryhope's way of communicating with the world beyond its edge. A passage in, a passage out; a connection between the first forest and the ever-evolving world.'

Jack was lost now. But it occurred to him that if his father had grown up inside a house that was the evolved version of such a gate, then perhaps it had been the Lodge itself that had called back George Huxley.

But these were wild thoughts, perhaps made wilder by the chemical brew that he had ingested, courtesy of the Iaelven.

They stood in silence for a long time, cool in the breeze, each of them thinking of a different world, each sensing the passing of this one. Finally, with a sigh and clapping his hands together, abandoning nostalgia, Steven said loudly, 'But I can assure you, I'm all human, and so was George. It's only my children who can step in and out of the shadow of the forest. How are you feeling now?'

'Very well.' Jack hesitated. 'Steven?'

'I like you calling me Steven. Better than Dad.'

The young man smiled acknowledgement. 'Steven: when this is over, when I find Yssi – and I will find her, I promise – when it's done, would you like to go home? Back to the edge?'

'Let's go in, Jack. I'm getting cold. Would I like to go back? With Gwin gone . . . you know what? Yes. Yes, I think I would. But that is for later.' He glanced solemnly at his son. 'For the moment, I'm guessing it's goodbye again.'

Jack kissed his father on the cheek, taking the older man by surprise. 'You don't belong here, Steven. Nor do I. I can't speak for Yssobel, but I inscribed a small broken silver clasp for her. Rune writing, of course.'

'What did it say?'

'*What we remember is all the home we need.*'

His father frowned. 'Not exactly an encouragement to return, then. Where did that sentiment come from?'

'Ealdwulf. He was doomed to wander, though his son is likely to find his own land and establish his own kingdom. He'll be gone soon, I'm sure of it. He has that faraway look.'

Steven had noticed and said so. 'It's true; this place is beginning to decay. Its life-force is fading. We built it up from ruins, but the ruins were from memory, shaped by need. Now the villa is being reclaimed, brick by brick. This is part of the land the Amurngoth claim as theirs, and I suppose they will have it back.'

Jack had noticed earlier how much the villa was in disrepair, despite the young Saxon's efforts, as if it had been storm-battered on too many occasions. The Amurngoth had been tolerant. They had hardly ever used the track that led from the hill through the villa's grounds, though perhaps they had used it at night. The Huxleys had avoided the hill, and the two communities had lived in respectful coexistence for many years. But now, as Steven was aware, everything that could sustain this particular landscape within Ryhope Wood was fading, weakening.

It made Jack's task more urgent. Haunter was a constant whispered voice of warning: that Yssobel was walking into danger. The green and the green were in distant, frail, but vital communication.

PART·THREE

Yssobel in Avilion

Armour of the King

As she reached the head of the valley, Yssobel turned for a last sad look at the villa. In the dawn light, it seemed so peaceful. She tried not to imagine the sorrow that would soon transform that silence into anguish.

She noticed that she had left no tracks, nor had the packhorse. Patting Rona's narrow neck she gave a silent thanks to Rianna. The High Woman's gift was endowed with a certain charm: it was as if Rianna had known that Yssobel needed not to be followed.

With a wave of her hand she turned again and rode into *imarn uklyss*.

After several days, she lost the packhorse to a band of Muurngoth but managed to save some of the supplies before galloping away from their stinging arrows. The journey was hazardous. She rode through the shallows of the river wherever possible, and camped where she could see in a wide arc.

And at last she came to the monolith.

It was taller than she had expected, taller than she'd painted it, but she recognised the rune snakes, each coiled serpent containing one of the four tales of Peredur. The monument seemed to whisper to her, to greet her. As she walked towards it in the night, it seemed to lean slightly, as if to embrace her. The illusion of welcome.

'I've found you,' Yssobel said quietly. 'And when the sun rises I know you'll show me the path to Avilion.'

Before she slept she ran her fingers over each of the rune snakes, puzzled to read *Peredur and the Song of the Islands of the Lost*. She didn't recognise it, though the song was familiar, a sad piece which her mother had often sung when she had thought she was alone and not being overheard. *Peredur and the Nine Eagles* was familiar. And *Peredur and the Shield of Diadora*, Peredur's prized shield, able to reflect what had been and what might be to come.

The fourth rune snake puzzled her again: *Peredur and Yssobel*.

'That can't be right,' she whispered to the stone. 'I don't belong to your time. This isn't the rune of my dreams. I dreamed of you at The Crossing Place of Ghosts.'

But she was too tired to think about it now, and after tending to Rona she curled up in the moon-shadow of the monolith and entered her own world for a few hours.

In the morning Yssobel stood for some while in the shadow of her grandfather's memorial, staring at the forbidding darkness of the forest to which the shadow pointed. Then she clicked her fingers and Rona came up to her. She stroked the horse's cheeks for a while, then, with a last glance at the monolith, she heaved herself into the saddle and galloped towards the wildwood.

As if she were a ghost, she passed into the gloom; as if she were a ghost, she rode through the frontier, red side surging with determination, green side drawing on the sap and succulence of the wood.

And she emerged onto a track, a holloway, that was deserted, unused, yet not overgrown. She could see the traces of stone, laid carefully in that road. Old, then, shaped for a purpose. Where would it lead her?

Yssobel rode for most of the day and was about to rest when she caught the scent of a lake. The wind had freshened. The smell of lake water was clear and sharp and clean.

The wind shifted and she stopped suddenly. In the distance, she could hear the scream and cry of battle.

The trail began to curve as Yssobel spurred Rona on. The horse was straining slightly. She could smell the lake as well. Rona was thirsty, no doubt. The ride had been long, but Yssobel hauled her back. The battle was very close now, and its sounds made Yssobel's stomach clench and her senses sharpen. The drumming and clash of shields, the ringstrike of iron, the wailing of men as limbs were slashed and life began to fade, the screeching triumph of killers, the noisy protesting of horses ridden through the fury; these signs of a vicious struggle waxed and waned on the air.

Yssobel's copper hair billowed out like a cloak behind her as the wind strengthened suddenly, bringing with it the sharp tang of blood. She took a moment to gather it and knot it to the side, using the silver ring-clasp that Jack had made for her, tying her hair as he had shown her. She briefly ran her fingers along the inscription he had made.

Avilion is what we make of it.

'Oh yes, brother. Oh yes indeed.'

She was about to kick forward again when a horse burst through the undergrowth above the bank and stumbled its way down and across the track. A man lay slumped on its back, arms dangling, features obscured by a small helmet that covered half his face, which now was red from a strike. As the horse leapt up the opposite bank, so he fell heavily to the ground, rolling back to the road. For a moment gleaming eyes watched Yssobel, a hand moved towards her. Then brightness became blur.

She rode on. The battle was loud now, and she dismounted, crawled stealthily up the bank and through the sparse woodland until she could see the hill, and the swarm of men on that hill. The sky filled with streaming pennants and clouds of fine yellow hair, blowing across the site of battle, glittering elementals engaged in the fray.

She saw the man at the centre of the action. His face-helm was black, his banner green. He was bloodied and raging. He rode with others as a troop, but was suddenly engaged in single combat with a bronze-armoured man whose white hair streamed from below a demon's helmet. This fight was contained within the ring of horsemen who rode at the centre, nose to tail, a mix of armies containing and respecting the duel.

There were no arrows in the air, just the forward surge and backward press of ranks of warriors, struggling at spear- and sword-point. Men fled from the wide, low hill, others seemed to appear from nowhere, shields sparkling, bone, bronze and iron shining, sometimes reddening.

Why did she recognise this fierce encounter?

In her red heart she knew why – the story she had been told often by her father. It took the green side to hear the sorrowing voices crying: 'Arthur – take care! Withdraw. He is too strong for you.'

'Stay with me!' came Arthur's reply, the cry of all war-chiefs who are certain that the moment of triumph or passing has come close and must be encountered.

And even as Yssobel recognised Arthur, so he plunged his blade into his opponent, who reeled for a moment, then struck back with his javelin.

The narrow spear found a home in Arthur's breast. He was pushed back. A sword strike followed, cutting through the face-helm.

As Yssobel watched, so he was struck again by the javelin, pushed back on his horse, falling from the saddle.

The protecting circle broke.

Ravens rushed towards him and the struggle over his body became fierce. The tone of the conflict had changed. It became static, pressing, urgent.

Yssobel pulled back. She had seen enough. But as she sat, huddled, at the top of the bank, she began to realise just what it was that she had seen. She looked towards the lake, remembering the stories she had been told by her father, remembering the dreams she had inherited from her mother. Quickly, she returned to the fallen rider and stripped the corpse of its armour and face-helm.

Yes, she would stay here tonight, in hiding, and watch events unfurl.

With a thunder of hooves, a dozen or so men rode away from the battlefield. Dusk was close. Yssobel watched them as they struggled down the bank, onto the old track, a rider on each side of a man slumped in his saddle, holding him in place. They raced off towards the lake and Yssobel, armoured and masked in the dead man's war-cloth, followed at a distance.

The track was rich with blood, the air heavy with its sour smell.

The horsemen thundered out of sight, two of them suddenly

turning back, unmasked, hair flowing freely, spears held low and at the ready. They were youthful men, shields on their backs, eyes bright as they came rapidly at Yssobel, who reined in and galloped up the bank and among the trees. They pursued her for a while, shouting in gruff voices, but the shadows contained her and when she stopped and looked out into the light she could see them sitting there, silhouettes, searching the gloom but failing to locate her.

They turned and disappeared and after a long while she cautiously urged Rona back to the holloway and at a gentle trot moved again in pursuit.

The lake was suddenly there. There was no sign of the escaping party, but Yssobel could hear the whinny of horses and the clatter of shields being discarded. A wooded knoll rose to her right. She dismounted and led Rona again into the gloom of the trees, tethered the horse and crept to where she could see down to the wide shore and the vast expanse of gleaming, reed-fringed water.

Her green side eavesdropped as she watched events unfurl.

Gwei eased the helm from Arthur's wounded face. The blow had cut through the cheek metal to the cheek itself, splitting the bone. Arthur's eyes were narrowed with pain, his wild red hair clotted. Emereth cradled him, kneeling behind him, glancing frequently at Gwei as his companion unlaced the chest armour. He put a finger in the first of the wounds there, then leaned down to kiss the cut, holding the flesh closed with his fingers as his tears fell upon the drying blood.

'It's done,' Arthur whispered. 'This is the dream. For me, it's over.'

'The wound is horrible,' Gwei said. 'Morthdred found the killing mark all right. You're done for.'

'I knew it when the point went in. But we held for a long time, didn't we, Gwei? We held strong.'

'We broke,' said Emereth.

'A battle too far,' murmured one of the others, who were all crouched in a semi-circle around the dying war chief.

'Morthdred was always going to break us,' said another.

'No!' Arthur shouted, then gasped with the agony of the

185

wounds in his chest. 'No . . . he was never going to break us. Not all of us. Don't you understand? For me, it's finished. For you, far from finished.'

'Then why are we sitting by this lake,' whispered Bydavere angrily, 'refugees from a blood- and shit-stained hill?'

Red rage grew fierce in the dying man's features. He had eyes for Gwei, and a severe look for his closest shield man, Bydavere.

'Who are these whimpering men?' he said to the sky. 'I don't recognise them. How many whimpering men? How many survived the iron task? How many fell? Answer me, Gwei.'

'Fallen?' said Gwei. 'Many! Scattered? Many! Of your shield ring, twelve are fallen. Twelve survive. We came out of it well.' He spoke with enthusiasm, recognising, perhaps, that his dying friend needed to be surrounded by men who were still strong.

'Twelve dead,' Arthur sighed. 'Twelve ahead of me, then. Into Avilion.'

'You'll meet them there,' Bydavere said.

'However they got there,' Emerith added.

'And all of us, in time,' Gwei whispered, 'wherever it is you're going.'

A new strength came into Arthur. Through pain-hardened eyes he looked at Bydavere. 'Morthdred has broken me, but only me. Do you understand what I'm saying? I do not wish to die in the presence of whimpering men. The sword at my side has his blood on it. There is a mark on his body, a cut as deep as his bone, that is Arthur-marked. The sword will find that place again. Do you understand me?'

'Yes,' Bydavere replied.

'Take it, then, and don't rest until the sword mark in Morth-dred is opened, and opened to the crows.'

Bydavere reached over and unbuckled Arthur's sword belt. He drew the blade; it was dulled with Morthdred's blood.

'Take it to the lake and wash it,' Arthur said. 'The blood is failure. It will find the place of failure, and fail again. The cleaned iron will find the traitor and pierce him true to its purpose.'

Bydavere rose and walked along the lake's edge, then waded through the reeds to clean water. He returned, the blade sheathed, and knelt among his companions.

'What's going to happen next?' asked Gwei, looking around him. Geese flew out across the lake. Evening was approaching fast and the wind was beginning to blow.

'Of that, I'm not sure,' Arthur said with a pained laugh. 'Except that I'll be dead before they come for me.'

'And coming for you? That'll be what?' asked Bydavere, staring back across the lake.

'A boat, a barge. The dream I had as a child wasn't clear. I believe there will be women in the barge, women of rare beauty and great kindness.'

The shield men laughed. One said, 'May I share your dreams? I'll pay.'

'I've always loved my dreams,' Arthur said when the laughter had subsided. 'There is promise in them, and pleasure.'

'So we wait with you . . .' Bydavere murmured.

'Yes.'

'For a boat or barge, you say.'

'Yes. You wait and watch.'

'To take you where? What *is* this Avilion?'

'The land of healing, Bydavere. I'll meet you there one day.'

Arthur caught Gwei's frown. 'What is it, Gwei? Old friend.'

Gwei took a deep breath. 'It isn't over. Morthdred's men are scattering. You fell, but the battle didn't end. Can't you hear the crows? Half of them are still hungry. I can't wait to get after Morthdred. Stay alive long enough for me to bring you his head.'

'What a keen man you are, old friend. I always admired that in you. Is the blade cleaned?'

'Bright as if it were newly forged.'

'Show me . . .'

From the look in Gwei's eyes it was clear that orders had been disobeyed. Gwei pulled the blade from its scabbard. Morthdred's blood remained, dark and crisp on the metal.

Gwei said: 'I want to return his own moment of failure to the failing life when I sever that neck of his. Why wipe away the moment of his wound? Rust on iron! Let the bastard suffer!'

Arthur struggled to sit up against his own killing pierce. Everything about him now was frail. 'Gwei: a clean blade, a clean strike. It's the certainty I want, the certainty of his silence in this life. Clean the blade in the lake. Let the blade shine as it strikes the traitor who brought me to my own end.'

Gwei withdrew, back to the reeds, back to the dusk-dark water.

'Light a fire,' Arthur said. 'Do we have supplies? Food? Enough for a dying feast?'

'Enough for a dying drink,' said Ethryn, the youngest of the surviving shield men. 'Food enough for twelve scavengers.'

'Scavenge after I'm gone. Just sing and laugh and wait until the barge comes for me.'

'Barge or boat,' Emereth reminded him.

'Whatever comes, make sure I'm in my war cloth, and that my face is helmeted, and my hair is tied tightly. Whatever happens, don't resist it. My friends, your other friends are finding their own way to Avilion. My dream told me the nature of my own transit.'

Emereth said, 'We won't interfere. We'll drink your health at the funeral games, and the health of Avilion as it welcomes Arthur.'

'Good man.'

Gwei returned from the lake, his face grim. Arthur said, 'Have you cleaned the blade?'

'No.'

'No? Why not?'

Gwei looked around at the others, then at Arthur. 'Because you're wrong. If I clean the blade, then the blade is new. We want the blade old; stained; hungry for vengeance. A new blade might seek new blood. It's old blood you want, and the blood trail. After the strike in the belly of your cousin, the bastard Morthdred, it will be keener for the rust stain. Keener on the scent. The final act, which I shall deliver with pleasure, my friend, will be the harsher and the more final for it. Do you understand what I'm saying?'

Arthur nodded. 'You're right. I see your point. Don't wash the blade.'

'It makes sense,' Gwei said.

'I agree,' Arthur replied. 'Sometimes what seems right isn't truly right. If we don't listen, we don't understand fully. Listening makes things right. I can trust you to do the final work for me. Like an old man trusting his son, even though we are the same age. And you will keep things right for me.'

'Yes,' said Gwei. 'I will.'

And Emereth added, looking round at the rest of the men. 'Shall we begin the funeral games? Is it too soon?'

Yssobel was watching from the tree line, the red side in her beating hard, the green side savouring this edge of worlds, the lake shore, the distance to another world. She had imagined it would be misty. In fact it was clear and vast, more like an ocean than a lake, stretching away to the horizon, a gleam of dusk grey and blue, with the first glimmer of starlight on its breeze-ruffled surface.

As dusk made shadows of all things that moved, so a shadow moved towards her, one of the companions, a burly, half-armoured man. He walked up to Yssobel's hiding place, and she drew back into the embrace of the coiled tree roots where she had been lurking, watching.

The shadow loomed and the man urinated, sighing with relief. For a moment as he tucked himself away he peered into the bosk, as if sensing a presence. It was Bydavere.

Yssobel practised the death breath, and held it for a long time.

With a curious sound, a grunt of dismissal, the man turned away and went back to where the war chief now lay on a bier of branches, his face and body armoured. Dressed again in the war cloth, face hidden, arms folded.

Two of Arthur's men had slipped back to the battlefield, to the looted baggage train, to the place of the dead and dying. They had joined among the scavengers. They had weapons, and the war chief's standard, which had been left, broken, halfway down the hill. They stripped the long banner from the shaft of ash and folded it between the silent man's hands.

They had also brought flagons of wine.

As their horses grazed the shoreline, so Arthur's entourage drank and became drunk. Night fell, and the men fell, curled by the lake, curled in their cloaks; men at the end of days.

Yssobel slipped out of cover. She shed the armour of Morth-dred's warrior and crept as quietly as possible to where Arthur lay on the bed of branches, enclosed and almost completely hidden behind his mask and cloak. Gwei stirred slightly, mumbled in his sleep, sat up and stared at the lake – a moment of alarm for Yssobel – then flopped back. He seemed to be crying in his dreams. So much had been lost that day.

For a moment Yssobel considered what she was doing. The lake was still. Stars illuminated its silent waters. The moon was hidden. Avilion, the place of her dreams, lay on the far side of this stretch of water, and she knew that a barge would be coming for the man who lay dead before her.

Gently, quietly, she eased Arthur from the bier. Step by step she pulled him from the wood frame. Breath by gentle breath she dragged him to the trees.

No one stirred.

When she was in cover, she dragged more fiercely, pulled the body deep into the copse.

By green light she surveyed the calm and handsome features of the man. His face was light with stubble, his hair tied elaborately. She drew out the small, open silver ring that Jack had fashioned for her, and copied the hair knot of the dying king, tying her own long locks into place.

Then she leaned down and kissed Arthur full on the mouth. His lips were cold, yet not death-cold. He didn't stir. She kissed him again, held the embrace, reached to hold his face in her hands. Bloodied, yes, but beautiful. A man of strength and certainty, a face of love and humour. She pushed back the long, lank hair from his brow, kissed him between the eyes, then let her face rest against his for a while; breathing.

'You don't need the passage,' Yssobel whispered. 'You belong here. But I know you won't forgive me for stealing your journey.'

Then she stripped him naked, every scrap of clothing, running her hands down his body, touching every part of him.

And then she stripped herself. The night was cool. She lay on Arthur's body for a while, embracing him with her limbs, enclosing him, thinking of this most audacious of acts she planned, letting the warmth of her body seep into the hardening frost of his own flesh. Her skin bristled with the breeze. She lay on him and held his face again, and kissed him again, wondering if the eyes would open and his hands reach round for her.

She almost hoped for it.

He lay quiet. Cool but not cold, though he was certainly on the death road.

'I'm stealing the armour of a king,' she whispered to him. 'I've dreamed of this moment. I never knew why I would steal the armour, just that I would have to do it. I do have a reason.'

Arthur lay silent. Yssobel sang quietly:

> *And I knew I had to hold on to what I had been given*
> *And that my world was changing. And that I had to hold.*
> *And everything that I had once been given was gone*
> *Yet everything I had been newly given was with me.*
> *Stay with me. For a mother's sake.*
> *I will embrace your armour.*
> *Hold on. Let me steal this little time inside your skin.*
> *I can't afford to break.*

'I will go to Avilion instead of you. But I will return and make good this theft. I promise.'

He lay silent.

There was no more time. His shield men lay sprawled and unconscious inside their cloaks, close to the lake. Ale-slumber was deep, but surfacing from that sleep was fast, as she'd often seen happen with Ealdwulf and his son.

She dressed Arthur as best she could in her own clothing. Rona was nearby, and Yssobel took the animal's blanket and covered the dying king with it. Then she released Rona with a kiss and a word, leading her quietly to the track and sending her back to where worlds changed, hoping that the horse would struggle into *imarn uklyss* and gallop home, home to the villa.

Arthur's clothing, his boots and armour were on the large side for Yssobel but not so much that she felt uncomfortable. She walked to the lake, lay down on the bier, crossed her hands and though the helm-mask watched the stars as they shifted in and out of clouds.

Her breathing slowed. At dawn, Gwei rose sleepily and stood by the lake, staring across the reeds, to where the mist was lifting.

And then he called out, 'The boat is coming. This is the time.'

Yssobel could hear the gentle stroke of oars. Aware that the shield men were lined up, watching the water and paying no attention to her, she lifted her head slightly. The reeds parted and a snub-bowed barge nosed into the shallows. It was wide and ugly, with a crude sail drooping around a roughly hewn mast. Two tall men stood at the stern, each with a long pole which they pushed easily into the mud. Two women in brilliant red and green garb, their faces veiled in white, held short oars. The barge was trimmed with purple, and the long, lean shapes of three hares, dancing in a circle, had been carved into the prow itself.

The two women rose to their feet and beckoned to the shield men to bring the bier onto the vessel. Yssobel felt herself lifted, then raised onto shoulders. One of the men cried quietly, others whispered words that might have been goodbye, or good fortune, or good journey.

Eyes closed, breathing hardly at all, Yssobel waited for the bier to settle into the barge. She lay between the two women.

The men dug their poles into the mud and pushed away from the shore. The two women sat beside the bier, staring ahead of them, unmoving, watching the land until the barge turned and faced open water. When they were out on the lake again, they lifted their veils, took up their oars and began to stroke slowly and steadily. They sang softly. Yssobel watched the clouds through the face-helm, experiencing a strange peace.

After a while the poles were placed down and the men crouched and took the oars from the women. The barge shifted on the water as a breeze came up and the crude sail unfurled and stayed. The men stared impassively ahead, but Yssobel was suddenly aware that one of the women was watching her from the corner of her eye. She tried to breathe as shallowly as possible, keeping her eyes closed, sensing the woman rather than seeing her.

A hand rested on her chest. A voice whispered so quietly that it might have been the passing hiss of a breeze: 'Stay still. Don't arouse the boatmen. If you do, they'll turn the barge around. They are dedicated to their task, and you are not the task.'

That same woman lifted her white veil. A pale, drawn face

turned to look down at Yssobel, a face without decoration and almost without blood; ghostly, yet kind.

Again they sang, this time in harmony, but they sang in a language that was obscure even to Yssobel's green side, though she sensed that its theme was life being rescued from the hill of crows and taken to the island of the lost.

She repressed all tendency to engage with these women in case she should respond without control and make herself known to the wrong eyes.

Night came and the stars appeared. The sail billowed out and the lake became choppy. She couldn't hold her bladder any more and hoped that the men would not notice the sudden release, though she was so thirsty that her body was preserving water.

With the new dawn the sail flopped, and the men tied it to the mast and picked up the long poles, pushing down into the shallows, feeling for the lake bed.

Suddenly the barge was passing through the upper branches of drowned trees. The women pushed with their short oars and the vessel at last came to a slow halt on the lake's bank. The men jumped down and hauled the barge further onto the land. Each then took one end of the crude bier, lifted it and carried it ashore.

Something was said. Angry words spoken by one of the barge-men. From his gestures it was clear that he was questioning the lightness of the corpse; that he was suspicious.

The other man reached down suddenly, lifting the helm from Yssobel's face, and the act of audacity was exposed. A hand hauled at Yssobel, dragging her upright. It was one of the women. The men glowered, reaching for the knives at their waists, but the two women shed their robes of red and green, exposing leather armour of the same colours. They were a striking sight, one, clearly the younger of the two, with luxurious black hair, the other with long braids of silver.

There was an exchange of shouts and threats. The older of the men leaned towards Yssobel, his pale eyes furious. 'What have you done?' he asked in a voice that sounded like a wolf's growl. 'What have you done with the man we came to fetch?'

'I took his place. I had my reasons.'

'Get back in the barge,' said the other. 'Do it now.'

'She stays,' said the younger woman, stepping in front of Yssobel.

The man nodded slowly, looking between all three of the women. 'But we don't. We'll fetch the man who waits for us, and when he arrives here you'll pay for this with more than your life.'

The boatmen spat on the ground, then turned away and pushed the barge from the shore, leaping aboard and taking up the poles. For a long while Yssobel watched them go, aware that hands were on her arms.

When at last she looked round, she saw that she was being greeted by warm eyes and warm smiles. The younger woman said, 'I'm Uzana. My sister is Narine.'

'Where am I? Is this Avilion?'

'It's a part of it, but remote,' Uzana said. 'This is one island among many islands. We know them quite well. And a friend of yours is waiting for you. Though he doesn't know it.'

'How do you know?' Yssobel asked, confused.

'We read your dreams.'

'Welcome to the place you've made your own,' said Narine.

During Yssobel's long transit across the lake, her red side had abandoned her.

Her green side, existing in a different realm, did not recognise at first the place to which she had come. As the barge drifted away, angry abuse being shouted from it by the men on board, Uzana helped Yssobel remove Arthur's armour and fold it carefully, ready to be stowed on the packhorse which Narine had fetched out of cover, along with their own mounts. There was a fourth horse, saddled and bridled, with green colours tied to its mane and fetlocks. Narine tossed Yssobel the reins.

'We have a long ride. Do you need to wash? Take relief?'

'Both. And food and water. That lake was a long crossing, and I was supposed to be dead. I held for a long time, but couldn't hold for ever. I need to get clean and feel alive again.'

The two women laughed at something private while waiting for Yssobel. Then they passed her a flask and a good-sized piece of cold beef, which she chewed as they started off at a slow pace.

They broke to a canter as they approached a narrow defile in a dwarf-tree-covered hill. As they eased their way through the narrow, treacherous and winding gap, Yssobel asked, 'If this is not the Isle of Avilion, what is it?'

'Wait!' called Narine, riding at the front.

They emerged from the hill and were looking down at a shoreline – rocky coves and short sandy beaches. The cliffs behind were riddled with caves, and there were bright, white-marbled structures scattered here and there.

'Which island is it?' Yssobel persisted.

'The island of the lost,' Uzana said, and Yssobel was startled, but pleasantly so.

'But I know a song about this place! My mother's song. She always called it the Song of the Islands of the Lost.'

And my grandfather is associated with the place, she thought. *It is the first of his rune snakes.*

Without thinking, without noticing the alarm on her new companions' faces, she started to sing the song that Guiwenneth had been so fond of. Almost at once, Narine had clapped a hand to Yssobel's mouth, silencing her. Uzana reared as her horse reacted with alarm, then reached out to squeeze Yssobel's arm. She was shaking her head, but smiling.

'Don't sing it! Don't ever sing it! If you do, then, like your friend, you'll be lost.'

Who was this friend? Yssobel wondered. And then remembered Rianna's sad words:

'She was singing that lovely song. The sad one. The one that suddenly bursts into joy.'

'Come on!' Narine urged, but Yssobel held back.

'I don't understand. There is something I don't understand.'

The other women turned around to look at her. Patient, now. Time seemed to stop; there was silence in the air.

And Yssobel said, 'You came for the dead, didn't you? That's what I was taught. You came for Arthur after his death.'

They laughed.

195

'Death?' questioned Narine. 'We come for *all* deaths. Even the living ones. We're collectors. Especially from battlefields.'

'Some of the dead hold on,' Uzana added. 'They value what they've been given and will not give it up.'

And Yssobel asked, 'Then what are you?'

'Waylanders,' Narine replied.

'We show you the way to other lands.'

'Sometimes we're called "waylands".'

'Guides, leaders, valks, morgvalks, peckcrows, morrikans . . .' Uzana added.

'So many names.'

'So simple a task.'

They laughed again, but kept their gaze on Yssobel.

Yssobel thought for a moment. 'And the task?'

Narine said, 'To take you to where you *have* to go.'

'And to take you carefully. We *care* about the journey.'

'But you came for Arthur!'

And Uzana said softly: 'We'll come for him again, if needs be.'

Narine went on, 'As we crossed the lake, our world changed. A world shift. It happens to us. We suddenly knew, on the lake, that we were coming for you.'

'How?' Yssobel asked, confused but not disturbed by what they were saying.

'I told you,' said Uzana. 'We read your dreams.'

Yssobel said: 'I still don't understand. In my dream, in my father's story, he was taken to Avilion by three queens.'

'Well, weren't there? Three?'

'That man, that warlord we came to collect,' Narine said fiercely, 'He *was* his armour. As for how much more he was than that – who knows?'

'And you wear Arthur's armour now! Queen and king in one.'

'Virgin beauty, soft-skinned, encased by bloodied leather.'

Narine agreed, smiling and glancing at Yssobel. 'Iron-cut, yes, and deeply wounded, but strong enough to bear the blows.'

'For a while at least,' the other woman added. 'Strength contained, concealed in strength.'

'Life, vibrant, in the vale of death. Which is why you will be tested!'

'Welcome to the place you've made your own.'

'Indeed!' said Narine. 'Now, let's get on!'

Yssobel in Avilion

Odysseus dreams

In his dreaming, he had seen her: the flame-haired girl, riding towards him.

In his dreaming, he had loved her. There was passion in his dreaming.

A cool sea breeze accompanied him as each day he walked to where the beach began, to the soft sea touch, and stood there; sometimes spear in hand, sometimes shield upon his back. In anticipation.

Eyes closed; asleep yet not asleep.

Not singing, now. Not here.

He had sung the song of the Island of the Lost, and was lost until awakened fully. In the half-awakened part of him, below Lethe's comforting, concealing shroud, below her sleep-veil, he knew that this was no more than rehearsal time.

This was his life in practice. This was the dream of the dream to come.

The flame-haired girl would rouse him.

And sometimes he whispered her name:

Yssobel.

'There he is,' said Narine. 'There's your man.'

I recognised him at once. He was older, though not by much. He was standing at the edge of the strand, leaning on a spear, a shield cast in front of him, half in the water. He was staring out to sea; wistful yet mournful.

I dismounted, flung Uzana the reins. 'Are you safe?' she asked.

'Oh yes.'

'He looks aggressive. Are you sure he *is* a friend?'

'Very much my friend. But stay close. There's something not right here. But yes . . .'

I looked at my horse-straddling companions as they leaned down to rest after the hard ride. 'Yes, I feel safe.'

Dear Odysseus.

He looked so confused, but recognised me as I walked up the shore towards him. I was unarmed. He dropped the spear. He acknowledged me with a quiet smile, and then turned away.

'Follow me,' he whispered.

Built into the cliffs behind the sea was the entrance to a palace; it was identical to the marbled gateway that had led to his cave in Serpent Pass, though beyond the pillars there was an open gate, not the grim mouth of a hollow in the hill.

'Do you know who I am?' I asked as we walked.

'I do. I do. Though memory is faint for the moment.'

'We were lovers. In a different place. Don't tell my father. I lied to him.'

'I think we were,' he agreed. 'Though I think a greater task, a greater love is coming to me.'

'You're right. I won't tell you her name. Nor the perilous journey you'll make to find her, though I've read of it. I know of it.'

'Don't tell me.'

'I won't.'

He paused, turned back. 'You know more of me than I know of myself, then. Though I already have an idea, as you'll see.'

'I will never betray the trust that comes with knowing you so much. I need you for a while. Be my friend, please; just for the time I need you.'

He looked at me, not so much confused as curious. Then he bowed his head. 'I accept that. Now follow me. I will take you to a frightening place. Perhaps I need you too. Who knows? Who knows where fear of the future grows?'

*

Broad-shouldered, dark-kilted as he was, I couldn't help but touch his spine.

Odysseus turned again and took me in his arms. The embrace was strong.

'I wish I could remember more,' he murmured as he eased his arms away, but still holding me. 'I seem to have spent my life on this abandoned beach.'

'Your future has much in store. Abandonment will be a part of it. Don't be frightened. At the end, there is enlightened vision.'

'Tragedy? Love?'

I closed his lips with mine, a brief memory of the past, a past that I knew could never last.

He smiled. He looked so beautiful when he smiled, a glimmer of delight in his dark eyes. I'd taken him by surprise.

I said, 'What we had we had; what he have we have; what will come to us will come to us.'

He laughed. 'Bad poetry.'

'Never claimed to be a good poet; just, if you can cast your mind back . . . a good lover.'

'Gods, I wish I could cast that line. To fish for those moments, a feast of memory. I remember bleeding.'

'Blood in our passion; yes, blood was the flood of love.'

And then he was stone again, as if some life-force had abandoned him. Glazed and sorrowful, he seemed to look into the void. He turned his back. Walked along the corridor.

'Follow me. But stay with me.'

And I followed; and stayed.

Yssobel dreams

Now Yssobel began to see what her companions had hinted: that this was a place she knew well. She took the silver hair clasp that her brother Jack had made for her and read the words again:

Avilion is what we make of it.

Yes. This was a part of the place she had dreamed of, when her mother had sung the song, the Song of the Islands of the

Lost. She had not expected to find Odysseus, certainly; but it began to make sense to her. And it made sense that she'd felt that sudden need, almost unspoken; the need for his help.

She would speak about it when the moment was right. He was walking through his own future, and the palace was a place of unfelt memory. She was alive here, vibrant. She sensed that he felt lonely.

There was a wide room with a table in it, and wine on the table, and food; chairs enough for a dozen or more. The walls – eight of them – were bright with flowing, terrible images, and Odysseus sat and looked around, then took Yssobel in his gaze. 'Is this my life?'

Yssobel sat and picked up fruit and olives. She was very hungry, and was also thinking of Narine and Uzana, still on the shore. 'May my friends have some of this? Is there enough to spare?'

'Of course,' Odysseus replied with a little laugh and a teasing grin, picking up a black olive and tossing it to Yssobel. 'I don't even know how it gets here. Someone takes care of me. Someone here, hidden in the darker rooms.'

'I'll take it later.'

She looked at the living marble walls. Strange creatures moved there, monstrous. And women of great beauty, walking as if in dreams, looking back across their shoulders; enticing.

And there was war. A great walled city, men engaged in a struggle no less violent but more heavily populated than the battle where she had seen Arthur take his final fall.

Yssobel suddenly shocked to see a woman being hauled up the steps of the city by hard-faced, hard-armoured Greeks. They clearly had intentions for her. Her infant son was taken from her arms and cast to his death from the high wall, screaming as he fell, screaming as she screamed. She was then subjected to the imperfection of love. And Odysseus himself, a much, much older man, was among the abusing men.

This was a heart-stopping scene. It took the anticipated delight of the fruit out of Yssobel's mouth. She stared at her young friend, already knowing, yet suddenly realising, what he would become.

A dark moment.

'So this is to become my life,' Odysseus said, as if hearing the unspoken thought, looking around at the reflecting room, before standing to face the wall that was showing the death of the child.

'Yes. I think it is. I'm sorry.'

He smiled with sadness. 'Don't be sorry. I've known it since I landed here. I'd hoped you could contradict me. Obviously not. It's hard to believe I will be that brutal.'

'Don't think about it. You have something to do before this even begins.'

'Yssobel.' He turned to look at her, a fierce, beautiful but frightened young man's gaze, not ready yet to face the violent days ahead, his arms crossed across his chest, as if holding in the fear of the rage and blood that he knew he must spill one day.

'I do not wish to be that man. I truly do not wish to be that man.'

'But that is the man you are. Though not yet. Don't think about it.'

'War? That I can understand. But that woman . . . what we will do to her . . .'

'Her name is Andromache. The wife of Hektor. Troy was the war. I painted images, some of them of you, on the back of the scrolls that taught me about them.'

Odysseus frowned, stood and searched the shaping wall.

'Hektor? I know him. He's here. He stares at me.'

He saw the man, pointed him out. On the shaping wall, metal-eyed Hektor was running towards him, shield held hard, sword hidden behind his back. 'Hektor. There! A fierce fighter. He terrifies me. All bronze terrifies me when shaped into the leaf-blade. But it's not my own weapon that will kill him. A ghost I know as Achilles will kill him.'

'That's right. Achilles will take him down. But the city will fall.'

The young man came back to the table.

He took Yssobel's hands in his. There were tears in his eyes. 'Not fallen yet. I've not even been there. It seems as if I've a long and dangerous path to walk.'

'That's right,' Yssobel replied. 'And I do not believe you are in any real fear of the leaf-blade.'

'If you think that' – he smiled thinly as he looked at her – 'then you don't know the twist and thrust of fear. But I do hope you're right.'

He sighed, looking thoughtful and anguished for a moment. Relaxing then, he returned his attention to Yssobel. 'Now: to you. What help is it that I can I give to you? I'll do anything I can.'

Yssobel hesitated for a long moment; her gaze was drawn again to the savagery of the Trojan Andromache's death by the Greeks, the child torn from her arms. It was a moment of doubt; whether or not to stay with this man, in his oracular palace. But she reminded herself: he was not yet the man that he would become.

She said softly, 'I need to find my mother.'

Suddenly, Narine was at the door, a horse held by the reins that she gripped in her hands. She was not happy.

'We're starving!'

She eyed the table where food was plentiful. Uzana peered over her shoulder. 'How long were you going to make us wait?'

'Come in,' Odysseus said gently. 'Leave the horse, though.'

They sat and ate like beasts, always watching the young Greek. They drank water, not wine. They settled back and looked around at this living-walled room. Narine noticed the beach charge towards the defences of Troy, and the men coming towards the observer. 'Quite a battle!'

'Quite a life,' Uzana added, looking around at the shifting images, the heaving sea, a crystal palace towards which a salt-soaked and beaten man was crawling. 'What strange beasts. What a journey this shows. Is this your life to come?'

'Apparently.' He glanced at Yssobel.

'Does it daunt you?' Uzana asked.

'Very much so. But I'll work out strategies to cope with it. Especially after the journey home after the war.'

'Well: if it is, I'd like to be there with you. There is excitement in your life; challenge.' Uzana looked round at the scenes. 'How does it end? Your life.'

'With slaughter, if the wall is to be believed.'

Uzana and Narine followed his hand to where it pointed at his murdering of several men in a small, tight room, where a tree was growing and holding up the ceiling. 'That is my home. Those men tried to steal it. But as yet, I haven't begun even to shape the home. This oracle is almost too challenging.'

Narine stuffed a fig into her mouth, looking quickly at Yssobel, a look that said: is he mad?

'We should get on,' Yssobel said. 'I have to find an army of ghosts called Legion. And there is a man to find, riding with it. I need to understand him.'

'Legion?' Odysseus said. 'Why would you want to find Legion?'

'Because they've taken my mother Guiwenneth.'

'Zeus! Legion! That will be a task!'

'You know it, then?'

His eyes had brightened. 'I've seen it several times. I don't know where it is now, but I know where to start looking. But getting there will not be easy.' He looked at Uzana. 'I assume you'll come with us?'

'Of course.'

'Then eat up. Eat everything. But not the table,' he added, with a smile. 'I sleep on it. I'll tend to your horses. Tomorrow we ride.'

'Where to? And how far?' asked Yssobel. 'We have to think of supplies.'

'To a set of caves, fronted by green porcelain. I've seen it. And yes, it's a long journey. But it contains a mirror to the world. We'll see things there.'

'The palace of green porcelain!' Yssobel whispered, almost to herself. It was the place she had visited often with Odysseus, on her long rides out from the villa. It was clear to her that he could not remember those Serpent Pass excursions. So she said only, 'My father talked about it. He'd read about it in an ancient book . . . a bound set of scrolls,' she added, when Odysseus looked puzzled. 'The story of a man who made a creature from metal and stone that could move through time.'

'Like Legion, then,' Odysseus said, intrigued.

Yssobel knew very little about Legion, but she agreed anyway.

And though she felt a touch of guilt about the way in which she'd used some of those scrolls for her paintings, the guilt fled from her like a startled hare.

Palace of Green Porcelain

In the morning, Odysseus was extremely cheerful. He was up early, saddling the horses – his own was a pure white mare – and was soon to be seen galloping away from the palace, down to the sea, where he turned and shouted something abusive, laughing as he did so.

He was dismissing his future, for the moment.

Yssobel and the others followed him on what was a long ride around the island's shore, to a narrow causeway that stretched across the ocean, vanishing into dawn haze. Lake had become sea here, though Yssobel had not noticed the moment of separation of waters.

'It's a dangerous crossing,' Odysseus said. 'If you slip into the sea, you're lost. Something below the surface is very hungry, and very fast. I saw it happen several times. That's why I have no friends left here. But so far I've been lucky.'

He led the way, keeping his mare under tight control. The causeway was only slightly wider than a horse's tread, and the ground was slippery.

Throughout a long and silent day they walked the bridge between islands, below a cloudless sky, stopping for nothing, keeping a steady pace, alert for danger.

Soon the island came into sight, rising like bull's horns from the water; two mountain peaks.

And the causeway widened and reached the narrow rocky beach, where a steep path led through the gorge between the mountains. Here, for a while, they rested and refreshed themselves.

'Not far now,' Odysseus assured them, though Narine seemed to know where she was.

After a difficult scramble up the stony path, the cliffs closed in; the passage became gloomy. Again, Yssobel recognised the place: Serpent Pass.

She took the lead, revelling in the eerie sense of familiarity. In just a short while she saw the first flash of light on green. As they came closer, so the carved effigy of a bull, shaped from glistening green porcelain, became clear in profile, its gaping maw the entrance.

This was like yet unlike the strange museum in Serpent Pass, behind the villa. Perhaps that particular manifestation of the mind had been her father's. This, perhaps, was a memory of her father's tale of the 'metal and stone machine that travelled in time', entangled with her own ideas. She had certainly noticed the exquisite statue of a bull that seemed to have been guarding the entrance to the museum.

Yssobel began to wonder what Odysseus had brought her here to see.

'More reflection,' he said when she questioned him. 'A shield!'

Narine and Uzana waited in the cool gorge. Odysseus led Yssobel through the open mouth of the bull. It was even colder here, and gloomy, but after walking for a while a green light began to glow, and shapes began to emerge from the rooms through which they passed. There was nothing alive among them; they were exhibits just as Yssobel's room in the villa had been filled with objects which she had collected. Just as her grandfather George Huxley had filled his own 'Oak Lodge', at the edge of the world, with objects that he'd collected.

But they were fascinating. And they were most certainly from her father's imagination.

'I love this place,' Odysseus said as they walked through the sometimes echoing chambers, descending steps into rooms lined with shelves of scrolls (at which Yssobel glanced with a fond guilt), ascending to where vast human figures stood, their arms upraised, their eyes wide. 'But what is this?'

He had led Yssobel into a wide room filled with dark metal

machines, some of which had wheels, wide wings and cross-pieces on their snouts. These were painted brightly, some of the decoration reflecting teeth. Everything here was a chaos of war. War machines. There were the more familiar chariots, two-wheeled and four-wheeled, and several of what Yssobel knew – from what she had learned – were guns. Massive pieces of war architecture, leaning heavily, or broken.

Odysseus said, 'You can enter some of these strange metal beasts. There is a space inside. Some have spaces big enough for several men. If they were in war, they would be a good place to hide, and this hard metal . . .' he banged his fist against one of the machines '. . . would stop a spear. I find these monsters fascinating.'

'War horses,' Yssobel said, remembering an expression of her father's.

'War horses,' Odysseus echoed. 'That's a good name for them. I'll remember that.'

The palace of green porcelain, this strange museum of past and future, dipped and turned, as if the earth itself had moved and shaped it. In places it was disintegrating, the marble cracked, the plaster falling. In one such place they passed a room of paintings, and Yssobel was entranced.

Here were men and women and children, all with strangely pallid and blank faces, holding hounds and horses, dressed in exaggeratedly ornate clothing, staring out as if to say: *Help me; I'm frozen in time.* And scenes of sea battles between huge ships, mast- and sail-shattered, but so many masts and sails! And a picture of a screaming woman, being dragged up steep steps by armoured, hard-faced men.

'I don't understand these scenes,' Odysseus said. 'Some I feel I know, some make no sense.'

'They're beautiful. Not all of them. But most of them. They put my own painting to shame.'

'Whatever your painting was like, don't ever let anything here put it to shame. Some of these people look miserable. And the horses are too big. And the ships are a nightmare of size. No ship that big could sail. Come on: let me show you where the monsters live, before I take you to the shield.'

But as Yssobel followed him into another gloomy passage, so

she glanced at a broad picture, a terrible scene, of men in strange uniforms walking through smoke, with short spears held before them, and walking not on a beach or a hill but over multicoloured cloth, which seemed to embrace the fallen bodies of other men. Beside it were words written on a piece of thin parchment.

She snatched this down, and her red side surfaced again for an instant, and she read the first line: *I walked for my life across a field of tartan.*

Not understanding, but feeling drawn to it, Yssobel folded the sheet and tucked it away. Odysseus was shouting for her and she followed.

This was a place of wonders. Odysseus was beside himself with laughter as he led her through a gallery of weird reptilian creatures, some small, some of enormous height and length. 'What strange, perverted god made these?' he questioned. 'All neck, tail and teeth. By Zeus, I hope my later journey doesn't involve an encounter with any of these echoes of a mad mind.'

'I hope so too.'

But as they left this display of forgotten night-born beasts, she looked again at the purloined parchment sheet.

A field of tartan?

And then he led her into the gallery of shields. There were hundreds, all slung from the rafters, turning and clanging against each other in a wind that blew from a narrow window, opened to the upper part of the gorge. Round, oval, tear-shaped, the geometry of these faces was astonishing and beautiful, as were the colours and the patterns, the animals and symbols, and the war-marks that had distorted, sometimes severed, many of these hand-held hopes against the coming blow.

'This is my favourite room,' said Odysseus. 'And this is my favourite shield.' He slowed the turning of a round shield with the image of a horse painted onto the outer leather. Thin bronze covered its face, but its weight came from wood and hide and wood and hide, four thick layers. This would have been heavy.

Yssobel remembered the shield that he had stared at so forlornly, half embraced by the sea waves. This shield was identical.

Odysseus was in contemplative, reflective mood. 'Does the

shield choose the man? Or the man the shield? I wonder. What does the shield – so many different shields – tell about the man who carried them? What does the armour of the man or the woman who wore it tell about the man or the woman?'

Yssobel was lost by his brow-furrowing thinking.

'Odysseus. My friend . . .'

'Yes?'

'Bad poetry. Stop glooming. Show me the shield that you brought me here to see.'

With a sly glance at her, and a wry smile, the young Greek beckoned Yssobel. As she followed him through the shield room he suddenly turned, caught her in his arms and kissed her, swiftly but with meaning.

'I do love you.'

'I love you too.' She pushed him away. 'Now. Show me the shield.'

'It's behind your back.'

It was a shield that could only have been carried by a man of enormous height and strength. When she stretched out her arms, she could not embrace its edges. It was made of rough wood in layers at the back, and again had leather pressed in between. But its surface, its shining front, was brilliant; patterned from some incorruptible metal, or perhaps a magician's way with powdered crystal.

And yet, as she looked at it, there was nothing but reflected light, and her own distorted image in the main shield, and in the green crystal boss that centred it.

'And this is . . . ?'

'Diadora's shield.'

Yssobel was stunned by its simplicity, having been shocked by its size. 'I've heard of this. There is a story about my grandfather – Peredur – that relates him to this shield. If this *is* the shield.'

'The shield of Diadora,' Odysseus said, and reached to swing the war-mirror to an angle. 'Don't look at it. Be aware of it. From the corner of your eye. Such strange visions can be seen. You'll probably understand them. I can't.'

Yssobel looked Odysseus in the eyes, remembering, remembering. But then, as he'd said, she started to see images in the shield, glimpsed from the corner of her gaze.

Her brother Jack, struggling to drag a horse and a boat along a river that was flowing wildly against him. She saw him drag the boat onto the bank, disguise it, then lead the horse to open space, and sunlight. She saw two boys sitting by a stream. They were alarmed at first, then calm. Jack, her brother Jack, knelt in the water between them and washed. He was bleeding. She could hear the murmur of conversation, but not the words. And she heard laughter.

Odysseus asked: 'Why are you smiling?'

'My brother found the edge of the world. Or will find it. His name is Jack. Does this shield look into time?'

The young Greek shrugged. 'No idea. But it shows other worlds, and they're happier than the world shown in my own palace. Which is why I come here when I can.'

'I need more. How do I get more?'

'Keep watching. Think of what you wish to see.'

'Everything. Everything. I wish to see everything.'

He was hugely amused. 'How long do you have? To see everything.'

'Everything, I mean, to do with finding my mother, Legion, and a man . . .' She hesitated, not sure of her words. 'A man who seems to have been resurrected. A man called Christian.'

'And he is? What, who?'

'My uncle. I need to understand him.'

Odysseus acknowledged that, and with a polite bow withdrew from the shield hall. 'I'll be outside, with the grave gobblers!' He laughed at his own rough reference. 'Take your time. This time is yours.'

Yssobel knelt by the Diadoran shield, staring ahead of her, letting the edge of vision entice the images. She called for her father, but to her surprise found that Jack was there again.

He was walking in a strange, unearthly land, an Underland, with the tall and hideous beings which they had come to call Amurngoth. There were some twenty of them, and a rough-faced, tousled boy, clad in deerskin trousers and shirt, carrying a short spear. He looked angry. Jack was walking with him, his face also set grim.

'What's happening, brother?' she whispered, and at once he

stopped. They all stopped. He looked around him, puzzled, then dropped to one knee, his arm around the boy, but staring through the shield. And she heard his voice, as if over a great distance.

'Who's there? Yssi? Is that you? It sounds like you . . .'

'Where *are* you?'

'Coming to find you. I believe you're in danger.'

'How are you finding me? How do you know where to look?'

'I can hardly hear you. We must put Haunter in touch with green. How did I know where to look? Huxley's journals. You're in Avilion, and I know how you got there. I'm coming through a different path. With the Amurngoth. We've come to an arrangement. I hope I'll be able to keep it. Are you safe?'

'Safe? Yes. For the moment. I have friends with me. When I find Legion, things will change.'

'Then I'll find you at Legion! Yssi . . . ?'

'Jack?'

'Do you still have the silver clasps?'

'Of course I do.'

'Keep them safe. I miss you, sister. But we'll find each other. Time isn't controlling us in this place. We control Time. Am I talking to red or green?'

'Red, I think. I thought I'd lost her.'

'Let green take over. I am more Haunter than Jack. So when you find wildwood, we can speak more easily.'

And he had gone, the image faded, his distant words of parting drawn back into time.

She slumped for a while, head on arms on the patterned floor, tears not quite flowing; but she felt lonely. The encounter through the mirrored surface had been wonderful. And yet her own words, until then thoughts unspoken, had frightened her.

When I find Legion, things will change.

Why had she said that?

Yssobel straightened up, her head banging against one of the other dangling shields, a moment's easier pain, before once more turning her edge of vision to Diadora.

But what to try and see? Her mother? Legion? She thought for a while, and then on impulse called quietly:

'Christian.'

He woke suddenly, and with a cry. He had been dreaming of Oak Lodge. In his dream he had been fishing on a pond with his brother Steven; their hooks had caught an old boat, a broken boat, but the lines had held and they had hauled it to the surface. He had waded in and pulled the wreck to the muddy bank.

He had been dreaming of their amazement, their inspiration: was this the work of pirates? Was there a body to be found?

He was dreaming about the discovery, and the story that might go with the resurrection of this sunken wreck, ten feet down in the millpond, close to their home.

But awake, and with a cry, he had roused those sleeping near to him. He stood, shivering, looking around at the low fires, the stacks of arms, the half-roused army sleeping here on the open plain. They were moving through time towards a battlefield, but as yet he had no sense of direction: forward or back; just that they were being summoned. Legion ploughed the earth as it ploughed time itself; Christian, waking up, was returned to his secret fear that they would be facing a future war, and not one for which this vast, mixed, strange and ghostly army was prepared.

Harsh, hard eyes watched him as he prowled, cloak around his body, a shiver in his limbs. He held tightly to his sword, hidden below the cloak. He knew that his leadership of Legion was something he would soon have to contest.

Fires burned, his mind was in flames. *Who's there?* he thought, unwilling to speak aloud in case his fear was shown.

Walking into darkness, away from the fires, he remembered the fire that had taken his life, the huge fire that separated his home from Lavondyss; from the place where the spirit ran with the wind; from the dreaming place, where he had been reborn.

Walking into darkness, he remembered Guiwenneth, and he hunched into himself as he remembered his passion for her, and how he had taken her, how he had killed his brother Steven, only to fail, to find Steven a stronger man, and a man who had come back at him with full fury.

He remembered his sense of loss at losing Guiwenneth, though he had abused her, though he had loved her; but he had abused her. He had been a lost man then. Now, suddenly, waking from this dream, he felt lost again.

Guiwenneth was watching him. Or was it truly Guiwenneth? The hair was the same bright, coppery flow, half shrouding the face, that pale, green-eyed face, that knowing, wonderful, silently smiling face; that loving face. But this was not her.

Who, then? He was confused.

Who's there? he whispered.

She stepped forward and he turned to face her. There was only darkness, the darkness of the plain, where Legion was encamped. But she was in the corner of his eye, and watching him.

Why do I know you?

She was silent, though. She was kneeling, now, her arms crossed, her head bowed as if in grief. She said nothing.

You terrify me. You ghost.

He had no sooner thought the thought than the apparition vanished. The air was fresh, there was a warm dawn light beginning to shimmer on the far hill, men were rising, and men were at his side, holding his arms, watching him with curiosity, but also with compassion.

He shrugged them off and went back to where his armour lay. Sensing their presence behind him, he turned, half unsheathing his sword. The four of them stood very still. They seemed alarmed and angry with his action.

The youngest of the four said, 'You seemed disturbed by something. If we can help, we will.'

These were his guard. They rode ahead of him, or beside him, four men he trusted. They wore dull-coloured tartan kilts and heavy deerskin jackets. They favoured weapons that he could not use himself.

The youngest spoke again: 'You need to be strong. We need to be strong for you. What is it?'

'I'm haunted by the past. I can't think why. There: is that enough show of weakness for you?'

'Weakness? Where's the weakness? What you took you took. What you take you take. What will be taken from you is what will be taken from you. You can do nothing about the first; the

214

second is something you can decide upon. The third is the excitement!'

He looked at this young, brash man, held his gaze. 'Bad poetry. But you're right. I can't remember your name.'

'Peredur. Not a name to forget. Remember it well.'

Reflections

The wind was freshening. The shield hall was a place of bell chimes as they clashed. The shield of Diadora, immense and heavy though it was, began to move.

Yssobel looked at it directly. Its surface was like an ocean; rippling. There were patterns in its face, movement that flowed. She became entranced by it, unable to tear her gaze from the silvered aquamarine beauty of it.

'Turn away!'

She reached to touch it, but a hard hand grasped hers and held it back.

'Look away!'

As quickly as he had been there, Odysseus withdrew.

'I thought you'd gone outside,' Yssobel said.

'Didn't trust you not to look,' he replied from behind her. 'Have you seen all you need to see?'

'I don't know. A while longer?'

'Why ask me? Take as long as you like. I have no immediate plans.'

There was a silence then.

Odysseus said quietly, 'Ask for what you truly wish to see. I'll give you a hint. It's your mother. It doesn't take much of a mind to understand that.'

'Be quiet! Go away.'

'The first, yes. The second, never.'

Yssobel waited until he had settled again, then called for Guiwenneth.

*

There was nothing of her but shadow. She walked through the camp, wrapped in her cloak, wrapped in her own arms. The moon was low; fires guttered in the light breeze. Men and women slept around the glow. She walked as a shadow.

Then, suddenly, an owl, white breasted, diamond-eyed, rose before her, wings spreading and folding as it flew from its roosting place. Such life in this death!

And as if the bird were the sound of new life, now she heard her daughter.

'I'm coming to find you. I'm coming to bring you home.'

'Yssobel?' She looked around, alarmed, searching the dusk. 'Don't. Don't. You never understood. Leave me alone. I am here to take care of an old wound, and if you interfere I'll lose my life again.'

'The resurrected man.'

Guiwenneth was suddenly aware that this was oracular contact. She stared at one of the fires. 'Call him what you like. Love him as you like. I need time to find and kill him. Go away!'

'I'm coming to find you.'

'You will never manage that. Even if you did, it would be too late.'

'I intend to take you home.'

The spectre of Guiwenneth laughed loudly. 'There is no going home.'

'You sang the Song of the Islands of the Lost when you left. You can *unsing* it.'

Guiwenneth turned slowly in a full circle, trying, perhaps, to get a glimpse of her daughter. She laughed. 'How do you *un*sing?'

'I don't know, mother. But there must be a way.'

'Leave me, *daughter*. Go back to where you belong. Find Odysseus and marry him.'

'Odysseus is here. We found each other again. Marriage is not a prospect. Our paths will soon draw apart.'

'A shame. A shame,' this vision regretted. 'He was a handsome boy.'

'My father is missing you.'

Guiwenneth sighed and dragged her long hair around her

face; in the mirror-shield she looked thoughtful and, for a moment, lost. Then the flash of hard-eyed green again. 'Steven will cope. He always knew that our life together would be a fleeting one. He's no fool, your father. Where *are* you?'

'In a palace, watching you through the edge of vision. From the corner of my eye. You seem so sad, Gwin. And so angry.'

'I'm here to do a deed, Yssi. If you wish to see anger, watch me in a while. This is a big army. Getting to its centre is hard. But when I get there . . .' Guiwenneth paused, tightened into herself. 'Leave me to my own devices! I miss you too; and Jack. But this is the end for me. Try to keep your paths together, you and the Greek.'

'That, I know now, will be impossible.'

'Then find life's pleasure soon. Leave me, Yssobel. Leave me alone. Don't follow me. Don't waste your life.'

And as if Guiwenneth's words could command the oracle, the Diadoran shield became just reflection and brightness. The image was gone.

Yssobel banged the surface with her fist, crying for a moment. Then that reassuring hand upon her shoulder, and when she stood, Odysseus was there.

'I heard your side of a difficult conversation.'

She wiped the tears from her eyes, angry at herself. 'My mother is stubborn. I *must* find this Legion.'

'Shall I hold you for a moment? Or shall we get on?'

Meeting his gaze, she saw warmth that she remembered, softness in eyes that could narrow to a glitter of fury. Eyes that would see death. Eyes that would become blind to the fury of the man, when Troy would be breached.

'Yes. Hold me. Hold me hard. Stay with me until I can find this night army.'

Was this the man she had known from the villa? Or had she created him, merely the memory of a man she'd loved, imbuing the 'change' with a faint memory of that love? The marks upon his body were the same as she remembered. The gentleness of his arms was as she remembered. The softness of his kiss was as she remembered. The sadness in him, the sense of being alone, was certainly that of the man who had been the Odysseus of her own days, before he had found the island where he would settle, where he would find the wife he loved – Penelope, as she had learned it from Steven – and father the son he would adore.

There were times when Yssobel despaired at being this half creature, half human; the red and green conflicting within her head and heart.

But she was green now, and so was this man-myth. And he was holding her with compassion and understanding:

I heard your side of what must have been a difficult conversation.

She realised she loved him, even if he was not the man who had danced with her by the fire, even of he was not the same young Greek who had brooded, future-pining, in the cave in Serpent Pass.

She had no hesitation. She invited his love. He welcomed it.

And after, he said, 'I watched you when you thumped that shield, when you cried. So I ask you: will you watch me now?'

Yssobel agreed readily, tying her hair into Jack's silver clasp, stepping back again into one of the dangling shields and laughing as she set off a chain of ringing. Odysseus clothed himself, and sighed. 'My life is a reflection. And I've done none of it yet! Palaces, palaces, walls, shields. Wherever I go I see myself reflected!'

'In my own eyes, you are reflected with affection.'

He gave Yssobel a knowing smile. 'So I gather. But alas.'

'Alas . . .'

'Stay with me for a few moments more. One more glance. There is a question I need to ask – and then we'll try to find Legion. This, for the moment, is your time, not mine. But please watch me as I've watched you. I need to know you're there.'

'I'll be here,' she said quietly.

She watched him as he crouched by the giant shield, his head bowed, his voice a whisper. And she heard the name. *Penelope*. He was seeking hope, hope in the woman who would be his homeward cause after the great war against Troy. This was ill-advised, but Greeks were Greeks, and Odysseus was a canny man, and no doubt he was building this painful vision into his strategy. Whatever he was seeing, it made him angry. Judging by his bodily actions beside the shield, he was killing men. Then he was whispering love.

My life is a reflection . . .

No sooner than having loved one woman with all his body and all his strength, he was loving another in dream and anticipation. Yssobel didn't find this easy, but she guarded his back. This had been her promise. And she took the clasp from her hair:

Avilion is what we make of it.

And looked at it, and used it as a charm of hope. Hope that she would return with her mother to the home where her mother belonged.

It rises. It rises. It turns face about, turning back, taken aback by the call from Yssobel.

The resurrected man gathers his commanders. 'We go back.'

'Back where?'

'There is something I have to do. We go back.'

'Time is taking us to a great confrontation. That's what we do. We cannot disobey the journey.'

Christian turned on the man who had spoken. He drew his blade, pushed it hard into the man's body. As the man sank, so Christian engaged the gaze of all the other men under his command. 'We turn back. Do we turn back? I say we turn back. There is something I have to confront. Are any of you prepared to argue?'

'We are Legion,' said one of the other men. 'But if you say we turn back, then we turn back. As long as we can return to serve Time and its demands. Will you agree to that?'

'I agree to that.'

There was general approval for the strategy.

They found Uzana in the room of monsters. She was holding an apple, eaten to the core, standing in front of the gaping, tooth-terrifying mouth of a huge reptile, staring at it.

'These are such strange beasts,' she said as Yssobel approached. 'There is life in them, and no life at all. This one could have snapped me in half in a heart's beat. It clearly doesn't want the remains of my apple.'

She tossed the core into the creature's maw, wiped her fingers on her skirt and looked around, all curiosity and innocence.

'If these beasts existed, I'm glad not to have lived in their world. The size of them!'

'Where's Narine?'

She focused again. 'Narine? She's found a room of oracles. She's trying to find Legion for you. There's a hard time to come, she thinks, and I agree. She's also trying to find Arthur.'

She grinned. 'If he's in a bad mood, we're all in trouble.'

Arthur wakes from the dream

A bird was sitting on his chest; dark-feathered, not pecking, curious. It flew off at the very moment when he opened his eyes, flying straight into the trunk of a tree, falling, then flying on; bruised but not life-abandoned.

Arthur sat up. The air was sweet with the smell of the lake. His wound was blood-congealed; painful. There was life in him, life he had thought taken. He was among the trees; his men were asleep by the lake.

He rose unsteadily, groaning with the discomfort of the deep strike that Morthdred had inflicted upon him. He realised suddenly that he was naked.

This was very puzzling.

He walked down to the lake's edge and kicked Bydavere. His close companion snorted out of sleep, looked up, then sat up, startled. 'Where in the name of the Good God have you just come from? We sent you off in the barge. With the women.'

'Clearly not. Give me something to cover myself. I'm freezing.'

'I don't understand it. How can you be here when we dispatched you to Avilion?'

'Clothes! Give me clothes.'

'A cloak?'

'Good thinking,' he agreed, with a cold, narrowed look at the other man. 'I don't imagine reeds and rushes would do it.'

Covered and warmed in Bydavere's cloak, Arthur crouched among his companions; they ate frugally. They all seemed nervous. They discussed the situation.

'We put *somebody* on the barge,' Bydavere said. 'A body that looked like you, same copper-coloured hair.'

'How heavy?'

'Quite light. Now you mention it.'

Arthur was neither angry nor amused. He shook his head. 'Bydavere: my death has been stolen from me. By whom I don't know. I don't understand it. And I dreamed a whispered voice: *I never knew why I would steal the armour, just that I would have to do it. Let me steal this little time inside your skin.* Strange words. But they have left me with life. What shall I do? Take revenge or show gratitude?'

Bydavere sank back on his haunches, his face a mask of confusion. He scratched at his lank hair. 'I know you value my advice, Arthur. But I confess that this is a difficult one.'

'I'd be grateful just to be alive again,' said Emereth. 'Though, of course, this could be a death trick. You look quick, which is to say, not dead. Which is a good thing. But possibly you're not. Though if you're not, then quite what you are is a difficult thought to think with.'

'Thank you. I assure you I'm alive.'

Emereth smiled and nodded, glancing nervously at Bydavere. 'Of course you are. Bydavere?'

Bydavere said, 'This was not a life stolen, nor a death. It was a *fate* stolen. Arthur: in my briefly considered judgement, you have been denied for the moment, only for the moment, the life after death that will become your – how can I put it, how to put it? – your life-after-death *heritage*. I have always thought that there is something about you that will last. God knows what that something will turn out to be, but something. Don't seek vengeance. Seek truth. And seek the person who – I suspect, from the smell . . . did I tell you about the smell?'

'No,' Arthur said darkly. 'You did not tell me about the smell.'

'It was a woman's smell. I'm sure of it. I'm not without experience in that arena. Even as we put the body on the barge, I thought: this is not Arthur. Women smell different to Arthur.'

'I sincerely hope so,' Arthur agreed quietly.

'We must find this woman. For whatever reason: she has claimed your death, and she needed to claim it. No revenge at first, therefore, just assistance. And *then* revenge. That's what we do.'

'It is indeed,' said Arthur, and reached to take his friend's hand in his. 'It is indeed. But she went across the lake. How do we get across the lake?'

'By the Good God, Arthur,' Bydavere sighed. 'Can't you ever ask a question that has an easy answer?'

In the oracle room, in the Palace of Green Porcelain, Yssobel pulled back from the whispering voices she had heard. The oracle was a rock-carved well of crystal water, its rim carved in the shape of three hares on their sides, limbs entwined, heads turned up to the listener. The eerie sounds of the conversation between Arthur and Bydavere shifted between the open mouths of these three stone-shaped images of the fast-moving animals.

Yssobel recognised the voices, even though they were spoken almost with a faintness that she might have associated with an echo on the wind. She had heard the men speaking as they had nursed Arthur, and later, as they had cried and joked before sinking into the drunken slumber that had given her her opportunity.

To steal his death.

Narine had called loudly for Yssobel when she had whispered Arthur's name into this particular museum exhibit and had begun to hear a conversation. The scene, again a reflection in this place of memory and reflections, had shimmered on the water.

'He's coming for you,' Uzana said. 'I've collected men like him before. They're confused at first, thinking they're still alive – when they're not! But at the end they just get angry. Your man is the other way round. But yes, as certain as a crow feeds on dead meat, he's coming for you.'

'He'll take the same barge,' Narine agreed. 'Those two men on the barge will tell him everything. They're just transporters. This way, that way. They have everything to lose if they fail.'

'This man Arthur, and his cohort; they'll have a long chase,'

Odysseus said thoughtfully. 'They will not know in which direction we've gone.'

Narine laughed, looking scornfully at the young Greek. 'Don't you see? Didn't you hear? Bydavere is a hound! He will follow Yssobel's scent like a hound!' And she added, with a small nod of her head. 'Oh yes. They'll know where to follow.'

'How can a man be a hound?' Odysseus asked. 'Are you saying he can beast-change his body? Man into dog?'

Narine laughed again, then put her arms around his shoulders, holding her mouth close to his ear, speaking softly, though the other two could hear.

'A hound is cunning; a hound uses strategy; a hound uses all its senses and its sense; it disguises itself in the wood; it waits for its moment. It slaughters. And Bydavere,' she added, 'is very much like you. Or what you will become, from what I saw in your palace.'

She pulled away. Yssobel saw the spark in her Greek friend's eyes, the hint of a smile; that hint of pride at having been compared favourably to a cunning animal.

'In which case, I imagine we have more work to do,' he said. 'This great army is turning, coming back. But back to where?'

Uzana was knocking gently at the thin crystal cage that contained the mummified corpse of a woman, sitting on a three-legged stool, a snake around her ankles. 'I don't think we're going to get much out of *her*.'

Narine consulted the three hares. The water shimmered, seemed for a moment to gleam with flashes of vision, but it revealed nothing. The Oracle of the Three Hares, as Yssobel decided to name it, clearly needed time to recover from the first effort.

On impulse, she lifted from her neck the silver clasp and finger ring that Jack had made for her. *Avilion is what we make of it*.

And on the small ring, crudely inscribed: *Here to there. There to here.*

She remembered what he'd said by the forge. How each of them would find a different world, and each return. Now she saw a different vision in the beating and shaping of the metal.

'Legion is coming to Avilion,' she said. 'It's coming here. But where is "here"? Where in Avilion?'

On an impulse, Yssobel threw the small ring into the air and let it fall onto the tiled floor, wondering if it would spin and roll to the appropriate oracle, an echo of a child's game that she and Jack had played with a pebble and a ring of childish treasures. But the ring fell dead and still. She replaced it on her finger.

And then, as they walked back towards the entrance of the museum, Yssobel discovered the answer to her question. As she passed the wide, slowly moving picture of the men running across the field, she was surprised to see that it had changed. Now it showed a deeply wooded valley, with the tall towers and broad ivy-covered walls of a fortress, almost growing within the forest. And slowly rising into that scene were the shining armoured shapes of men and horses, visible among the trees.

Narine said, 'That's the Sylvan Fortress. The windows of the towers all look out towards different worlds.'

Yssobel knew that well enough. She had created the castle in the forest at the very heart of her paintings of Avilion as she imagined it. Once a beautiful castle, the land in which it stood had suddenly risen up and consumed it. Tree and stone had mated and become a single entity. She watched the slow movement of the army: tiny figures, but a multitude of them.

'If that's this army called Legion, then my mother is somewhere in the chaos.'

'And to get there we need a boat,' said Narine. 'And there are boats in this place, if we can find them.'

They searched the galleries and soon Uzana's call brought them to a vast chamber, where a huge, strange ship lay crumbling on its side, its deck rotting, the tatters of sails hanging from broken spars. It dwarfed all the other vessels, but there were hundreds of them, from longships and a galley with eyes painted on its prow that Odysseus recognised as a warship from his own land, to canoes and tiny coracles. Yssobel found a barge that seemed solid enough to take the four of them, and they hauled it slowly from the chamber, and pulled and pushed it to the entrance of the green palace. They rested before taking the boat across the beach, heaving it half into the water before gathering their belongings, weapons and supplies. They let the horses go, then launched the craft and hauled themselves aboard, taking up the oars.

The Sylvan Fortress

The crossing had not taken long. Soon high cliffs emerged from the sea mist and they rowed towards an obvious ravine, a narrow entrance. Now they rowed against the flow, and in heavy shadow as the rock rose sombre and sinister above them. But quite soon they emerged into the shallows and into the light.

Leaving the boat, they walked on. There was an eerie silence about this world, and even though birds flew and flocked, they seemed to make no sound.

Walking and resting, they made their way inwards and suddenly, startlingly, they were at the edge of a steep decline, and staring out over a thick green canopy of forest. There, distantly, were the towers and the walls of the deserted Sylvan Fortress.

Narine turned to Yssobel and smiled. 'This is where we leave you.' She looked at Odysseus. 'Goodbye, you hound.'

'Why are you leaving?' Odysseus asked.

'Because we smell the coming deaths, and we will have a different role than as your guides.'

Uzana embraced Yssobel, but said nothing. The two collectors, the two queens of the dead, turned and walked back the way they had come. Yssobel watched them for a while and then, quite suddenly, they seemed to rise into the air, the brightness of their clothing now turned black.

It was a hard descent to the wide valley. There were human shapes in the trees, some male, some female, all slender and very tall. All forests were inhabited by such beings. Odysseus referred to them as dryads. Yssobel knew them as trunklings, her father's word for them when he occasionally encountered them.

Soon, the massive wall of the fortress emerged from the screen of foliage. The towers were astonishingly high, each with four windows. And indeed, as the painting had shown, where the fortress joined the earth the forest had joined the fortress, wood into stone. The foundations were massive roots, four man-lengths across. The dryads that lay within the bark were giants, naked and gnarled, eyes closed as they slept, though as Yssobel crept past them, sometimes forced to walk over them, eyes would open and the head would emerge slightly to see who or what was intruding on its slumber.

The gateway to the courtyard was an oval slash, like a deep wound in bark. Faces were carved around the slit, but they were ugly, some skull-like, some clearly daurog, the summer form of what Steven called the green man, some intensely un-human.

Yssobel had brought no defences against the daurog, should they appear, but she could make them easily enough in this place.

'We're here too soon,' Odysseus observed unnecessarily. 'Which encourages me to ask the question: how do we know they're coming? Perhaps they've already been. Perhaps they will be here a long time from now.'

'They're coming,' Yssobel said quietly, looking up and round at the massive structure. 'I'm the focus. I'm the crossing place. Narine and Uzana called themselves Collectors. I knew the moment I saw my mother in the shield that I'm a Caller.'

Odysseus shrugged, half in agreement. Yssobel smiled at him. 'While we wait, I'm going to see what can be seen.'

She climbed a tower. She was exhausted by the time she reached the first of the four windows. But when she looked out she saw a view that took the rest of her breath away, a stunning landscape of mountains, rising sheer, snow-capped, with beauti-ful, ornate buildings covering their faces, clinging to the rock, delicately shaped elegance against the harsh, rugged stone. She stared at it for a long time, letting her red side absorb its power and majesty.

From the second window she saw a sight that shocked and startled her. A woman was being transformed into a tree, her mouth open in a silent scream as branches grew from her, and her body grew within the forest around. She aged as rapidly as a meteor passes across the sky, then broke and fell. Snow was suddenly coating the land, and a man with a stone axe cut a chunk of the fallen tree and carved it, forcing it into the ground beside his crude leather tent.

Yssobel was disturbed by the sight, with the violent way in which the woman had been transformed. It all suggested a time very much in the past. It had nothing to do with her own dreams.

She moved to the third window.

She was looking out over a bleak land, at the edge of a bleak and cold sea. A great hall had been built there, with smaller buildings around it. The hall was magnificently decorated and vibrantly painted along its walls. Shields hung from the eaves and hundreds of swifts flew between them as if in a game.

From the fourth window she saw Amurngoth, many of them. They were walking in their ungainly way through the under-world, along a passageway illuminated by the torches they carried. As they passed her point of view, so she saw Jack, holding the hand of the boy she had seen earlier.

She called to him, but this time he didn't hear. Perhaps he was Jack for the moment, with his Haunter side subdued.

As he passed she blew him a kiss, then returned to where Odysseus was waiting, seated on the steps that led up to the main entrance of the Sylvan Fortress.

'Did you see anything?'

'Nothing I could understand – except that I saw my brother.'

Odysseus nodded. 'That's twice, then. Is he close?'

'I don't know. Space shifts, and time shifts. He looked a lot older and more beaten than when I last saw him. I think he's been on a journey.'

Legion was culled from all of time, selected from armies across the world. It was an army of the dead, formed in antiquity to service those who could summon it. The summoning usually came from a king's request at an oracle, or from the horn call, or from the shaman or druid who was confined within a besieged fortress.

Legion had been moving backwards in time, and towards the land of the Gauls, to a place called Alesia, summoned to help the men and women held there under siege by an army from Rome.

They had answered the call and were close to their task – to take the Roman army from behind – when Christian heard the whispered voice that frightened him.

And turned the army round.

Ghostlike, they moved through earth, but they made a noise, a din, a racket, of dogs and cattle, and the squeaking of un-oiled wheels; and songs, a cacophony of sound as the marching songs of so many worlds combined in harsh dissonance.

Christian was at the army's head, on horseback, leading the way. He was following a whisper trail, the whisper of the woman who had called to him.

As they covered earth, so they rose in time.

Disorientation suddenly occurred. The land ahead of the army stretched and twisted, almost seeming to part. Beyond them lay a star-studded darkness, as if they'd reached the edge of a cliff and were looking straight ahead at the night sky. Several of his commanders were edgy, implying that they had come the wrong way.

'No! This is a boundary to another world. I once passed through a boundary to the same world, only at that time it was through a wall of fire.'

'What other world?' asked one of his men.

'I know it as *Lavondyss. The place where the spirits of men are not tied to the seasons.* Meaning tied neither to life nor death. It is a form of Avilion: the place of healing and resurrection.' He was speaking softly, as if in a dream. Then suddenly he came awake: 'We'll press on.'

The army moved. It walked and rode and drove through space, through a void where there seemed to be no ground underfoot but which was firm to the step. Soon the stars faded and a forested landscape emerged, a wildwood of immense span and age.

Christian tasted the air, closed his eyes as he rode, listened for that ghostly whisper. If he heard it, he didn't know it, but for some unknown reason he shifted the direction of his army towards an unseen, unknowable goal.

*

Night fell and Yssobel walked out of the fortress into the cool damp of the forest. The massive dryads were emerging from the roots of the foundations and moving into darkness. She could hear their crashing progress for some time as they hunted for their prey, searched for whatever night encounter they wished to find.

The tall, slender forms were gathering in circles of thirteen and singing in birdsong, a beautiful sound. Yssobel watched them from hiding. Soon, the birds came and settled on the shoulders and outstretched arms of these strange creatures. The red side of the woman observed with curiosity; the green side listened, then walked out of hiding and approached them. Startled for a moment, they admitted her to the circle. Soft hands held hard. Two small birds settled on Yssobel's shoulders. The talking between the dryads was fast. She followed its source with ease, as each mind expressed its thoughts.

Danger is coming. We will be broken. We will be fire-stuff. We will be cut. We will be broken by anger. We must protect our trees. I have lived in mine four hundred leaf-falls. I will die if I cannot drink the sap that rises at leaf-burst. All of us will die. Birds, be vigilant. Beak, claw and bird-screech will be needed. This stranger among us is no threat. She is not like us. She is less than us, but some of us.

It went on like this.

Danger was coming! The tree guardians were in chattering, frightened mood. And they had sensed the arrival of the army.

A different voice broke through the anxious exchanges of the dryads.

'Yssi? Yssobel? Is that you again?'

For a moment she didn't recognise the distorted voice. 'Jack?'

'Haunter. Are you green or red?'

'Green. Very green.'

'Stay that way. I almost know where you are. I'll follow the earth call. Are you in danger yet?'

'Not yet. But danger is coming.'

'Yssi! I reached the edge of the world.'

'I know. I saw you from a place of strange magic. It looked a beautiful land. And you were talking to two boys.'

'You saw *that*? Strange magic is the word for it. That was

when I'd just arrived. I have one of those two boys with me. I hope to get him home. Are you safe?'

'No. I didn't expect to be.'

'Are you . . .' But his voice became faint, and the babble of the dryads was again very loud.

Yssobel stepped out of the circle, fell to her knees and burst into tears. She suddenly felt very lost, very alone. She suddenly missed the life in the villa.

Then hands were on her shoulders, comforting her, and she looked up at Odysseus, the dark ringlets of his hair brushing against her cheeks. His eyes were kind, questioning. Without a word, she stood and led him back into the cold hall behind the courtyard, and to the skins they used to keep themselves warm.

Yssobel was touched awake, the gentle brush of a finger on her cheek. It was before dawn and the air was damp and rank with the odour of musty stone and rotting vegetation. She opened her eyes and sat up, heart pounding, as she met the gaze of two dryads who were crouching over her.

One was male, one female. The touch was not of hard bark but soft, like flesh. Their eyes were very wide, their stare constant. Odysseus slept on, face down, arms stretched out by his sides.

The green in her engaged with the fear of these slender and beautiful wood nymphs.

The female touching Yssobel was thinking the green-thought that Yssobel understood. 'There is danger approaching from deep in the earth. It is a monstrous thing. It consumes all that is on the upper world. It is already at the edge of the forest and coming this way, though it moves slowly. You have time to flee, to escape to the high ground where there is nothing to consume, nothing to burn. We are lost. We cannot move. Our death is certain. But you can go.'

Yssobel asked: 'What is this beast made of?'

'As many of your own kind as there are leaves on my summer branches. But you are not like this hateful monster. I would give you shelter. But soon there will be no shelter, only fire.'

The male touched Yssobel. 'I believe you have a reason to stay,' he said, and Yssobel sensed his understanding.

'I do.'

He seemed almost sorrowful. 'You will be split by lightning, and by the stone and the metal axe.'

As he murmured, she could feel the anguish he felt, a pain passed on through the generations of his kind as they faced fire and the axe-blow. In their darker moods, dryads would ensnare human life and draw it inside them, feeding off its vigour, especially in times of winter. But they were more far more vulnerable than their occasional prey. This dryad was concerned. 'The tree that is in you has no protection against such sudden death,' he whispered. 'We protect the tree in which we were born, and in which we sleep. But this encroaching beast will be too powerful for us. You should flee now.'

'Thank you. But I'm staying.'

His eyes were wide, unblinking. 'Then you have little time. To prepare.'

The male dryad looked up and around. The hall still displayed the carvings and rusting shields and shreds of banners that had once made this a place of noble gathering. 'This did not belong here,' he said. 'It grew from the rock, like mould, like tree fern. It was white and filled with human beauty and display. It was full of wonder. Full of song. But it did not belong here. We took it back. That wonder remains within us, sleeping. Below. We visit it often just to look at it. We preserved it, ready for a time when we would send it back. Now all that was and is here will be destroyed.'

They rose to their feet and walked from the hall. Yssobel shook Odysseus awake. He grumbled, turning to look at her. 'What is it?'

'They're coming,' was all she said, and at once the Greek was alive and active, and strapping on his leather armour.

Odysseus was tired. He had worried through the night, trying to think of a strategy to hide Yssobel from the resurrected man when he arrived, to keep her safe. When she had referred to herself as a 'Caller', he thought she meant she was calling to her mother. But as she climbed the tower, leaving him to his thoughts, he realised she was calling to this man Christian. And every instinct suggested that Christian was a wild and angry creature.

The cunning that Odysseus had been informed he possessed eluded him. His only thought was that if the army coming out of Time was going to surface through the earth, then Yssobel should surface with it, not confront it.

He had prepared an earth grave for her in the courtyard of the fortress, a shallow grave in which she would lie in the direction of the approach. When he showed her what he'd done she stared at the long narrow pit, then looked at the man and laughed out loud.

'Are you mad?'

He seemed taken aback. 'Not yet, I hope. But perhaps,' he agreed, 'not a good idea.'

And so they waited. The long day was very still; the woodland was silent. The air itself seemed motionless, stifling. And then the air was drawn away from them, a strange gusting blow that made Yssobel shiver and the woodland become animated. When this strange and eerie moment had passed, there was stillness again, before the sudden eruption in the sky of birds, great clouds of them, flying not in circles but in a formation, as if fleeing. And animals also fled below the birds, making no sound save for the beat of their flight upon the earth.

And the earth began to shake. There was a deep sound like drumming, but muffled. It grew louder. Then a strange whisper, a thousand ghostly voices whispering. The distant sounds of horns, the creak of wheels, the rattle of harnesses, all growing louder and more coherent until quite suddenly—

Heavily built men on great warhorses reared up through the courtyard, throwing off mud, struggling to find their ground, ghostly yet very tangible. The horses almost screamed and the men shouted, urging them up, up.

Yssobel fled through the gate of the fortress, Odysseus in quick pursuit. They leapt for cover among the giant roots and stared in dismay at the scene unfolding before them as the whole forest became a rising ground for this immense army. The forest filled with human activity. A cohort of Romans marched out of the earth, shields and helmets slung behind them, their eating and drinking utensils clattering as they moved. Nearby came riders on elegant black horses, the men clad in brightly coloured jackets and trousers, with strange curved helmets over their trim faces.

The din was deafening. There was movement for as far as Yssobel could see through the forest.

In the castle root behind which she crouched, the giant tree-being shifted and groaned. She saw its eyes as it turned to look at her. It was confused and seemed frightened. It groaned again as a racing group of yelping, youthful Gauls rode on their ponies across the roots, playing a game, it seemed. They hurtled over Yssobel, not seeing her.

For hours this army rose and passed by, though many groups settled and started to make fires. Trees were lopped and Yssobel glimpsed many of the slender tree-forms running for their lives. Some were noticed, but so rich and varied was this Legion that they might have been a part of it.

All the while, Yssobel searched among those that she could see for her mother, but without success. Guiwenneth might have been at the far edge of this army for all she knew.

The task would be long and hard unless she could find a way to speak to her through her green side.

A large band of black-skirted Greeks passed by, noticed Odysseus and Yssobel and stopped, curious. Odysseus at once rose and went to greet them and be greeted. Conversation was animated for a while, and the Greeks cautiously circled the man who would one day be a hero. Then laughter erupted and one of the band, the oldest-looking, took Odysseus by the wrist and slapped him on the arm. Weapons were placed down and the area marked for their camp for the night, or for however many nights they would stay here.

As groups and cohorts moved on, many settled, and soon after nightfall the forest was alive with fires and the smells of cooking.

Yssobel crept back to the strange entrance to the Sylvan Fortress and went inside. The courtyard was ablaze with fires and crowded with what seemed to be the nobles and leaders, low kings and champions; all of this she assumed from the array of banners and decorative shields that had been erected on poles, or hung from windows. There was light inside the hall, and in the towers. Horses were tethered at one end. Five tents of different style had been put up.

When she went to return to her huddling place she found Odysseus standing behind her. 'Tie back your hair. You're very conspicuous,' he said. 'Then come and join us. They're intrigued by you, but you're not in danger from them.'

She did as he'd suggested and then followed him to the group, which didn't rise to welcome her. But all nodded greeting. She sat down next to her friend.

'Who are they?'

'Athenians. The dialect is difficult, but I believe that's what they are. They are all brothers and cousins, the survivors of a family defeated in battle somewhere in the north of the land. Though there is something about them that suggests they are not survivors at all. The army was heading towards a summoning, moving up through Time to break siege-works surrounding a great hill, when they were suddenly drawn round to return the way they'd come, still rising through the centuries.'

'How do they know? How can they tell?'

He spoke to them, and the oldest of them replied. His speech was an echo of that of Odysseus, but thicker. Odysseus was clearly having difficulty understanding, but he said, 'To rise is to feel age; to sink is to feel a touch of youth. They have been back as far as a time when there were no metal weapons and sometimes so far forward that the world they glimpsed in passing was incomprehensible to them.' He turned to Yssobel. 'The army has been led by different men; they contest the leadership. In the time these Athenians have been with Legion, the leader was first a man called Culloch – something like that. But a close compatriot of Culloch's, who had been a great friend before leaving Legion, returned suddenly and killed him, taking over.'

'And that man's name?'

'The dialect is difficult. But there is no mistaking the name "Christian".'

Odysseus was watching Yssobel, his eyes full of concern; he could have such a narrow gaze, a hard look, but now he was watching his friend, gauging her reaction to a truth that she had already suspected. The Athenian was still talking, his companions, propped on their elbows, watching Yssobel.

236

'He says Christian is a violent and unpredictable man. He is hated. But he comes from outside the army. He says that there is something more foreign than the stars about him. He breathes different air. He knows the future.'

Odysseus's hand was on hers, his gentle gaze intense. 'Are you certain of what you're doing? Are you sure you want to find this man?'

Yssobel felt a shiver pass through her body. What was it her father used to say? As if a ghost had just walked over her grave.

'I was impelled to find this place to find my mother. To find Gwin. But I know that I also came here to find my uncle. I'm not sure at all who is calling to whom. All I know is that when I saw him in the shield he was frightened. He could sense me watching him, and he was uneasy at being spied on by a ghost.'

'You told me,' Odysseus reminded her, 'that you'd also seen him brutally murder one of his commanders.'

Yssobel was silent for a long while, though when Odysseus made to remove his hand she reached to keep it clasped over hers. 'Ask them if they know where in this chaos he keeps his own camp.'

The reply was that Christian always moved at the head of the army, his men spread out to either side of him, riding slowly. But as it approached the time when they would rest, he withdrew to the centre and formed his palisade.

Two more Athenians suddenly appeared, carrying supply sacks and a roll of furs. They were curious about Yssobel as they placed their tarnished helmets alongside the others and lay down on the inside of their shields. They had been to the baggage train to fetch supplies and bedding for the next few days. Words were exchanged among the Greeks, and agreement was reached.

Odysseus made a sign of thanks.

'We've been invited to eat with them. Dried goat's liver, and guts stuffed with olives, almonds and cheese.'

Yssobel hadn't realised how hungry she was and raised an appreciative hand.

Quite suddenly, as if on command, the forest army was silent. Everyone was at rest. Odysseus too had curled up some way from the fire and closed his eyes. Woodland shapes emerged now, walking quietly between the sleeping forms. A hand touched Yssobel's shoulder and she turned to meet the wide-eyed gaze of the female dryad from earlier.

'Your thoughts are disturbed,' the dryad said sympathetically. 'You are anxious. Part of you has the scent of blood. There is also the scent of sap from a wound. Your uncertainty entangles with ours. Do you need help?'

Yssobel embraced the night air. Smoke-tainted, the breeze was chilly. She submerged the red in her, the echo, the fragment that remained, and let the whole of her mind and body become part of the forest.

The wood nymph led her to a young oak, its branches strong, only one of them lightning-struck. 'I guard this tree. It's what we do. My tree is yours while you search. You still have time to escape to the stone hills.'

'I abandoned my life to find this place. How could I run from it to save the life I've abandoned? Besides, why are the stone hills any safer? This army consumes everything in its path, from the underworld to the mountain. That much I've learned.'

Disappearing into night shadow, the female had slipped away as Yssobel's words reflected back the dryad's suggestion. Now Yssobel leaned against the oak, closing her eyes. Her skin hardened, her head was drawn back, and slim, thorny fingers touched and nicked her skin, drawing her deeper into the sapwood.

She entered a noisy and confusing world of overlapping memory, and life and dreams.

She could hear the distant sounds of voices, and some of them called her name. Was that Jack? Was that her mother? Nothing was clear. The earth moaned, the network of roots below her raged with movement, sparked like fire where they touched. The hollow dreams of this ghost army were a raging argument between fear and pleasure, anticipation of adventure, and loss of that which had once been loved.

So many dreams, so many languages, so many fleeting images of youthful summers and the hard graft on the land, and the hard push of war.

Legion itself was a living being. It became aware of her, an outsider, a parasite that had crawled below its skin. She was being watched, studied, there was a presence around her that was curious, although it was not threatening. It probed and assessed. There was no definable shape to it, no elemental presence, just the looking and listening, as if Yssobel were being explored by fingers that did not touch her, an animal cautiously sniffing and watching, without blinking, to see what this strange arrival from outside its skin might have been.

After a while the curiosity waned; she entered Legion's dream, if only for a moment, and at the periphery. In the blink of an eye, she was on a vast plain, among other armies, facing the glittering shields on a far hill. Horse-drawn chariots twisted and turned on the bone-dry earth as the moment of attack approached. The air was stifling, hot. The shield hill flashed brilliantly. When the attack began, in a furious charge of horse and chariot, there was sudden screaming as men and horses plunged into a great chasm, a rift between the armies that had been concealed by the play of light from the hill.

Legion, called to support, did not suffer the same fate, but plunged to safety, its mission failed.

Yssobel was treated to glimpses of other actions, some in wastelands of snow, some against dark hills, high-walled and alive with fire, some on open plains where banners blew in strong winds and the sudden attack was desperate and savage, and on a scale she could not comprehend. She had seen Arthur torn down by a spear stroke, but the armies there had been small compared to these vast gatherings of war.

The memory of Legion retreated as quickly as it had come. Yssobel was inside its boundaries. She had been accepted. Perhaps it now expected her to become a part of its fighting force. Time would tell.

The oak held her tightly. Her limbs had spread through the earth. She probed and sought, and still she heard the distant sound of familiar voices. They whispered to her through the whirling pool of Time and recollection that was Legion, the anguished voice of a multitude of the dead.

A little touch of the red side in her murmured: focus on one voice. Find Guiwenneth.

Yssobel in the Green thought strongly of her mother, brought her image to mind, remembered laughter and anger, engaged her in her mind's eye with that fierce yet gentle gaze. Inevitably, it was a confrontation that presented itself. The two women were standing in the snow, arms crossed, facing each other, arguing about Christian. The argument was loud and intense, but to recall it, and to recall that emotionally charged moment, seemed to open a path through the forest network, and Yssobel in a huddle in her oak-haven saw her mother sitting cross-legged by a fire and watching her, from somewhere in the heart of this beast.

There was nothing forlorn about Guiwenneth. Her hair was tied back in a leather band, and her face was patterned in blue and green, though this might have been paint rather than tattoo. She was protected by scaled armour from throat to breast, a dull sheen that could be seen through the dark bearskin wrap that was drawn around her shoulders. Her eyes were hard. There was no love in them.

'So you followed me after all. And you expect me to greet you. Go away, Yssi. Your mother is not quite dead. But before dying she has a task, as well you know. You will not interfere with it.'

'It's too late to tell me that. Where are you in this heaving mass of war? Where are you hiding?'

Guiwenneth laughed, but without humour. 'I'm not hiding, just lost inside it. As with any battleground, finding your way through chaos is a hard challenge. Yssi, go home, if you can. Do not confront Christian. Oh yes, he's here. Avoid him! And do not try to find me.'

'I don't know how to go home,' Yssobel whispered through the earth, green embracing green.

'Then how do you expect to take me home with you? I don't even know how you arrived here. There must be an ingenious spirit in you.'

'Inspired,' Yssobel said. 'From a dream. And with help from a man who is not very well pleased with me.'

'Odysseus?'

'No. Someone else.'

Across the distance, in this still, moonless night, Guiwenneth was silent for a while. Then Yssobel heard her say, 'You think you've come for your mother, to rescue her from her folly. But the truth is you're here because Christian has called you. He might even be watching you now. You have put yourself in jeopardy, Yssi. It only makes my anger strengthen. Be careful. Be watchful.'

Odysseus's very words, reshaped by her mother. The red in Yssobel vibrated for a moment, a pulse of anguish. But the green was stronger. She could slip and slide among the sylvan shadows. But there was doubt again, and she could not deny that uncertainty. She wished to heal the wound with Guiwenneth. But she was profoundly intrigued to meet the man who was her mother's *life-bane*. The sad and sorrowful man of whom she'd dreamed throughout her childhood; or the murdering commander, lost in his own insecurity and desolation. She had come too far to turn back now.

Where was Jack?

Yssobel reached through the network, scouring the night-woods, summoning him to sight and mind, but though she imagined she could hear him, and the grim chatter of the boy who came with him, he was elusive here. She had created the outskirts of Avilion, a world of visions and reflections from her own imagination, and constructed simple links with the strongest elements in her life; but Legion was not hers, and it was a barrier to the network outside its confines.

She began to emerge from the dryad's home as, in this deep part of the night, the forest was beginning to stir again and torches were being lit. She was cold. Turning to look at where the Athenians were sleeping, Yssobel could see Odysseus sitting up and watching her, although after a moment he stood and relieved himself away from the fire. Everywhere the silence of the night was breaking into the murmur of a new activity.

The slender dryad, the beautiful nymph, slipped back to her tree, smiling, shivering. 'Was it a help to you?'

'Thank you. But I don't know. I spoke to my mother, but it was not a good exchange.'

'Our feeling is that this intrusion of men and fury will soon be moving on. The destruction was less than we'd feared. Will you stay? There are many havens here, and you are half like us, and vigorous. We like your spirit.'

'Thank you. I have no idea where I'm going at the moment. Though I spoke with someone I love. Thanks to you.'

'Good, good,' the lovely dryad said, and touched gentle fingers to Yssobel's dew-damp face. 'Something, then. Something achieved. Please stay.'

But before Yssobel could answer, before she could respond to this strange, almost desperate invitation, a man was standing before her, though not physically, just in her mind's vision. It was Arthur. His face was masked in iron. His eyes gleamed with anger. He was very calm. His words were distant, blunted, but there was something of nemesis in them.

'You stole my death. I will have it back.'

Then the flash of vision had gone.

Shaken by the suddenness of it, Yssobel stepped back into Legion and found her Greek companion.

Peredur and Christian

When he felt he could trust those around him, when he felt safe among his guard and his commanders, Christian would erect a small protective palisade at the heart of the army, and with his aides and advisers he would discuss the visions and the calls that would come to them. He called it 'scrying', but the youthful woman and blind, ageless man who murmured the calls from out of Time and from across the land called it 'gathering'.

They gathered the screams of need and anguish, and the army responded. They were mercenaries who fought for no monetary pay. Their pay was the extension of their warlike lives after death. There was a hunger in Legion, and it was ill-disposed to beauty.

That had been then. Recently, everything had changed. Christian no longer felt safe; there was a vulnerability in him which came from his instinctive awareness of the way his men looked at him. He no longer erected the palisade wall but camped in the open below a roof of stitched skins to protect against inclement weather, a crude shelter from which he could see the army around him.

He often woke with his mind a turmoil of dreams, lucid and vivid and terrifying, not in the sense that they were nightmares, just that they recalled a time in his earthly life when he had been deeply happy. He and his brother Steven had been close, friends in exploration, protective of each other in the local school, and later where they boarded, in one of the big towns far from Ryhope Wood. The war in Europe had intervened and life had changed for ever.

Guiwenneth, the mythago of a Celtic princess, had arrived at the edge of Ryhope, and the scene was set for terrible confrontation.

Even then, Christian had been confident. But some part of him, some part of his heart, his head, had twisted. Lost, then forming his small band as he explored the realm of Ryhope, he remembered the long journeys along the tracks and trails of the forest, the way a simple oak could catch and turn his small band of hawks. He had loved his hawks. Fighters from a time of stone and bronze, they were athletic, lithe, fierce, never removing their hawk masks, eating and drinking through the thin slits in the beaks. They burned the woods when they attacked, running through the flames. They had been faithful and they had been all the assistance needed to find Guiwenneth, those many years ago, in an age which might have been future or past, he had no way of knowing.

The hawks were gone; all his early companions were gone, long before he joined Legion. Now, overweight and suspicious, he was not regarded well by the brash, youthful men who rode beside him.

Three of them had served the previous leader of Legion, the hero Kylhuk. When Christian had found Legion, he challenged Kylhuk, who had come to regard him as a friend.

Kylhuk had departed the death world by what was regarded by many as 'the cheating blow' from Christian – a strike made when the opponent had signalled for a moment's truce. That Christian had not been challenged himself was because Kylhuk had not fought fairly either.

That had been then.

Christian's act of spontaneous cruelty earlier, when he had been questioned by the more arrogant of his commanders, had resulted in a silence that he found difficult to deal with. The man he had stabbed would no longer meet his gaze. The wound was healing, but he was in pain, and he brooded quietly as he sat among the others. It had been a mistake. Christian knew that they felt their leader was out of control; but that ghost! That echo of Guiwenneth. He had been so shocked by the apparition that he had become blind to reason for a while.

Lost in thought, he did not notice the younger of his

commanders walking towards him, stooping under the canopy and crouching down. The man took off his sword belt and placed it, hilt away from his hand. This was Peredur.

'I haven't been with you long,' the young rider said. 'Long enough to know that something very deep is troubling you, though.'

Christian met the steady, icy gaze. Peredur was clean-shaven, his hair hanging to his shoulders, simply combed, two slender golden clasps tying a single lock on each side of his face. Like his decoration, his armour was simple too, just leather stitched with ivory tusks, and striped flannel trousers with a leather kirtle. Christian judged his age at no more than twenty-five.

Words from his school days came back to him, a memory of a play. 'The head lies uneasy.'

'Very clear to see. That was an unfortunate blow you inflicted on Maelin. If you had killed him, matters would be worse.'

'I will make amends to Maelin. Perhaps you will be able to advise me, since they no longer communicate with me.'

Peredur bowed his head. 'If I can, I will.'

Christian regarded Peredur coolly. It was the man's calm, his certainty that was disturbing. He wasn't used to it. Christian was conscious that he trusted no one now; perhaps he would always find a reason for mistrust. There was madness in the thinking. He asked, 'How long had you ridden with Legion before you came to me to offer your services?'

'Not long.'

'Where were you recruited? What battle?'

'It was not a battle. I was shot by an arrow while trying to save my daughter from being stolen from her mother's arms. All the memory of it happened in a dream. How I came to be here, I don't know. I was alive. I took on the form of an eagle to save my child. I almost succeeded, then the arrow struck and I was at unwelcome liberty and in the world of the dead.'

'You took on the form of an eagle? You can shape-shift?'

Peredur smiled but shook his head. 'It was a briefly received gift. The gift did not last. I had to pay a high price for it. Well, as you see! The price was my life.'

'And we collected you recently.'

'I remember your passing. That great, dense cohort of men at the head, and the backwards-walking army that guards the rear. I simply entered the body of the beast and rode.'

There was a brief pause in this soft conversation. Peredur asked suddenly, 'Who is the ghost you talk about when you're half asleep?'

Christian was startled by the question. 'I talk about a ghost?'

'Yes. A ghost that terrifies you.'

'I use those words?'

'You do,' Peredur agreed, and whispered, 'It's hard to stop a dreaming man speaking, but these words do not sound good to the hearing of the men, your personal guard, who might want to challenge you.'

'I agree. You don't have to tell me.'

After a moment, Christian decided to open his heart a little to this confident young man. He said, 'The ghost is no more than that. She is someone I once knew. Do you never have bad dreams?'

Peredur laughed. 'Oh yes.'

'And what do they consist of?'

'I told you: losing my infant daughter to a Roman. Legion is full of Romans, and I avoid them. Losing my daughter, yes. I was carrying her and I dropped her as the arrow struck; but a kindly goddess was watching over me and my friends caught the child.'

'What was her name? The child.'

'My lord: I hold that child in my heart. I will hold her name there too. Forgive me.'

Christian raised a hand: nothing to forgive.

'Peredur,' he said, thinking hard. 'I turned this army round because I saw a woman I once . . . loved. She was alive again. And yet – this is difficult to explain – she was not the woman I had known. The same, but different. When I first met her, under strange circumstances, I was drawn to her at once, attracted to her very powerfully; though in the end I was denied her, which was heartbreaking. But now I'm drawn again. Can you understand this? I feel she is close again. I turned Legion round. Yes, yes, yes! For my own ends. But when I find her, we will return to the task. How do I convince this vast army to follow me on such a personal quest?'

246

Peredur laughed and stroked the bristles on his chin. 'Well, I'm not sure that you can. Therefore perhaps it would be better to say nothing. Is she here, then? This woman. Where are we?'

'Lavondyss. Avilion. Call it what you like. When we crossed the void, we entered a different world.'

Peredur nodded sagely, still half smiling. 'I think we'd all realised that. Let me ask again: is she here? This woman? This ghost?'

'She has copper-coloured hair, eyes as green as oak leaves in spring, a pale complexion, and a smile and a laugh to take your breath away. And yes: I believe she is here. Quite how, I don't know. But she is close. Peredur, find her for me. I need to be rid of the ghost.'

'She sounds beautiful.'

Christian turned away, staring into the past. 'She was.'

And the young rider asked, 'If you find her, will she know you?'

With a wry laugh, Christian answered, 'I imagine she will remember me. Yes.'

A while later, one of the young 'gatherers' walked slowly towards the awning, and the grouped men who commanded Legion. She was almost ephemeral. Peredur had slipped away, and though Christian was puzzled by his absence he put it down to the young man's agreement to look for Guiwenneth, though he would not have known the name.

The gatherer was dressed simply in green and black, the lower half of her face covered with a veil. Christian didn't recognise her. There were hundreds of such entities in Legion. Scourers, recruiters, gatherers, alert to the loss of life and the importance of bringing in the best of any broken forces to be a part of the army.

'Those who called to us for help are now dead,' she said simply. 'They called many times. The siege was fierce. The walls were broken and the besieging army took the town, and took all life that had not at that time taken itself, all but the women, who are now without family or home and are in chains. The last call was a dirge of despair. They had seen us, summoned us, put hope in us, and too late realised that we had abandoned them.

You should know this. You turned Legion around. I hope there was purpose in the action.'

'Thank you.'

The woman's eyes were angry, perhaps because of Christian's dismissive words, his lack of explanation. Her gaze was unblinking. 'There is another call. It is from Time future. When you are ready, my father and I will describe it to you.'

She turned without bowing and walked away, a stiff and angry creature, betrayed in her talent by the man who led her.

The three men who crouched with Christian stared at the ground, hardly breathing. The hilts of their swords were pointed towards him. He wished the young rider was here. This would be a difficult time.

Maelin said, 'My lord, I will not consider the consequences of your wound to me if you tell us why we have turned around. Tell us what you have come to find.'

Christian considered the statement, but shook his head. 'I have nothing to say on the matter. In due course, Maelin, we will discuss your grievance in the company of the others. And in due course we will turn round and resume our duty. For the moment, we rest.'

'While you search for a ghost,' said Aelroth bitterly.

Christian rose to his full height and pulled his sword belt round his waist, bringing the sheathed blade to his right hand. Staring down at the man he felt a flush of blood and anger. His skin sharpened and his vision cleared. 'Yes! Yes! While I search for a ghost.'

Aelroth stood and faced the warlord. Hard gaze met hard gaze, uncompromising, challenging; there was no friendship here, no sense of respect.

'And this ghost is? Describe the ghost, and we'll search for her. We'll bring its flimsy carcass to you. Throw it at your feet. Let it become dog feast. Anything for you, my lord. Anything that will help us get to war.'

The others stood, picking up their swords, holding them by the scabbard. Christian decided that he had no choice.

'Her name is Guiwenneth.'

He repeated the description he had given to Peredur. 'I do not wish her harmed if you find her.'

They backed away, each bowing briefly and without sincerity. Christian summoned his personal guard, watching through the thin rank of men as the warlords on whose support he counted, and which he was losing, talked briefly among themselves, then went away in different directions.

When he thought he was at a safe distance, Peredur stopped and looked back at the guarded but open-walled camp where Christian lay, brooding and angry. He was puzzled. The description of Guiwenneth was not a description of the woman he knew. Then again, Christian might have been remembering the past.

He found his horse and rode the long way across Legion to where he had last seen the woman. His two comrades were there, restless after being abandoned for so long, and they greeted Peredur with sullen smiles. 'You've been gone a long time.'

'I'm a commander. It took some persuasion, but the man at the head of this army is open to persuasion.'

'In what way?'

'He's desperate to feel protected. It would be a simple matter to challenge him, but there is something – I can't define it – something that keeps him in charge of his own life, and of this army. He's an outsider. That probably accounts for it. Guiwenneth? Don't tell me she's abandoned the place.'

One of Peredur's men jerked a thumb over his shoulder. 'There's a lake. The women and children are bathing. Don't try to get past the guard if you value your masculinity.'

'And please cease this charade of not knowing each other's names! We're tired of pretending. It's tiresome, especially for not knowing the reason for it.'

'You're right.'

The lake was beyond a narrow defile. Peredur could hear the laughter of children as they swam and jumped into the fresh water. Four women crouched at the entrance, playing a game of dice and shouting with each throw. As Peredur approached, they looked up, two of them standing and gripping short fish-hook spears. Their eyes narrowed, one of them holding his gaze, the other looking him quickly up and down, assessing him.

'The men bathe later. This is the time for the children and their mothers.'

'You don't pass.'

He smiled and raised placatory hands. 'I'm looking for a friend. Red and white hair, a leather band stuffed with hawk's feathers, bone-scale cuirass, blue tattoos or paint all over her arms. Unmistakable.'

'Who is she to you?'

Peredur wondered what to say, then decided: 'My mother. Guiwenneth.'

'Leave your weapons here. Call to her.'

He walked through the defile. The lake was below a high wall of rock, shaded by overgrowing trees. The water was so churned by the pleasure of the youngsters who travelled with Legion that it might have been the frenzy of a fishing expedition. Peredur saw Guiwenneth and beckoned to her. She was dressed, drawing a wide-toothed comb through her hair. When she saw him she gathered up her belongings and walked towards him; there was irritation in her look.

'I'd thought you'd abandoned me. Do you know how long you've been gone?'

'You look refreshed. I could do with a swim myself.'

She glanced back. 'I hadn't realised there were so many children with this army. And these are just a handful. Here.' She squeezed water from her hair and smoothed his cheeks, smiling impishly. 'The lake is very deep. And cold? It's freezing!'

As they passed the guard, one of the women looked up from the game and said, 'If your son's available, he'll know where to find me.' There was laughter. The young rider bowed. It was not like him to feel flattered. A moment's weakness, manipulated by the guile of his peers.

As they drew away from the lake, Guiwenneth looked up quizzically, not necessarily without amusement. 'My son?'

'A small lie to allow me to find you.'

She shook her head, a half-smile on her lips. 'Strange to say, I do feel an affinity with you. But my son is Jack.'

'It was a lie.'

Guiwenneth was very quiet as they walked through the wood, and through the groups of waiting men at arms. Eventually she said, 'I wonder who you are. I don't know your name. You don't know mine . . . Or do you?'

They had stopped. The older woman, not much shorter than Peredur, engaged his look powerfully. 'You know who I am,' she stated.

'Guiwenneth.'

'I've known it all along. I've known it all along,' she repeated. 'From the moment you surfaced, that strange conversation: the crossing place. Strange poetry from the mouth of a young rider; you were so knowing.'

'I didn't know immediately. Earth voices call. I remember being called to that villa; I had dreamed of the encounter. In this world, we don't follow our dreams – dreams are the path we take.'

'But I am not your mother.'

'No. Far from it.'

'Although, when we met at the wall, I felt as if I knew you. There was something familiar about you.'

'There is a twist in fate here that I can't reconcile. What I can tell you, though, is that I have found your man. Why have I been gone so long? Because your man now trusts me. I am one of his commanders.'

Guiwenneth crossed her arms uneasily, turning away from the young rider. 'You *are* talking about Christian. Aren't you?'

'Of course. You discovered that he leads Legion. I have made myself close to him. He doesn't trust me fully, but he listens to me.'

Guiwenneth stared at Peredur, confused, her heart racing as her suspicions were confirmed. She was suddenly anxious. 'Why have you done this? I thought I could trust you.'

'You can!' he insisted. 'You must. Guiwenneth, what you have in your heart cannot be expressed with vengeance. He's too strong. I know what you intend. But you can't succeed. Not alone.'

'I told you what he did to me.'

'You told it to me. And it breaks my heart to think how very few wonderful years you had when you were found again by your Steven. You've lived a life in the shadows. I'll help you change that. But you can't do it alone.'

251

Guiwenneth watched him carefully for a moment. Then she dropped her gaze, thoughtful, coming to a decision. She laughed quietly. 'Your companions keep trying to call you by name, then biting it back. "Poet" sounds amusing, but that's their way of keeping the secret that I know already.'

She looked up at him quizzically. 'Your name is Peredur, of course. My father's name. And a younger version of him than my daughter once dreamed and painted when she was a child. And you are the same age as my daughter. We have all been drawn together. You are right: there is a twist in fate here.'

'There will be an iron twist in your guts if you try to take on Christian,' Peredur said bluntly, expecting a rebuff. He was surprised when Guiwenneth looked away and almost seemed to agree.

PART·FOUR

Avilion Alive

Fire Dance

'You cannot steal someone's death!'

Odysseus paced around the camp, stepping over the reclining Athenians who watched him with some alarm as he raged in a muted, uncomprehending way. Yssobel watched him silently.

'You can steal someone's life. You can steal their land. Their home. You can steal their wife, their animals, their children. You can even steal their dreams. You cannot steal someone's death. It makes no sense.'

Why was he so angry? 'That is what he said. "You have stolen my death."'

'A flash of vision. A moment's glimpse.' Odysseus shook his head. 'This is your own guilt talking, not this Arthur.'

'It was him. I know it,' Yssobel replied, remembering the way that Arthur had been cut down in battle, and the tranquil, scarred features beneath the facepiece of his helmet.

'You seem very sure.'

'It was him. I'm certain.'

Odysseus sighed, shaking his head again. 'But how can you be certain? Did you see his face when you borrowed his armour?'

'Of course I saw his face. I took his helmet along with his armour. I kissed him for thanks.'

Odysseus frowned at that, arms folded across his chest. He was breathing very deeply.

'You kissed him?'

'Yes! I spent time with him, as he lay dying.'

'Time with him,' he repeated, almost sarcastically. 'It sounds so innocent.'

'It *was* innocent, it was guilt-free. Apart from stealing his death. Are you jealous?' Yssobel's smile mocked him.

Odysseus waved her quiet with a gesture that said everything about his annoyance. 'But a mind in turmoil,' he went on, 'can conjure fear. How can he have spoken to you? Here? No shield, no reflecting wall. Voices don't just come out of nowhere.'

Yssobel replied simply, 'I made this place. Not Legion itself, but the place we're in. Avilion. I dreamed it as a child, from what my father called my "red side". The human side of me. It's all a reflection of my memory of the stories he told. I can summon what I want, what I imagine, though I don't wish to. This is not the true Avilion. This is my dream.'

Odysseus laughed. He crouched down to face Yssobel as she sat, huddled. 'I'm a pragmatic man, Yssobel. I'm learning two things that will help me to live to an old, old age.'

'Lessons, always lessons.' Irritable in her turn. 'Strategy; the man lives for strategy.'

'Yes. I do. And so should you.'

'And what have you learned?'

'That pragmatism is nothing without imagination; and imagination is wasted without pragmatism.'

She stared at him for a long moment, then shook her head. 'What does that mean?'

He shrugged, half smiling. 'Would you create a goat so tall you couldn't milk it, only hang on to its tail? Would you create a horse so huge you couldn't ride it, only hang on to its belly?'

Yssobel was so confused that she almost laughed out loud. 'Are you mad? I have no idea what you're talking about.'

Odysseus took her hand. 'We must try to imagine where in this confusion your mother is hiding; and where it is likely that this Christian has his guarded enclosure. Then we think of the best way to find them both.'

'Strangely, I'd already come to that conclusion.'

There was something else, though. The way he looked, the way he frowned, these were clear signs that he was the same Odysseus she had known in the villa; older, yes, but not a re-creation here. He was the same. How he had come to be here she didn't know, but he remembered her, and had almost certainly recognised her when she had first seen him on the beach, his shield in the water.

'Did you truly not remember me when I came to your palace?'

'It took a while,' he confessed. 'But it came back to me. All those years, Serpent Pass, that warm and cosy cave, your visits; your silly but engaging songs. Your family. And everything else we had. Yes. I remembered you.'

'That warm and cosy cave in Serpent Pass?'

He leaned forward and kissed her gently, eyes gleaming. 'There's a word for it in my language. It implies "the opposite of what is being said". That said: your presence there, under the furs when you were young but old enough to put flesh to flesh, did make it warm.'

With a wan smile, Yssobel replied, 'And a well-remembered warmth. But not to last.'

'I know.'

'I'm tired. I don't know where to begin.'

'Where we begin is here. Well, not exactly *here*. Every one of these bastards has his eye on you.'

Yssobel glanced quickly at the Athenians. 'They look formidable. They look ferocious. But they can look all they want. When they have to fight, eyes will be on the enemy, not on me. We start here, then. And we go – where?'

Before Odysseus could respond to this moment of challenge – a question that Yssobel could see he had not anticipated – from somewhere deeper in Legion came the sound of a stringed instrument. It was tuneless, in the process of being tuned. A drum thumped like the call for the dead, another rattled as if in a mad rage; a woman's voice quavered, wavered, coughed and tried again. Quite soon the murmur of voices and laughter suggested that something was happening: a wedding, perhaps, or a birth, or just pleasure in the peace between missions.

'Let's dance,' said Odysseus. 'Just for a while. Let's dance.'

They went into the forest, darting among the camps, following the sound trail.

All but two of the Athenians followed.

And they found a strange party but an exciting one, with a ring of torches arranged around a central fire, and between the two sets of flame a pirouetting, swirling game of 'come here/get 'away', with bronze-bright discs around the necks and waists of the women, and much clapping of hands and shoulder-shrugging by the men, and a movement of bodies that was hungry and passionate, at the same time suggestive and amusing, a feast of movement in the pause in Legion's ever-onwards tracking through Time and the call to war.

Five musicians pulsed out the rhythm and the string tones, and the drum tones, and the delicately voiced words. Odysseus was in his element, as was Yssobel, and they leapt across the torch ring, turning to face each other, finding an embrace, a lissom shift of limbs that matched the hard, fast movement of the music.

The green side of Yssobel felt rather than understood the words: *Can you hear the music move you? Can you feel alive today?*

And in this sudden vibrancy – the smells of torchwood, of cooking, of spilled wine, of sweat and breath and pure ebullience – she indeed felt suddenly very alive.

'It's hard to love you so much,' she said, 'when nothing will come of it.'

Odysseus held her face in his hands; his gaze was sad but proud. 'It would be hard not to feel love when we've had so much of it.'

'Everything, yet nothing,' she said quietly.

He kissed her, she kissed him back. They held each other closely, almost dropping into a dream, all rhythm gone now, just the holding.

And I will hold on to what I have.

And yet, she knew: *I must let go of what has gone.*

'Everything we had, we had,' Odysseus whispered in the dream. 'Everything we lose we lose. Everything that will come to us will come to us.'

'Everything, yet nothing,' Yssobel replied, drawing in his warmth, breathing his body smell as she rested on him.

He whispered to her: '*Ola ke eapandou.*'

Embracing him in movement as the dance raged between the fires, she asked, 'And that means? What? What does that mean?'

'Everything, It means "everything". Let's not talk about "nothing".'

'Omnia. Everything. That's the Roman. My father insisted we learned a little Latin. As if we weren't surrounded by the manifestations of everything that speaks in strange tongues and lives in strange ways. But Latin-speakers often came by the villa for hospitality. Omnia. Like this music. Like the musicians. Everything together.'

Odysseus held her hard. The drumbeat was ferocity incarnate. The singing, pure and clear, strident and beautiful, a call to love voiced with challenge. He was shaking. Danger was near, and Yssobel sensed that he sensed it.

'All we have we have. Let's be alive for it. Tomorrow, the Grim God alone knows what the wood will expose for us.'

But whatever 'grim god' he was referring to was closer at hand.

A young man was walking towards her. As the dancers got in his way he stopped, but his gaze never left her. As Odysseus danced, moving around the ring, the stranger followed. He wore a short green cloak, pinned at the shoulder, and knee-length trousers, brightly coloured. He was not armed.

His hair was copper-coloured, side-locks tied with long thin gold clips. Though there was hair on his face, it was scarcely more than a day's growth.

Yssobel felt his presence very powerfully. He was elegant and refined, and in the dark and the firelight she was sure that she recognised him. Odysseus soon became aware of her distraction. He drew back, puzzled, glanced around and then seemed disappointed, though perhaps he was suddenly facing a truth that he knew was coming.

The young man came up to her, glanced at the Greek, then bowed to Yssobel. 'I suggest you leave the dance. And quickly.' He spoke quietly and in earnest.

Yssobel was taken aback by the intensity of his command and the narrowness of his gaze, though there was no hostility in that look. 'Who are you?' she asked

'Never mind who I am. Go back to where you are camped. Go now! I'm urging you for your own good. And tie your hair tightly; it catches the flames and looks like a beacon.'

Yssobel started to look around, her whole body responding to the man's sense of urgency. He snapped a finger by his waist. 'Please! Ask your friend to follow you and leave the circle.'

'But I *do* mind who you are,' she whispered. 'Why are you looking for me?'

He was irritated for a moment, or perhaps it was anxiety. 'I didn't know anything about you until you spoke to Guiwenneth—'

'My mother?' she said in surprise.

Again he urged her to be quiet. 'That was when I saw you; but so did he. I've searched for you and found you; he's searching too; go back to your camp and cloak and hood yourself. I'll lead him a dance.'

Confused and quite apprehensive now, Yssobel shook her head, but in agreement. 'I'll go. But who are you, and why protect me?'

'I work for him. Or so he thinks.' He put a finger to his lips and gave her a smile, and a glance that appraised her. She suddenly recognised him.

'Peredur! Peredur was your father! I dreamed of him, and painted him.'

'Whisper, don't shout!' he urged again.

But she was still looking at him. The resemblance between this haunting young man and the image of Peredur that she had dreamed was striking. And he had seen Yssobel talking to her mother, here in the sylvan army, an encounter that had been through the roots of the forest. Had he seen her in the flesh? 'Where's Gwin . . . Guiwenneth? Do you know where she is?'

'Safe. I think,' was his unnerving reply, but before she could question him further, suddenly, like a bird alarmed, he turned away, walking into the night, lowering his head as if to hide himself. Yssobel moved steadily out of the fire ring, Odysseus following behind her. And yet she could not resist a quick glance back.

On the other side of the dance stood a small band of armoured men, shadowy and sinister. They were looking around at the festivities. The one in the centre had eyes that seemed to blaze; and for a moment he saw her, or so she imagined. There was anger and fear in that look, in the time-hardened face.

*

260

That was when I saw you, but so did he.

Caped and hooded, Yssobel sat among the Athenians, most of whom had returned to the camp. Odysseus kept watch over her shoulder. He had alerted their hosts to the possibility of defending Yssobel, and they had merely shrugged.

Yssobel kept thinking that she had not even asked the young warrior's name, though she was certain it would be the same as his father's.

Legion was alive with music and dancing, and the dryads moved restlessly in whatever shadow they could find. The trees writhed with their shapes as they tried to conceal themselves and protect their charges from the wilful, drunken carving of runes and names, or the stripping of bark to feed the fires. But the female suddenly put her light touch on Yssobel's shoulder.

The men around her all rose to a crouch, watching the tree nymph with dark-browed interest. 'My nest is yours if you wish. If you wish to speak to the person you love. I have found a night-place among the roots of the fortress for a while.'

She slipped away towards the high walls; although Yssobel could see her, Yssobel's red side saw only a slender young oak tree, receding in the mind's eye until it became a part of the earth.

Odysseus suddenly leaned forward and whispered, 'Armed men. Coming this way. I count five, and one is clearly searching.'

Yssobel closed in on herself and feigned sleep. The Athenians, already back in relaxed position, talked quietly, while Odysseus poked at the fire. The flames flared slightly as the band of men passed, their longs cloaks swirling. They walked towards the fortress gates; two of the band glanced back to where Yssobel was concealed, but the small camp they had passed was one of thousands, and they saw nothing new.

As soon as they had entered the fortress, Yssobel shrugged back her hood. 'Why would he come here, of all directions? He's aware of me. I'm certain of that.'

Odysseus agreed. 'And yet he can't quite see you.'

There was a brief exchange then between old Greek and new; the Athenians were asking about the cause of the concern. The most grizzled of them glanced at Yssobel, laughed, and made snipping motions with his fingers against his hair. Odysseus clearly agreed.

'That young man at the fire said your hair was like a beacon. Why do you keep it so long, so free?'

It was a moment of truth. Yssobel lay back for a while, staring at the night sky, where the first faint hints of a new dawn were catching and brightening the very tops of the trees. The air was freshening.

'My mother always wanted me to keep it long. She liked to comb it; she liked to braid it. There was such affection when I was younger.'

'She was holding on to something she'd once had herself. And there is nothing wrong with that. But our friend here is right: you shine like a bronze shield in bright sunlight.'

'And I was nearly seen because of it. Ah well; since your friend agrees with you.' Yssobel reached for her knife and passed it to Odysseus. He checked its edge, pulled a rough stone from the fire and honed the blade. He worked quickly, shearing her hair to shoulder-length, gathering the thick locks and passing them to her. As he worked, she watched the gates to the fortress. She had been unnerved twice in the night, and she did not feel ready to meet the man whose group had swept past earlier; the look in his eyes had been frightening.

When Odysseus was done she wept for a moment, then laughed quietly. From her belt she undid the two silver clasps that Jack had fashioned.

By looping the twisted hair through the wider one, then tying it tightly using the smaller, she made a new belt that she could step into and tighten at her waist.

Odysseus grinned as she tried it on. 'Not practical, but very beautiful.'

Yssobel laughed at his words. She was not mocking him. She wanted to ask: '*Are you talking about me? Or my belt?*'

Odysseus did not have tears in his eyes, but there was loss there, loss in his gaze; And there was the sign of loss on his lips, that knowing smile, the small twist of the mouth that says: *This is it; this is the end.*

He knew that she was now thinking of young Peredur.

'Am I beautiful?' Yssobel asked.

'Very.'

'Am I practical?'

Odysseus laughed aloud, shaking his head. 'Are we talking about belts? If so, no. If not, then yes. You will hold hard in difficult times. I've always known this. You came out to Serpent Pass on the hardest of days, those ice-days, bringing me your life and supplies. You never asked me why I was there, what I was doing. You came because that is what you do: you hold hard to what you have; and yet are prepared to share it.'

She stared at him, not quite understanding his words. 'I came to Serpent Pass because I was fond of you, and concerned for you.'

'You loved me, Yssobel, and you knew it wouldn't last. There is an agony – don't deny it – there is an agony in holding on to something that must pass away. I don't know how we know it, but we can see the end of love. And yet the end of love is not the end of fondness. You must pass on. I have murder to commit. Your life is love; mine is the knife, the blade, practicality without beauty.'

Yssobel knelt before him and took his hands in hers. 'How can you be so young and think so darkly? Maybe things will change.'

'It is for the simple reason that I *am* so young that I can think so darkly. When I'm an old man, I can learn from my young mistakes.'

'I'm a mistake?'

'Certainly not! You are the surge of water on the shore; you reach, you drag a small part of me; just as I reach and drag a small part of you. We are just the flow of tide. For me? Murder and a life I hardly know, though I have seen its reflection. Penelope. And how beautiful she is. What love we shall have. How practical she will be as she waits for my return from murder. I know her. We were children together. Our parents were neighbours. The sand shore of our home island is imprinted with our childlike traces. The footprints of innocence, Yssobel. Our life will be long and beautiful, though only after difficulty. It's very hard to live with the certainty that your dream will come true. You? That is for you. If you hold on to what you have, you will find that you have more, far more, than you are holding. That is practicality! That is strategy.'

Yssobel reached for Odysseus's face, kissed his mouth, whispered, 'May a woman ask a man to take her to a quiet place and say goodbye with gentleness, warmth?'

'She may.'

Later, she sat in the tree and entered the earth.

The Crossing Place: Crow Choice

Bydavere had returned to the battleground. He had approached it cautiously, and on foot, aware of the crying of men's voices and the screech and confrontation of carrion birds. He stripped clothing and armour from a fallen man, and all the time he was attacked by birds; they did not want him there. The field was theirs.

He came back to where Arthur had made a temporary enclosure, in the woods away from the lake, where his dying body had been dragged by what he called 'the kiss that stole my death'.

'They've gone,' Bydavere reported, and Arthur accepted that without expression.

'I wonder who won the day.'

'Not the field of carcasses that are left. There are no gatherers that I could see, no women, no sons; only crows.'

'We fought,' Emereth reflected, 'in a strange place. Morthdred must feel the same, if he has survived.'

Arthur said nothing for a moment, then agreed. 'All of my life had led to that hill, that final skirmish. I don't suppose it matters where it happened. It was meant to be the end, and so it happened in a world of its own. I feel for the good men who rode with me. Where are they now?'

'Scattered. Finding their own paths,' Bydavere said.

This discussion was happening in the early hours of the day, and a new sun was beginning to bring dim light to the horizon across the reed-fringed lake. It was suffused through mist. Arthur stood and stretched, then took Bydavere by the arm, and the two old friends walked to where the water was still and cold against the bank. Crouching, they reached between the reeds and splashed their faces.

'You were talking loudly as you slept,' Bydavere said. 'It disturbed my own sleep, not the others, though we're all restless.'

'You don't know what to do.'

'We'll find our own ways. Half of us are young, only a few of us old and weary.'

Arthur glanced at Bydavere, recognising the mocking tone. 'Weary enough to be unable to avoid that bloody blow. Old enough to know to escape the field. And nothing about you – a man older than me – seems weary; or ageing. You have a good future.'

'I wish I could see it, Arthur,' answered Bydavere wistfully, looking up into the dawn sky. 'Just a hint of it. A torch in the dark, telling me where to ride.'

'The torch will come. Just don't expect it to be a torch. Or in the dark.'

Bydavere laughed. 'A dark-haired, dark-eyed woman on a proud horse, riding from the edge of the woods and beckoning to me. "This way!" she cries. I'd settle for that.'

'You'd follow her?'

'I was not born to follow, as well you know. I was born to be a knight-in-arms, and to assist. I was born to be a friend and a war-friend, and a shield-friend, though always acknowledging his warlord.'

'But you'd follow that dark-haired woman.'

'Faster than I can throw a spear. Why not? Torches burn out.'

'Everything burns out, my friend. But I hope she comes for you.'

The air was fresh; the reed bed stirred with a breeze and a sudden flight of small water birds broke the heavy dawn silence. 'That could have been a meal for all of us,' Bydavere said, shaking his head as he watched the birds descend further out on the lake.

'What was I saying in my sleep? What deep secrets did my lips murmur when I was caught between here and the otherworld?'

'You see her. You see the woman who stole your death. You

266

were raging at her. You kept on and on about the kiss that stole my death.'

'Did the others hear this?'

'I don't know. I don't think so. But there is something else: you were making a sound.' Bydavere looked hard at his friend. 'It was the sound of despair.'

Arthur crouched in silence for a while, letting his fingers play with the muddied water at the lake's fringe. Then he said, 'Thank you for telling me this.'

Bydavere took his knife from its sheath and cut a reed; he cut two sections of the reed and crossed them on the ground.

'We go our own ways, Arthur. I cannot accompany you on your pursuit of death.'

From behind them, Emereth shouted. 'Arthur! The lake! The boatmen are back.'

The lake fog was lifting. The small craft was appearing. The two tall boatmen plunged their poles languorously into the increasingly shallow water. Two huge dark-feathered birds perched on the wide prow, watching the land, the only signs of life in them the occasional lift and flutter of their wings.

As the barge came closer, so these birds rose almost effortlessly into the air, wings wide, catching an updraught that Arthur could not feel. As they rose higher they came into a tumble of an embrace together before plunging into the lake, ahead of the boat.

Arthur had no time to ponder on this strange scene. Behind the boat, land was rising. It loomed large through the dawn fog. It seemed to grow from the lake. It was a wide island, and verdant. The reeds began to shift as the lake was disturbed, ripples becoming waves that began to surge around his feet.

The waves consumed the shore, the lake spreading inland so that suddenly Arthur and Bydavere were hip-deep in water.

The island was not growing; it was approaching. It seemed almost to float on the lake. Soon it was so vast in his vision that Arthur could see the narrow paths between the steep wooded slopes. There was the gleam of marble deep within, the hint of structures, the sharp glance of new light on old walls, deep within the forest.

And it was a forest of yews, evergreen and gleaming, reaching out beyond the island, massive and ancient, splattered with the blood red of their fruits, their apples. The trees reached forward, as if grasping the air in front of them, and as the barge came to a slow halt in the reed bed, so did the island come to a stop, sending a massive wave of water that knocked down all Arthur's men, surged into the tree line and the camp, then withdrew to leave a sodden and muddied bank.

The island towered high, filling the horizon. The boughs of the yews, hundreds in number, looked to Arthur like arms, reaching out to protect him as he craned his neck to see the full extent of this apparition. Silent and strange, it was waiting, floating; watching. And Arthur knew that it had come for him.

The two bargemen had lowered their poles and crouched down in the craft, one on each side of the mast and the furled sail. They became a part of the boat; they might have been carvings in its hull.

Standing on the saturated bank, feet buried in the mud surge, Arthur waited, breathing shallowly; and Bydavere, trusted Bydavere, waited equally calmly.

The reeds were suddenly disturbed. With a double birth cry, the waters were broken and two women surged into the air, rising suddenly and spectacularly, their bodies draped with black cloaks, their hair spraying widely as they shook their heads. One was young and one was older. Waist deep among the reeds, they met each other's gaze and laughed, then turned their look on Arthur.

They walked through the reeds, stepping ashore, the lake draining from them, the brightness in their eyes and smiles extending as their gazes embraced both the men who waited for them.

The younger woman winked at Bydavere who whispered, 'By Brigga! I'm in love. Quite suddenly!'

'Easy,' Arthur warned, and the lake nymphs laughed again.

The older woman, so sure in her gaze, so certain in her posture as she lifted her cloak and squeezed the lake from its fabric, said to Arthur, 'Do we seem lovely to you?'

'Yes. Of course. Yes.'

'And yet you know we are carrion eaters. You saw us as

ravens, now you see us as women. Which are we? How do you see us?'

Arthur thought quickly. 'As ravens, terrifying. As women, beautiful. As woman-ravens, terrifyingly beautiful. I know why you're here.'

'You do?'

'You came for me before. You took the wrong person.'

'Then who are we?'

'Two of the three who will take me to Avilion.'

'And in Avilion?'

Arthur took a deep breath, holding his chest where Morthdred's spear stroke was still hurting but had not yet taken his life. 'I will go to Avilion. The island of Avilion. In Avilion my wounds will be healed.'

'Will they indeed?'

The woman had pulled back her hair, wringing out the water, watching Arthur all the time. There was a hawk's look in her eyes, no beauty now, sharp and bone-drawn. She said, 'I am Narine. This is Uzana. We are two of the three. Where is the third?'

Confused, Arthur thought hard. Bydavere was frowning. Uzana had turned her youthful, mischievous smile to a grim look, and was also appraising Arthur.

Narine repeated the question. 'Where is the third?'

In a dream vision, when he had come of age, and had listened to the words of older men who had been able to see beyond his own world, and had listened to the words of women who had communicated with past and future, Arthur had been told – and had spent his life believing – that on his death three women from the isle of Avilion would come for him, and take him, and heal him. He had never questioned the nature of that healing. He had assumed that he would live again, but beyond the human realm.

As if she could hear his memories, Narine said, 'You have dreamt the dream of kings. You never questioned the consequences of that dream; nor the dilemma of the dream; nor the life that lies beyond the dream.'

There was power in her gaze; it was as hard and sharp as a

sword. But Arthur would have nothing to do with her statement.

'You talk in riddles. I'll have nothing to do with that sort of talk. The consequences of my dream? Only that I'm dead. The life that lies beyond it? The life I find when I get there.'

'What makes you think that you're going there?'

Narine came up to Arthur, took his long hair in her hands and tugged it, pulling his face back, playing with him. Her hands were weapons, manipulating the king. As she twisted him this way and that, her gaze following her movements – Arthur remained calm – she whispered, 'The dilemma?'

'That,' Arthur agreed, 'is what I do not know.'

'The third?' Narine asked.

'Again: I do not know.'

Narine kissed him. Her breath smelled of carrion but he didn't recoil. She kissed him for a second time, her gaze holding his own, and this time her breath had the perfume of flowers.

She said, 'Uzana is the bright road that begins. I am the quiet grove where it ends. Between us is the stealer. The third one always steals, then steals away.'

'I see.'

'Her name is Yssobel,' Uzana murmured, with a frown. 'I liked her.'

Arthur responded at once. 'I've seen her in my waking hours. I see her from the corner of my eye. She has hair the colour of copper, and a face of pale beauty. Is that this Yssobel?'

'She is everything you dreamed at dawn. And she stole your death.'

'I know.'

He released himself from Narine's grip and walked to the lake's edge, looking up at the rise of the island, the green of the forest. He threw off his cloak and stepped among the reeds, wading into the lake until it was deep enough that he could submerge. He held his breath for as long as possible, his hands in the mud. When life called for it, he emerged, gasping for the scented air, shaking the water from his hair.

Arthur returned to the crows, cloaked himself again and crouched to feel the stolen armour. Looking up, he asked Narine, 'What are my choices?'

Although Uzana giggled, Narine looked pained. Behind her, Arthur's companions were standing in a line, armed and nervous, watching events unfold. Narine took her own damp robe and lifted it, brushing at his body, drying him. 'A difficult question. Why did you immerse yourself in the lake?'

'Practice,' he said with scarcely a thought. But there was humour in his eyes. 'At taking the plunge. Which I imagine is what I'm about to do. What are my choices?'

'Same answer. A difficult question.'

'I shall give you my answer in an instant. Give me the options.'

Narine smiled. Grey-green eyes held him hard. 'You can stay here, alive. Why not? Life has been returned to you. You are still a handsome man. You will live a long life, but at the end of it you will not be remembered. You will be a king covered in earth, lost among all the other forgotten kings, bone white below the chalk mound, below the grass, one more shallow shape in the land. If you choose to come with us to Avilion, to walk into the yew forest, to find the third of us – the stealer of death – then you must take back your death by taking her life.'

'And the consequence of that?'

'To be remembered. To be remembered well.'

Arthur glanced at Bydavere. 'Do I go alone? Or may I take a shield-man? This man.'

'Alone, of course,' Narine said.

Without taking his gaze from Bydavere, Arthur said, 'That saddens me. We were born four years apart, but we have fought side by side, we have suffered the same bleak winters, we have each lied to protect the other; we are brothers.'

'Shadows in the mist,' Narine said, and Arthur agreed.

'You have my answer.'

'Which is?'

He looked at Avilion, at the loom of the island. 'To be remembered.'

'A man in every way.' Narine laughed. 'But that is what we are tasked for. We don't just gather the dead, Uzana and I. We gather memory. We gather eternity. You'll need to dress.'

Arthur collected the armour. Without a further look at his men he returned to the lake, flung the metal and leather into the barge and hauled himself onto the deck. The boatmen rose from their sleep. The beautiful crows took their form again and settled on the prow, wings spread to catch the breeze, watching as Avilion was approached, finally flying up and seeking among the narrow paths for Arthur's best route through the tangle of the trees.

As the barge slipped onto the water, Arthur looked back at his brother. Bydavere reached behind his back and drew the sword that he had kept. He raised it high. The sun caught the iron.

'Use it well!' Arthur shouted.

'I have every intention of doing so!' Bydavere called back. 'I will slice through the mist. I will make shadows in your name! Though in another land.'

Field of Tartan

Jack was walking in fear of the Iaelven. He could not understand their click-whistle language, but it was clear they were discussing him, and their options. The boy was subdued. Perhaps the very fact that Won't Tell had ceased to be a nuisance to them had made them question the point of this expedition.

Silver ran ahead of them as they progressed, then hid in the rocks or the woods, darting out to make brief contact as the party moved at a swift pace down the pass, through *imarn uklyss*. The Amurngoth hardly ever paused, and the stench they exuded was sometimes overpowering. They walked as a group, two abreast at the front, two a long way behind them watching the flanks, two behind Jack and Won't Tell, slender spears and bows held ready. And talking all the time. When Silver came back into the ranks they listened to her eagerly, though they never seemed satisfied with what she reported.

They slaughtered as they moved. Muurngoth blood stained their clothes. Muurngoth flesh was threaded on thin branches and the hafts of their weapons, for later use in eating. They had cut thick slices of liver and haunch for Jack and the human boy, but Won't Tell was growing weaker because of his resistance to this frugal, brutal fare.

Now they are standing at the stone, the marker of Peredur. The death stone. He sees the rune snakes, the marks within the pattern, the life within the coil.

Silver reached and touched: 'These are stories,' she said. 'These are a man's life.'

'They are. They are my grandfather's life. And this is where Yssobel found her way to Avilion.'

The Iaelven formed a circle, gazing at the monolith. They too seemed overawed, fascinated. The boy crouched against the face that could be seen from the valley, the edge that looked towards the villa. Silver walked dreamily around the stone, her slender fingers tracing a line through the enigmatic marks that shaped the story of Peredur.

It was night, and she gleamed. She was bright frost in darkness, and yet the air was warm.

The Iaelven chattered. Silver waved a finger: don't worry. 'Nothing of importance,' she whispered.

When the sun came, the shadow came, and the path was shown.

Silver danced in the dawn, a simple movement, arms outstretched, her voice a thin song. Won't Tell laughed as he watched her, but when she dragged him from his sitting position and made him dance he complied. The Iaelven regarded this calmly and without comment. They weren't curious. In their own tradition, dancing was not strange.

Silver came to Jack and whispered, 'I can't go much further. But this is the crossing place. This is hinterland. Do you understand me?'

'The region between regions.'

'I can go so far and no further. But I would like to go a little further. The track is open. The Amurngoth will take you so far and then abandon you. They are afraid of Avilion.'

'They agreed to take me.'

'To get rid of the boy. Without a name he is useless to them.'

'Their time is past.'

'They know it. They don't accept it. But only their time at the edge. There are more lands to explore than you can imagine.'

'And they will steal, of course. They will take life.'

Silver cocked her head as if she were watching a child. 'Jack. Jack. It's what they do. It's Iaelven. It's what they do. Why do you question it?'

'Because I don't understand it.'

'Jack: I don't understand *you*! What did you find at the edge? An answer?'

He looked at her, dazzled by the moon-bright glow of skin and hair and eye and smile. This was a beautiful woman, and she was from a time long past. 'I saw a strange world.'

'You didn't understand it.'

'I saw life, reflection of life. I saw stone and loss, anger and gentleness; I found hospitality.'

'Did you find Caylen Reeve?'

The question startled Jack. Silver's look was cunning, searching. 'Well, did you?'

'Yes. I met him. How do you know of him?'

'Because I know of him.' She turned away, then danced again around the monolith. 'I can't see how he looks, your Peredur! But he lived well, and lives well now.'

The sun had shown the way. The Amurngoth were restless. Won't Tell had eaten and was looking gloomy. He was very smelly. They needed water: a lake. The tallest of the Iaelven was waiting where the stone's shadow cut its path into the trees. Whatever the chatter sound it emitted, it was clear that they were now ready to move on.

Silver came with them as far as the lake. She disappeared like mist once they'd arrived there, though not before a whispered word to Jack. 'Courage.'

Before that they had passed the field of tartan.

How Jack knew it was hard to say, but he knew that Yssobel had passed this way before. It wasn't her scent, or message, or any trace of her: just knowing. And in knowing, he came close to her; and in coming close to her he could feel her anguish.

There had been a battle somewhere here, a dreadful force of arms. There was no blood smell, but the trees were silent with the watching crows.

The track was old. Silver whispered: 'I smell water.'

It was Won't Tell who came scampering down a high bank, cut with briar and bruised, eyes wide. 'Skeletons!' he cried. 'Hundreds of skeletons.'

The Iaelven led the way, pushing back the underbrush as they climbed, until they all emerged onto the low hill.

This battle had occurred a long time ago.

Banners of all colours had become entangled with the dead.

Bone white, the fallen revelled and remained in tartan. The wind made a restless performance of the tattered cloth. A spirit dance, woven in the breeze. Colour and movement in a field of silence.

The Iaelven gathered trophies, mainly skulls. Silver stood in the shadows, arms crossed, mournful. Jack circled the hill before walking to its centre, gathering the strips of kilt and shirt and banner, tucking them into his belt. Yssobel's presence was everywhere, as if she were watching even now. She had seen this field. She had been shocked by it.

Sitting down among the bones, Jack rammed fingers into the earth. One of the Amurngoth noticed this and came towards him, breathing raggedly, curious, holding its trophies in the crook of its arm, but perplexed at Jack's forlorn expression. The creature crouched and click-whistled.

'If I knew what you were saying, I'd answer you. I think – I'm certain – that this is where a king met his end. Do you smell the lake?'

Click-whistle.

'The lake is where he crossed to Avilion. My father told me the story. Three black-robed queens in a beautiful barge. He went to the place where he would be healed.'

Click-whistle. The cat's eyes narrowed, the grim mouth pursed. The Amurngoth rose and departed.

Jack watched it go. It walked to Silver and spoke briefly.

She beckoned to him after a while. She would not leave the thin shelter of the brushwood that circled the hill.

'I will have to leave you at the water's edge,' she said. 'This is an old place. The Amurngoth will have to go under, but there is something about this valley that they don't understand. They are prepared to take you under, but they are walking beyond their limits. They have asked me to ask you: if they have to abandon you, will you keep the boy? They have made a promise that nothing will be done to harm him, not now, nor if they go to the edge again.'

Jack agreed. 'How do I get back to the edge?'

'The one you spoke to, the old Iaelven . . .' Silver used her eyes to signal the creature she referred to, the mournful Amurngoth who stood among the bone ruins. 'He will take you back. If you can find him again. He will be in the hill.'

'Is he dying?'

'Dying? He's already dead. They all have time after death to create a time to be remembered. A story, if you like, in human language. He was the Iaelven who found you at the old house. At the edge. He would like to be remembered for that journey. It was his own *change* that was left behind. He would like him back.'

Jack stayed silent. He risked a glance at the ageing creature. Was it possible to feel sadness and sympathy for such a being? He could still smell the sour stink of whatever it was that had flowed in the Change's veins as Caylen Reeve had struck it in two.

What should he say?

Silver was touching his chin, her finger's stroke as light as a breeze. 'I'll come with you when you go. I would like to see my land again.'

'That land has changed.'

'To you, perhaps. But nothing changes. Not if you know how to see it.'

'And you wish to see Caylen Reeve.' It was a rude and testing assumption, and Jack immediately regretted his words.

There was the smallest of smiles on Silver's lips, the quickest glance that said she knew that Jack knew.

'Yes. How clever you are.'

She was suddenly alarmed. One of the younger Amurngoth had appeared from the path. Its long, sinewy grip was painful as it grasped Jack's shoulder. Click-whistle as it shook lake water from its hair. The stink was abominable. It looked at Silver as it spoke.

'We have to go,' she said. 'There is something you must see.'

The Iaelven gathered up their bones, threading ivy through the sockets, slinging them over their backs. Jack took Won't Tell's hand. Silver came behind. They walked the long track to where the lake was quiet and calm. There was no horizon, but the wood that bordered the sloping bank was a dense stand of yew trees, branches high, trunks thick, a grove so tightly packed that it seemed and looked as unnatural as it was.

Other sparkles of steel gleamed and glinted from the rough wood as Silver weaved her way between them.

Masks in the form of helmets; and in the helmets, sleeping faces.

Silver played a child's game, appearing and then disappearing as she darted between the trees. The Iaelven were not amused. They crouched, all eight of them, watching her antics. Two seemed more intent on the lake. Won't Tell stood in front of one of the helmeted faces.

'They're dead. Not sleeping. They're dead.'

Silver heard the boy's words and came running to Jack. 'There has been a change here. He's right. These are dead. But something, someone . . . I don't know . . . I can only feel it. Someone has been taken. A death has been stolen for a life.'

And after a moment all joy had gone from the pale features of her face. She was so old and yet so young, and she was shivering as the light grew dim. The Iaelven had drunk from the lake, washed their lank hair, and now seemed concerned.

'I have to go,' Silver whispered. 'This is where it ends. The old one will come with you, back to the field. He needs Avilion. He can speak in our own tongue as well; don't be fooled by him.'

Jack was startled by this quick elfin chatter from the woman. 'The field? Back to the field?'

'Go back. Go back! It's the way to cross.'

The younger Amurngoth had begun to depart along the road. They seemed to have no time even to acknowledge Jack. Silver walked behind them, constantly glancing over her shoulder and beckoning.

Jack and Won't Tell followed at a distance. The boy, for some reason, seemed excited. His walk had become a jig and he looked up at the sky and smiled. When Jack quietly questioned him, all Won't Tell said was: 'We're on our way.'

Both were sad to see Silver disappear into the dusk, back along the road that had led from Peredur's stone. But they walked back into the forlorn field, disturbing the last of the scavengers, those bone-eaters desperate enough to try and find a feast within the armour. They croaked and screeched and settled in the trees. Jack walked through the wind-flow of colour, the rags of the fallen.

Won't Tell was nervous despite his new-found excitement. 'This was a great battle.'

'An important one,' Jack said. 'I wish I knew more. This is where a king died and was taken to a place of resurrection.'

'Arthur?'

Jack was surprised. 'Yes. Arthur. What do you know about Arthur?'

Won't Tell stared at him as if looking at an idiot. 'Everybody knows about Arthur,' he said. 'Everybody.'

For a moment Jack was torn between concern that his bodyguard had gone and his realisation that he had spent too long in the woods.

The elder Amurngoth was already kicking its way among the bones.

'I have been too long away from the edge. I do not know what is known,' Jack said.

Won't Tell took his hand and held it tightly. 'But you got there, Jack. You're a wood haunter. You can go anywhere. You don't have to know things, just do things. You will take me home, won't you?'

'I will take you home. I promise. Just don't tell anyone your name.'

'Not even you?'

'Not even me.'

Click and whistle sounded from the field. The Iaelven elder was beckoning. Jack hastened towards him, aware that the whole hill was moving.

The creature motioned him down and Jack dropped to a crouch, the boy beside him. The wind was strong now and there was a howl to it that suggested the cries of the dead. The tartan strips were alive with movement. A deeper movement was surfacing.

As they crouched among the dead, so the hill began to grow into a forest. It sprang through the earth, a writhing of life that encompassed and gorged upon the bones, drawing them in, white matter and the terrible beauty of tartan drawn into the dark of bark, shattered fragments gleaming in the spreading leaves of the branches; this was a yew forest, and it emerged out of old time, and each thick gnarled trunk was shaped and carved and battered by the lives and deaths that had happened within its bounds.

Resurrected, Avilion came to claim Jack and Won't Tell. The Amurngoth screamed as he was absorbed into one of the giant trees, but his last glance was one of peace and pleasure.

Avilion did not choose between those it took. This Iaelven, whatever he had done in his long life, had done enough to deserve the island.

As Jack and Won't Tell huddled together, a grove formed around them, thick enough to contain them as prisoners. The banners and strips of clothing hung from the branches, draped across shields and broken weapons. But it was not a place that Jack felt was threatening.

There was no sense of movement, just the rich growth and a warm stillness. Then the boy whispered, 'Someone's approaching.'

There was a rustle of the undergrowth, a muttered curse, and a man in light, tarnished, weed-racked armour stepped into the grove, facing Jack. His hair and beard were wet, as were his boots. His strange eagle-face helmet had been pushed back on his head. Jack saw the design of the raptor as the man bent to cough up water before sitting down slowly, leaning back among the roots.

When he had recovered from whatever ordeal he had just experienced, he pointed down to the ground. 'Avilion,' he grunted. Then his hand waved about the grove. 'Avilion.'

He said something else, closing his two palms almost together. A small part of Avilion.

Because of the boy, Jack's human aspect had surfaced, protectively and anxiously. He let Haunter back, and the mythago side of him seemed to wake and yawn. It looked around and was impressed.

This is the place that Yssobel dreamed about. Does it feel strange that we sought the edge of the world and have ended up in one small part of its heart?

Yes. But the edge was not my home, no more than Avilion is my home. The villa is my home. The icy wind from Serpent Pass; and the strange winds from the valley that brought Guiwenneth back, all those years ago.

We will not be settling again at the villa. Not for a long time yet. Nor Yssobel.

I know. Not for a long time.

We're moving. There is a shift occurring. And Yssobel is close. She is very close.

Do you have any feeling or sense about the man sitting so close to us and looking so mournful?

Only that the armour is not his. And that he is not dead and crossing to his otherworld. He's red like you.

Jack stared at the silent man. This was not Christian, but there was a great deal of similarity to Yssobel's painting of their grandfather. The man was of much the same age, and looked weary and wounded.

But Huxley had written: *and she stole the armour of a king . . .*

Jack was about to whisper his other thought to the boy, but Won't Tell was asleep, curled up like a cat.

The Riot of Her Blood

Yssobel had hoped to find her mother as she embraced the dryad tree, to find the woman with whom she had shared love and anger, and yet the earth was both friend and enemy and she was drawn deeply down.

She felt herself extended by finger and toe, and sight and sound, and by the riot of her blood as both red and green conflicted within her.

She flowed through the dank, drear earth and was life-charged by the vibrancy of the underworld. She could hear the sound of the dead who had been long consumed there, and the sounds of those in the act of fighting and dying and soon to be bloodied in the field of clay.

And all of this because she was mostly sap-green. Jack was there fleetingly, travelling with Haunter, and her mother was there fleetingly, by a lake; and the fierce man whose purloined death she now owned was watching her.

Another man watched her although he stared at her in fear from the tower in the stone castle that rose above the wood and all of which was a part of her—

(—and reflected her childish dream and was entwined with that which was not a part of her because—)

Legion and its ghosts had existed for an age or more and moved through times and spaces that she was able to sense distantly, as sharply as a wolf senses snow, as she toured the earth mass below her, with her blood-body in the tree and the sap in her mind in the deep flow. Legion was entwined with her.

And she was screaming and searching for her mother, but

finding only the confusion of her own mind and memory, and the terrible acts of Legion that it had performed in its eternal age, and the sense of Avilion *alive* and rising and coming towards her, with yew grove and oak grove and orchards, and a great heart at its centre which was beating out a rhythm of hope and restoration.

Avilion: rising towards her and bringing with it the desperate man whose life she had denied by stealing his death.

A very angry man, she was aware.

Avilion, however, was without concern as it came to claim back the small part of Yssobel's childish vision that had *mis-created* this land of silence, and the silent sound of long-lost music, and the music of silence and the peace that comes with life in new colours; and the reflection and the yew groves and the ash groves and the high cliffs with their green cover and their small pathways, and the crossing places; and she felt all of this—

Felt it in her heart her head her belly her sap, the flow of memory, the reflection of herself as a child.

Painted wonder, painted fantasy. The memory of wonder . . .

Avilion Alive is curious about her. She has stolen its dream. It has come to take it back.

Yssobel became aware that Odysseus and several of the Athenians had formed a ring around her. She was drenched with sweat and incontinence. The tree would not let her go. Its bark had become a lover's embrace and its tendrils wound into her flesh and held her hard. For a moment she was frightened as consciousness returned. But when Odysseus drew his sword and asked, 'Shall I cut you free?' she answered, 'No.'

The group crouched down, a circle guard as she was absorbed again into earth and time.

Though Guiwenneth was close, Christian was closer, and it was to him that Yssobel went in her sylvan dream.

The Riot of His Blood

Two of the towers had shown Christian nothing more than other lands, and he had dismissed them, magnificent and strange though they had appeared to him. In the third he saw her. The ghost.

Peredur and Aelfrith stood behind him. The others waited below. For a moment it seemed as if Christian would plunge through that window to his death, but he gripped the carved stone that surrounded the window, head lowered, gasping for breath, holding on. 'Who is she? Who IS she?' he whispered.

'We have no answer for that,' Aelfrith said coldly. Christian turned on him.

'How many ghosts haunt you? How much of your own night is spent running from your own actions?'

Aelfrith thought hard for a moment, finally answering, replying quietly, 'I lost my son. I lost my life. Two losses in one skirmish. My son did not make the journey to Legion. I did, however. So life, even in death, goes on. My life changed. I haven't the time to deal with ghosts. You, my lord, seem different.'

Christian returned the hard look, but with a smile. 'I envy you, Aelfrith. Your death has indeed bought you a life. I've seen you in action. I would not wish to be your enemy.'

Aelfrith remained silent. Cold.

Christian held his gaze. 'You asked me how many ghosts haunt me. The answer is two. And I can't tell them apart, except that one sometimes seems older. They are two shadows from the same shade. One is like the light at dawn. The other closes in on me like night. One loves me. One will kill me.'

'Which one is which?' Peredur asked diplomatically. 'Can you tell the difference?'

There was desperation in the man's face as he thought about the question. Then he took a deep breath. 'The old one intends to kill me – that would seem the obvious answer. Old enemy. But the young? I'm not sure. I don't know who she is. I cannot reckon with her thinking.'

'May we see through the window?' Aelfrith asked. He was standing at his full height, and though his hair was turning to the colour of new-forged iron he was not intimidated by the strange man who led him. 'I would, my lord, like to see what you have seen.'

'The ghosts?'

Aelfrith shrugged. 'Whatever you have seen. Ghosts or enemies. We follow you. We need to know the task.'

Christian walked up to him, glancing at Peredur. 'You think I'm weak?'

Aelfrith didn't flinch. 'No. I think you're haunted. Your own words, not mine.'

'Am I weak? Peredur?'

'Haunted,' Peredur replied calmly, aware that Christian had not looked at him as he had addressed him. 'We are all haunted.'

'Will you stand by me when the killing time comes? That is all the truthful answer that I need. Will you both stand by me?'

Aelfrith answered without a pause. 'I will always stand by you.'

Christian looked now at young Peredur. 'And you?'

Peredur slipped his sword from its scabbard and let it fall. With a look as cold as the ice-flows of the north he answered: 'I am not the man you think I am. I do not follow. I do not serve. I fight, yes. Sword and shield. But the truth lies there on the stairs. Return the blade or use it.'

For a moment Christian was uncertain. Then he reached down and picked up the weapon by its tip, passing it back to Peredur. 'I don't trust you completely, but I think I know you. You are not natural, not even here. You are, as you rightly say, more than the man I think you are. But what is that, I wonder?'

'I am one of nine eagles,' Peredur answered easily, and with a grim smile. 'I am one of nine stags. I am one of nine men lost in the forest, guarding a child. I am one voice among nine. I am all of the life that went before me. I am nothing in this form but the father of a woman who was stolen from her life twice in her life, but came back. As you are lost, so am I. As you are raw, so am I. Nature has claimed us. The *nature* of that nature differs, but we are of the same family of wanderers.'

'Nature. Yes,' Christian said, with a frown. Peredur's strange declamation had almost startled him. 'I believe you're right. Nothing will prevent you from protecting your own.'

'Nothing will stop you from killing what you fear,' Peredur replied.

'Then should I kill you because I fear you?'

'If you fear me, then kill me. In this life I live to protect. I am a shield man. What sort of man slashes his shield in half when running into battle?'

Christian considered this as Aelfrith fidgeted. 'Perhaps a man who is torn in two?'

Peredur said sharply, 'Perhaps a man torn between two worlds. A man changed. That is what you are, is it not? A changed man? You crossed the edge, inwards, and change happened. You left only a memory behind.'

Christian was silent for a long while. Then he walked past Peredur, back down the steps. His passing whisper was the words, 'Who are *you*, I wonder?'

Peredur stepped up to the window and looked through it. What he saw was the spread of Legion, putting out the night fires, gathering their baggage, feeding and saddling what horses they had and moving the wagons and chariots into position to attach them to the beasts that would drag them as they advanced.

But at its centre, and in the distance, a woman with short-cropped auburn hair was walking towards a lake, where an older woman, cloaked and hooded, arms crossed over her chest, was waiting for her.

Peredur's heart unexpectedly raced as he realised what was going to happen now that Christian had seen this scene.

He turned to follow the others down the steps of the tower.

Aelfrith's sword blow narrowly missed him because he saw it coming. The older man had not expected, perhaps, that Peredur would spend so little time at the window. But the following blow with the flat of his blade was furious and skull-cracking. As Peredur tumbled down the stone steps, Aelfrith chased after him. Christian's earlier words had been cautious, but his mistrust had been total; he trusted Aelfrith, however, perhaps alone among his retinue.

Dazed and bruised, Peredur had no choice but to accept the deep, thrusting blow from the burly man, though he was lithe enough to twist so that it cut into his body's edge. He immediately rolled into a ball and again fell and tumbled down the steps to the next landing.

Aelfrith cried out. He had slipped on Peredur's blood and came down in a similar fall. The two men embraced without meaning to, Aelfrith's face startled and grazed, a mask of sudden fear.

Peredur killed him instantly with a knife strike.

It took him some time to disentangle his body from the other man's heavy limbs.

Outside, the courtyard was alive with activity, yet no one else had been in the tower to look at the strange scenes from the windows. Though they would most likely have fled before helping. Peredur went to the nearest cart and asked for water, but was turned away by the rough-faced man who was loading it with the help of his family. The wound in Peredur's side was hurting, but he was holding it closed. His fear was that he would collapse into a death dream. His head was singing but without melody or harmony, a screech of pain and noise; and his eyesight was beginning to blur. He was becoming confused.

He stumbled over the great roots at the base of the fortress, falling heavily. The last thing he knew was that he was lying on an enormous face, not so much carved in the root as living in it. The eyes of this giant blinked awake, then closed again, just as Peredur's eyes began to close and his hand ceased to grip the wound in his side.

Through the haze of vision he was aware of four men running towards him, long cloaks flying. He had no strength left to defend himself. He went away into darkness.

When the light came back, Peredur flinched at the face so close to his own. Then he recognised the dark-eyed, thin-bearded man who had been dancing with Yssobel. He knew the man was Greek, but couldn't remember his name. Peredur's body felt comfortable and the wound had been strapped. There was strength in his limbs again. Around him, noise and chaos.

He was helped to his feet by this man and one of the others from the group.

'Yssobel,' the man said, and pointed deep into Legion. 'Gui-wenneth. Hurry!'

Then he picked up his helmet, shield and leather pack and indicated that he would not be coming.

A cavalry group in bright colours came galloping by. Horns were being sounded, drums beaten. Everything was getting set to move. In a place where all of time combined there wasn't much time. Peredur nodded to the Greek and retraced his steps across the expanse of Legion to where he knew Guiwenneth had made her own small camp.

The Lake

Yssobel had come out of the earth dream with a cry and a struggle for air. She had seen her mother. She knew where to go.

She tore herself free from the dryad tree. Her skin was ripped through her thin clothing and her hair was torn. She stumbled for a moment, aware that she was surrounded by movement and noise, and that the land was shifting. From what she had learned about Legion, she was aware that it was preparing to move through time.

Everywhere the rattle of armour being piled onto carts, the laughter that comes with a fresh task, the dogs that howl; the children making mayhem, or crying. The thunder of hooves. The rattle of chariots and the soothing voices of men, calming the nervous horses.

The female dryad was standing close by, holding Yssobel's armour. In the language common between her and Yssobel's green side, she whispered, 'I'm sorry for your wounds.'

Yssobel shook her head. *It's of no matter.* The slender woman turned away, as if ashamed. Yssobel called, 'Thank you. All this will be gone soon.'

'Good,' the tree nymph said. Her eyes glistened with sap. She returned to her own place, leaning back into the trunk, and became as the tree she guarded, disturbed for only a moment as she touched a strange stain.

Yssobel's blood was still on the bark.

Yssobel checked her wounds quickly, licked the more persistently bleeding ones and then smeared mud onto them. She was more grazed than torn. It did not occur to her to look around for Odysseus. She had seen the lake and seen her mother and she was determined to fight her way through this heaving riot of army to find her.

She put on the armour. Then she heard her name called.

Cloaked and ready to travel, Odysseus stood before her, the Athenians grouped behind him. His horsehair-plumed helmet was hanging by its strap from his right hand.

'These men lost their families in wars between cities. They like the idea of fighting new challenges on strange beaches. So do I. We have joined forces for the moment.'

'I'll miss you,' Yssobel said wanly. 'I'll miss Serpent Pass.'

Though, truthfully, she had long since come to terms with the loss of her friend from the cave in the deep hills.

He nodded. 'It was by exploring further up that pass which had come to the river that brought me to the island where you found me. There is so much connection in this world. I'm sure our paths will cross again.'

'I hope so.'

They did not approach each other. Yssobel raised her hand and Odysseus bowed his head.

As she weaved her way through the confusion, she was approached, laughed at, challenged for her cropped hair, followed; mocked. She could feel the sense of the words: a woman who wears her hair around her waist!

Yssobel ignored it all. As once before, she had scented the freshness of a lake. She pushed through the forest, following her instincts. Campfires were being extinguished, skins rolled up, iron, bronze and stone being checked, honed, polished, all depending on the ghost who carried it.

Noise and mayhem: but ahead of her, the laughter of children swimming, their last dip in the pool, perhaps, before they were required to rejoin the baggage train.

The lake lay beyond a screen of drooping willows and was reached by a narrow path where two women crouched on their haunches, observing with hostility anyone who approached. Further away, sprawled on their sides, were two lightly armed men whose expression suggested they were not content. They watched as Yssobel walked past them, one of them sitting up and frowning as if he recognised her.

The two women guarding the path stood and quickly barred the way. They were dressed in short black tunics over loose highly patterned trousers. Their expressions were fierce. They carried short bows, each with an arrow notched, ready for a quick and easy strike. Their dark hair was shaved high above the right ear and they wore ear guards, suggesting the way in which they used their small but effective weapons.

But they too seemed to recognise Yssobel.

'I've come to find my mother,' she said.

Whether they understood or not, they nodded, glancing at the belt of auburn hair, one of them even half smiling as they let her through the willows and along the path.

Guiwenneth was emerging from the lake as her daughter approached. She was wringing the water from her hair as she caught sight of Yssobel and for a moment was startled. Then she gave a shout of what sounded like despair. She walked to where her clothes were strewn on the bank and tugged them on. This was a small lake, and its cheerful human content was being hauled out, with reluctance, by mothers of all ages.

'Why did you follow me?' Guiwenneth asked in a whisper, frowning. 'I told you not to.' There were tears in her eyes, and a touch of anger in her look.

'Why did you go?' Yssobel retorted, taken aback, unable to prevent the anger in her own voice. This was a different Guiwenneth to the one she had seen reflected in the Palace of Green Porcelain, and yet she was most certainly the same woman. 'Why did you leave the villa?'

Guiwenneth, her face like pale stone, walked past her daughter without a word. Yssobel watched her return along the path to where the army was preparing for the move. Then she followed as quickly as she could. She saw the two armed men stand and accompany her mother, each of them glancing back at Yssobel and shaking their heads in warning.

Guiwenneth's small camp was hidden and sheltered well, pitched between three trees, covered with a broad square of canvas. It was a short walk from the lake's edge. Four horses were tethered nearby, blanketed, saddled, bridled, ready for the ride.

The woman herself sat in the gloom of her own cover, and her own fear.

When she sensed Yssobel approaching, she rose and whispered again, 'Why did you *follow* me?'

'Because I love you,' Yssobel said. 'And I couldn't understand why you left. I'm free to make my own choices. I choose to hold on to what I have. I don't know how we'll do it, but we can return from this place.'

Arms crossed, the older woman stared defiantly up at her daughter. 'You never understood! You never listened. You never felt for me, for what he'd done to me. You broke my heart!'

Yssobel wanted so much just to take her mother in her arms. They faced each other, separated by a confusion of anger, joined by memories of their years together in the villa.

'When I first saw him—' Yssobel began.

'You saw him?' Guiwenneth was suddenly hard-featured again.

'When I *sensed* him! When I was young. When Steven took me to the head of the valley. You know this!'

'What about it?' her mother asked.

'Gwin . . . he seemed so lost, so lonely.'

'Your father?'

'No. Christian. The resurrected man.'

It was the wrong thing to say. She should have known it. Guiwenneth went into a silent fury. She stood and came up to Yssobel, reached out and took her daughter's cheek in her fingers, green eyes sparkling with tears of frustration, almost snarling as she said, 'He was not lost, you young fool. He was playing the game he plays so well. To look sad, to seem weak, to look for sympathy. "Find your prey and catch it." And rape it! You were duped! Your fascination was a haunting – in his hunting ground. If he's close, I'll kill him. If you try to stop me . . .'

She pushed Yssobel down to the earth, standing over her, hand on the belt where her sheathed blade was slung. 'I'll kill you too.'

'You don't mean that. You couldn't do it.'

'Perhaps you're right. Perhaps you're right,' Guiwenneth repeated forlornly.

She looked up, smelled the air, glancing around nervously. A strong wind was blowing, and the movement in the earth was powerful once more.

But this was a different movement. This was not the tension of departing, the tremor of Legion moving off through time, but of something rising, all-encompassing.

To both women's astonishment, the lake began to flood its banks, flowing towards them. Distantly, children ran excitedly as the waves and the reeds, detached from their resting place, lapped and brushed at their heels.

The sky darkened.

Then the earth itself gave birth.

Guiwenneth dreams

I had come to the edge, I knew it. I was lost, but I found Steven.

We could hardly understand each other except for the fact that we knew each other, having never known each other. As if from a shared dream.

He was young: so was I. I remember the wide-eyed consternation and delight in his face as I first approached him. I had walked from the edge of the wood into a small compound, beside a large villa made of red and black brick. I had never seen its like before. A tall and beautiful home. A house which echoed with time and laughter, but also with a darkness that I could not comprehend.

Steven was shy, gentle, funny; and very curious about me.

Our languages combined to create an understanding and he told me stories of his life, and I tested him with riddles from mine. He seemed to know the answer every time, and I knew that when we laughed, one evening, sitting outside the strange villa and drinking a dark wine that made us laugh even more – I knew that it was he who had called me from my dream.

I loved him there and then.

It was so short a time of love and contentment. The edge of the wood burst into fire. Hawks came tumbling through, bronze-metalled men, savage and screeching, the hawk-masks they wore taking on a life of their own. And the horsemen followed them. And the fat and ugly man came through last of all, his hair burning, a crown of fire. He ignored the flame that scarred his head until one of his comrades reached out and brushed the fire away. It was as if he had not been troubled by the heat – though the marks were there.

His eyes were on me, and on Steven, my lover, caught by those Hawks and held down.

Others dragged me and tied me. I was slung over the broad back of this burned man's horse. He lifted my face and kissed me, grinning with triumph. He said words that made me sick. He turned to Steven, his brother, and the last I saw was Steven being hanged by the neck from a rafter.

I knew later that he had survived that execution.

I had been told tales of 'eternity'. I came to know its meaning. Eternity is not endless; it is pain and despair for what seems to be a lifetime. But there is peace at the end of it.

The long trek through the great wood, the growing desire in this burned-haired man to exercise his strength upon me, which finally he did, all of it lasted an age.

There was no desire in him when done, no pleasure, just disappointment.

It was Steven who had called to me, not that man, that Christian. And Christian knew it. He went through agony. I could see it in his face and in the screaming of his words, in his anger at having found what he thought would be love, finding only eyes that were cold and hard. I was a ghost in his world; but I was Steven's ghost, not his. And I was glad to be Steven's ghost. Not his.

He carried me far, a prisoner, bound and protected, cherished yet hated.

Then we were in snow, a winter place, although a wall of fire burned by my father's stone, where my father's life was carved; and Lavondyss lay a few steps away if you knew how to get there.

Christian was lost, desperate, alone. He had no purpose, he had no desire.

He had me killed.

As I died, I remembered one of the songs that the Jaguth had sung in my later life. It was my father's song, though he had perished before I ever knew him.

Such is the nature of all men.
Shallow defies their depth
When tenderness and anger come surging as a flood.
Deep-rooted uncertainty, and the need for love,
Conflict within the riot of their blood.

And where am I now? I have met the man who is my father and yet who is far younger than me. Where am I now? Is this a death dream?

I ache for the need to kill the man who haunts me. I also ache for the need to love. And my daughter haunts me, as if I'm some resurrected ghost . . .

Yssobel suddenly took her mother by the right shoulder and backside and threw her into the lake. The woman came up, spluttering and angry, but woken loudly from the spoken and savage reminiscence. Her daughter stood on the bank, furious. 'Stop dreaming, Gwin! Why did you leave? The true reason!'

Guiwenneth shouted back, 'Because I'm dead!'

'You don't look dead to me,' her daughter replied coldly. 'Get out of the lake, mother. Something is happening and I don't like the feel of it.'

The earth was birthing a new forest, a forest of yews. The children ran screaming. Horses panicked. The world became darkened with green, even the lake draining down as the wood consumed Legion.

But within this new growth surfaced old hate.

Christian moved through the burgeoning underbrush without effort, stepping between the rising trees, his eyes fixed on Guiwenneth. Behind him came five men, their long cloaks flapping as an autumn wind blew cold and hard. For a moment he saw Yssobel and hesitated in his step. Guiwenneth ran for her sword, but Christian was faster. He pushed her into the water, her second drenching, following her in.

Yssobel stood defiantly before the five men. Peredur suddenly stepped among them and they all seemed alarmed. They had been expecting Aelfrith, no doubt. Peredur's face was dark with anger and pain.

'If any one of you enters the lake,' Yssobel said quietly, 'they must pass me first.'

A furious struggle was taking place. Peredur stepped forward. 'What happens in the water happens. I promise you there will be no interference.'

He came and stood by Yssobel, turning to face Christian's companions.

Guiwenneth and Christian were below the surface. There was a gush of red among the rushes. Guiwenneth surfaced and screamed, then dived again. Christian came up, howling like a hound. He too sank again.

When he came out of the water he was blood-bedraggled and opened. He held himself together, kneeling carefully, looking up at his companions and at Yssobel. Such sadness in his eyes.

Christian seemed to come to a sudden understanding. 'It wasn't her. She was not the ghost I kept seeing. You were the ghost.'

He was a torn and forlorn man. Yssobel went to him, crouching down, lifting his chin. She contemplated him for a long moment. 'I dreamed of you. I even painted you.'

'You haunted me.' Regret and confusion softened his scarred features. He shook his head, gazing at the woman. 'You are so like Guiwenneth.'

'Her daughter should be just that!'

'Her daughter . . .'

'Everything must end,' Yssobel murmured. 'Dreams end the fastest.'

'I suppose it must.' He looked up, still holding himself tightly. Then he smiled. 'Why did you cut your hair?'

'You were going to damage me.'

Christian shook his head. 'Never. I would never have done that. I was a man afraid, and my men knew it. I was a man who took a wrong direction at the crossing place. But I feared Guiwenneth.'

'You killed her once. What have you done now?'

The wind was becoming fierce. There was confusion in the

air. The widened lake heaved against the reeds. Christian's men had backed away, drawing their long cloaks around their bodies.

Yssobel looked at the man who she knew to be her grandfather.

'What do I do? I have a greater task ahead of me. What do I do with this man?'

Peredur drew in his breath, then shook his head. 'Whatever you must. Whatever seems right.'

Then from behind them: 'You'll do nothing!'

Guiwenneth emerged from the lake, bloodied and furious. 'Leave this to me,' she growled, and walked to where Christian was sprawled.

She stood over him, the weapon in her hand held low. Her look was determined as she pushed back her saturated hair. She was holding her side. With a long and searching stare at her daughter, she asked: 'Have you finished charming him? I hope so. I don't think I have very long, thanks to his blade.'

The blow was quick and clean. Christian was gone in an instant.

Mother looked at daughter, softly now. 'Don't try to find me again, Yssi. Go back and care for Steven. If there's any finding to do, leave it to me.' Hesitating only for a moment, Guiwenneth came forward and put her arms around Yssobel, leaning her face against her daughter's. 'I was here before, and came back. I'll come back again, I promise. I always loved you, Yssi. I was only ever angered by you; and that anger came from fear.'

She kissed her daughter without meeting her tearful gaze, then stepped back. She tilted back her head and uttered a series of eerie wailing cries. They had the effect of making everything go still, except for the birds, which rose in panic from their roosts in the forest.

Legion, in the distance, was still moving in its slow, cumbersome, rhythmic way.

Again, Guiwenneth gave voice to the call.

The sky darkened and the wind changed, still fierce but now bringing with it a powerful animal smell. From the shadows among the yews, five huge ragged figures emerged, draped in layers of hide and fur, and wearing the masks of deer, antlers cropped to stubs.

Guiwenneth said, 'I felt human for a long time, but I am green; I am *mythago*. I always was. It's time for me to return. If only for a while.'

And with that, she walked towards the Jaguth. One raised its mask. A face neither human nor animal watched her, and a hand reached out for her. 'Magidion!' she cried. 'I knew you would not be far away!'

She shook the Jaguth's broad shoulders and the group clustered protectively around the woman, turning and disappearing with her into the darkness. For a brief moment her pale features could be glimpsed, staring back at the lake.

The face faded like a dying flame, and Guiwenneth was gone.

After a while, Yssobel addressed a question to Peredur. 'Why did you not protect her?'

He shook his head and said softly, 'Because it was her end; and she knew it. In the form that I am, I am not yet quite ready to sire the small beast that will be your mother. Don't question Time. Question the danger that is coming to you.'

'Then how did you recognise her?'

'We recognised each other. Legion, led by Christian, was drawn to her, though he didn't see her. But I did . . .'

Yssobel, too, was drawn: to this young man with the easy smile and the hard but kind eyes.

'Will you help me, then?'

'As best I can.' Peredur looked around at the rising storm. 'Legion is moving. Avilion is alive. I cannot tell where the next and last event will take us.'

Avilion was the lake, within its island of yew trees. Deep in its waters lay all of death and all of life. To break those waters was to return to life.

In the yew-green forest, as Legion moved away, Yssobel clung to the memory of her mother.

'We are not part of the army. We stay here.'

The dismembered body of Christian lay in a posture of agony, some of his men grouped around it, insecure now, confused. They looked to Yssobel for direction.

The woodland was stripped as Legion moved away. Who was leading it now? she wondered. One of Christian's men, perhaps; the truth, and the tale, did not matter at that moment.

The lake was calm.

When the waters broke, it was Arthur who emerged, rising rough-armoured and angry, flanked by two women in long black robes. He stepped through the blood-red rushes and came onto the bank, pushing back the shallow mask of metal that concealed his face, throwing it aside, stripping the false armour from his body, standing naked and furious as he stared at Yssobel.

Yssobel slowly dropped the armour from her own body. She brought it to Arthur, placed it down. The armour of the king returned.

The dark-cloaked women revealed their faces, and for a moment Yssobel felt joy as she saw Uzana and Narine. But they shape-changed into giant birds, rising on outstretched wings above the lake. There was no movement in their flight, just the ascension. They hovered there like hawks, looking down, waiting for the kill to fill their ghost-led desires, rising on Avilion's strong breeze. Watching with the eyes of those who know that soon there will be flesh to eat and soul to take.

Yssobel stared up at them. They returned the gaze with the hard focused glitter of the predators they were. She called out, 'I liked you. Uzana? You were fun to be with.'

The dark women in their bird forms had no time for memory.

Arthur looked like this:

His auburn hair was unshaped, draped about his face, long and lank. His eyes, green and angry, expressed a fury that was as alive as fire. His bearded face was grim, his fine lips held tight with anger. His shoulders were scarred, his breast was scarred, the deep slash on his body oozing guts. His thighs bled again from the wounds of battle. His feet were strong, his long-fingered hands as strong and pale and beautiful as flowers.

With the flowers of his hands he reached for Yssobel, but gently.

'Why did you steal my death?'

She shook and shivered, then reached into Arthur's cold and damp embrace. 'I had to pass the crossing place. The idea came to me in an instant. It came from the memory of a story that my father told me.'

'Concerning what?'

'Concerning you,' she said.

'My death? My passing?'

'The way you crossed to Avilion. I knew for certain that my mother was here. She called it Lavondyss. She would come back here if she died, she said. The young rider had taken her.'

His arms were warming her. The earth trembled as Legion departed, but the yew forest remained. It was as if the ghosts of the long-dead, the fallen spirits of courage, were evaporating around them. The Avilion lake surged.

'I have to regain my death,' Arthur said. 'To do so means I must take your life. I could choose life but I would be forgotten. I can't have that.'

'I know. I saw it in your eyes when I dreamed of you.'

Flesh against flesh, life and death held hard for a while. Then Arthur stood back, reached down and picked up the sword that Yssobel had taken from the field of battle. He turned the blade in his hand, inspecting it. It was as if he were thinking: is this worthy enough for the bold and brilliant woman?

There was a sudden movement. The two crows screeched as they now circled overhead. Arthur came forward. There was regret in his gaze. Yssobel waited, ready to parry the blow, but the lake heaved, the waters broke again. Avilion gave up its living, and Jack walked onto the bank, a young man beside him, tall and proud and hard-featured.

'I'll give you the death you seem to need.' He glanced at his sister. 'What happened to Christian?'

'Dead. Disposed of. I have no right to keep life when I stole this man's death.'

Peredur threw Jack a sword, which her brother caught with astonishing skill. He checked its edge as he advanced towards the naked man who stood between him and Yssobel. 'Is it death you want?'

Yssobel had never seen such fury in her brother's gaze. There was something of the feral hound about him.

Arthur replied, 'May I armour myself first?'

When Jack stood still, Arthur put on his purloined leather and the iron from the killing ground, covering himself where it was vital. The only part of his own armour that he drew, from where Yssobel had placed it, was his face-helm. The mask of the king, with its scars and memories of survival. It was as if he wished to deny everything else in the armour of the king.

Lake water ran from Jack like sweat. Yssobel reached down and picked up the belt-ring of her hair, bound with its silver clasp. She tossed it to her brother, who caught it and slung it around his neck, grinning as he recognised his own fashioned jewellery.

'I thought you looked a little cropped,' he said, with a smile. 'It will take a year to grow it back. Meanwhile, I'll start to lose mine through natural causes.' He shook his head. Then, more serious, 'Cover yourself, Yssi. You'll catch a cold.'

Arthur looked at each of them. He was in confusion. 'Brother and sister?'

'Brother and sister,' Jack said. 'And again: if it is death that you want, you come to me.'

The resurrected man said, 'It was your sister who stole my death.'

Jack approached him, his arms loose at his sides, no threat implied. 'I've travelled to the edge of a world to find why my sister left my home. I discovered that she was in danger. I mistook that danger. I misunderstood the man. If you want death, you take it from me. What have you got to lose? To die? Not to die? Either way you win it back, your life in the afterlife.'

'You speak as if you know me.'

'I speak of the legend that is Arthur. But first: we must settle the matter. Yssobel is not involved. Please give that statement your approval.'

'I do.'

'Then a moment, please, before we enter the lake.'

Jack came up to Yssobel. 'Cover yourself!' he whispered again. This was the human side of her brother. Peredur tossed his own cloak from where he crouched with his men, watching the surreal scene. Yssobel drew it round her shoulders, shuddering. She was forlorn and sad. 'Let me do this.'

'No. What other purpose was there in my journey? I found Huxley, I found the edge, I found the world where our father was born – and Yssi? I could not enter it. All I have brought back is the certainty that you were in danger. All I can offer is my life for yours. The youth is called Won't Tell. Whatever happens, take him back to his own world. But stay in the villa. Stay at the head of *imarn ukylyss*. "Where the girl came back through the fire." Where Gwin came back. Whatever happens, promise me that you will stay and remember where the girl came back through the fire.'

'And deny my life?'

'You have Odysseus.'

'I do not have Odysseus. But the villa is a crossing place.'

'It is,' said Jack. 'And at the crossing place we find what we need, find what we want, and find that it's not just a passing place but a settlement.'

'He'll kill you. He's a very strong man.'

'I think we shall leave that to fate. Yssi: I can't let you die for the sake of a man's immortality. Won't Tell might even tell you his name. But he must go home. I made that promise to him. And there is a woman called Silver. Look for her. She talks the common tongue, and she would like to journey to the edge, even if only for a moment.'

Jack stepped back. The group of men, in this restless wood, were crouched and watching, not understanding.

Arthur said, 'We should do it now. Avilion is waiting for one or both of us.'

With a quick kiss, Yssobel let her brother go. Green listened for Haunter. He came as a whisper. 'Whatever happens, Jack will always be with you through me.'

Separated by several paces, Jack and Arthur entered the lake, walking through the mud until they were waist deep in the water. There they began the combat.

Soon they sank. The reeds were blood red. The crows screeched and hovered in delight.

Won't Tell

I will never tell you my name. Jack called me the 'Hawkings' Boy'. He promised to take me home. I came to trust him.

In the yew grove he protected me, but he had put his arms around me much earlier, when the tall creatures had taken me. When the yew grove was flooded by the lake, time seemed to race by. I grew, like young thorn, fast and furious, and when Jack and I stepped from the water I was a man. I wanted to protect him as he had protected me.

One glance, one small shake of his head, and I knew that what was happening to him was none of my business.

He entered the water with the armoured man and there was a fury of striking blows, but below the surface. When the waters broke it was Jack who came up first, screaming and dying. The other man surfaced a moment later, silent and despondent. Then he too went down into the blood silt.

The crows made their sound, and one descended, reaching and drawing out the limp body of Jack's opponent. It carried it into the sky, and disappeared.

I waded into the lake. It became deep very fast. I found Jack there, floating as if asleep. I gathered him up and carried him to the shore. The woman called Yssobel knelt by him. She touched his face, his lips, his eyes. She cried for a long while. Then she looked up at me.

'Where is your home?'

'Shadoxhurst.'

She seemed to understand, nodding forlornly.

'I've heard of it. My father talked of it. My brother longed to

303

find it. I'll find a way to get you there.' She kissed her brother's mouth. 'I'll keep his promise.'

Her expression was suddenly curious. 'In a dream, I saw you as a boy. You seem to have grown since I saw you in that dream.'

I cannot, and will not, tell of the experience when Avilion took me, and took Jack and the old Amurngoth; and took the man called Arthur. Not until I understand it myself. Except to say that Avilion itself whispered to me that I was too young for the journey home; that I would have to grow. That I would shed years of my life to find the strength I would soon need.

Waters were broken once, she told me. Waters would be broken again. I would have to live with the loss of youth.

I lifted my friend. Jack was lighter than I'd thought as I carried him in my arms, then moved his body across my shoulder.

The second crow came down, wings spread. But the wings folded and the woman appeared out of the bird-form, dressed in black, a feathered cloak.

'I will take him,' she said.

She was old. She reached out her arms.

I denied her. 'No. I'll take him myself.'

'Then I will lead you,' she said, and I agreed.

'To the edge?' she asked.

'To the Villa,' I replied. Jack had told me of the Villa. And Yssobel nodded her approval. 'And to the Amurngoth,' I added. 'They will take me to the edge.'

'And I will have the man?'

'No,' said Yssobel angrily, confronting the shape-changer. 'The man is for the earth.'

The crow flared, for a moment, in the face of the woman, then calmed. Old engaged young, and there was a silent word spoken. Yssobel whispered, 'Narine . . . help us . . .'

And after a moment's pause Narine answered, 'Why not?'

Her fingers were a feather's touch upon the face of the young-man-grown-older, as he held the limp body of his companion.

Then she took Yssobel by the hand. 'Follow. Follow. Do as I say. I'll get you away from Avilion.'

The Fury of Survival

'Take him to the edge.'

Yssobel sat with her father in the dusk garden of the villa. They had cried; they had comforted each other. All that had happened had been told. Won't Tell stood respectfully distant, waiting, as did Peredur and his men. In the distance a semicircle of Iaelven crouched, watching, Silver among them.

'Why not bury him here?' Yssobel asked. 'It's where he grew up.'

Jack lay pale grey in death, his body still wrapped in Peredur's cloak, only his facial features showing. Steven leaned down and rested his face against his son's. 'No. If you can bear to, take him to the edge. He longed for it. Besides, this place only exists because of us. When we're gone it will be reclaimed.'

'Jack will go with it.'

Steven looked up, forcing himself to pause in his grieving. He shook his head. 'I can't speak for Jack. I can only speak for myself. I would like my son to rest in the garden where I spent my own childhood.'

The Amurngoth rose suddenly from where they had been sitting. Silver had been listening intently and translating for them. Now she approached, moon-radiant and gentle.

'They will take the body,' she said, 'and give it earth. They will take the boy. They will fetch back the Change they left behind. There will be no difficulty.'

Steven bowed his head in acknowledgement and covered his son's face. A moment later, with a bird's cry and a swirl of wind,

Narine arrived, though from where she had come it was hard to tell.

As the dark-robed queen she stood over Jack's body, looking at it hungrily; but she addressed Yssobel.

'I've listened to your talking. I've listened to your grief. I feel for this man, your father, and I feel for his wish to send Jack to a place where he might have wanted to spend his life.'

She was silent for a long while, eyes narrowed, lips tight as she considered an option, her gaze shifting from the dead body to Yssobel. Eventually she said, 'I feel for you too. Uzana and I were impressed by the audacity of your trick with the man Arthur. So I will make you a bargain.'

There was a sudden spasm of pain in her face. This bargain would be hard.

'As *morgvalk* and *morrikan* I take life. As a *wayland* I transport death to the place of healing. And as a *wayland* I can *give* life, but that weakens me.'

What bargain? Yssobel wondered, watching the shadow of the crow flick and flitter in the otherwise beautiful face of the woman. *What have I to bargain with?*

Narine continued: 'Give me the "wood" side of the man, the Haunter in him, the ancient part – and the man part, the blood heart, will find what he wishes.'

For a moment Yssobel was too stunned to speak. She heard a whisper from within Jack, as if a child were emerging from a disturbed sleep.

'You can do that? You can separate the two sides of my brother?'

Narine inclined her head. She was still showing pain. 'Yes. Of course. I can turn lives upside down, inside out. I make a habit of it. Though this is an unusual situation for me. This blood and sap. You are both very strange forms of the lives I've gathered with my sisters over the many generations.'

It was the red in Yssobel who was talking to the gatherer. Now the green in her took over, submerging the human.

Within the body of the young man, Haunter was terrified for the first time in Jack's life. He became a forest shadow, darting through the earth, pressed against the looming boles of the forest, ascending to the canopy where the air was always fresh and moist. It was a time of terror. He engaged with what he could: the musty floor of leaves, the flower-filled dells, the animal sanctuaries within the groves, the old tracks that he knew so well by an instinct drawn from the very wood itself.

Eventually he came back to the edge, drawn there by the cold home that was Jack-in-the-flesh.

Green slipped into the shadow and crouched down beside him. In the garden of the Villa, Yssobel was kneeling in her cloak and belt of hair, eyes closed, unmoving. Narine stood silently, some way away, waiting with a bird's patience.

Peredur's horses were restless. Perhaps they sensed the tension in the air. One of his companions led them away from the uncomfortable arena.

Haunter said, 'When I died, heart-stopped, I was surprised to find that I continued to be in his dream. I felt the blow and called for you—'

'I didn't hear,' Green said. 'Yssi was in a rage of fury, trying to be aware of everything around her.'

'When the boy reached for us and drew us to the land, I just let go. The deep earth abandoned me. I couldn't hear the sounds of stone any more. I gave in quietly. But to find I'm still alive! And though I feel a part of this strange forest, I *am* Jack, with all his memories and affections and irritations – at Yssi's birthday songs! Things like that. But I am *not* Jack. I am the ancient in him, the echo of the beginning. So hard to define it . . .'

'Don't bother. Green feels the same.' She reached to stroke his hand. 'So what do we decide? For Yssi and Jack. For the *red* in Yssobel. For the red in Jack. Haunter: the decision is yours.'

He thought long and hard, always looking towards the garden of the Villa, away down the hill. They were sitting at the edge of the Iaelven wood. Torches were being lit in the garden, and were being placed around the body of Jack Huxley. He had been laid on a bier, but was otherwise unadorned.

'With Haunter in existence,' Haunter said, 'Yssobel could still be in touch with her brother. Through me, through you. If she stays at the head of the valley, stays in the Villa, she would have the small comfort of connection.'

'But if Haunter is taken by Narine . . .' Green said quietly.

'Then Yssobel has nothing. Unless she goes with Jack to the edge.'

'She won't do it. She thinks she will, but she will not.'

'I know. And if she stays here, she will be isolated once her father dies.'

'Not long to that. He's drying up, soon to shed.'

'I know. I know.' Haunter grieved. 'I can feel the withering in him myself. He's been sap-lost for a long while.'

He paused. 'Perhaps the red in Yssobel *could* be persuaded to go the Lodge? To the edge?'

But Green shook her head, a rustle of disappointed certainty in her thoughts. 'No. Your instinct was right. I exist with her. I know how she feels. This is where she belongs. If she goes anywhere at all, it will be back to Lavondyss. Assuming she can find a new way to get there.'

'The red. So restless, so restless.'

'I know.'

Jack on his own, assuming that Narine's words implied resurrection and were not just a trick to allow her to collect her death-meal, would be confined to Oak Lodge and the world beyond.

Green said nothing. She had patience. Yssobel was in a trance. Narine was wrapped inside her cloak. Won't Tell was sitting next to Silver. They were talking quietly. Night had come and Peredur had found more torches to make this garden gathering behind the wall into a place of ceremony and respect.

With a feeling of immense sorrow, a dismaying rush of thought and realisation, Haunter came to terms with that simple truth: that if he went with Narine, Jack could achieve the target of his boyhood dreams. He could be free to live in the world which his father had taken for granted, until Guiwenneth had come into his life and he had lost himself in despair and hope. At the heart of Ryhope Wood.

'Goodbye,' he whispered to his sister. 'Go back to Yssi. Tell them that Narine may have me.'

And with a silent kiss, Green had gone.

*

308

Yssobel woke with a surge and a cry of anguish. For a moment she was startled by the fires around her. Her heart was racing and she felt an immense sense of loss.

Green confronted her. *The decision has been made. We live with it now.*

Narine was triumphant. She raised her wings and began to beat the air. The woman in her was gone. She rose suddenly into the night sky and began to croak.

Jack's dead body twisted and writhed for a few moments, and then was still and grey again.

Yssobel saw a human figure walking down the hill from the Iaelven wood. It was hard to make out features, but Green illuminated the night. The sylvan form of Jack, grey-green, skin gnarled like bark, hair lank like overhanging ivy entwined with arms and legs. He was naked. He approached the tall garden wall, walking unsteadily, and began to raise an arm towards the Villa. It was a gesture of finality, a final call for comfort.

The dark shape of Narine dropped out of the night and took him in her talons, as swift as a hawk takes a hare, sweeping him aloft as he struggled and screeched in dreadful pain, gathering him into her own cruel custody.

Narine had tricked them.

Jack lay cold in death and Peredur and the others moved the body to the coolest room in the Villa. Yssobel felt betrayed and angry, but had already come to terms with the loss of her brother during the Under-realm and Over-lake journey under the direction of the Crow-queen, Narine. It had been a timeless journey, in permanent twilight. No sleep had been needed, and the world around them had existed in silence. They, too, had travelled in silence, only Peredur's horses – he would not abandon them – making sounds of protest when they were made to swim through the gloom behind the barge that Narine had summoned.

They might have travelled for a day or so, or a week. The air was cold. Jack had become corpse-grey, but stayed only as if he was asleep.

In the dead and dark of night, the Iaelven gathered their bows and quietly returned to the entrance to their realm, at the top of the hill. Silver followed, hand in hand with the tall, rather gawky figure of the Hawkings' boy. It was at the insistence of the Amurngoth that Won't Tell stayed with them, a reversal of their earlier desire to shed him. In some part of their Iaelvish minds they perhaps saw the human as hostage to future fortune.

Won't Tell had not complained, however. Yssobel had heard the laughter between the young man and the glowing, ancient, never-ageing Silver. They had found more than a common tongue of language.

At dawn, Yssobel walked to the head of the valley. She stood on the rock where she had balanced as a child, staring into the enigmatic and forested curve of the gorge. She missed Odysseus. She was losing Peredur. She felt bleak and alone, but she belonged here, and her life would open to new events and new challenges. It had been impulse that had set her following Guiwenneth into Lavondyss. But behind that impulse had lain the curiosity about her grandfather. She had created a faux-Avilion. But Peredur had been drawn to it – blood drawing blood, green summoning green.

Only the mismatch of unbound Time had led to their meeting at a similar age.

Yssobel was holding his portrait. She looked at it now. The sky was beginning to brighten, a rim of bloodlight in the darkness. Red could not see the portrait, but green could, and she stared at the face that she had made when she had dreamed of her mother's past.

As she walked back to the villa, Peredur and his two shield men rode slowly towards her from the gate. He was equipped and clearly moving on. Dismounting, he embraced Yssobel awkwardly, then took the picture and stared at it in the dawn light.

One of his men called, 'No songs. Please? Nothing poetical, I beg you! We have a journey!'

Peredur grinned but ignored his friend, still staring at the portrait.

'I'll go through the wars, by the look of it.'

'I expect you will.'

'In a dream I saw my death, shot down during a flight from an invader. I was not this old.'

'You cannot tell age by the scars of life.'

'True enough. May I keep this? Or is it so precious that you must keep it for me and for my final moment?'

'It's yours. Take it with a granddaughter's kiss. Survive the bruises and the scars.'

'I'll do my best.'

Peredur looked around, scenting the dawn, the breeze, the forest. Sighing, he said, 'I have to leave now. Your father told me of a ruined fort, somewhere in the hills behind, along Serpent Pass. I plan to see if it has potential as a defensive base.'

'Dun Peredur,' Yssobel said quietly.

He smiled again. 'Dun Peredur,' he agreed.

'My mother knew of it. It was a haven to her.'

'Indeed? This Serpent Pass is a place of surprises. I plan to explore it.'

'I plan to explore it too.'

He bowed deeply. 'Then we shall find a new crossing place. A place of meeting.'

Peredur saluted her, remounted, and the three of them rode slowly away. Yssobel had toyed with the idea of telling him that the fort was already his, explaining why it had been a sanctuary for Guiwenneth over the years, but she decided to stay quiet.

She watched him until he was out of sight, the new sun reflecting off his shield long after his shape had become obscured by distance.

Back in the Villa, she saw four Iaelven making their way back up the hill. She found Steven sitting by his son, who was now shrouded in some strange fabric, knitted from plant stems and coated with a sticky, waxy substance.

'To preserve him for the journey, as I understand it,' Steven said, looking up as his daughter entered the cold room. 'They appear to want to leave at the moment of moonset, which is in the early hours of tomorrow.' He glanced up. 'Will you go with them?'

Yssobel smiled even as she sighed and shook her head. 'You know I won't. I can't. I belong here. I've said it before: the Villa is my home. Serpent Pass is the challenge to my curiosity. But dad – *you* should go. Go home. Go back to fresh earth and human company.'

'And leave you here alone? And lose you again? How could I do that, Yssi? Rianna is almost dead. Hurthig left while you were away. This is a dead place. How could I leave you here?'

Yssobel kissed the crown of his head. 'Yssi,' she said pointedly, 'has plans.'

'I'd be in the way, you mean.'

'Never. But you'd see very little of me. Follow in the tracks of Grandfather George. Write books. You are a collector of timeless moments, timeless events. Share that wonder with the "fresh earth" world.'

'Perhaps,' he said, holding her hand. 'Perhaps not. We'll see.'

They closed the door to the cold room and went their ways to a brief and restless dream-broken dawn sleep.

When Yssobel woke, it was the middle of the day. Her name was being murmured. As she opened her eyes she was aware of breath that smelled of rotting vegetation, and a pale moon-glow of a face, so close to her own that as she turned to stare into its watery eyes her nose brushed with its nose.

'Yssi!' the apparition hissed again. 'Yssi!'

She scurried away from the foul form, holding in her cry of dismay. And gradually, as her moment's panic passed, she recognised the pallid but very much vibrant features of her brother Jack.

But Jack was not vibrant in his mind. He was vacant and soon became ill. For a day he lay curled and in pain, sometimes screaming, sometimes crying, at other times retching violently before wrapping his arms around his legs and mewling like an infant.

Rianna, in tears, tried to feed him a thin soup, but he turned his head away, eventually slapping the clay mug so that the warm broth splashed across the floor of his room.

With nightfall, Steven and Yssobel helped him to his bed, and Yssobel lay down below the furs with him, her arms around his shuddering body. He lay, his face away from her, and cried until she could bear it no longer. She woke Won't Tell and asked him to keep watch, and the young man agreed willingly, sitting on the wooden bed, a hand resting on the weeping man's shoulder.

Eventually, Jack managed to sleep, a sleep so deep that he did not emerge from it until the middle of the following day.

He suddenly sat upright. The grey pallor had disappeared from his cheeks, though his eyes were wide and startled. 'Hungry . . .'

Rianna raced from the room and came back with a bowl of the same soup. Jack drank from the bowl, groaned loudly and threw himself sideways as the food refused to stay down. But there was now something of true life in him. A while later he ate again, then seemed to recognise those around him.

'Yssi,' he whispered hoarsely, and then, 'Dad. What happened to me? I feel like a ghost. I'm not real. What's happened?'

Steven and Yssobel exchanged a nervous glance. Then Yssobel took Jack by the hand and hauled him to his feet. He was wobbly, unsteady, and he smelled very bad.

'We're going to get you shaved, bathed and into new clothes.'

'I'm a ragged man. I can tell.'

'Worse than the worst mythago. But we'll soon have you right.'

And later, when he was kempt and clean, and had found his senses, Yssobel told him of Haunter's sacrifice.

He slumped forward, and tears came again. 'I knew it. I could tell he wasn't there. I feel like a ghost, Yssi. I'm not complete, just rag and bone.'

'You're Jack,' she said, taking his hand. 'All blood now. And the journey that lies ahead of you is your final journey, and you'll be able to explore your human world.'

Yssobel explained what had happened. Jack listened, shaking his head, but gradually began to accept what had occurred. When Steven came and hugged him, he breathed very softly and whispered, 'Do I go or do I stay?'

'Do what you must. Do what feels right.'

Jack stepped back, his face a grimace of indecision and confusion. Then he said, 'I don't – I don't feel I belong here any more.'

Steven's own face was a mask of repressed grief. 'I know. I know. I always knew. Even with the green side inhabiting you, the call of the old home was stronger in you than in Yssi.'

'I've lost something that I loved. I cannot feel the earth any more.'

'Don't be closed down by lost love. Find new love. Go to the edge. Rebuild my old home.'

Jack turned on his father, and Steven was shocked by the way his son had grabbed him by the arms, a blaze of fury in his eyes as he said, 'No! Not without you! We rebuild together. All of us – you, Yssi, Rianna. We can find the way home.'

Steven disengaged himself carefully from the furious grip. 'The Amurngoth have agreed to take your young friend back to his family, in exchange for the Iaelven child they left behind. Your friend will be safe, and you should go with them. How can I go back? What would I do there?'

Yssobel said quietly, 'Take over from your father. Write books. Understand the way things began. Address the mystery from a place where a man can think without the intrusion of the need to survive.'

Jack became aware of Rianna, her arms folded, her pale, drawn face creased with a frown. She turned away and walked back into the Villa. Steven glanced round, as if the sudden breeze of her anger had caught his attention. Without looking back, he followed Rianna into the crumbling building.

Yssobel came up to her brother. 'You must, you truly must! Take him with you.'

'I think he and Rianna . . .'

She closed his mouth with her finger. 'Don't ask. Don't think. Take him with you. He belongs where his father dreamed.'

'And you?'

Yssobel drew a deep breath, then took Jack's hand and walked with him to the gate; and through the gate to the head of the valley.

'What do you see?' she asked. There was a stiff wind blowing. Cloud shadow made the gorge indistinct; it was almost in darkness where it curved out of sight, where it began to drop towards the monolith to Peredur, and the track to the lake.

Without Haunter, Jack could see nothing but the land, the crags, the cliffs, the forested edges of the winding river, the silver thread that flowed in no particular direction, a life-force of its own existing at the edge of the conscious world.

'She came from there, she has returned. What else can I say? Guiwenneth has made this path her own.'

314

'And she will come back,' Yssobel said, with a smile. 'And I will be waiting for her.'

'She will not come back. She exists in you!'

'And you.'

'No,' Jack said, with a grim look at the distant shadows. 'No longer with me.'

His sister caught his hand again. 'She *will* come back. But Jack, you and I now live in different worlds. Please go home, and take Steven with you. Dear old dad. So lost now. And think of me fondly. And dream wonderful dreams.'

He had no words for a moment. Then he asked, 'Yssi: what dream do you have? To wait for the return of a mother created out of bark, flower and cold earth? Is that all? What dream will sustain you until the woman comes back through *Imarn Uklyss?*'

But Yssobel had an answer for him. 'Serpent Pass.'

Jack was instantly intrigued, half smiling as he remembered his sister's encounters with Odysseus, in the Greek's adolescent cave, in his place of preparation. 'You're going to find him again?'

'Who?'

'Odysseus.'

'Absolutely not. Odysseus has embarked upon a journey far greater than mine. No: Serpent Pass is a place of mystery. It is endless, and I will never be bored, or short of a challenge. Nothing will decay in me as fast as the brick in our Villa, so long as I have a valley to explore.'

After a moment, Jack asked, 'What do you expect to find there?'

'Whatever is to be found.'

He laughed, looking back to where their father was still in a state of perplexed indecision. Yssobel queried his response. He explained about his father's request for artefacts from Oak Lodge.

'He wanted a story book. I found it in a pile of musty old volumes. It had his name written inside it. It was called *The Time Machine.*'

Yssobel shrugged with recognition. 'He was always talking

about it. Grandfather George had given it to him as a birthday present.'

Jack accepted the fact without acknowledging that he hadn't known it. 'I hadn't realised until I found them – the books, that is – how compact they were, how . . .' He tried to find the word. 'How useful. They're tiny! They would hardly make a fire. You can hold them in the palm of your hand! And yet they are a source of visions and adventure. I read the story on the way back from Oak Lodge, following the Iaelven.'

Yssobel asked about the nature of the tale, and Jack explained: it was about a man who had created a machine that could visit the future. 'His journey was remarkable. I was overwhelmed by it.'

'What did he find there? This man. According to the book.'

'A form of life that was in fact death.' Jack struggled to remember the events, written by a man called Wells. 'Handsome people in the future, called Elwe, or something like that, but living for nothing but beauty. But living in an under-realm, there were dead creatures, Morloks, or Morlgoths, I can't recall clearly. And they were very much alive and living for the kill. They had design in their lives. They fed on the Elwe, slaughtered them. He described a dead world where nothing had its true place. An end of life as we know it. An end of everything. Why did Steven want to keep this book, I wonder?'

'Perhaps for the pure wonder of it?' Yssobel murmured after a moment. 'But it sounds miserable.' She dragged her brother back to reality. 'And I don't know why dad wanted such a piece of misery. Unless something written in it addresses hope and a dream fulfilled.'

'We're back to dreams.'

She giggled. 'And on that note, a song comes to me . . .'

'Oh no.'

'Oh yes.'

Yssobel found her singing voice, hoarse and harsh because of what had occurred recently, but the words were rendered with affection.

Brother Jack, brother Jack, he's lost his shadow, but hears
  my cry;
Our brother Jack is back!
And he will find his place upon the path, and one day he
  will die,
But Jack is back,
The Haunter's gone,
A new world waits in terror for his clumsy life,
His special dreams, new strife, new fears,
But a sister will love him from afar, and there will be
  loving memory in her tears.

Jack groaned but couldn't help but laugh. 'The final verse? I sincerely hope so! It's not even my birthday.'

'The final verse,' Yssobel agreed, with a kiss. 'I'm finished with songs. And in a way: yes, this *is* your birthday.'

'Good. Then there will be dancing until moonset! Will there?'

'Hold me in the dance,' sister said to brother. 'What is it you said to me, long, long ago? What we remember is all the home we need.'

'Here to there. There to here,' Jack added.

The Time Machine

Steven: *I am finished with this place. I hadn't realised it until Yssobel talked to me. She's quite right. There is a small future for me at the edge of the wood. I will emerge as a ghost. I will write in the scrawled fingerprints of my father. Perhaps something will occur to me that will illuminate my life. I shall kiss Yssi goodbye, and after that, she has her own path to follow.*

And so I will travel with the Iaelven, and my half-son. And with the boy with no name, and with the ancient girl who glows by moonlight.

Rianna will stay. She has been strength and certainty in my life. She is the timeless mother, the caring friend, who always, like the Beloved One, is by your side; in passion, yes, or singing you to sleep. She is the archetype of love. I shall miss her too. She is the counter-side to Yssi; yet they form a whole. Young and old, they are the Villa; they are the home. At the head of the valley, they are the end of the walk from beginning to end. The valley exists because of them. It is not the place of resurrection. It is the place of return. And it is the place of death. It is the place of forming, shaping. It is the crossing place. They will define their world in ways that ordinary blood and flesh cannot conceive.

I am so proud of her, my Yssobel. Pride in my daughter will be strength to this ageing 'Change', this old man called Steven. And yes, I will write about her when I return to a place I once knew well.

All done now. The path is open. The crossing place is left behind. I will go with the ghost of my son. I will follow the shadow trail to the echo of my home.

One of the Iaelven was standing over him. He had noticed the stink, but was so familiar with the strong smells and scents of the world around the Villa that he had not noticed the quiet and careful arrival.

The Amurngoth, old and gaunt below its layers of skins and feathers, seemed strangely nervous.

Behind him, the shining face of Silver peered quickly to signal her presence. She was otherwise in darkness, wrapped tightly in a bearskin. Her eyes shimmered. She tugged back her hood. 'Steven,' she whispered.

'Yes.'

'We are ready to go. Where is Jack?'

'Sleeping, I think.'

'We must find him. Steven . . .'

'Yes.'

'The Iaelven will keep their promise. The boy will be returned safely. The Change that they left behind will come back and be nurtured. The Iaelven wish me to tell you something so that you will not be afraid.'

Where was Jack?

Steven hauled himself upright, facing the stern creature that waited to address him in this room, this private place in the Villa.

The only light came from the girl's smile. She seemed glad of something. There was a sense of desire and hope in her face, as if she were waiting for a change in her own life.

Steven called for his son. Soon the shaking but increasingly more robust figure of his son, naked but for a loincloth, appeared in the room.

'This is a representative of the Iaelven. He wants to speak to us.'

Amurngoth and young man exchanged a quick glance. Steven said, 'Won't Tell will go home safely. All they want in exchange is the life they left for him. Do you remember the life they left for him?'

'I remember it very well.'

319

'Will there be a problem?'

Jack caught the quick look that his father gave him and shook his head, not to indicate 'no' but to indicate 'yes'.

Steven said, 'Take silver. Hurthig fashioned a great deal of it before he disappeared. These creatures will die from silver, we know that.' He looked at the shining girl. 'Are you going to repeat what is being said?'

'No,' she said. 'I'm here only to tell you what the Iaelven want you to know. What you resolve at the edge of the wood is up to you. I am nothing more than an old woman, stolen and changed.'

The Amurngoth was suddenly restless and irritated. It turned on Silver and made a sign for her to be silent. Looking back at Steven, and at Jack, it began to click-whistle.

Silver spoke its words for it.

'The Iaelven and your own kind never existed together. The Iaelven were always present. It is from their own magic that humankind came into existence. They were unprepared for the power of their nightmare. The beings they call by a name that means "violent children" consumed the world. The Iaelven were submerged beneath the flood of the life they had dreamed into existence. It is their desire to remain separate from that nightmare, but to understand and dream of their creation they must sometimes leave one of their own and take one of yours.'

The Amurngoth was almost agitated in its strange speaking, its mouth moving so fast that Silver was struggling to keep up with her interpretation.

'They had never meant harm. They have always acknowledged that loss is necessary for understanding. They have always hoped that the changeling left would be welcomed by the human community. It often comes as a shock to them to find the way their offering has been treated.

'They are, after all, the originators of all of life. That is what he says.'

Steven said to Jack, 'Their offering is dead?'

'Cut in half.'

'There will be difficulty.'

'I'll be armed with silver. Keep this thing happy. We need to get to the edge first.'

'I agree. Does this thing truly believe that his ancestors imagined the human race into existence?'

'Don't argue with it. Anything is possible in Ryhope Wood. There is no such thing as truth here. Whatever this monster believes is true, is its own truth, insofar as it's true to itself. Right now, agree and smile.'

'Just as soon as I've worked out what you just said.'

Steven for a moment was taken aback. His son's humour was back. The human quality was surfacing at last. 'I'm coming with you.'

'I know. Yssobel isn't.'

'I know.'

The Amurngoth had continued to speak, but now withdrew like a shadow from the dark, dank room that was Steven's private place. Silver remained for a moment. 'The Iaelven are not without intuition. This one is old and has detected that there is a problem. We must be on our guard. While you were talking he was explaining that he and his kind would like an acquaintance with their nightmare creation that might be more comfortable. They have kept themselves out of sight for many generations. Your species is not the only type of creature that they have brought into existence through their dreaming, but you are the most hostile to the Origin.'

Steven and Jack listened without comprehension. Both were thinking of the task at the end of the journey.

But Silver smiled. 'Once at the edge, they are beyond their true territory. And I have a friend there. Don't look so concerned. We leave shortly. Just enough time.' She glanced at Jack appreciatively. 'Enough time for you to find some clothes for the journey.'

She laughed, and with a final few words had vanished, scampering up the hill as the moon began to set.

'Don't forget the boy. I will find out his name! And he will find out mine.'

No goodbyes, daddy. No goodbyes. I will love you for ever. I will find wonder in the valley. Who knows, I may even find a way of sending you a message from the unknown! Just go. Take care of Jack. Compose birthday songs for him and take no

notice of his moaning. And if you see either of my grandfathers,
remind them to talk to me again. Ancestors are such delights.

—Stay safe, Yssi.

Oh, yes. I intend to. Go on. Moon-set is past and the Iaelven
are waiting for you on the hill. They are impatient for your
company. Go away. Go home!

—If she ever comes back . . .

Daddy, she WILL come back. Everything turns. Everything
returns. That is the pure beauty of the crossing place. We meet,
we part; at the crossing place we test the heart. We go away.
One day we'll find ourselves back where we began. And that's
where you're going. Go on! Go on, now. Those ugly elves won't
wait for ever.

—Find a way.

If I can, I will. Daddy, I'm of the wood. I belong here. Jack is
you. He belongs with you. This is how it has always been. Just
because we lose each other does not mean we lose love. What
have you done here? Nothing except raise two children. What
can you do at the edge? Wonderful things. Now go. Please go.

—I'll listen for you. I'll look in legend.

Go! I'm sorry to cry but, daddy, the crossing place does not
exist for ever. And I need to be in my new life.

—Bye, Yssi.

Bye.

'When the Time Traveller sent himself millions of years into the
future, he found a world that was not just different from his
own but reflected the divide in the nature of men. The animal
and the intellect. But he fell in love with a woman who gave him
a flower.'

'And he went back,' Jack said. They were in the Under Realm,
and the Iaelven were stalking through the dank caverns, ahead
of them. Behind Jack and his father, Won't Tell and Silver were
following and laughing. They were arm in arm. There was the
sweet scent of passion in the grim stink of the cave.

'The Time Traveller went back because he thought he could
rescue a brief beauty from the world in which she was nothing,
in one sense, *but* a flower. In the story – you said you'd read it?'

'I read it.'

'He brings the flower back, an unknown species. But the flower is a dying thing, and he has no hope. He follows the flower back to the future in the hope of finding a love that can't exist. How can it? There is nothing human in the future world he travels to. That is why I love this book. It implies that there is hope. In fact, it creates a fiction of ultimate destruction; an ending of all that we had hoped for. The Iaelven believe they created us. We believe we created the Iaelven.'

'Losing me. You're losing me,' Jack said quickly. 'I just want to get to somewhere to put my feet up and smell fresh grass, not this Iaelven stink.'

Steven put his arm around his son. 'You're right. Enough thinking. I'm so glad you're back. Although you know I only ever related to the "red" side of you. The Haunter bit was denied me. Jack, you have a wonderful life ahead of you. And it will be boring and difficult, and somehow we will have to make money. Money! We've traded in livestock, crops and Egwearda's brain-blinding ale. At the edge, everything will be different. Hard times ahead.'

'But anew vision.'

'Yes. Oh yes. I can't deny that to you.'

'How did the Time Traveller survive in his long-distant future?'

'I have no idea. All I know is that when the Time Traveller went into a strange world he found an absence of life. He brought back a flower and a dream. All my life, since Guiwenneth was taken from me, and since she returned as a shade of herself still shadowed by the cruelty of my brother, I have held on to the dream; and the flower. The flower was remembered love. The dream? Simply that something might come true. Real life in an unreal world. It didn't happen.'

'Returning to Oak Lodge isn't a dream come true? It must be. I don't understand.'

Steven was silent for a long while. When he spoke it was with a dark and sad tone to his voice. 'A dream without Gwin? Do you have any idea how much I loved her? Are you not aware that she came into being not by birth by a mother, but by me? She emerged from my mind!'

323

'I know. I do know. I've lived with that knowledge since you first told me,' Jack said.

'She was my child, my wife, my life,' his father raged, suddenly and unexpectedly angry, though the fury was no more than frustrated memory. 'Oak Lodge will be brick and garden! For me, Jack, there will be only shallow life. It's for you that I hope the home will come alive. It will never come alive for me again.'

'You've just said it will,' Jack said gently, putting his arm around Steven's shoulder as they walked. His father was breathing and perspiring heavily.

The Iaelven were disturbed by this sudden burst of emotion. Jack calmed his father. Won't Tell came up and assisted. Steven was not in a good state of mind, and it occurred to Jack that the claustrophobic conditions of this long walk home were part of the problem.

The youth, Won't Tell, was wonderful. 'I'm going home to my family in Shadoxhurst. I'd like you to come with me. I'll find it difficult to get back with them. I hope you'll help me.'

Steven shook his head. 'Don't count on me. If I can, I will. But don't count on me.'

In the long years that Steven had waited at the head of the valley, for the return of Guiwenneth, the earth had entered him. Just as Jack had found it difficult to move too far from the edge of the wood, when Haunter had been tied to the ancient realm, so now Steven found himself struggling against the journey outwards.

When Jack realised this, he asked the Iaelven to slow their pace. The Iaelven troop was twelve strong, all young and heavily armed. They were not happy with the delay, but because they had been told to be tolerant they allowed a brief pause in the journey.

'It isn't easy,' Won't Tell said to Steven, his hand on the older man's shoulder. 'I don't suppose that anything will come easy from now on. But you can make it. Just hold on to me.'

'Thank you.'

Won't Tell took Steven under his arm and walked with him through the Iaelven underworld, and stayed with him until there

324

was the glimmer of daylight ahead of them, and the scent of new forest, new land. And Silver had walked behind Won't Tell.

Jack had noticed how their hands touched, how they whispered. There was love in the air, even if that love was a little uncertain; love separated by centuries; love combined across an age of difference. But passion in the look. The glance, the quick kiss that youth always assumes cannot be seen.

Won't Tell was a man now, and he carried Steven with a man's strength, and walked towards the light of the outer world with a confidence that had not been demonstrated by the small boy, angry and protective when Jack had first met him, by the sticklebrook, so long ago.

When they came into the light, Won't Tell eased Steven to the ground, scooped water from the brook and moistened his mouth and face.

'Welcome home.'

The Amurngoth hugged the tree line. Silver stayed with them.

Silver

Yes, this was the land in which she had been born. She walked quickly into the green. This was the air she knew, the hill she knew, the old oak, standing proud on the skyline, the tree that had been called Strong Against the Storm. This was the land of her childhood.

The Iaelven were restless behind her. She turned and click-whistled reassurance, even though the language she spoke was a language of lies. She had no intention of returning with them.

Where was the man who had protected her?

Caylen! Caylen! Caylen Reeve.

She sang the old song, standing away from the wood, away from the Iaelven.

Soon, summoned by the song, Caylen came towards her. He was dressed in his long black cloak and his wide-brimmed hunter's hat. He recognised her at once, but also saw the danger. He was circumspect in his approach. He hid the silver weaponry he carried. Recognising Jack, he made a sign for Jack to do the same thing.

At the edge of the wood a man was reunited with the girl that he had lost.

Silver stepped into his embrace.

'Little Bethany. Little Beth. How beautiful you are.'

'You've spoken my name. What happens to me now?'

Caylen Reeve looked around at the armed band of Iaelven. The stink in the air was overpowering. Won't Tell was searching the skyline, listening for the sounds of the town from which he had been abducted. He was suddenly as a child again, rosy-cheeked and with wild unkempt ginger hair. Caylen Reeve, watching him, suddenly recognised him.

'The Hawkings' boy.'

But Won't Tell held up two hands in a defensive posture. 'Stay away from me. Stay away. I know who you are. I know what you are. Let go of the girl.'

Silver turned to him. The day was bright, her face darkened by the sunshine. 'My name is Bethany Reeve. This man is my foster father. I was taken by the Amurngoth. I am not like you, Won't Tell, not completely. But neither am I half and half, blood and green. My mother and true father have been dead for many years. My other father is . . .' She smiled at Caylen. 'Old Oak.'

Jack said, 'There is a small touch of the Green in you.'

Silver glanced at him. 'A small part only. An inheritance of nature. The Iaelven took me without understanding me. They took this handsome man here, this nameless boy, without understanding him.' She gave the Hawkings' boy a knowing look. 'The Iaelven are past their time. It's only the Iaelven who don't know this.'

Caylen Reeve said quietly but very deliberately, 'The Iaelven will kill us all. Look at the flush on their skin. That flush means they are now in killing and taking mood.'

'They want the Change,' Jack said.

Caylen could not restrain his bitter laugh. 'The pigs were fattened long ago on that piece of sour meat.'

One of the Amurngoth, a young and supple creature, half again as tall as Jack himself, strode forward and picked up Silver by the waist. A second Amurngoth darted at Caylen Reeve and took him by the neck, twisting him back over its knee, whistling in a triumphant and terrifying way. The priest abandoned himself to death.

Silver screamed. Jack reached for his silver arrowheads, flinging one at the Amurngoth that was strangling the churchman. The metal strike caused the creature to pause. Then bony, frighteningly strong hands had caught Jack by the neck, pushing him down. He was surrounded by the Iaelven, one of whom crouched and stared at him, raising a burned, pointed spear towards his throat.

Click-whistle!

Silver shouted. 'They want the Change! Give them the Change and you can go free. Otherwise this will end badly.'

'The Change is dead!' Jack shouted. 'Tell them that. And tell them that unless they return to the wood, it will end badly for *them*!'

The spear point came into Jack's flesh, but he pushed at it. 'The Change is dead!' he shouted at the Amurngoth.

He twisted the wooden weapon from the creature's hands, threw it in its face. Fierce eyes studied him. Hard hands still held him.

And then a voice from nowhere, or so it seemed to Jack.

'Tell them that they have their Change. Tell them that the Change will go with Silver. Tell them that they must never ever come back to this part of their world. Tell them to stay in the Under Realm.'

As Silver click-whistled this statement, Won't Tell pushed his way through the aggressive circle of the Iaelven, reached for Jack's hand and pulled him to his feet.

'What are you doing?' Jack asked.

The youth smiled. 'Silver!' he called, and the girl came to him. She reached around his waist and he took her hands in his. 'I'm going back,' Won't Tell said. 'I will find a way to be free of Iaelven rule.'

'What about your parents?'

Won't Tell sighed as his gaze dropped. 'I don't know. They live in another world now.' He looked up and into the distance, towards his old home. 'I just know that I've found . . . what? How can I describe it?' His eyes as he turned to Jack were almost imploring. 'I've found a change that has changed my life.'

'And you are prepared to stay for the rest of your life in the wildwood? It's a rough and winter life, and you will bring life forms into existence that might well be dangerous. Especially with your temper.'

The young man thought about this. 'Yes, I am. Prepared to stay inside. And I promise: these creatures will never come back. Does my decision surprise you?'

Jack had no answer. His father was watching, listening; the old man shrugged as if to say: why not?

'We're at the edge,' Jack said. 'I stay, you go. I will explain everything to your parents. You are all red. You are the Hawkings' boy. You can come home at any time.'

'I know. Just as long as you never ask me for my name.'

'I never will.'

Silver Dreams

I have found love in the form of the boy. Caylen Reeve found me when I was a child, abandoned by my parents, dropped like a rotten log on the highway. He found me, he fed me, he found a mother for me, and a place that I could call home. I was not liked, but people were kind. I was well fed. I crept into the church sometimes and slept below the seats, and Caylen would find me and give me water, and meat and bread, and he educated me. And I accepted his name, as if he were my true father.

I knew from the moment I became aware of men that he was not a man like other men. He was wild. He was ageless. There was nature's compassion in him. He treated me as a flower, nurtured me and supported me and gave me the space to grow.

The Iaelven took me on that night, that dreadful night. There were six of us stolen. We had been hiding in the church. Armed men were stalking the streets of the village, shooting at random, crying out that they were for the people and not for the king. It was a confusing and terrifying time.

They broke down the doors to the church. The discharge of their muskets shattered the statues and the glass of the windows. The priest ran towards them, his arms stretched out. He was crying tears of fear, screaming words of distress. Not this place! Not this place! A musket struck him, and two of the steel-helmed men crouched over him and cut the sound from his throat, cut the blood from his heart. They ransacked the church and left, and when the sound of their horses had died away, Caylen Reeve rose from where they had seemed to kill him, but he was weak and dying.

We watched him with astonishment as the dead man blos-
somed, his flesh growing green, his hair briefly shaping itself
into leaves. He rose, strong like an oak, but then sank to his
knees and whispered, 'I have lost my strength.'

Evening came, and the edge of the wood was ablaze with
light. The soldiers had gone but, as if they sensed the weakening
of the edge, the elves came. They stalked up the hill and brought
the small changes that would be left as dolls for the grieving
women. They found us in the church. We were brutalised and
stripped, then taken like livestock, slung over their shoulders,
carried back to the forest.

The last I heard was Caylen Reeve screaming as he pursued
them. He shot arrow after arrow, and the creature that carried
me stumbled and died, the silver point embedded in its back.
Another picked me up, slapped me into silence. But I took the
silver from the other monster, concealed it carefully, and have
held it with me ever since.

That silver point, fashioned by Caylen Reeve, is all that
helped me survive the abduction.

Silver took the fire-burned spear from the Iaelven and broke it
with astonishing strength across her knee, throwing the two
shards to the ground. She spoke to the Iaelven and her voice
ended in a screech of agonised anger. They stepped back. Sap
flowed from their faces. Won't Tell walked towards them, then
through them.

The Change was returned.

Caylen Reeve called out, shouting the boy's true name,
adding, 'You don't have to do this!'

'Now that you've revealed my name,' the Hawkings' boy
called back, 'I think I do. Silver!'

She ran to him, took his hand. The Hawkings' boy smiled.
'Thank you for everything, Jack: I'm sorry for what I said about
you when you first came to my home town. You are a good
man. And I hope you find love in this world. Thank you for
helping me find love in the strangest place I can imagine.'

He embraced Silver and kissed her, and she laughed and
glanced at the open sky, a last glimpse, and a moment later the

two of them had stepped into the sticklebrook and disappeared into the gloom and wonder of the wood.

The Amurngoth backed away from Caylen Reeve. Soon, they too were no more than shadows. The late-afternoon sun died away; the forest fell silent. Reeve checked his wounds, inspected Jack, found all was well. They went, with Steven Huxley, into the ruin that was Oak Lodge, and by dawn the garden at its rear was bright again.

Overnight, the sentience that governed Ryhope had withdrawn enough to allow new planting, not just of seeds and tubers, beans and the flesh of fowl, but of life again.

Steven sat quietly at his father's desk.

Julie came down from the town with exercise books. She came into the Lodge and, with a smile and a tear, greeted Jack.

'Caylen told me you were home again. I've brought you some cans of food.'

None of them were labelled. Jack couldn't help smiling. 'So again,' he said, 'I guess at the contents.'

'Aren't we all always guessing?' Julie said.

After a moment she reached up and kissed his cheek. It was a nervous gesture, and Jack took her by the arm. He noticed how she went still; the stillness of indecision.

'Thank you for everything,' he said.

'More to come. Of everything.' How shining her eyes, how curious and wanting. 'Have you had a hard journey?'

'Very hard,' he said, slightly taken aback by her first comment. 'My sister had it harder. The Hawkings' boy, well: he'll find a strange life, but I think he'll be happy.'

'I didn't know you had a sister. Is she in the wood?'

'Very much so.'

'I hope she fares well.'

'So do I,' Jack said.

And Steven shouted from the study, 'It's time to start again! Come on, Jack. This house needs work. The garden needs work. We have to leave what's left behind. It's time to start again!'

'I'm coming, dad. I'll be with you shortly.' To Julie he said, 'Oak Lodge is not that young that it can't wait for a few minutes more.'

'Oak Lodge is made of brick,' came his father's reply. He had heard the comment 'It lasts longer than flesh. I have work to do! Get the romance settled and come and talk to me.'

I miss Haunter. I miss the feel of him. I miss the scent of the ancient of days. And I miss you, Yssi. But now I can walk into the town without the wood strangling me. Caylen is a good man, though of course mythago is in his bone and blood. I had not realised how easy it is to find new love where old love is dying, and yes, this relates to Julie. A very human affair.

My father works, my father explores. Sometimes he goes back into the wood for weeks at a time. Searching for Gwin. He returns dishevelled and unhappy. But he is convinced that he can bring her home, even though by now she must be old and frightened and staring at the brilliance that is twilight. But my father has found new hope and new life, and though he misses you, Yssobel, with all his heart, he is glad to be home.

The everyday contact with the people from the villages is stimulating him. The common language is his own.

And he has started to keep a journal, just as his father before him did.

He longs for Gwin, though. I hope he finds her.

Yssi, this is for you. I have no other way of sending it except that the young-old priest, my close friend Caylen, cuts his limbs and cuts the bark of the willows by the sticklebrook, and we sit there and he enters the wood, and he cries and dreams and screams and sings, and attempts a return to the place from which he emerged more than a thousand years ago. He is a change-hunter. He truly is a man between worlds. And he is the postman to my sister, and to the Villa.

Yssi: I miss you! And I always loved your teasing songs, though I pretended not to. And though I can only speak for myself and Steven, I hope that your life is vibrant; and that after the winter shedding, there is the green of Spring in you. And that a tide of change will always be the way.

I have love here. And I have life. And that young man – you remember? – who would not tell us his name: he is now seeding the wood with his own dreams. And he has brought new life to a girl who once lived in an ordinary world, and who now has an extraordinary love. They are coming back to you.

Yssi: dream me well. I promise you, every night I dream of you, and always hope you will find those challenges you mentioned: in your journey along Serpent Pass.

Yssobel's Last Song:
The Crossing Place

The crossing place is where we meet, and where we part.
The crossing place is where we test our heart.
The crossing place is where we turn and turn:
It is the moment's pause;
The road where we make selection.
Yes, this is the Shaping Place!
Yearning comes strong here.
At the crossing place we find our next direction.

The wind from the valley was strong. Yssobel stood in her furs on the rock where, as a child, she had stood when her father had told her of the legend of her mother, Guiwenneth.

Rianna was long in her grave. The Villa was intact and fully weatherproofed. Over the long span of years, since Jack and her father had left, many travellers had passed by, and Yssobel had known affection and friendship, and some had stayed and helped to build and maintain the fragile structure that Steven had drawn and shaped from his dream.

She was old now, and Serpent Pass was no longer accessible, though it had revealed many of its secrets in her years of exploration.

There was no sense of loneliness in her. No longing for lost time. No passion for lost love. The valley blew through her, and its changing breezes were sustenance enough. On the wind came memory and joy. There was no sadness in her.

Today, though, something was different. There was a shadow in the distance, a small movement where the dawn sun was illuminating the edge of the river. There was brightness, shifting as the sun rose. And a small shape approaching through that gleam of light.

It suddenly seemed to see her, as she stood on the rock.

Across a great distance, an arm was raised in greeting. From where she stood, Yssobel raised both her arms, and indicated that the woman should hurry home.

The Crossing Place

(Verses and memories that are embedded in Avilion)

The Field of Tartan

(For my grandfather. Who walked across this field on the Somme:
July 1916.)

I walked for my life, across a field of tartan.

The Scots went first. They had it worst.
The First, the Twenty-First.
Highlanders.
They sowed the seeds, the soft touch
Of fabric-woven earth, over which we walked.
They had been mown down to a man.

They made a field of tartan.

Before they went, they sang.
The songs were haunted.
We joked about their skirts; they took it in good part.
There was a sense of peace,
Resignation!
That touch of Spartan in each heart.

(He walks for his life, across a field of tartan.)

No mud when the top was crossed,
When the iron wind blasted and counter-crossed,
Seeking the marrowbone, the head, the heart,

Taking us down into that field of tartan.

It was so strange, so savage.
Astonishing to find no earth, just fallen flesh;
To briefly meet a dying gaze,
A last remembered highland day.
To walk over limbs clad in scarlet tartan.

And we slipped and slid upon the patterned cloth, but made the
other line.
There was killing, then.
No charms, just arms, the sinking down, the frightened frown,
Flesh suddenly shaped into dirt, life dearth,
Blood silt,
Nothing to hearten us
Except our unwanted luck at walking over hand-weaved kilt.
Not sinking into earth.
Walking across a field of tartan.

Robert Holdstock, March 2008 (revised September 2008).

He regrets that his dreams are not fulfilled, yet dreams

And in the stars, in the silence of that silent world,
Sky-stretched above me as I stretch in sleep,
Earth pillowed,
The small, much dazzling gleam of eternity, the infinity
That embraces the wide-eyed wonderer,
The wanderer in the void of thought;
There, yes there! There is the moment; there the dream.

I lie on earth. Soon earth will lie on me.
Will I see through chalk, clay; through the finger's dusting
On the wood;
Through the small whisper of parting; the salt drop?

Will I see the trip I need, I wonder,
Find it among those rusting
Fire-rustling echoes of eternity?
Some so old. And some so new. New words.
New worlds of stars,
Where thoughts, like and unlike ours, perhaps begin to queue,
And radiate,
Hoping to be heard!

Night sky, wrap me round
Hold me in your fire, your future, the memory of fire.
I do not need the sound of fury to be in your embrace,
Only the transport to your echoing, soundless space.

340

Memory

I am not closed down by lost love.

There is a passion in me, once expressed,
That flew with laughter, ecstasy,
Not so much
The gentle cooing of a dove,
But the ringing sound of singing, emblazed, inflamed;
Bleeding beneath a loving touch.

I do not like this flesh-old distance,
This hollow heart, emptied of dreams
Harsh-beating with old-year's rage.

Come fire, come flame: torch me—
I'll play the game, shed the skin of age!

Yes, I've changed my mind:
Bone strong, blood strong,
Lost love is lost; we hold
To that which now is precious.

Into each other's arms we fold.

The Crossing Place

The crossing place is where we meet, and where we part.
The crossing place is where we test our heart.
The crossing place is where we turn and turn:
It is the moment's pause; the road where we make selection.
Yes, this is the Shaping Place!
Yearning comes strong here.
At the crossing place we find our next direction.

Acknowledgements

My special thanks to Jo Fletcher, Howard Morhaim, Abner Stein, Gillian Redfearn, Maura McHugh, Alison Eldred (I made it!), and Sarah – as ever – for listening and supporting the ups and downs; and Garry Kilworth for his frankness about the non-prose parts of the book, and for letting me draw on his poem 'The Bull'; and to OMNIA, for PaganFolk musical influence that set more than my mind dancing: (www.worldofomnia.com).

And in fond memory of Leena Peltonen, long-time friend and translator, who I think would have liked this tale. And with much love for my father, Robert Frank (1924–2008), who would have liked to have listened to it too. (Sorry I took so long, old boy.)